The Empress Emerald

The Empress Emerald

J. G. Harlond

www.penmorepress.com

In memory of P.A.H., who taught me to observe

PART 1

INDIA
1900 - 1918

Chapter 1
Goa, India, 1900

Millicent Cleaver, well accustomed to snail-slow Malabar trains sighed as they came to yet another halt. She tapped the fingers of her right hand on the window ledge and watched a family of women in bright saris and a large, moustachioed patriarch who were gathered around a plump young matron in western dress holding a baby. Each of the women kissed and fussed over the baby, then kissed and fussed over its mother. After some minutes, the patriarch, now bearing the child, paced down the narrow platform with a railway employee at his heels. The door to Millicent Cleaver's compartment was opened and the railway employee entered with an expensive leather travelling valise.

"Madam! Madam! So sorry, madam. There is confusion. This lady, she has no seat, madam. Is it possible for you, please, to allow her here?"

Millicent Cleaver sighed again. "If there is nowhere else."

"Not first class, madam. Not a ladies' carriage, no, madam."

"Then what choice is there?"

The ticket had been more than Millicent could afford, but

she had paid believing the status of the compartment would ensure her some privacy; something unobtainable in her normal employment. Knowing she would have to scrimp later and now had to forego that which she had purchased, she was angry. "Well?" she said, fixing the carriage servant with an icy, school-ma'am stare.

The railway servant was lost. "Does that mean yes or no madam? Sorry."

"Yes," she hissed.

He placed the heavy leather valise in the rack above the free seat and stood by the open internal door. Noisy flies began to swarm in, he batted at them idly.

"Please do not leave the door open," Millicent said in cut-glass English. The railway employee looked at her blankly. "The door," she repeated.

"This door, madam?"

"Yes," Millicent hissed.

Eventually, the young mother arrived at the carriage, pushed a bulky carpet bag into the train and climbed in after it. Unaided, she lugged the bag into Millicent's compartment then returned to the outside door. The patriarch handed up her squirming child and stood back to wave farewell.

The railway employee, flushed with nerves and relief at a catastrophe averted, grinned broadly at the ladies, bowed twice, and closed the door to the stuffy compartment. Once safely back on the platform, he wiped his brow and blew his nose on a square of red rag then wafted it energetically in the air, shouting, "All aboard the Bombay Express! All aboard!"

The old engine struggled back to life, ready for its climb up the Western Ghatts.

Millicent Cleaver glanced at the young woman adjusting the child on her lap opposite. It was a boy, less than a year old she calculated, but large for his age. The boy caught her eye and wiggled his plump arms in the air. Millicent swallowed hard and turned to stare out of the window.

The family on the platform was now waving furiously, the women dabbing handkerchiefs to their eyes. Such a palaver over catching a train: all money and no manners, as her father would say. Millicent pursed her lips and attempted to focus on the flamboyant scenery slowly streaming past the murky window. She made no attempt to converse with her intruder because she loathed long-journey companionship. Talk, talk; talk about nothing. If one was never going to meet the person again why bother to be nice?

Nevertheless, Millicent's eyes were drawn back to the young woman and the boy on her lap. She studied the mother through half-closed eyes. Seated sideways on the seat opposite and gazing at the retreating figures of her family, the woman looked remarkably like a black-haired Queen Victoria. Small head, small hands, ample curves.

The mother murmured something in her son's ear and kissed the top of his head then looked across at her. Millicent managed a watery smile then closed her eyes and pretended to doze, trying to ignore the two flies that had sneaked into the compartment to compound her annoyance.

After some minutes the baby became restless. The woman placed him on the seat beside her and ferreted in the carpet bag at her feet for a wedge of bread and an embroidered bib. The bib was tied around the child's neck as he opened and closed his mouth in anticipation of food. He was, thought Millicent Cleaver, exactly like a cuckoo; large compared with his dam and getting larger by the day. The mother caught her eye and looked embarrassed.

"His ayah left this morning. It is so inconvenient. I told her two days ago we were going to Bombay and this morning she was not in her room. I shall have to do everything for him now, until a suitable girl is found."

"Oh dear, what a chore," replied Millicent, who was a

governess by profession.

"We are going to meet my husband. He is a diplomat. In the new Russian consulate, in Bombay."

Oh Lord, thought Millicent, *here we go*.

"I stayed in Goa to be with my mother you see, until Leonid found us a nice big house on Malabar Hill. Then I stayed for the lying-in. Do you know Malabar Hill?"

"Yes, very nice."

"And he's got one. A little palace he calls it. A little perfumed palace, with jasmine. And servants already installed, although no ayah. But at least I can go there and the furnishing is ready. Do you, by any chance, happen to know of an ayah in Bombay?"

Millicent shook her head. "I'm sure you will find someone soon."

"I hope so. You see my husband is Russian, and a diplomat and I shall have to accompany him to social occasions not stay at home like an ordinary wife. My husband gave me some beautiful clothes, western clothes, for our wedding, and one of his mother's own jewels, you know. I have a lot of course, from my own family. My ancestors were Portuguese, obviously, and we have a famous Italian ancestor as well, although some say he was a pirate."

The woman smiled a conspiratorial smile across the narrow space between the upholstered seats. Millicent returned the revelation with silent acknowledgement then looked out of the window, determined not to encourage her. But it was to no avail.

"I have a pendant necklace. It is *very* special. My husband's family are high class and well-educated – of the Russian Empire. Would you like to see it?"

"The necklace? Oh, no, really, please don't bother."

"No bother. Look."

The young wife opened the top buttons of her blouse with

one hand and pulled out part of an elaborate necklace. Millicent just caught a flash of a huge emerald before the baby seized it.

"No, no, not for you," the mother laughed, prising it from the baby's podgy fingers and tucking it back between her ample breasts. "Safer there than in a bag, don't you think?"

"Oh, yes, assuredly," Millicent replied.

For a few moments there was silence except for the regular rhythm of the wheels and engine. Millicent began to genuinely doze off. Then the girl started again.

"Leonid says it could have belonged to an empress, you know. A tsarina – imagine!"

Millicent sighed, opened her eyes and gave a reluctant nod.

"Leonid's father was an explorer, you see. He came to India many years ago, then he returned to Saint Petersburg – I think. Where are you from?"

"My father is Welsh."

"Ah, the British Empire. Like me."

"As you say."

The baby saved Millicent from any further and more embarrassing revelations by spluttering out yellow masticated pulp, sending soggy crumbs across his mother's white blouse.

"Leo!" His mother pronounced the name the Latin way.

Portuguese descent 'obviously', thought Millicent. She gave a sardonic smile. It explained the family fussing over the baby. Millicent had resigned her post as governess in a Goan household that very week. The children were spoilt, unteachable.

"We should be introduced." The young matron extended a sticky palm. "My name is Catalina Figueroa da Silva. Oh, sorry," she wiped her fingers on the boy's bib and settled him back on her lap. "We are pleased to meet you, aren't we

Leo?"

The baby looked up at his mother, grinned then closed his eyes and promptly fell asleep, but that did not deter his garrulous mother. "He's big for his age, isn't he? Ten months now. Born in the hot weather. I cannot tolerate hot weather very well. Perhaps I shall like Russia, when we go. My husband says I shall visit his mother as soon as Leo is old enough to travel. It is a very long way to go, of course. I don't know if I shall like the travelling, and they have snow. Imagine! Have you ever been in snow?"

"I have seen it, in the distance."

There was a pause while Catalina wiped the baby's mouth with his bib then she said, "Do you have children?"

"I'm not married."

"Oh, sorry. No offence."

"None taken."

For the next hour Catalina chattered on intermittently and Millicent Cleaver tried to avoid gazing at the baby. She was not married, no. And never likely to be now: nearing thirty and obliged to work for a living. She continued to supply discouraging monosyllabic replies to her travelling companion's persistent questions and eventually the train pulled into a station. Tea, fruit and water sellers were lined up along the platform singing out their wares. The carriage servant came into the compartment and said the train would be in the station for ten minutes but he would be stopping here. The two women each handed him a few pice.

Catalina moved the heavy child off her lap. Her blouse was soaked with sweat under the armpits and the boy's nappy was so sodden it had stained her skirt. Millicent looked at her with some compassion, "We'll be here much longer than ten minutes. Why not take advantage of the station's Ladies Waiting Room facilities?"

Before Catalina could respond to the offer, a woman

selling guavas, mangoes and fresh limes tapped on the window.

"Oooh! Delicious guavas! Would you like some Miss . . .? Sorry, we travel together and I do not know your name."

"No thank you," responded Millicent. "But let me hold the boy. You go and freshen up, and buy some fruit before we set off again."

"Yes, how kind."

The damp child was transferred into Millicent Cleaver's long, thin arms. He looked into her face with big dark green eyes and blew a bubble. His mother extracted a dainty reticule from her carpet bag then alighted from the train.

"Now then young man," said Millicent, "let us see if Mummy has a clean nappy in that bag for you, and if I know how to change one."

Catalina hastened into the First Class Ladies Waiting Room, holding her reticule in front of her to hide the embarrassing stain. The cool air of the room was pleasantly scented with lemon leaves. She set her small bag on a narrow shelf beside an enamel basin and poured scented water from a jug provided. Quickly, she unbuttoned her blouse, folded down the collar and began to splash water over her face. But in doing so, nervous and hurrying, she knocked the bag off the shelf. Bending to retrieve it, she suddenly felt dizzy. On standing upright again, she staggered and fell to the stone floor, cracking the back of her head. A young woman who had no right to be in that particular waiting room bent to help her. Catalina Figueroa was unconscious.

The impostor looked around. They were alone. Swiftly, she exchanged her cheap fabric bag for the soft leather reticule on the floor then bent down to see if the woman was wearing jewellery. She opened the woman's blouse and gasped. It took an awkward moment or two to unclip the emerald necklace from under the high-necked collar but no one disturbed her. Catalina's necklace with its huge emerald was hastily stuffed into the stolen reticule and the thief returned to the platform.

The platform was a dense cloud of hot air and heavy steam. No one saw her go.

Millicent Cleaver's heart pounded as the train gathered speed. But the little boy on her lap found its rhythm soothing; he popped a thumb into his mouth and closed his big eyes.

A different railway servant opened the compartment door. "Tea, madam?"

"Yes, please."

"What a nice boy you have, madam, very healthy, very round."

"He is, isn't he," responded Millicent Cleaver proudly. "He eats up everything."

Chapter 2
Bombay, 1904

"It's more than a question of trust, you see," said the Reverend Reginald Johns, a moon-faced Englishman. "We can accept the child to be educated, but you will have to pay a proportion of his tuition."

Millicent Cleaver stared at the man. She hadn't considered this.

"But this is an orphanage," she said.

"It is. It is also a school."

"The Bombay Anglican Boys' Orphanage. For orphans, correct?"

"Correct. It is also a school, remember. We educate more boys than our resident orphans here, and our staff has to be paid. It is my belief," said the Reverend Johns, folding his soft hands over his stomach, "and I am sure you will agree, Miss Cleaver, that those of us who *have*, have an obligation to help those who *have not*. It is our Christian duty. That is why we are here in India, is it not? Not living comfortably in Hove."

The reference to Hove made Millicent nervous. Where or what was Hove? The man was clearly trying to trap her into a confession or a financial commitment beyond her means, or both. "Reverend Johns," she said, "I will sign a document swearing under oath – on the Bible, whatever you like – to say that I am not the child's mother. I repeat: I am not the boy's mother. I found him. That is to say the child was abandoned in my arms. I am simply trying to do what I can for him. It is my Christian duty, as you so rightly say."

The principal of what was known locally as the BABO inclined his head but said nothing.

The indignant spinster took a deep breath and looked out of the window at a wall: clerical grey stone covered in exotic, sinful colours. "I could just leave him with all the other little urchins in the street," she continued. "Lord knows, there are enough of them, nobody would notice. Nobody cares about *them*. I could just walk down a busy street and . . . Obviously, I am not going to. The child is innocent. I must do what I can for him. But I cannot pay you." Her breath came in gasps. "I thought this school belonged to a Christian organisation." She hoisted the heavy child into a more comfortable position on her lap. "And I will not be morally brow-beaten. He is not mine."

The principal nodded, "No, no, of course not."

"Good heavens man, look at me! Do I look like the brat's mother?" Millicent gave a small cry, realising what she had just said. She loved the child, had never, not once in four years, thought of him as a brat.

Reverend Johns glanced involuntarily at the tight-lipped, thin face before him. Then he looked hard at the chubby features of the quiet child sitting on the woman's knee. It was, indeed, most unlikely that Millicent Cleaver had brought the boy into the world. He took a form from his desk drawer and tapped it gently with a finger, "But there remains the question of identity; name, date of birth, nationality."

Millicent moved the boy off her lap. He stood beside her, gripping her grey skirt in a tight fist and stared straight at the round face in front of him.

"He's like an owl," the boy said. "Like the owl in

Grandpa's garden."

Reverend Johns raised an eyebrow, "Grandpa?"

"It's what he used to call my father." Millicent bit her lip then added, "The owl he refers to comes every evening to sit on a tree stump in our garden – what was our garden. Owls have kind faces, but they are not always kind." She looked the school principal in the eye then leaned down to extract a small sheet of thin paper from her cracked leather music case.

Reverend Johns read it through twice. "Leo Kazan Figueroa da Silva. Quite a name for a little chap. Registered in Goa, I see. But the Kazan? The father's nationality is not registered? Do we classify him as Eurasian or Indian? Or would you call him Anglo-Indian?"

Millicent Cleaver's tight lips pursed out of sight, "Figueroa da Silva is clearly Goan-Portuguese. Kazan, I am not sure about, Armenian perhaps or Hungarian. It could just as easily be British. I am told England is teeming with foreigners these days."

Reverend Johns acknowledged the defensive parry. "I'll put Indian, then. That covers another multitude." He dipped his pen into an inkpot and began to scratch at the form on his blotter.

The boy's large, greenish eyes watched him closely, but apart from repeatedly clenching the hand holding Millicent's long, plain grey skirt, he made no other move.

"Now, I just need your full name and the name and address of your bank. Will you fill in this form for us, please?"

"So, in order for this child to be saved from the streets I must open a bank account. Mr Johns, I do not have a bank. My father dealt with all financial arrangements."

"Then your father's name and address."

"My father died three weeks ago today. That is why I am

here; that is why I can no longer care for this child. I have to obtain employment to support myself. I am a governess you see and I can hardly take this boy . . ." Millicent swallowed hard.

Reverend Johns had the courtesy to be abashed. "I'll call Miss Tibbs. She's in charge of the under-fives. Perhaps you would like a cup of tea?"

Millicent lifted the sturdy child back onto her lap. He snuggled into her arms and placed a pink thumb in his mouth. It was gently removed. Millicent breathed into the boy's soft black hair and unthinkingly kissed the top of his head.

The school principal watched her. "A strange case," he said softly. "Not a typical orphan, not even for us, and we have quite a collection here, as you no doubt already know."

Millicent nodded but kept her eyes focused on the boy, knowing the principal suspected something was amiss; that she wasn't entirely innocent. For all that he was being business-like and logically needed to keep charity within manageable limits, however, it was evident he was not a hard man. The thought helped calm her. The orphanage at least had a compassionate principal.

Reverend Johns got to his feet, "While you are having tea with Miss Tibbs, you can tell her all you know about this young man. I'll go and fetch her myself." He smiled and left the room, closing the door gently behind him.

Leo cocked his head on one side. "Not nice," he said.

Millicent smiled at him and kissed the top of his head again, worrying what she going to tell this Miss Tibbs. The truth? She hadn't actually told a lie so far, but evasion had not been easy. Now he was gone, she was tempted to confess to Mr Johns. Explain to him how an adorable little boy had come into her arms for just a few minutes – and why she had kept him for over four years. Why she hadn't pulled the emergency cord on the train all those years ago.

One hot, airless night about a week after the admission of the Kazan child, the Reverend Reginald Johns, principal of the Bombay Anglican Boys' Orphanage, woke up in a cold sweat. The name – Kazan – he had remembered. It had been in all the newspapers! The next morning he contacted his bishop. The bishop advised him to say nothing to anyone and contact Sir Lionel Pinecoffin, a senior Indian Political Service officer, immediately.

Looking at it from the point of view of the Indian Political Service, Reginald Johns could see that this was indeed a very delicate affair; the abducted son of a Russian diplomat had been living with a British family – or at least a woman with a British name – for over four years, and was now in *his* British orphanage. It would start an embarrassment, a scandal. The Indian press would go to town. The Indian National Congress would have a field-day making mischief between the two nations. More than a scandal, the whole thing would be blown into a major international incident.

"Least said, soonest mended," said Sir Lionel. "He is in good hands after all: won't starve. And if someone does discover his identity, well that will be wonderful. A happy ending for all involved."

Reginald Johns stared at the IPS officer, who was perfectly relaxed, leaning back in his chair lighting a cigarette with cool hands. The walls of the wood-panelled office pressed in on him. The office belonged to the Raj – and the Raj, in effect, had spoken. "Yes, I suppose so. What can I say?"

"Nothing, dear chap, nothing at all. Although you might just check the entry register when you get back, I think you'll find you misspelled the boy's name. *'Leonard Curzon'*, wasn't it?"

Sir Lionel appeared to find this amusing. The child was to be named for the British Viceroy of India.

Reginald Johns went straight back to his orphanage and took out the entry register. He dipped his pen in his ink pot then put it down again. No, the boy had a name, his own name, and a genuine birth certificate. If he were to be found by his true family, that *would* be a blessing. A happy ending, as Sir Lionel had said. In the meantime, young Leo would be well cared for and receive as good an education as the BABO could offer. The boy had been taken from his parents; he would not take his name as well.

Chapter 3
Bombay, 1912

Leo kept a pet python and fed it on frogs. It was not a wholly benevolent arrangement; the python was expected to guard Leo's treasure. The treasure was in a biscuit tin. On the lid of the tin there was a lady in a poke bonnet and a young man in plus-fours riding a penny-farthing bicycle. The decoration meant nothing to Leo; he was only interested in the tin's contents. The tin and the python lived in the hollow bole of an upside-down banyan tree in the orphanage grounds.

One illicit evening, while eating sweet pastries in the bazaar, Leo heard an old man spinning yarns for his supper. He talked of the fabulous wealth of the independent princes. They had palaces three miles long and electricity and telephones (he called them speaking machines) and white concubines. They were so rich they kept their treasures under nests of cobras. They had so many rubies and diamonds, the old man said, they only knew they had been robbed when a thief dropped down dead before their very eyes. This, thought Leo, was a splendid idea, and the python had been in the banyan maze for years.

The following Sunday afternoon, he and Skinny Eddie Sartay walked out of the orphanage servants' entrance, down to the dead-end of Lime Grove, then cut off down a rough track leading into the tall grass of India. They passed a group of houses, where chattering children played around women bent over cooking pots, and went on until they came to a track bordering a rice paddy. They were on a frog hunt. They were of course expressly forbidden to leave the orphanage unsupervised, and under no account was any boy ever allowed out on the Sabbath, but Leo had to go frog hunting. Sunday afternoon was best – watchful masters snoozed, so he only had to give his bored dormitory companions the slip, which was usually quite easy. He played the role of the dorm fat boy to perfection. The butt of jokes and jibes, Leo was quite content to demonstrate how little intelligence he possessed. It was a relatively painless means of liberation. He kept Skinny Eddie as his best friend because boys who were loners aroused suspicion. Loners were scrutinised. Leo had also, reluctantly, come to accept that lone frog hunting was unwise. Not all snakes were as benign as his python. If he were to be bitten, his companion could run for help. Or, better still, his companion would be bitten instead.

"What d'you want frogs for, Leo?" Skinny Eddie asked, skipping along beside his big friend.

"To put in Matron's bed."

"Oh."

They ambled on down the track to where a dike would keep them out of sight. It meant walking one leg up, one leg down, along the slippery embankment, tricky but fun. Hiding in flat scenery had its challenges. For some time they crouched and grabbed, splashed and squelched, until Leo's dirty linen bag was bulging with juicy frogs. Then they climbed up onto the top of the muddy bank and shared one of the Latin master's evil cheroots. Skinny Eddie was sick almost immediately so Leo finished it off while poking his bag now and again to make sure the fodder was still alive and kicking.

"Hey," said Skinny Eddie, pointing, "Look."

Two memsahibs were strolling down the track, twirling frilly parasols. They were very pink in the face and giggling like schoolgirls. Leo pulled Skinny Eddie down into the warm mud and the women passed them by. Then Leo was up out of the mud and mincing at a safe distance behind the mems – an imaginary parasol in one hand, his precious bag of frogs tucked onto his hip like a baby.

"Now then, young Sartay," Leo declared, "recite me your nine times table and you shall have jelly for tea."

"One nine is nine, two nines are nineteen, three nines are . . ."

Leo slapped his free hand over his chum's mouth, "Get down!"

One of the women had dropped her parasol and bent down to tie a bootlace. Across the tall grass on the other side of the paddy there was a dark ripple, a breeze of movement on a windless afternoon. The boys froze, watching a ridge of dark spots shimmer closer and faster in the direction of the women. Suddenly the boot-tying lady sat down on the track, laughing. And then she wasn't laughing, because she too had seen the grass move.

"Aaaaaagghhh," screamed Leo at the top his voice, charging towards the women.

"Aaaagghh! Yeaaaayy!" He was running full tilt, waving his arms in the air. The leopard burst out of the grass and leapt straight over the track, down onto the other side and into the paddy. Leo stopped. Nobody moved. The air stood still. Then the lady on the ground slowly raised a hand. Leo looked down at her, "I think it's gone," he said.

The other woman started to cry. "It's all right lady, don't be afraid."

The tableau stayed in place, staring in silence at a retreating ripple of bright spots.

"Hey!" came a voice from behind them, "You dropped your frogs."

The two boys were invited back to Lady Hermione's colonial bungalow in Acacia Avenue for tea. They had jelly and cakes, and tea with fresh milk in porcelain cups, on the veranda. They were introduced to Lady Hermione's children, two snivelling boys in white-drill safari suits. Then came Lady Hermione's Scottie dog called Hamish, who took too much interest in Leo's bag of frogs and had to be shooed into the garden by the house-boy. And then, just as they were about to take their leave, Sir Lionel Pinecoffin arrived.

"Lionel, come and meet a hero. This is . . . I'm sorry," the beautiful lady looked down at the boy, "you haven't told me your full name."

"Kazan, ma'am. Leo Kazan. But everyone just calls me Leo, even the masters at school, ma'am."

"Leo's different," piped the knowing voice of Skinny Eddie Sartay.

Lady Hermione looked across at her husband to share her amusement, but all his attention was focused on the boy. "Well," she said, "a meeting of lions! Leo, this is my husband, Sir Lionel Pinecoffin. He is the District Political Officer, if you know what that is?"

"Lavinia," the tall Englishman turned to his sister-in-law, "what is this all about? My wife is positively babbling."

"This young man," answered Lavinia, "is a hero. He saved Hermione from a leopard!"

"Good Lord. What happened?"

The story was retold and elaborated; the leopard brushing past them as Leo waved his arms in the air to deflect its murderous dive.

"Goodness gracious! I shall have to reward you. One cannot let one's wife's life be saved without compensation.

What can I do for you, Leo Kazan?"

Leo cocked his head to one side, noting a silver cigarette box on a low table, "Actually, sir, nothing, thank you. That is, I would rather you didn't do – or say – anything."

"Out of bounds, were you?"

"Mmm." And there was a thin, silver dagger-shaped thing on top of an envelope on a pretty silver tray. Leo looked up at the District Political Officer, a person of authority, and gave a sheepish grin. "I like your house, sir."

"And I like your cake," said Skinny Eddie, helping himself to another slice of Victoria sponge.

It was now time to leave. Despite Leo's protestations, Lady Hermione insisted the garden-boy accompany them back to the orphanage. However, once out of the bungalow's ample grounds and on the tree-lined street, Leo easily negotiated a deal that left them free to return unescorted. It cost him the last of the Latin master's cheroots.

Leo and Skinny Eddie sneaked back in through the servants' entrance. Eddie went straight up to the dorm and Leo went to feed the few remaining live frogs to his python. He pushed his way under the upside-down banyan roots and branches and untied the linen sack into the hollow. There was space in his round tin, he thought, for the silver box, but he wasn't sure the funny dagger knife would fit. He would have to find an oblong container. There was time, though; he'd have to leave the new treasures in the bungalow for at least a few days to avoid linking his visit to their disappearance.

The following Wednesday was Sports Day, the last outdoor event before the monsoon. The tension that had built up during the humidity of May over-spilled into over-excitement. There was a general disruption in school routine – masters were relaxed; boys and servants were all over the place; Matron was in a constant panic trying to be everywhere at once. Leo was delighted to find exactly the tin he needed on a table in the dining hall. It was a long rectangle: the lid was covered in red tartan and had a man with bulging cheeks blowing into a contraption made of a sack-like bag and pipes. It was a sign. He helped himself to a finger of sugar-coated shortbread, stuffed his pockets with two more, and tipped the rest into an empty dish. Then he put the lid on the tin and placed it on top of a used plate. Dissembling the helpful schoolboy, he made a pile of dirty plates and headed in the direction of the kitchen quarters. Nobody stopped him. Nobody asked him what he was doing.

On the evening of Sports Day, the orphanage entertained local benefactors. There was whisky and bonhomie. Pupils were sent up to their dorms a little later than normal. The runners, jumpers and throwers all fell asleep as soon as their heads touched their pillows. Leo, who had been in charge of tying finishing lines and measuring long jumps, was not in the least bit sleepy. He waited for the snivels, snores and mutters to form a steady rhythm, waited until a cloud obliterated the almost full moon, then slipped out of bed and pulled on his darkest clothes. As he crept down the back stairs, he double-checked his toffee supply. Still there and getting stickier. By the time he reached his destination, it would be just the right consistency. Then he was out over the servants' gate with an agility that would have surprised many. It was quite a long walk to Acacia Avenue, and once there he had a little difficulty identifying where they had actually drunk tea from paper-thin cups. All the houses seemed the same in the dark.

And then he knew he was in the right place. The two women were sitting on the veranda steps sipping from tall glasses; Sir Lionel was leaning back in a low chair behind them, his hands cupped round what looked to Leo like a begging bowl. Keeping close to the bushes but not making a sound, Leo crept close enough to hear their conversation: something to do with a Cicely and a wedding. Where was the dog?

He was lucky: he almost always was. He was lucky now because he was able to get round into the garden undetected, and the back door was unlocked.

Which room first? Would the house-boy be waiting for the family to finish their drinks? Did the ayah sleep in the house? Would the two boys be awake?

First a bedroom: two boys sleeping under cathedrals of netting. Another door. A dressing table: a trinket box, a brooch, a long hat-pin with a star at the end. A low growl: Hamish.

"Sshh . . ."

The dog growled again, yellow teeth suspended in darkness.

"Shut up, you stupid dog," whispered the thief in street Marathi. He bent down and offered the squat demon his hand to smell. The growl ceased, the teeth disappeared and the tail stump wagged. "Good boy." Leo extracted a lump of toffee from his pocket and popped it into his mouth, all the time stroking the smelly creature's stiff fur. Then he removed the softened toffee and stuck it firmly onto a canine tooth. The dog licked. 'Mmm', it seemed to say, lick, lick. Leo considered using more toffee on the other tooth. He took another lump from his pocket, popped it in his mouth – and left it there. Why waste good toffee? He'd be out in two wags of the dratted dog's tail.

He checked the dressing table – nothing out of its place except the starred hat-pin, now pinned to his shirt – and made for the door, shutting it sharp on a black nose. Then out through the back door, round once more to the front of the bungalow and under the shelf of the veranda. They were still dribbling on about Cicely. He squirmed into a comfortable position and finished his toffee.

Leo didn't have long to wait. Cane chairs were shuffled, English voices said, "Goodnight." He pulled himself into a crouching position, *ready, steady*, "Sweet dreams," *go*. He was at the bottom of the steps. Between the English leaving and the house-boy arriving, Leo had grabbed the silver box, but the silver tray and the dagger thing were no longer visible. Never mind, another time. Then he was off up the path, over the gate and into the road. Hamish started yapping. A bigger dog barked. A voice shouted, "Who's there?" Then a long awkward run, hand closed like a clamp over a pocket, and then he was climbing the stairs to the dorm, out of breath.

He flopped down on his bed.

"That you, Leo?" asked Skinny Eddie.

"Mmm."

"Whatsamatter?"

"Collywobbles."

"It's 'cuz you're greedy."

"I know."

There was silence. Leo pushed his loot firmly under his lumpy pillow, all except the sharp hatpin. He tried to sleep, but he was too excited. Outside, the moon pushed through a cloud and glinted just once on the star in his hand.

Would she like the pretty things in his tin? He felt her bend over his bed and tuck the sheet up under his chin; he felt her soft face against his and heard her say, "Good night, my darling", the way she said it every night.

"Come and fetch me, Mummy. You said you would," he whispered.

Leo gulped back his tears and the moon went out.

"Leo, I have here a request from Lady Hermione

Pinecoffin. She wants you to go her home this afternoon." Reverend Johns looked at the twelve-year old standing to attention in front of his desk. "I have to admit, I was not aware that you were socialising in such circles. Do you know the way to Lady Hermione's home?"

"I think so, sir."

"*I think so* . . . So you have been before?"

"Yes, sir."

"When?"

"Only once, sir."

"When, once?"

"With Sartay, sir."

"When?"

"With Sartay, on a Sunday, sir."

"Leo I am not conducting a quiz, nor is this meant to be an interrogation . . ." The boy's shoulders relaxed. "I am simply trying to ascertain how an orphanage boy has got into – how shall I put it? Oh damn it! What on earth have you been up to now, boy?"

"I expect it's because I might have saved the lady's life, sir. I didn't mean to. That is I didn't mean to be in a place where she was in danger of being attacked by a man-eating leopard and having to save her. It just happened, sir. Ask Sartay."

"Lady Hermione hasn't included Sartay in her invitation, so we can leave him out of this interview."

Leo couldn't help grinning. If this wasn't about the shiny box and the star pin then there would be more cake, just for him.

"Well, I shall accompany you. I cannot allow my charges to go running off to the civil lines on Sunday afternoons without ensuring they are in appropriate company for the Sabbath." Reginald Johns watched his pupil's face and there was just the faintest tweak of a smile, a dimple appeared and disappeared. He had to bite his lower lip and fuss about in a drawer until he was sure he could maintain his serious demeanour. "In the mean time young man, I should like you to write a composition entitled 'How I Saved a Lady from a Man-eating Leopard'. Dismissed."

Leo came back to attention. He didn't actually click his heels because the mission school was not a military academy, but he did march straight-backed to the huge black teak door. "Thank you, sir. Goodbye, sir."

"Half past four at the main entrance, clean uniform and the composition."

"Yes, sir."

The door closed. Reverend Johns leaned back in his chair and chuckled. He wrote a note and sent for a runner. Then he sobered. An unfortunate set of coincidences, if indeed they were coincidences. But surely not even the scheming Sir Lionel Pinecoffin would – could – arrange a leopard attack.

Chapter 4
Bombay, 1912

After that first visit, Leo was detailed to 'accompany and entertain' the snivelling Pinecoffin sons at weekends, before they were shipped off to their English boarding school. Miles and Percy did their best to make his task as onerous as possible. Leo, who coveted his independence, was forced to invent and participate in games, accept perpetual defeat at interminable rounds of gin-rummy, and tolerate a name-calling and physical abuse that would have shocked even the toughest BABO bully. That he did so was to his credit – and to his benefit. He swallowed his ouches because he knew Sir Lionel was watching him.

Leo knew his destiny as an orphanage boy was in the balance. If he passed muster, Sir Lionel might take him on, albeit in some very menial capacity. If not, he would be apprenticed as a life-long under-clerk in some British Bombay shipping firm, or, worse still, in one of the stifling cotton mills. Charity boys were a source of easily trained clerical labour. Only those well above average in mathematics ever reached the more comfortable offices of cotton exporters or shipbrokers. Leo was not above average in mathematics: the very thought of dealing with three columns of figures made his head spin. The most he could hope for under normal circumstances was to be a filing clerk.

And if he didn't mind his Ps and Qs this was going to be quite soon because he was already over twelve.

Occasionally, one of the brighter boys who shone at Latin and Natural Science was given the chance to stay on at school until he was sixteen then, if he was a very special scholar, he might achieve a bursary to study in Britain or at Bombay's own university. Not that this appealed to Leo, either. Sitting still for hours on end, stuffing one's brain with facts and figures, seemed a waste of time. The facts and figures had already been gathered and documented: what was the point of memorising something one could find in a book if needed? Studying filled up valuable space in your head that could be used for something far more rewarding.

So, reasoned Leo, if putting up with Miles and Percy were to be his test, even if it might only lead to fetching and carrying for Sir Lionel, he would do all that was required of him. Over and above that he would, of course, prove himself to be resourceful and reliable. This regrettably prevented the little lords from having any damaging accidents.

Sir Lionel sat down beside Leo on the top veranda step, "I see you get on famously with Ayah, Leo," he said

Percy and Miles had gone to change their wet clothes. They had been playing monsoon hide and seek in the garden; they did the hiding and sheltering, Leo did the seeking and soaking. Sir Lionel knew this; he also knew Leo had triumphed despite his sons' mean tactics. From his chair on the sheltered veranda, he had seen Miles and Percy slip into the gardener's shed to keep dry. Leo waited a while under a tree, then went up to the hut and tapped on the closed door. "I say you chaps, I hope you aren't in there, garden-matey told me he saw a cobra this morning." The boys were out of the door in a flash and off toward the house. Leo watched them go, his face expressionless, then slipped into the hut himself and shut the door behind him. Now he was sitting on the top step of the veranda next to Sir Lionel like an old-time friend.

Leo cocked his head on one side, and responded to the question about the boys' ayah. "Oh, yes, I get on very well with Ayah: no chap should ever miss an opportunity to butter up a maternal woman, sir."

Sir Lionel choked back a laugh. "What language do you use?"

"Language? I'm not sure, sir."

"But you obviously understand Ayah very well, and you do not use English."

"No, I think it is the language they speak in the kitchens, sir."

"In the orphanage?"

"Yes, sir."

"And are there other languages spoken in your school, apart from English?"

"Oh, yes, sir, many."

"Leo, how do you know that there are many?"

"Well . . ." Leo hesitated. "Well . . ."

How much is he going to tell me, wondered the Oxford graduate, who had passed his IPS entrance exams with flying colours because he, too, had what his chums had called the gift of tongues. "Mm?" he nodded encouragingly.

"Well, there are the languages some boys use with each other in the dorm, when . . ."

"When they don't want anyone to listen in?"

"I suppose so."

"And?"

"Well, sometimes it is more convenient for chaps to just speak to each other – without everybody knowing what they are saying."

"Absolutely."

"And there's the language they speak in the kitchen. The sweeper and the gate-keeper, and the principal's syce and the gardeners, they all speak a similar language."

"Similar?"

"I think some words or phrases are different. They come from different villages, you see. Some are from the coast and some are from up-country. Anyway, they speak differently when they are together than the way they address Mr Johns and the other staff."

Sir Lionel placed his old-fashioned pipe in his mouth and spent a while lighting a match, then puffed until the tobacco took hold. He watched Leo watching his every move while apparently shifting an ant from one foot to another.

"I see. And you can speak to these people, the boys in the dorm and the servants, in their own languages?"

Leo looked at him and grinned a half-dimpled, conspiratorial grin. "I seem to, sir, yes."

"Tell me, Leo," said Sir Lionel, "how do you get into the kitchen? And don't say through the door – I know about Indian kitchen ramparts – they can only be breached by a full scale Agincourt strategy."

Leo transferred the ant to his other foot. "Cakes, sir, I'm very fond of cakes. We only get them on Sundays for tea. But you see, the cook's assistant has got a brother who's got a pastry stall in the bazaar, and they are excellent, sir. I mean I know I shouldn't go, sir, but you see sometimes I – well, I just escape. The bazaar is out of bounds, very strictly out of bounds, but *I* can get there. And I get those lovely sticky pastries with honey. And then once I got punished. But cook's assistant has got a sister who's a cleaner and she lets me into the kitchen . . ." Leo slowed down then added quietly, "now I can never go back to the bazaar."

"So the boy who knows cook's assistant has been banned from the bazaar. And does this boy take it as a life ban?"

"Oh, no, sir! It is a temporary ban, while . . ."

"While you grow out of your school? Or while you think of a strategy? Hamish come out of those rose bushes," called Sir Lionel. The man pushed a hand out toward the orphanage boy, "Go and get him, he'll bring mud into the house and there'll be hell to pay."

Leo ran his tilting, swaying run down towards the rose bed. Sir Lionel Pinecoffin watched him cross the sodden lawn. The bustling backside was ample testimony to the story of the cakes. And a lad who could learn a new lingo for a sweetmeat was a lad to nurture. But this particular lad came with an embarrassing family history. He would have to be very careful. He would have to play this one *very* carefully. The role he had in mind for Leo demanded absolute, unconditional loyalty.

There was no great hurry, however, for the next month Leo could continue to keep the peace between Miles and Percy. After that, the boy could stay at the school for another few months, or at least until he'd discovered more about Millicent Agnes Cleaver and the man whose name was written on the birth certificate in his desk drawer.

Chapter 5
Bombay, 1913

Some months later, Sir Lionel Pinecoffin arranged for Reverend Johns to send Leo to him one evening after school. He wanted to interview the boy properly and put him to a couple of small tests before they sent him on to the next stage of his education.

The house-boy showed Leo into Sir Lionel's study and shut the door quietly behind him. Leo was evidently excited, but he maintained a calm expression, an expression that Sir Lionel watched turn to disappointment as the interview proceeded.

Sir Lionel – in his role as the District Political Officer, not as Miles and Percy's father – opened with a few polite enquiries, then launched into a serious lecture on Anglo-Indian politics. It was heavy fare for a boy of Leo's years and limited experience, he knew, but he could see no way round it to achieve what he had in mind.

"Take a seat, Leo. Would you like something to drink, some lime and barley water perhaps?"

"Yes, barley water, sir, if I may?"

Sir Lionel pushed a pewter tray across his desk, "There you are: help yourself. Good day at school?"

"Er – well, I suppose so, sir." Leo poured barley water into a tumbler and remained standing as he took a polite sip.

"Not keen on school studies, Leo?"

"I like some subjects, sir. And there's a good library. Reverend Johns gets us topping books to read."

"*Coral Island, Treasure Island*, that sort of thing?"

"Yes, sir."

"Are you reading anything at the moment?"

"*The Old Curiosity Shop*, sir."

"Are you begad! Dickens, eh? Bit hard going, isn't it?"

"The beginning was, but I like the people – well, not *like* exactly, but they are . . .

"Convincing characters? Indeed. Right, take a seat here. Make yourself comfortable, but not too comfortable: I need you to pay attention."

Leo wriggled his round frame into a wicker chair pulled up beside Sir Lionel's desk and gazed about him.

"Ready?"

Leo nodded.

Sir Lionel leaned back in his chair behind his study desk. He drummed his fingers on the leather blotter then began. "Back in 1900, Britain granted Russia permission to open a consulate in Bombay. Russia and India have well established trade links: Russia imports tea and exports kerosene for our kitchens, and so on. Because of this commercial link, Russia has wanted to set up a trade mission for a long time, but viceroys such as Lord Curzon held out, always saying 'no' because Britain needs to protect her raw materials. Do you follow me?"

"Oh, yes, sir. India is the jewel in the crown. There is great rivalry for our Indian resources: we learn this at school. The geography master is very thorough, sir."

Leo smiled eagerly, although Sir Lionel had his doubts as to how much the boy actually understood. He drummed his fingers again and gave him a piercing look. Leo responded by sitting up straight and putting his hands on his knees like a model student.

The Empress Emerald

Sir Lionel swallowed a smile and continued, "Monitoring trade from a political point of view, as far as *we* are concerned, means not one Ivan – er, not one Russian – moves in or out of our new Gateway to India here in Bombay without me knowing about it personally. This, as you must see, requires constant vigilance. I have to keep a team of what we might call 'watchers'. It's a standard arrangement; goes on all over the country and in other countries too, no doubt. In India, of course, we all have to accept it. Everybody watches everybody in India; rajahs and parliamentarians, nabobs and businessmen, they all maintain a string of informants. Natives in the professions, particularly the politically inclined – lawyers, professors and the like; begums and maharanis out of purdah; memsahibs and white box-wallahs; ministers of religion; princes and schoolboys . . . we are all subject to scrutiny."

Leo gave a knowing grimace, "I know, sir."

"But you have found ways round it, haven't you?"

"Sometimes, sir."

Sir Lionel took a large monogrammed handkerchief from a trouser pocket and wiped his brow. "*Sometimes* and at *different times* that is all that's needed – sometimes. Anyway, where was I? What do you know about the autonomous princely states?"

"I don't think I know anything, sir, not very well."

"Well this is where it gets interesting, although you're a bit young for all this yet. Nevertheless . . ." Sir Lionel paused, replaced his handkerchief in his trouser pocket and sipped from his glass of boiled water. "Eccentric rajahs, Leo, have kept British sub-secretaries scribbling away for generations. Humble clerks from Clerkenwell and Tunbridge Wells spend their poor, dull lives minuting oriental peccadilloes. Unpleasant perhaps, but it has to be done."

Minuting, sir?"

"Writing reports."

"About what, sir?"

"Well, not to put too fine a point on it – erm – extravagances."

"Money?" Leo furrowed his brow.

"Not money exactly, no, although some of these rajahs are as rich as Croesus. No, it's, erm, what they get up to – such as stealing Hill State maidens for, erm . . . dubious erm – ceremonies. This means nothing to you now, I know, but believe you me, if a Hill State tribal leader becomes an aggrieved father or, heaven forbid, suffers a loss of dignity, retribution will be sought and that could lead to interstate trouble, which in turn upsets our delicate balance. The Mutiny proved how vulnerable we are. Terrible, terrible business. Learn about it and never forget it. All those innocent women and children, all those poor soldiers – on both sides, I might add – all murdered because of a . . . Well, I'm off the subject. Here, drink your barley water."

Sir Lionel paused for air and drank some water. As he lifted his glass, he noticed the boy looking at his cuff links. It unnerved him so he began again, rather too hastily, "As a direct result of that dreadful affair, we Britons attached to the Indian Civil Service and Indian Political Service all want to know what's going on everywhere, all the time. It's perfectly reasonable and necessary. And now, watching who does business with the Russians has become part of my brief as well. Leo," Sir Lionel paused, his tone changed, "I do not expect you to ever reveal what we are discussing today – ever."

"No, sir, of course not. Why might I want to discuss it, sir?"

"Hmm – time will tell."

Sir Lionel's particular brief was to 'monitor commercial enterprise in the light of a changing diplomatic climate'. In other words, he was to watch and note and inform the India Office in London the moment a foreign diplomat or a Russian sub-secretary stepped out of line. He was also supposed to keep a close eye on intellectuals, and any cultural exchanges between Saint Petersburg and Bombay. London was very nervous about what was happening in Russia politically and feared Indian students might be too easily drawn into what they'd termed 'insurrection'. Basically, they didn't want young Indians getting ideas. The Tsar was weak and there had been bad harvests; Russian peasants, organised by student agitators, were apparently ready to revolt. Trouble was contagious and if the peasant class caught it there would be an epidemic. It was in the best interests of all concerned, he'd been told, to prevent Mother India's children from mixing with undesirables who spread germs. Hence the most diligent watching and reporting. Knowledge was power.

Sir Lionel had a modest office near the Bombay Stock Exchange, he also rented rooms near the Sassoon timber docks and maintained a network of remunerated beggars among the warehouses: old men and young, who spent their days and nights hunkered down in ones and threes, chewing betel nut and apparently gazing into space. His principal observation post operated from dockland premises. It had a ground floor office where new arrivals from the ocean-going liners, visitors and commercial travellers of all nationalities, could insure their luggage for overland journeys, and where, if in need, they could consult a firm of 'Legal and Contract Translators' that operated from rooms above: rooms with a panoramic view of the harbour. Sir Lionel rarely entered this building, and very few British officials even knew about its connection to him.

This is where Sir Lionel planned to send Leo, if the boy passed muster. For a moment he leaned back in the chair and studied the boy, then he said, "Leo, put your hands over your eyes. That's it. Now, tell me what's in my study."

"A memory game, sir."

"Exactly. But with extra details. Describe things for me."

Leo smiled, pushed his thick black hair off his face and put two plump palms over his eyes. "There's a cricket bat and a cap on the wall behind you, sir. There's a photograph of Lady Hermione on your desk. I think she is wearing a straw hat. The cushion on my chair has dog on it like Hamish. There is a green leather blotter on your desk and a letter. The curtains are pale yellow, I think, or a cream colour. They are open and you can see the back garden from your chair, at least I think you can. There's a wicker paper basket . . ."

"Anything in it?"

"A torn up envelope – I'm not sure if it's from England, I didn't see a stamp. There's a rug in front of your desk, dark red . . . it's got an intricate pattern. Can I stop, sir, please? My face is very hot."

"Yes, but first tell me what's in the letter."

"Oh – um, I shouldn't . . ."

"No, Leo, I want to know exactly what you've seen."

"I didn't mean to look."

"And I didn't know you had – well done. Now, tell me, where is the letter from and what's in it?"

"Um . . . It is from a school sir – Wincaster?"

"Winchester."

"Your sons have the measles, sir. It is from the headmaster's secretary, I think."

Sir Lionel pursed his lips, rested an elbow over the letter in question and steepled his hands.

"I'm very sorry, Sir Lionel." Leo was staring at the rug beneath his feet, clenching and unclenching his hands. "Shall I go now?"

"No. You will stay. And my cufflinks?"

"Like knots, sir, and gold – I expect. There is a shield device on your ring . . ."

Sir Lionel nodded and pushed the boy's barley water towards him. "Take a drink, Leo, while I explain what we plan to do with you."

Chapter 6
Bombay, 1914

When Leo left the orphanage he was provided with a small leather case, a new set of summer weather clothes, and an orange box from the kitchen that he'd begged for unspecified knick-knacks. He carried it carefully so as not to rattle the contents, using an ingenious string handle. All the domestic staff made a fuss of him, even Matron. Reverend Johns patted him on the back, congratulated him, and put him in a hired tonga that was directed to an office on Sassoon Dock.

Within less than twelve hours, Leo was not at all sure congratulations had been in order. Contrary to his hopes and expectations after his interview with Sir Lionel, he discovered he was to be a skivvy, a tea boy in an office where no one ever smiled.

During the first week he made vast urns of tea, all day, every day. The second week he was trusted with some filing. The following week, however, his life changed forever. After the offices were closed, one of the employees, a quietly spoken native of Bombay, gave him an evening class in written Urdu followed by half an hour of formal Hindi.

During his second month he began Russian. From six to seven each morning, he was tutored by a middle-aged Eurasian called Sidney Tamchian, who managed the translation business in the upstairs rooms. After this lesson was over, Mr Tamchian kept him busy for another twelve hours or more with clerical copying tasks. Once his working day ended, Leo returned to his box-room at the back of the building. He had been provided with his own room, which initially delighted him. There was a bedroll with a rough sheet, a bucket and a brass washbowl that had once belonged to somebody's grandmother, and a door that did not lock. It was the first time that Leo could remember having any space to himself. Unfortunately, he spent precious little time in it.

As to meeting his various friends in the evenings, even if he could have found a way out of the building unseen, he certainly had no spare time or energy for clandestine trips to the beach. There were no more visits to pastry stalls in the bazaar. Each and every night, Leo practised his Russian grammar for the next day and fell asleep before his head hit the lumpy bedroll.

Leo came to hate Sidney Tamchian. Yellow-skinned, slant-eyed, slope-shouldered, the boy saw him as a typical Conan-Doyle villain, the sort that lived in a netherworld of unlit tunnels and hissed as he spoke. Despite his status within Sir Lionel's personal raj, Tamchian believed Life had dealt him a severe blow and was anxious to share its pain with his pupil.

"Those of us of mixed race are always set apart," he stated bluntly, expecting Leo to react. "Second-class citizens we are, and never forget it, boy. You might think you're special here, but you're not. Next time you pass a mirror take a look – that *pukka* English accent won't convince anyone."

There was no mirror in the building. Leo pushed the matter aside. He didn't think his appearance or his accent was the real reason Mr Tamchian and the office staff treated him badly. He assumed it was normal for apprentices and menial juniors to be given the rough end of the stick and hoped that as his clerical skills improved, so would his life in general. Unfortunately, his rapid progress in everything had a negative effect on every employee in the dockland premises.

Leo learned too much, too quickly. Sidney Tamchian reported it as a failing to Sir Lionel. The office scribes employed as legitimate clerks made Leo's working day as difficult as they could out of sheer spite. As a result, Leo never had a day off. That meant no free time to enjoy his collection of treasures, and certainly no time to add to it. And that was another worry – sooner or later, his precious tins were going to be discovered, nothing was private. During the first week he had rolled them into his sleeping mat before leaving the tiny room. Then he found a loose floorboard and tucked them out of sight. But he had good reason to believe some of the clerks came sniffing around, looking for clues to his identity while he was elsewhere. He moved his tins as often as he could but he was rapidly running out of hiding places. Leo lived in dread of discovery. Life was unbearable, his head swam with verbs and he was losing weight.

One evening, after Sir Lionel had made a rare visit to the Legal and Contract lawyers and left the building, Leo ran after him.

"Sir Lionel!" he called, waving an arm.

The man stopped in his tracks, furious. "Are you completely stupid, boy?"

Leo was taken aback; he had never heard this tone before. What had he done?

"You will never call my name aloud like that again. Do you understand?"

"Yes, sir." Then, dismayed, Leo shook his head, "No, sir."

"Look," Sir Lionel sighed, "I'll explain one day. What do you want?"

"Nothing, sir. Just to say that I – um, er – I'm, er, learning the Russian verbs, sir."

"And doing very well, I hear. As it should be."

"So can I stop now? Please."

"No, Leo, not yet."

The boy's face fell.

"Why do you want to stop when you are doing so well? Does Tamchian keep you on short rations?"

Leo lowered his head and nodded.

Sir Lionel controlled a smile and his tone softened. "No, you can't stop learning, especially not Russian. Not if you are going to be of any use to me. You might need it yourself one day, you know. You might even be grateful."

Leo thought that was highly, highly unlikely but said nothing.

"Shall you tell Tamchian you have spoken to me?"

"I don't think so, sir," Leo replied.

"That might be wise. A lot wiser than keeping me here talking." The tall Englishman looked around then ostentatiously reached into his pocket, took out a red leather change purse and gave Leo a four-anna piece. It was the standard tip for well-behaved servants and deserving vagrants.

Leo stared at the coin placed in his hand, confused by the short interview and its termination.

"There, now run off and buy some of those disgusting fried cakes you used to like so much." Sir Lionel took a step away from him. "Go on, or I'll ask for my money back."

Leo did what he was told. Forgetting everything, he ran down the quayside clutching the coin tightly in his fist as he passed the betel-nut chewing beggars. Some of them made a mental note of his passing. One of them informed a man, who told another man, who knew the porter of the Russian consulate.

Chapter 7
Bombay 1915

"Leo, I'm moving you out of the translation business."

Leo, who had been watching rain lash Sir Lionel's office window in the centre of the old city, turned around, a smile scythed once across his face and disappeared.

"Tamchian feels you've become too much of a threat to him. Quite a compliment. What are you now, fourteen, fifteen?"

"Fourteen until August. My birthday falls under the sign of Leo."

"Does it? Have you ever had your horoscope read?"

"No. I needed a birthday and it seemed appropriate to have one in August."

Sir Lionel was tidying his desk, putting documents, papers, pens and pencils under lock and key. The blotting paper on his desk pad was carefully torn to shreds over the waste-paper basket. Leo watched him.

"Blotting paper absorbs," Sir Lionel said. "It absorbs and can inform. Do you follow me?" Leo nodded. "Like you, eh?"

Leo smiled and gave a polite shrug. "I used to wonder about having *our* horoscopes done. Lady Hermione was very keen to see someone about the boys' birth dates, but you know, people say they are frighteningly accurate, so I said, 'no, better not'. Ignorance is sometimes wiser in personal matters." Sir Lionel closed a desk drawer and locked it.

Leo waited a moment or two then said, "Where am I to go, sir?"

"Mm, well I suppose I'd better tell you." Sir Lionel sat down in his high-backed chair and fiddled with a cufflink, he seemed distanced, distracted.

Leo waited by the window, wondering what was about to come next.

"Where was I?" Sir Lionel ran a shaky hand through his fair, thinning hair. "Ah, yes your future. Well, sit down, sit down. And just for future reference, if you are going to stare out of a window it is better to do it at an angle, and make sure there's no light behind you first."

Leo looked round sharply then moved to the bent-wood visitor's chair. Sitting closer, Leo could see Sir Lionel was shivering. "Do you have your quinine tablets, sir?"

Sir Lionel laughed out loud, "Malaria, my old friend, come to call again. I do. I do. You are very observant. But first we'll get your future sorted out then you can make sure I get back to the bungalow before I become a dithering wreck." He lit a cigarette, the match jittered; the smoke became a spiral in the thick air before he spoke again. "Right then, you mastered the translation tasks in double-quick time, but you'll have to keep up with the Russian. I'm going to arrange private evening-classes. However, for now I want to send you in a different direction. Have you ever heard of The House of Craven?"

"Is that a Sherlock Holmes?"

"Do you read Conan Doyle now, Leo?"

"I used to, sir. Not lately."

"Oh, yes, I remember, you enjoy fiction. Do you still manage to read much? I wouldn't have thought you had the opportunity."

"No, not since I left the school, sir. I miss it."

"Because?"

Leo gave a slight shrug. "I miss . . ." He had never thought about it before. "I suppose it was a way of being on my own. People got used to me being in the little library or under the banyan tree by myself and left me alone. A couple of the masters used to lend me their magazines and books, sir."

"Yes, that's right, you told me. Adventures!" Sir Lionel chuckled to himself. "Here's a boy whose life is the stuff of novels and he prefers the vicarious word. Life's a conundrum."

Leo cocked his head on one side, "In what way, sir?"

"Mmmm?"

"Is my life the stuff of novels?" Leo was becoming impatient to find out about his future but kept his voice calm and polite.

"Did I say that? Rubbish, ignore it. Malaria talking. Back to the task in hand. Craven's shop is a real place, although it would make a good setting for a murder mystery. The Cravens, father and son, are perfectly real. Except Old Man Craven isn't altogether real. He's neither normal nor . . ." Sir Lionel wiped his handkerchief across his brow. "I'm sweating. Brain fog's rolled in." He took a deep breath. "The House of Craven is a group of connected businesses dealing in precious stones, jewellery, antiques, that sort of thing."

Leo swallowed. Did he know after all? Had he found his collection and not told him? That is just exactly what Sir Lionel would do. Find the evidence then set a trap for him. "What am I to do in the House of Craven, sir?"

"First, you will be in their Oriental Curiosity Shop. Dust the ornaments, help at the counter, keep an eye on the customers – who comes in regularly, who leaves items to be repaired and sends someone else to pick them up. Keep a mental note of who comes in selling loose stones, uncut rubies, emeralds, that sort of thing." Sir Lionel swivelled his chair round to look out of the window.

Leo didn't know how to react. His first impulse was to shout 'hooray', his second to say 'spy'. He said nothing.

"So, that all right with you? Start tomorrow? I intended to take you there myself this evening on the way home, introduce you." The chair returned to its normal position. "But I feel so terrible I don't think I can. Let me get down to the street, see how I feel." Sir Lionel opened the middle drawer of his desk and withdrew a strong buff envelope, a leather wallet and a set of keys. "Shall we go?"

Leo went round the desk to help him to his feet. "Where shall I sleep, sir?"

"Tonight you can stay at the bungalow with me. I'm on my own. Lady Hermione won't be back until the cool weather. I got a lad to pick up your stuff from the dock office. It's all quite safe in my boys' room."

So he did know. It must have given Tamchian great satisfaction to reveal that the boy who was too clever by half was also a thief.

"If you give me the keys sir, I'll lock up as we go out."

"Keys? Yes, here you are. Make sure you give them back before we leave the building."

They stepped out into a world of steaming dampness and pushed their way down to the Stock Exchange and into the commercial district. There was a mist that was not a fog but a palpable cloud of humidity. Sir Lionel indicated a shop front, a wide step flanked by mullioned windows: Craven's Oriental Curiosity Shop. *Straight out of Dickens*, thought Leo. Would Quilp be inside, threatening to bite him if he didn't do as he was told?

Sir Lionel was now shivering so much they did not go in, but hired a tonga, tucked themselves under the leaking canopy, and the pony trotted and splashed them all the way back through the city out to Acacia Avenue.

J. G. Harlond

As soon as they arrived at the bungalow, Sir Lionel's bearer adopted his traditional role of field-nurse-cum-bodyguard and Leo was left to his own devices. He went straight to the boys' room to see what had been collected from Tamchian's rooms. His battered biscuit tins had been placed side by side on the white coverlet of a bed. He checked their contents. All his shiny objects were there, each item wrapped in tracing paper and each layer separated by a filched lawn handkerchief. All there – but no longer a secret. Would, could, a serious bout of malaria erase a recent memory? A few days of fever would give him just enough time to establish himself at the curious curiosity shop, and find somewhere for his collection that was safe, safer, safest.

The next day, Leo set off early for the House of Craven. He was there at nine on the dot. The shop was opened by a very tall, disjointed, ageless man who reminded Leo of the whippets he had once seen at the race track: pink-eyed, anaemic, but athletic. This was Young Mr Craven, who ushered him in through the door as quickly as possible telling him the staff entrance was 'round the back' and never to use the customer entrance again.

The interior of the shop was ill lit, perhaps by design. The poor lighting came from wall-bracket kerosene lamps, whose fumes added to the strange mélange of odours that Leo noticed before his vision had adjusted itself. There was the lavender and beeswax of furniture polish, the old, rather damp smell of floor boards; there was incense and sandalwood, and a cloud of bhang that hung about a sweeper as he pushed his broom around the back of the shop. Having identified some of the odours, Leo took stock of his surroundings. Above him were crystal chandeliers; to the right of the doorway, a small filigree cage containing a stuffed goldfinch hung from a brass stand. On the floor to his left, two green, square-faced Chinese dogs barked at his intrusion. Behind them stood a small jade lioness carved into a perpetual growl. There were a pair of less than oriental King Charles spaniels made out of porcelain; a stone toad; and two flat marble cats curled up on a counter. A mangy stuffed mongoose challenged a bronze cobra on another. Around the outer walls were large tureens and elaborate urns made for umbrellas; there were waist-high, wax-faced dolls in oriental costumes, their tiny deformed feet nailed to wooden plinths. Behind a bamboo screen there was a commode decorated with scenes from the *Kama Sutra* and a pair of crimson Persian slippers. And there, behind the long, polished teak counter, under the only electric light in the shop were rows of sparkling stones nestling in beds of crimson velvet. There were ruby rings and sapphire brooches, pearl-tipped hat-pins and onyx tie-pins, emerald necklaces and diamond bracelets, gold collar-studs and silver cufflinks. Aladdin could not have been more pleased with his cave.

On his first day as a shop assistant, Leo was introduced to the staff and given long-winded instructions on how to clean the ornaments, how to register watch repairs, how to fill in forms for this and that, which envelopes to use for items to be valued and which for bracelets and brooches needing safety chains. Then, having spent the morning giving him instructions, Young Mr Craven said he could have a bowl of plain rice and fruit for lunch. Nothing spicy, nothing smelly, understood? At all times he must put customers first. After a half-hour break, Leo was handed a small, lined exercise book.

"Write down what I told you this morning, boy. Do it in categories: ornaments, stones, watches, brooches etc. Let's see what sort of memory you've got."

So Leo sat in the back room and visualised the contents of the next room, and filled the pages under more categories than he was instructed. Young Mr Craven showed neither surprise nor pleasure. "You'll do," he said.

Two weeks later there was a change to the quickly established routine. Leo was told he was being given the opportunity to increase his knowledge of the business. He was led out of the back door and Young Mr Craven's other shop boy whistled up an urchin, "Follow him," Leo was told.

First, he was led down the narrow side-alley that led back to the main shopping street. They wandered among the colourful clients of The Fancy Mahal Bazaar for a few minutes and then they stepped out of the Victorian gothic of colonial Bombay into a very different land of commerce. Colonial emporia gave way to sari shops and trinket markets: out of this they crossed to a street of palladium and minaret facades, then they were among street vendors and cooking pots; the smell of sizzling cardamom seeds and onions frying sweet golden brown in ghee. Then suddenly they were in a labyrinth of tall wooden tenements, stepping between bags of bones begging for life and painted boys lurking for business. Leo followed the urchin and knew that if he were abandoned or assaulted the outcome would be the same; he could run in any direction and never get back to British India a quarter of a mile away.

They turned into forbidding alleys that became canals in the rainy season. The tenements above seemed to lean in to suffocate the intruders. A rat ran down a gutter in front of them for a number of yards, a flea-ridden Pied Piper in reverse. They turned again, and again and again. The underfed urchin skipped and slipped down alleys that had never seen the light of day. They turned again, this time into a closed courtyard. A dead end. The urchin pushed open a door and the noise of Bombay, the clamour of humanity, stopped. For one single moment there was silence. The urchin beckoned Leo to follow him into the empty black entrance. And then Leo jumped out of his skin.

A giant was hiding behind the door. The genie had escaped from its lamp. A huge, turbaned head lowered itself to examine him. Leo's eyes were on a level with a wobbling belly overlapping a sashed waistline, and a scimitar.

"Hah!" breathed the creature.

"Huh!" retorted the urchin.

"The water-rat returns, and with a fine fat frog for supper," whispered the giant, knocking Leo sideways with inhuman halitosis.

"The water-rat returns," said the urchin in his street Marathi, "on legitimate business."

"Legitimate!" exploded the giant, tossing the little guide some coins.

"Legitimate. What would you know, freak? Your mother was an elephant, your father was a toad, your arse is covered in warts and you fart like a . . ."

The giant lifted the urchin by what remained of his shirt. The shirt collar tore apart; the urchin fell, landed like a cat, looped beneath the archway of bandy legs and was through the door. "I have to take him back, you devil worshipping lump of pig lard! Call me." And he was away before Leo had a moment to realise he was on his own. But then he did, and he was terrified.

Leo had read about trolls but didn't know they existed in India. The creature lowered itself again to scrutinise him, then reared up and a haunch of wobbling oiled flesh that was an arm stretched out to inch the door open a little further. Leo stood motionless, his white drill suit almost luminous in just one ray of light.

"Good Lord above and bless my heathen soul," said the monster in perfect schoolboy English. "A young sahib. Or yes, or no?" He turned Leo with a plump, ringed finger. "The clothes say you are, young sir. But my nose tells me something else. Hmmm . . . Fee-fi-fo-fum – not the blood of an English mum!"

The creature sniffed Leo's hair, stared into his sea-green eyes and tweaked his nose up and down then he straightened up to his full height and adopted a quite different attitude. "Now, please follow me," he said.

The turbaned doorman stepped into a foetid stair well and began to rise. "Follow me. Follow me. Come along, chop, chop, and take care to watch your step."

Leo watched his step – and it was as well he did, for many of the steps were not there at all. A banister appeared as if summoned by the genie, and then they were on a landing and going up a more solid, safer set of steps. And then they were on another landing and the giant knocked delicately at a stout door. It was opened by a midget.

Leo was ushered into Victorian England. Velvet and chintz, tassels, hunting prints, three large-globed oil lamps and, in the centre of the room, a carved mahogany table. On the other side of the room, an ancient, seated mummy – a collection of leather-clad bones dressed in a burgundy smoking-jacket and wearing a fez – was propped behind a large, ornate desk beside a narrow window. It was Old Mr Craven.

"You are Leo Kazan. Welcome, welcome. My son says you have the makings of an excellent apprentice. Come here, where I can see you better."

Leo stood rooted to the spot. Light filtered through the barred window, illuminating the old man in profile. His nose had been eaten away. His mouth had disappeared, but his eyes bulged out on stalks. The urchin had brought him to a house of freaks and – lepers. The man moved. It was a mask. He was in a madhouse. There were bars on the window; this was Bedlam in Bombay.

"Come closer," beckoned the decrepit creature that was to be his master. Then, with two yellow claws, Old Mr Craven removed his bulging eyes.

Leo felt the floorboards disappear beneath him. He was falling, falling through the floor. He would land on the genie and . . .

The old man tutted. "Arnold," he said, addressing the small man who had opened the door, "call the Pathan back and get the boy some water. Then get back to Lionel and tell him my apprentice has arrived as arranged."

Eventually, Leo yawned a huge air-gulping yawn and found himself sitting in a high-backed armchair flanked by the vast doorkeeper, his arms folded across his chest, a scowl on his face, and the immaculate midget in a frock-coat. The diminutive man offered him a glass of water from a tiny tray. The room swayed back into focus but reality lay just out of reach.

A distant voice said, "Well, now, young man, if those two flights of stairs are too much for you I do not think we have a future together. Hmm?"

Leo looked up. It was just a normal old man. Thin and wrinkled but neither wasted, shrunken, nor leprous. "I am most sorry, sir. I am – I'm not a weakling."

"No indeed, you look very well-fed to me," said the elderly antiquarian, coming over to the chair and patting the boy on the shoulder. He nodded at the doorkeeper, who said something under his breath in English and left the room. "Shall we start again?" Old Mr Craven asked Leo with a smile.

"Please."

"Well, come over to my desk. Can you stand? Good. You are here to learn about precious gems, are you not?"

Leo drained the water and handed it back to the diminutive man holding the tiny silver tray whom he assumed was a servant. Then he dropped his shoulders, took a deep breath and levered himself out of the deep armchair. "Yes, I have been sent to learn. That is, I want to learn." He walked over to the desk. Nothing seemed quite right; he was still a little woozy. "I am most dreadfully sorry about this disturbance, sir."

"Tut, tut, a momentary failure." Old Mr Craven was back behind his desk replacing his magnifying goggles. "Nevertheless," he said, gazing at Leo with sightless eyes, "nevertheless, being quite serious, I shall say that this is something that you may not let happen. Not if you are to work for the House of Craven. If you are employed to take valuable items from here to there, you need your wits about you. A slip, a trip, a stumble, whatever the environment, you will be stripped. Do you follow me?"

Leo nodded and went closer to the desk. On its green leather top there was a large sheet of pink blotting paper. On the pink blotting paper were two sheets of white paper. And on each sheet of white paper there was a small pyramid of irregular, dull pebbles.

"Your task, young man, is to tell me on which sheet lie the more valuable stones. Shall we begin?"

Four hours later Leo was back in the labyrinth of alleys, trying to keep up with the underfed urchin, who demanded four annas when they reached Victoria Terminus. Leo gave him two. It was still too much because they were probably of an age, but one of them had a future and the other faced mere survival. Two days later, Leo learned that the tenement occupied by his master had another doorway into another alley, and at the end of this alley lay Craven's Oriental Curiosity Shop, and the land of the commercial box-wallah. In less than a minute he could be back among the pompous emporia of the Raj. Leo revised his ideas; a street urchin who could protect a business investment deserved respect.

The Empress Emerald

Exactly one week after that, Leo was standing behind a vast teak counter trying to thread soft, soggy string through the tiny holes of cardboard price tags when his attention was drawn to a face pressed up against the shop window. It was a woman. More than that it was impossible to say, so flat was her face against the glass. He had already learned that women could spend ages gazing at the baubles Young Mr Craven put on display in the window (anything of real value was kept behind the counter), so to start with he was not at all disturbed by her interest. But she didn't go away. The fiddly price tag task was tedious and the woman's presence began to irritate him. Leo tried staring back at her, willing her to go away. It didn't work. He left his task and went to drink a glass of water. She was still there when he returned. He resumed his task; she stayed in place.

Unable to resist the temptation any longer, he lowered himself from sight and re-emerged with crossed-eyes, and lolling tongue like a dribbling idiot. She had gone. The door bell tinkled and he nearly swallowed his tongue.

"Yes, madam, can I help you?" Leo's voice squeaked up and down, out of control.

She was tall, thin, and wearing a spinster governess's outfit of high-necked blouse and long grey skirt. "May I look around? I want to buy a gift for . . ." She bent to examine a mother-of-pearl box on a three-legged table, "How pretty."

Leo tried to get his features and voice back in order and came round from behind the counter to be of assistance. She looked up at him almost in fright.

"Oh dear, oh dear, yes, well thank you. Another day." She was gone.

Leo shrugged and went back to the price tags. He tipped the box containing the cut string pieces into the box containing the cardboard tags and pushed them to the very back of a drawer marked 'watch repairs'. The incident had unsettled him. A memory jiggled uncomfortably, like a loose tooth. The woman in his head said: *'There's a good boy – Mummy's boy.'*

Leo pushed his hands through his hair as if to clear his mind. He needed a more demanding task; he didn't want to think about her or anyone like her.

Chapter 8
Bombay, 1917

Sir Lionel Pinecoffin was taking afternoon tea in the Taj Mahal Hotel. He enjoyed taking tea at the Taj. The absurdity of the place amused him. It was an ostentatious, French-designed building, erected on an unwanted swamp once gifted to England in a Portuguese princess's dowry, and the only establishment in British Bombay where the raj and wealthy citizens of all creeds could meet informally. The hotel also served the best tea-cakes outside the Home Counties. It was absurd, it was amusing. It pleased him to sit among the tall, cool columns and watch rajahs and their retinues; ranis in gold-edged saris clinking priceless bangles as they lifted their cups; American businessmen in safari suits; Indian spice-merchants smelling of turmeric, selling entire cargoes. He liked to see how other nationalities conducted their lives, albeit the sheer expense of the hotel set them on different social strata to the rest of their fellow countrymen. Each and every visitor was in some way atypical. If the city of Bombay was a social melting pot, the Taj Hotel was where the wealthiest and best dressed of each race mingled.

On this particular afternoon, Sir Lionel had just ordered tea with lemon and Madeira cake from one waiter, when another came to his table bearing a business card on a tray.

"The gentleman to your left, sir, sends his regards and asks me to give you this."

"Thank you."

The man sitting to Sir Lionel's left was examining his finger-nails. The name on the card was Leonid Kazan.

"Please convey my respects to the gentleman and ask him if he would care to join me."

The waiter crossed between the tables. Leonid Kazan looked in Sir Lionel's direction, inclined his head in acceptance and rose from his seat. He was a large, thick set man of indefinable middle-age. His hair was straight and black, his collar exceptionally white against a swarthy skin. Something about him reminded Sir Lionel of a seventeenth century courtier, the sort who ill-advised his monarch for personal gain.

"Sir Lionel, how charming. Well met by lamplight, as your Bard nearly said." The Russian lowered himself into a chair and smiled around him. "*Midsummer Night*, or was it *Twelve Night*? Yes, yes, charming. I have been meaning to make an appointment to see you for some time." His English spilled out in unpredictable bursts, like rusty water from an aged watering-can. "So very congenial to see you in these delightful surroundings, I cannot understand at all why the architect suicided because the hotel was not quite altogether just what he wanted. Such a perfectionist must have a sad life, don't you think?"

Sir Lionel smiled, "Perfectionists are their own worst enemies, by definition."

"When one has to contend with so many petty enemies, why bring trouble to oneself through mere dissatisfaction? Not being satisfied is just a trivial excuse, don't you think, for being miserable?"

Sir Lionel inclined his head in agreement. "Are you resident in Bombay, Mr Kazan, or just visiting?"

"Both. I have come from Delhi on business, but also to see my house. I bought a charming property on Malabar Hill some years ago. The view – the jasmine – a little palace. Staff is a nuisance, of course. They don't have anything to do when I am not there and expect to be paid. It defeats me."

A waiter brought fresh tea, and a cup and saucer for Sir Lionel's guest. The Russian lifted the lid of the teapot and peered into the hot liquid. "I only drink leaves," he said. "None of that dry powder you English think is tea." He stirred the pot with his teaspoon. "A proper home is so important, don't you agree?"

"Indeed, and your family are here or in Delhi?"

"I may re-marry very soon. We shall live where I am posted, if my lady accepts, of course." The Russian gave Sir Lionel a winning half-grin and cocked his head to one side.

"Congratulations. Your new wife is from Bombay?"

"God forbid it, no! She's Russian – from a most excellent family. Pedigreed."

"Yes. Well, that makes life easier; chatting to one's spouse in a foreign tongue must be a chore. Your first wife passed away? I am sorry to hear that. Not the best of climates, Bombay."

"No, not the best of climates, nor perhaps, I may have to say it, always the best of people. Traders!"

Kazan spoke the word 'traders' with such disdain that Sir Lionel wondered if he had heard 'traitors'.

The large Russian then leaned back to watch someone enter the room and, addressing the room in general, said, "My first wife went mad." Then he turned back, and lowering his voice very slightly said, "She had delicate mental health. She was born in India, of course. Her father was a trader. Perhaps, as you say, the climate." He shrugged and sipped his tea. "It is a sad case. And it has taken me *years* to acquire the divorce."

J. G. Harlond

Unsure whether he wanted to hear anything more about the first Mrs Kazan, Sir Lionel moved the conversation in a new direction. "Forgive my curiosity, but you clearly recognised me here. I regret I cannot recollect us ever having been introduced."

"Yes, yes, many years ago. At a vice-regal reception. There was some little joking about my name, some of your young fellows calling me Lord *Curzon*. A silly joke, of course. It was you, Sir Lionel, who put a stop to the embarrassment, very smartly."

"Ah, yes, I think I remember. Your name wasn't . . ." Sir Lionel took a sip of scalding tea to silence a foolish statement. A political officer of so many years standing and he could still put his foot in his mouth. Hermione would laugh. He thought about her waving goodbye, waving her wide-brimmed, white hat like a flag of surrender, and for the first time in many years wished that he, too, were on the ship going back home. Surrender to the climate, the constant vigilance, give in to indigestion, mosquitoes, scorpions in slippers – give in to the whole caboodle and go back home, saying: 'Pax, India – you have won.' But of course he wouldn't. Nor, thinking about it, would the gentleman stirring a third sugar lump into his tea. So why the silly chit-chat?

Sir Lionel placed his cup on its gold-rimmed saucer. He was about to speak, but Kazan said, "Interesting thing, these names we have. Take mine for instance, fairly obvious its origin: Kazan, from the khanate, now considered a province – on the Volga. My ancestors were the Khans of Kazan, naturally."

"Naturally."

"Your name, too, is interesting. You attend many funerals?" The Russian chortled, and some of his tea spilled into his saucer.

Sir Lionel smiled as was expected and said, "No – that was an old school joke. Also, that I am a good sort deep down." The word play was lost in subtlety or translation, or both.

The Russian said, "I still have land there, farms and villages. They bring me a comfortable income. Not princely, but something for a son to inherit. Which leads me indirectly, in this roundabout way, to why I wished to meet you. However, I pause. I see more people coming in to take their tea and perhaps this conversation should be less conspicuous. We are watched, you know. Shall we meet quite by chance in similar circumstances for an early *aperitif* in three days' time?"

"You were going to make an appointment to see me in my office. Why not come there?" Sir Lionel could see no way out, so decided to play it out on home territory.

"Yes, yes, less clock and dagger. Our Empires are no longer enemies; they are brothers-in-arms in this tragic war. The habits of our old Great Game die hard. I was so used to you chappies keeping an eye on me I stopped noticing, until . . ." The big Russian leaned forward, straining the button-thread of his double-breasted suit. Then he decided to withhold the comment and sat back, cocking his head to one side and giving a dimpled grin. "Shall we say Wednesday?"

"Yes, I believe I am free."

"Good. Wednesday: the day of Woden, the warrior god, the transformer, the poet. Do you know Norse mythology, Sir Lionel?"

"No, I regret I don't."

"You should read myths and fairy tales, my friend. They are the keys to our cultures. Every people have them and with similar stories: *The Magic Beans, The Stolen Child.*

They also serve to explain our origins. Names have meanings; they give us our – *belonging*."

"Yes, quite."

Sir Lionel was abrupt because he was trying to formulate a response to what had become a diatribe of innuendo. He was saved, however, by Kazan himself. The man was suddenly on his feet, saying, "Well, thank you for a pleasant tea. Goodbye."

Sir Lionel rose from his seat, but the swarthy Russian was already striding out. Tugging his napkin from his jacket front as he went, he tossed it onto an unoccupied table and nodded to a family coming in, but never once did he look behind him.

Lionel Pinecoffin returned to his seat, exhausted. It would all have been quite absurd, he thought, if there hadn't been a quite definite element of menace. Origins, an estate in Russia. A mad wife and a house on Malabar Hill – a little palace, no less. And the stolen child of myth, legend and fairy tale. What did Kazan know?

Sir Lionel's sense of loss without his wife was compounded by his need to tell her what had happened at the Taj Hotel. Hermione was in every sense his helpmate; she would listen and perhaps offer suggestions. He *could* let Leo go. Kazan was right, the two empires had, albeit perhaps only temporarily, set aside their rivalry over the Indian sub-continent. The role he had in mind for the boy wasn't strictly necessary anymore, in the short term. Leo's return to his Russian father could be stage-managed as a glorious re-union. It could even be used in the press as confirmation of how the two nations had come together. The whole thing could be presented as a terrible mistake. Reverend Johns had mistakenly rescued a lost child, who in fact had a family. The family had finally been located. End of story. And whatever the press did with it, no one could deny the orphanage had done its very best for the boy.

He would get Arnold Mackay, his personal secretary, to locate Millicent Cleaver – she was the weak link. Johns would mind his Ps and Qs, and do what was instructed. But the governess woman would have to be dealt with: a gentle threat of prosecution might be sufficient. The Cravens were not a problem: discretion was their family motto.

Sir Lionel decided to take a stroll down the only sweet-smelling dock in Bombay, the Sassoon timber terminal, and call on Tamchian for a chat. There were two important details to be ascertained before the Wednesday interview: the whereabouts of the mad wife, and how mad was mad.

Chapter 9
Bombay, 1917

During the early months of 1917, Leo was sent on three sea trips in a fishing boat to a tiny harbour some miles down the Malabar Coast. On the first two occasions, a gaunt individual wearing the yellow scarf of Kali gave him a stitched-up, rag-wrapped package. The rag packages were ridiculously easy to unstitch. They each contained a small quantity of uncut diamonds of varying sizes and a minute roll of paper containing a list of names. Leo read the lists then selected a stone. Just one. Not the smallest, not the largest. Just one very average, dusty, uncut diamond.

He assumed he was acting indirectly for Sir Lionel. He and Old Mr Craven were as thick as thieves. He'd have to report in to Sir Lionel, in any case. Make his weekly witness statement on whom he'd met and where, what they had said and what they had not said. It occurred to him during the third return voyage, that this might have been one of Sir Lionel's tests. Test or no test, however, he was going to have his cut. On this third trip, the bag was significantly bigger than the previous two. So he took significantly more stones.

Sitting in the prow of his evil-smelling bark on his return, Leo watched white birds swooping between the blue sky and the green sea. Noisy gulls harassed the fishing boat for part of its catch. They bullied the more delicate terns, stealing shiny little fish from their beaks. A couple of years before, a gull had dived out of the sky and stolen a cake from Leo's hand as he walked along the beach. He had been more scared than he cared to admit. They were brazen, abusive thieves: vicious, noisy, no style, no saving graces.

Leo enjoyed being at sea, though. The boat trips had been a revelation. He had lived near the sea all his life and never really noticed it. Out here on the water, he felt clean. It was everything the city was not. Despite the clamour of the gulls and the lurching of the small boat, there was tranquillity. The patched sail flapped and the woodwork creaked, and Leo thought they were the finest sounds he had ever heard.

The gentle surge and dip of the boat lulled him into a reflective mood. He normally avoided introspection, tried not to look back at the past because what he saw there was too upsetting. But this wasn't a question of reviewing the past; he was examining the present. Uppermost in his mind was the image of a yellow Kali scarf looped around a dirty brown neck. These men in offices, Sir Lionel and his ilk, who wore starched collars no matter what the heat, these men who drank tea at five and only ever mixed with their own, had no idea who they were dealing with. Or, more to the point, who *he* was dealing with. Had they never heard the Hindi word *thag?* Did they know anything about the cult of the goddess Kali? Or was that why he had been sent? Because he was disposable: an orphan boy no one need seek or claim.

Thinking about it, Leo lost his sense of calm and became angry. These ignorant colonials had sent him to men who were obliged, compelled, to kill – to make regular sacrifices – human sacrifices. It was not as if he even had a chance of escape if he were chosen. Kali's men worked in threes: one to confound the victim, one to hold the victim, one to slaughter the victim. Leo shuddered. He had been sent to collect rag-bags of uncut stones from known killers. He was sure that the man with the yellow scarf had not been on his own. Old Mr Craven had some dubious contacts, but these were just plain dangerous.

Leaning over the side of the boat, Leo watched the white spray grow taller, and with it grew his sense of resentment. He was always being sent here and there; do this and that 'and not a word to anyone'. Not that you could talk to anybody and expect them to take your words at face value, not any more. Nothing could ever be taken at face value. There was no one to trust and nobody was what they seemed. Even the hillsmen from Kashmir, Srinigar and Peshawar who sent the rubies down from the frontier 'for Mr Craven, sahib, only' had interests beyond purses of rupees. That's why the mad Pathan was employed. He translated their cryptic messages into English and passed them on to Arnold Mackay. Then little Arnold Mackay, the tame P.A., set them out in official form for Sir Lionel, who then sent them on with his IPS dispatches to the India Office in London. Yet, as far as Leo knew, all those messages ever contained were a few lines on who had been seen off the beaten track in remote areas. The Great Game with the Russians, the geopolitical struggle for the right to pass unchallenged from Afghanistan and travel down into India for trade, was not over yet. International politics all tied up in scruffy bags of rubies. But, oh, those rubies! The gem of gems: the lord of stones, worth three times more than these trifling diamonds. Rubies to protect a man in war and peace, to keep body and soul safe from injury and evil.

And the emeralds – so cold and clean to the touch. Emeralds the colour of a temperate spring, symbols of hope and beauty, and eternal love. It was written in the *Veda*, the book of life, that emeralds had the power to heal and brought the wearer good luck.

The Empress Emerald

And now these dusty diamonds . . . diamonds had their value, he supposed, because they were all things to all people. They possessed not one colour but all colours in the universe. Learning and working with Old Mr Craven in his stuffy room was fine. Handling the uncut stones, weighing them, pricing them, that was fine. Cleaning up antique jewellery, watching lights glint off facets, examining unusual settings, this was more than fine. Learning juggling and disappearing tricks with the Pathan giant was also fun. But was this fetching and carrying what they had been training him for? Had he spent the best part of a year in captivity learning Russian and Urdu, only to be sent on these crazy, dangerous errands? Was he of so little value that it mattered not if he were killed in the process?

The closer the boat got to the Bombay docks, the more indignant Leo became. The thought crossed his mind that he ought to pocket the rag package for himself and when he reached the docks buy a passage to . . . anywhere. Or stow away on a liner. Stay at sea for a few weeks. This was the life for him.

Or he could get a job on a boat, sail away, and live his own life. Everybody wanted something from him and nobody gave him anything in return. It wasn't fair. Even his grandfather . . . But he wouldn't think about that. He stepped across to the other side of the fishing boat and watched silver-scaled fish swimming too close to the net for their own safety. His mind started to replay a scene and he couldn't stop it.

"Don't wriggle dear. You'll fall off the wall like Humpty Dumpty."

"Fidgety bottom, never still. Tell him he'll fall off. Crack his head one side the wall, drown on the other. That'll stop him."

Her arm tightened round his waist. He could smell her warm hair and skin, like vanilla and the roses in Grandpa's garden.

"Millie, for God's sake, put him on the ground, and leave him there. Nobody will notice. You can't keep him forever. Fidgeting like a cuckoo, shifting his fat bottom until he's pushed us out of the nest, eating us out of house and home."

"Down, down now."

"I've just put you up, dear. Look at the pretty boats, Leo. Off they go for the fishies, bobbing up and down. No, don't bob, dear, you really will fall and drown like Grandpa says. Look at all the boats. That's right, big boats going to other countries. Ships, they are called ships. We'll go on a ship one day."

"Will you? And where'll you go, I'd like to know? Millie, you put more nonsense into that child's head than is good for you – or him."

"Down, down now."

"All right, let's go to the beach."

"I'm not going to Chowpatty, I told you I wouldn't and that's final. Hordes of bloody children and squawking women."

They walked along beside the sea wall instead. Mummy bought him a stick with a wooden monkey at the top. Grandpa carried him on his shoulders. They stopped to watch a fleet of little fishing boats coming in. The sea had been calm that day.

Now the sea had begun to heave and churn. His head ached. For reasons he could not name he wanted to scream, shout. Further out, the water had begun to boil up; black waves tumbled into a tumult then threw themselves in an ecstasy of spite at his vulnerable little vessel. The spray soaked Leo's shirt and dampened his lank black hair. He brushed it back off his forehead. He would wear his hair brushed back like this now. It would make him look older. He felt older.

Leo stared into the ocean, willing it to drench him, daring it to knock him over. As if in response, a huge wave hurtled straight at him, leapt into the boat to clasp him with monstrous claws, sink its frothing fangs into his throat. Involuntarily, he stepped back. "Coward," he said to himself. The wave, accepting defeat, licked his feet in submission. He stamped on it. Killed it dead. Then he returned to his seat on a greasy coil of rope and folded his arms across his chest: he was too old for children's games.

The boat got back into port at sunset. Leo stuffed the small rag-bag deep into his right-hand trouser pocket and stepped onto the foul smelling quay. The reek of the dying catch, combined with the overpowering stench of drying Bombay duck, nearly knocked him flat. Clamping his hand over his trouser pocket, he swayed down the quay and into the city. Keeping to lighted paths whenever possible, he hurried straight back to The Oriental Curiosity Shop and entered through the back door.

Young Mr Craven was doubled over a ledger, doing accounts. Leo placed the package on top of the ledger, slightly smudging a group of numbers. Young Mr Craven tutted like his father but said nothing. Not a word. So Leo had no opportunity to comment on his errand. A long-fingered hand waved dismissal and Leo was sent on his way.

Outside the darkened shop, the night was cooling. Nocturnal street-life was crawling out from warm, rotting woodwork: every delight was up for sale, and so much to choose from. Leo returned to his room in the building guarded by the Pathan, changed his sea-drenched clothes and was back down the rickety staircase in a trice. The gatekeeper wasn't there, but Leo left his cheroot offering on top of the door frame anyway.

The night was now wide awake and eating a hearty breakfast. Everywhere there was the smell of food: frying onions, cumin and coriander, ghee and cauliflower. A thousand curries crowded the narrow lanes.

A painted boy called to Leo from a balcony. "I'm here Leo, my love. Come and get me for perfect minutes of perfect delight."

"Minutes!" screamed an elderly whore from another balcony. "I can give you an hour, boy, if you've got the energy!"

Leo called up, "It'll take more than an hour, beloved – I'm a eunuch, remember!"

The two whores laughed. They were joined by a small group of pretty girls on another balcony, tittering together like colourful sparrows. They all knew full well Leo had all that was required.

Walking backwards down the lane, Leo shouted, "A cookhouse supper for the first to tickle my fancy." The painted boy instantly disappeared indoors. Leo squealed in mock horror and skipped off down the alley, through the tenement labyrinth, and out into the shopping streets.

Some, but not all, of the money in his pocket, was quickly spent. Then he slipped into a curtained doorway and joined a group of much older men in an elaborate den. Their headwear spoke of their religious differences, but not their conversation. He shared their hookah and listened to their gossip.

"Hari has been in a fight," he was told quietly as he passed the pipe.

"Ali Sayid has been called up to fight for the English. His younger brother has returned to their village."

"To scratch a living out of dust."

"Gupta has met some boys from Hyderabad. He's found a place for them to meet the Bombay nationalists. It's been agreed he can buy small stones for polishing, but he mustn't sell them in the city."

"Who told him this?" Leo asked.

The men shrugged. "Things are said. Who says them is not our business."

Leo felt suspicious eyes on him. Nevertheless, he said, "Send them to sell in England with someone safe."

"And who might that be?" Gupta asked.

"Me."

The men laughed. "You aren't safe, Leo, and you aren't going to England. It's too dangerous on the sea, anyway."

"You'd be sunk by the enemy."

"Well, I am not going anywhere," Aziz declared, leaning back and stretching like a long, lithe cat. "I've found a girl with three breasts."

"Three!" the men chorused.

"What did you do?" asked Hari, his bruised eyes shining in the twilight dusky den.

Aziz leaned forward to whisper, "I fondled two, sucked the third and made her wriggle in my lap. What do you think I did?"

The men laughed, guffawed. "Where? How much?" they asked.

"Under the Towers of Silence."

There was a collective pause, eventually broken by quiet Hari, "Is this a joke?"

They do not joke about sacred places. They do not offend.

Leo left and wandered through the bazaar, bought a cone of puffed rice and found himself on the seafront. Fishermen holding long bamboo poles were angling for a catch before the storm finally broke. A very thin street urchin appeared from a shadow and grabbed Leo's hand, "Hey, Leo, sahib, an anna and a toddy and I shall be your friend tonight." Leo handed him the half-empty cone of rice and pushed him away, then squatted beside a beggar sitting cross-legged on a bench. The urchin hunkered down on the ground beside them.

"Here child, go and rot your guts and don't blame me." Leo handed him two coins. The urchin jumped up with glee and ran off.

"So?" said the beggar.

"May the gods be good to us and bring us rain," said Leo.

"The gods will be good to you, never fear. The rain comes because it must. Sit with me and share an old man's thoughts."

Leo sat and listened and paid the old man for his intelligence. Then, as if pulled by the retreating tide he returned to the sea wall. The tide was pulling him, pulling him out beyond the rows of fishing vessels, out beyond *the pretty boats, Leo.* Out beyond the sea lane to the Gateway of India; out, out into the deep, deep sea. Now he was on one of the big ships. He was leaving the stuffy intrigues of Bombay, living his own life, voyaging to the lands of camels and dry sands; travelling over the sand to the land of donkeys and olive trees where Christ was crucified; now up to the snowy lands where Christmas trees grew and a man called Santa made toys for good boys who sat still and ate their bread and butter nicely. *Such nonsense you put in his head, Millie.*

A sharp pain split his forehead in two and settled in the left temple. He leaned over the sea wall to vomit. His head ached, his body ached. It was time to go.

"Not yet, Leo. Not yet."

Sir Lionel Pinecoffin looked at the young man seated in front of his desk. He was tall, well-set and good-looking in a swarthy way. He held himself straight, did not slouch in the chair. He was as close to being a gentleman, when he was dressed appropriately, as became his circumstances. He was like his father only in build and certain mannerisms. There was a lot less bluster about young Leo. He had learned to measure his words. But then he had always known when to keep quiet, nobody had ever had to teach him when *not* to speak. And by his own admission he was a loner. The ideal 'intelligencer'.

Getting up, Sir Lionel busied himself in a filing cabinet, extracting a sheet of paper to cover his discomfort. Seeing Leo from this corner of the room, however, he could visualise the young man dressed in furs, riding across the Steppes, a crossbow-shooting khan. Leo could also pass as a Balkan count, a Portuguese merchant, even, in a silk turban, a green-eyed, up-state prince. In scruffy pyjamas, he was another Bombay coolie of indefinable heritage. What he was not, and never would be, was an Englishman, which was inconvenient, given that he spoke English as his mother tongue. And that was something that would have to be dealt with sooner or later.

Sir Lionel had found Millicent Cleaver. He had her address in his desk drawer. Leonid Kazan's little palace on Malabar Hill had been located. The wretched mother, Catalina Figueroa da Silva, had been traced to her parents' home in Goa. She was, as her ex-husband had so unkindly stated, quite mad.

Mad or not, however, Leo had a real mother. He also had grandparents and a real father who was heir to a wealthy estate in his homeland. And what about the broken Anglo-Indian woman who went to sleep every night clutching a blue shawl she had once knitted for a baby boy now living not five miles away from her? If he chose to reveal what he knew, he could send the boy to any of them.

But it was too late now. There never had been a right time. Firstly, because of the scandal and its political repercussions, then because Leo was doing so well in his apprenticeships, and now because Leo was an invaluable watcher. He mixed and went unnoticed. So many reports were going to London based on Leo's observations. The information he was currently picking up about members of the Indian National Congress, the INC, was pure gold. Leo had become an essential part of his machinery and he did not want to part with him.

Sir Lionel looked at Leo, then looked away and sighed. "I can't let you go anywhere yet. Not yet. And don't tell me it isn't fair, Leo. You're complaining like a child, and you're not a child anymore."

"That's what I'm trying to tell you, sir." Leo's voice had changed, settled into a gentle baritone timbre.

Sir Lionel kept his face averted and shuffled documents in his filing cabinet. "None of us gets much choice when it comes to it. No one offered *me* a choice regarding my future. Winchester, Oxford, Indian Political Service. I'm a second son; I'm supposed to think myself lucky I have an interesting, meaningful career and wasn't packed off to the Army or Church. Do you know, right at this very moment I would like to be walking the home farm with a couple of gun-dogs, then back to a roaring fire and supper with Hermione. Who can say life is fair?" The colonial administrator sighed and turned back to his protégé.

Leo bowed his head, unsure how to react to these personal revelations.

"The fact is, Leo, I have been waiting for you, waiting for you to grow up, so to speak. I have some rather special plans for you. I wasn't going to tell you yet, but as you seem so low perhaps I can cheer you up with what is to come. But, before you get too excited," Sir Lionel braced a fair, freckled hand in the air, "I'm not sending you to England until this damned war is over. Too many ships are being attacked."

He returned to his desk and stood behind it, drumming his fingers lightly on its polished surface, deciding how much he could reveal and phrasing the words carefully. "There *will be* a good deal of travel. I didn't send you to Tamchian for no reason. Your Russian will come in handy. More so now than when I first decided you should learn. Perhaps we should find a way to top you up; you are probably getting a little rusty."

As Sir Lionel sat down he could feel Leo's piercing gaze on him. Not for the first time lately, the boy – young man – was making him nervous.

"We haven't had you wasting your time with jewellery and curios either. You needed a trade. You needed to learn how to make an honest living." He looked the boy straight in the eye. Leo did not bat an eyelid. "I have tried to help you learn the ways of the world, and I can see that you now want to be out in that world. Normal reaction at your age. So yes, Leo, you can go, but I don't want to lose my investment: your skills and abilities. There is an important, perhaps even exciting, role ahead for you. But we are talking about the future. I do not want you to leave Bombay, yet."

Chapter 10
Bombay, 1917

Sir Lionel realised that when he had insisted on Kazan coming to his office he had not specified a time. He made sure Leo was with the Cravens, ancient and modern, on the day in question, instructing the doorman to say he was unavailable if the boy did appear.

He assumed the Russian bear would make his appearance during the lunch hour when the office building was empty. He was right. The lift clanked to a halt on the second-floor landing. Its metal cage scraped open and there was a tap, tap on the office door. Before going to open it, Sir Lionel entered an adjoining, interior room. A very small, immaculately dressed man was perched on a chair writing in a ledger.

"He's here?" inquired the scribe, lifting his head.

"Think so. I'll call if necessary." Sir Lionel straightened his jacket, adjusted his cuff-links and strode over to open the door to his offices himself. "Mr Kazan, come in, come in."

The Russian was more subdued. He wore a dove-grey tie and had a matching silk handkerchief in his top pocket. He was carrying a crocodile-skin briefcase. A little too elegant, thought the Englishman, yet not vulgar.

"Good to see you. Please take a seat." Sir Lionel ushered Kazan into an overstuffed chair in the corner of the room before seating himself in another, which he had placed at a suitable angle earlier. "Comfortable? I can send out for some tea, or would you care for something a little stronger? I have a bottle of vodka, a gift from a member of your consulate when it was first opened. It'll be rather aged in the bottle by now, I fear."

Kazan looked at a silver timepiece on a chain. "It's after one, yes, why not? You show me the vodka bottle and I shall decide."

Sir Lionel poured the Russian a measure and waited for his approval. Kazan nodded and held his small tumbler out for another. The vodka was poured and the two men settled back as best they could in their uncomfortable chairs.

"Now, Sir Lionel, I shall not be beaten about the bush, I am going to come straight to the point. This is in our both best interests and we are both to suffer if we cannot resolve the issue *tout de suite*. So here it is . . ." Kazan paused, looking at the door to the adjoining room then inclined his head in its direction and raised a bushy eyebrow.

Sir Lionel followed his gaze, "My private secretary. Trustworthy. Has to be."

Kazan sniffed, "In both our interests, but not for secretaries, Sir Lionel. I must insist."

Sir Lionel rose, stepped through the open door and, out of sight of his visitor, tapped an ear. The small man clambered down from his cushioned chair, took a stethoscope from one desk drawer, a small pistol from another, then went to stand by the dividing wall. Sir Lionel nodded, turned and closed the door as instructed behind him.

"Diamonds," stated Kazan the moment Sir Lionel retook his seat.

"Diamonds?"

"A fortune's worth of diamonds."

"Diamonds, here? Where? I understood Indian diamond sources were mined out last century. Very few or none left."

"Alluvial diamonds, picked like pebble stones on a beach. A riverbed in Hyderabad."

"Good Lord! Are we talking about Golconda diamonds, by the way?"

"No, not Golconda. I understand it is a dry stream and someone found some interesting stones and he went to see somebody, who spoke to somebody else – you know the way these people are. My informer, I regret, is rather too shy with actual facts. However, I do know that the Nizam of Hyderabad, this very short man who is so rich man, doesn't know his peasants are selling them to an agent. And he would have a blue fit if he knew this agent has links to a Bolshevik group in Moscow. Into the bargain, this agent is a Hindu and brother of a man in the National Congress."

"Sounds a bit of a rigmarole to me," said Sir Lionel. "You have, I am sure, checked the veracity of the claims."

"Naturally, Sir Lionel, we are not colonial amateurs. I am also informed by a safe and honourable, very concerned source in a high position." The Russian picked up his drink, but before the glass could touch his lips he exploded righteously, "Independence, Home Rule League agitators with more money than sense, now putting ideas to some damn stupid college boys in my country."

"Yes, well that link is nothing new, is it? Marx did after all stress the *international* aspect of class struggle. Are the gems going to Saint Petersburg, do you know?"

Kazan huffed, "This English cold blood. I bring you this information as a small gift in good faith. A way to improve our relations – diplomatic and personal." He paused for a moment then continued, "Some stones get to the diamond exchange in Antwerp."

"Excuse me?" Sir Lionel, who on hearing the word 'personal', had been following a completely different line of thought, was lost. "Antwerp?"

Kazan looked at him meaningfully and nodded, "Antwerp. Diamond centre of the known world. I do not know how, in this war, but I am told these uncut diamonds are traded for good prices. They are the best ones, they tell me, the ones that get to Antwerp. The small ones go straight to Russia, apparently. It is ironic, but they are very useful for our new industry machines. A complete waste, if you ask me."

"You seem very well informed."

"We have our patriots, Sir Lionel. There is mischief in my country . . ." The Russian diplomat searched for a word, "Disturbances. Strikes! Factory workers, farm boys, they are marching in the streets causing trouble. And who is organising this? Students! There are groups of students and ex-soldiers with weapons, guns and God forbid it, bombs. And to get these guns, these damn nuisance students need finance. And some cheeky coolies here in this very country, India, are providing it. Now it is *your* job to find who is organising this and why." The Russian tossed back his vodka with a flourish.

Sir Lionel adjusted his position, said nothing and waited for Kazan to pick up the thread again.

"The student threat in Saint Petersburg, I regret to say, is very strong. These diamonds are helping to finance a rebellion against the very Tsar of Russia."

"And you need our help to bring it to a halt. I see." Sir Lionel drummed the fingers of his left hand on the arm of his chair. "If the information was that they were being sold to finance the Home Rule for India campaign here, it would make more sense. Do you think these two groups of revolutionaries are actively collaborating that closely?"

Kazan laughed, "You do not seem surprised, Sir Lionel."

"Well, yes and no. I mean I am surprised and not surprised. If anything, I am surprised at the apparent sophistication of a group of coolies discovering what must look like ordinary stone chippings, examining them then hiring an agent who has links with Antwerp. Naturally, I appreciate your situation. And, as you say, we are wartime allies now. It should be easy enough to stop at source, if we know where that is, though. And we'll trace any Home Rule financing back to members of the National Congress if we can." As Sir Lionel spoke he was wondering how soon he could inform Old Mr Craven, and if indeed, the old man had known about the Russian connection all along. Using the deals to flush native agitators out into the open, or at least learn names, had taken a very unfortunate turn. Looking Kazan in the eye, he said, "So the small diamonds go straight to Russia: overland, then by boat across the Black Sea and through the Ukraine?"

The Russian shrugged his shoulders, "The usual trade routes. My country drinks also a lot of tea. We think they go with the tea. Or maybe with rice."

"And the end-users of the finance – in Moscow? Do you have names?"

"Our enemies, Sir Lionel. Mutual enemies. I told you. Revolutionaries who will kill our royalty. Yours and mine. The same maternal line from your good Queen Victoria. This is a disease. A plague of rats. It will spread. These students will commit regicide as soon as they get into the palaces."

Sir Lionel sighed, "Yes, absolutely, but names would quicken the – erm – extermination process." He was distracted, still wondering how all this was going to lead back to the unspoken personal issue and innuendo of a gift, requiring, no doubt, a reciprocal favour. He reached for the bottle and refilled the glasses.

The Russian tossed back his drink and said, "This war has shown them the power of the ordinary *ignorant* with a gun in his hand. Any uneducated son of a butcher can kill people like pigs these days. I told you, they are even marching! Thousands of killers are out on the streets every day, they pretend to be waiting in bread queues, but they are in lines for pistols. These men and boys are not in uniforms on our battlefields, oh, no, these *hoi polloi* are waiting their chance to stir up trouble in their very home. Sir Lionel, we need to identify our enemies within, we need the leaders. Look what happened to beautiful France. Destroyed forever by unwashed *culottes*."

"Indeed." Sir Lionel wanted to laugh, but the implications of the matter were too grave. He placed his glass on the low table before them then smoothed the creases in his trousers. "Tell me," he said slowly, "the Nizam of Hyderabad, does he really not know about the alluvial diamonds? He would intervene on your behalf, you know."

"Independence for India is not in his favour. This I know. But Sir Lionel, this is for you to do, this is not my country."

"Yes, absolutely, I just want to be sure of the facts before I go any further. This may just be a – well, a coincidence. Some coolies find some stones and someone who has Home Rule sympathies and knows a couple of your Russian students gets involved. I cannot see how a few industrial-value stones can really be that significant."

"High quality as well! They go to Antwerp, I told you." Kazan looked exasperated. His neck had gone red and he was clenching and unclenching the fingers of his left hand. "But this is not the matter. We are talking of revolution. Look, Sir Lionel, let me add a little more explaining to you. The Nizam is a *prince*." The Russian pronounced the word with reverence. "He is wealthy from the tributes his peasants pay. He may know – or not know. You need to locate a boy of the Kapasala family."

"The Rajah of Kapasala – in the Punjab? Is he involved, too?"

"His second son." Kazan leaned forward, "You British educate these boys in your own schools, you know. You teach them and – here is the rubbing – you give them education but they get bored, and like all naughty boys, they like to be with the less desirable types. Then they get ideas: political ideas, which they do not exactly understand. They should be kept at home. Quite honestly, Sir Lionel, it has to be said, your government has an unnecessary sense of generosity regarding this country. It is education to blame. You let them go off and learn, any Tom, Dick and Hari! You even teach them here in Bombay in your missionary schools."

Finally, thought Sir Lionel. He fidgeted with a cufflink and waited.

"Look what happens, Sir Lionel," Kazan continued. "A born prince who supplies revolutionaries, it is not natural. It simply should not be permitted. You cannot educate these boys to use their brains and then expect them to be docile like coolies. These young chaps are looking for trouble."

"I cannot believe the Rajah of Kapasala would permit it."

"Perhaps he does not know where his son is, or what the boy is doing."

"Possible."

"Possible, yes. Fathers can be the last to know these things. And you know yourself, what you British say and do here in India, in Bombay itself, is not always what it should be."

Sir Lionel kept his eyes averted. "I will contact my superiors forthwith." He made to stand; it was time to terminate the meeting, but Kazan spoke again.

"*We* have identified *our* enemies. *I personally* know *my* enemy. Unfortunately, we need your government and police to cut these students and their league down, in the bud, root and branch."

"You may be right, but I am still confused regarding some of your details. Princes, rajahs, maharajahs – none of them, or at least very few, are interested in Home Rule, it would ruin them. They stand to lose income, land, status – their entire lives are rooted in the ancient laws of tribute."

The Empress Emerald

Kazan looked at him as if he had just failed a spelling test. Sir Lionel proceeded regardless, "Can I ask why you have come to me with this and not taken it straight to Delhi?"

"Do you want an honest answer or a diplomat's answer?" Kazan got to his feet and stood with a wide, well-manicured hand on the back of his chair. Speaking more quietly, he said, "My family stand to lose a very great deal in Russia if there is a revolution, Sir Lionel. I believe this is a very dangerous matter. I have colleagues who . . . Let us say they do not take this seriously because they have less to lose. . . They foolishly refuse to act." Kazan pulled the grey silk handkerchief from his pocket and wiped his forehead. "I am taking a big risk to tell you this. Being honest is not what a diplomat should do. But I believe you and I, man to man, can see a matter through – together. For my family's sake, if that is not too emotional for you as an Englishman?"

Sir Lionel was sobered by the man's tone. For as much as he wanted to see Kazan as a pernicious buffoon, there was something very genuine about his concerns. He opened the palm of his right hand, encouraging the Russian to proceed.

"If there is a revolution and these Bolsheviks win – if it is known that I was the one to cut a supply of finance here, once they are in office I shall have no job. I shall not only lose everything I possess in my country – that goes without saying – I shall lose my post here in India. If this happens I can never return to my family estate, and I have no income here, either. I am, as you say, batting a sticky wicket and I have very strong reasons for not wanting to leave India until a certain personal matter that has come to my ears becomes resolved."

Chapter 11
Bombay, 1917

The beast that is Malabar Hill lies crouched, lapping the ocean, its head to the south licking the salty surf, its tail alert, wagging up country. Colonisers and better-off natives built houses along the beast's spine to escape the Bombay swampland and enjoy spectacular ocean views. They built in every style and ostentation: pagodas and Palladian mansions, medieval castles, gothic horrors with more turrets than structure. The Hendersons' property was someone's idea of Ancient Rome – in its decline. But this was not out of keeping with the bacchanal planned that night as a fundraiser to help send Indian boys to the European Western Front.

The cab driver kept his bony pony at a trot behind the other conveyances also taking party-goers up the hill. Leo sat back in his tonga, thoroughly pleased with himself, especially his appearance. His silk tunic lay smooth and comfortable across his broad chest, its long, pearl-buttoned front line made him appear even taller than his current six foot one. He was especially delighted with the pigeon-egg ruby pinned in his sky-blue satin turban; borrowed for the one evening only and to be returned to Old Mr Craven before noon next day. For this evening – there might be more, he was told – Leo was Karan Singh, a wealthy young Sikh recently arrived in Bombay and looking for chums. The second son of the Rajah of Kapasala had been placed high on the Hendersons' mixed guest invitation list and had accepted in writing. Leo was detailed to attach himself to the Kapasala crowd.

Leo had been briefed at length about both the son and father. The Kapasala estate was virtually bankrupt, thanks to the entire family's extravagant life-style, and the rajah now feared independence would bring a halt to the tributes he extracted from his peasants. This money paid for his sons' education, for his sisters' Parisian dress accounts, for French brandy and Havana cigars and family entertainments such as tiger hunts, not to mention the vastly expensive week-long weddings of their numerous offspring.

The son Leo had been told to befriend had his own spacious apartment in Bombay overlooking the ocean; he paid his tailor and drove an Italian-built four-cylinder automobile. Leo found it difficult not to admire and envy him, despite the fact that Sir Lionel insisted he was not to be trusted with a glass of water, and Leo had better take care — because if the Kapasala boy got wind they were watching him, he could find himself in a very disagreeable situation. Young Kapasala, who was almost certainly personally involved in the very lucrative diamond link to Antwerp, had some nasty acquaintances — as Leo knew only too well from his recent boat trips down the Malabar coast.

As Leo's tonga drew to a halt on the gravel driveway of the Hendersons' pillared mansion, he noticed Sir Lionel being admitted through the large front door. Leo counted to sixty, paid the driver then held out more money, saying, "I will pay you this extra to wait for me." He handed a small portion of the extra money to the driver, whose eager face told him what he wanted to know. "Wait until this is the last carriage, then wait a little longer. If after that, I do not appear, you may return to the city."

Leo then strolled across the gravel drive to mingle with a mixed group of youngsters who were gathering forces for their third sortie of the evening.

"Fundraising for the Front is such fun!" a girl in a pink-fringed frock and silver shoes squealed at him. Neither she nor the other gay young things appeared to have any understanding of the fundraising's real purpose – or if they did, they were ignoring the darker implications. Not wanting to be drawn into the party before he had had time to take stock of who was arriving and who was greeting whom, Leo stepped into the porch and leaned against a pillar with his arms folded as if waiting for someone.

Inside, the Hendersons' huge, circular hallway was lit with Venetian chandeliers. Liveried servants were stationed at inner doorways like museum attendants. Envelopes, empty for the filling, lay on a marble-topped table, carefully scattered around a grotesque centre-piece cornucopia of soggy fruit and wilting flowers. Mrs Henderson, a robust matron dressed in swathes of rusty taffeta, a perfect match for her hennaed head, was crossing the hall with what appeared to be a dishcloth in her hand. She stopped in her tracks and cried, "Sir Lionel! Oh, it is nice to see you! You're quite the stranger these days!"

Leo watched Sir Lionel make a short half-bow in response.

"How is Lady Hermione? We do miss her on the committee, you know. She's the only one who ever managed to keep us in order." There was a burst of girlish laughter.

Out of the corner of his eye, Leo watched Sir Lionel and kept track of the silver-shoed girl and her little group. One of them was a Sikh in western evening dress and turban. Two of the other men, also in western clothing, were carrying bottles of champagne. The Hendersons' butler scowled his disapproval. A waiter, hired for the evening, appeared not to notice and proffered a tray. Leo sauntered in and took a flute of tepid champagne then found a suitable spot on his own and remained where he was, listening to the Henderson woman twitter on at Sir Lionel.

"Let me just do this," she indicated the dishcloth, "and I'll go and find Albert. He'll want to show you the gala he's got laid on himself. I'm not supposed to know some of the things he's arranged out on the terraces. I do, of course, but it wouldn't be right for me to admit it." She cupped her free hand round the side of her mouth conspiratorially. "'Edna,' he says, 'you keep quiet or you'll get expelled from your own knitting circle.' Hee, hee, hee. . . 'All in a good cause though,' he says, 'and if tonight we don't raise enough to win the war, we'll just have to come up with something that will.' Mind you, after this I can't think what. Oooh, you just wait and see what he's got in the garden!"

Sir Lionel waited until the woman had finally tottered off with her dishcloth, put down the warm wine he'd been holding, picked up a pink gin and wandered out to the top terrace. Leo followed at a distance, curious to see how his mentor behaved; he was evidently not enjoying himself, but it was early yet.

The night spangled around him. Men and women of all ages and creeds conversed in what Leo came to know as the particular cocktail hush that heralds a long evening of sweetened alcohol and tasteless canapés. Sir Lionel was collared by an earnest couple and grilled about his family, his plans for the near future, the distant future, his pension schemes and what would happen if they all had to quit India. He was polite, charming, bored. He extracted himself and made his way to the steps that would take him down to the next terrace. Leo followed.

Albert Henderson called from a distance, "Sir Lionel! Good-o! Off to find the fun. Edna said you'd arrived. Good-o, enjoy. There won't be another night like this for a long time."

Leo was accosted by the squealing girl who was having so much fun. "Come with us," she commanded. Then she stopped, turned in a whirl so her fringes shivered around her and peered up into Leo's eyes, "What's your name?"

"Karan Singh. And yours?"

"I'll tell you that later, if I still like you." The girl hooked an arm under his. "You look interesting. Stay with me."

The girl's friends were now gathered around the other young Sikh. He was regaling them with a bawdy version of the 'Charge of the Light Brigade'. Leo laughed, waited until the Sikh got to the chorus then interrupted in mock-classroom la-la-la, adding, "And climbing on top, 'Again, again!' she cried. 'Up, up, and oooohh, ooooh, up the Night Brigade.'"

The Sikh slapped Leo on the back. "Who's your new gem?" he asked the girl.

"He says his name is Karan Singh. I say his name is Adonis."

"Adonis was blond," snapped a pasty-faced Anglo-Indian standing behind her.

"How do you know that?" the girl retorted. "Greeks aren't blond – or are they? Well who cares anyway."

A waiter arrived and, in the lull of choosing fresh drinks, Leo stationed himself a little away from the group to pick up nearby conversations. A hunched group of older men were saying, "Bad business, these disturbances in Petersburg."

"Yes. Not unexpected, though. It'll spread to Moscow of course."

"They say Tsar Nicholas has abdicated. *Daily Chronicle* says the entire royal family is under arrest, even the Empress!"

"Where'll it all lead? That's what worries me," said a stooped greybeard.

"Up the Khyber without a paddle."

"Trouble is, our children here think Russia might be their great deliverer from the north. If these hot-heads, workers, students, whoever they are, do succeed, *we* are done for."

"Good Lord," said the greybeard, "I didn't survive the Mutiny and this blasted climate to hand over power just like that." The old soldier tried and failed to snap his fingers.

Another greybeard shook his own arthritic index finger, "And certainly not to a bunch of native amateurs."

"Coolies setting fire to godowns and threatening to booby-trap public services, where will it end?" the stooped greybeard shook his head in despair.

Leo sipped his flat champagne and watched a tall, barrel-chested foreigner with a mane of black hair pushed back off his face descend the steps to the terrace, then walk towards Sir Lionel and his group. He wasn't English and he wasn't Indian; Leo couldn't recall having met him before, but there was something familiar about his appearance. Sir Lionel knew him, though, because he excused himself and greeted the newcomer quietly. Leo wondered who the man was and decided to find out. But not at that moment, because the nameless girl with silver shoes was now towing him down more paved steps to another grassy terrace.

In acknowledgement of the United States' entry into the war, gaming tables had been laid out like an American saloon: roulette and twenty-one, black jack and poker. Young Kapasala joined the roulette table. Leo was about to seat himself next to him when something caught his attention. A woman in a gold frock was piling chips on a number. As she leaned forward, a heavy green pendant fell away from her neck. Whether by accident or design, the stones of the pendant formed the profile of the late Queen Victoria: the head was a lustrous pearl; the body a plump, pear-shaped emerald; the long neckband was studded with smaller emeralds, diamonds and pearls. The necklace was called the *Empress Emerald* and it was worth a fortune – Leo knew, he had seen it before, in Old Mr Craven's secret safe.

Leo grimaced involuntarily as he looked at the woman. She was no beauty, her skin aged by the sun; her voice roughened by whisky and cigarettes. She did no justice to the fabulous ornament. The woman, oblivious to his gaze, was playing roulette with the intensity of an addict, watching the wheel like a hawk scanning for rodents. A sharp English voice brought Leo back to the present.

"I've just lost the equivalent of a month's income, I should have stayed indoors."

A dapper man, whom Leo thought might be a doctor, got to his feet. Leo hovered by the chair, waiting to take it the moment he left.

"Well, playing a few tables has kept me *outdoors* quite a lot recently," replied the emerald woman's husband. "Last summer in Simla, I picked up a whole new string of polo ponies at a table."

"Yes," said a pretty woman across the table, "we can see you're on one hell of a winning streak." She pointed a long finger nail at the necklace lying on his wife's flat, sallow chest. "Where *did* you get *that*?"

The husband laughed, "Right here in Bombay, at Craven's. The old chap can get you anything – if you're prepared to pay."

The woman wearing the Empress Emerald stroked the stone with a nicotined finger. Leo flinched again and stepped back into the shadow. He brushed shoulders with Sir Lionel. They did not speak.

"Hey, where's Johnny Sing-along?" cried the silver shoe girl. "Come and sit with us."

The Empress Emerald

Leo was dragged across to another gaming table. From the poker table, he could just make out the burly black-haired foreigner watching Kapasala. Sir Lionel was watching them both. He shuddered, then decided Karan Singh needed to forget all about them and concentrate on having a good time with his new pals as briefed – until later. He only hoped the polo pony husband had enough cash or chips to see him through to the very end of the party.

Eventually, after losing a few games of Black Jack, the youngsters returned to the house for some food. Despite his intentions to enjoy himself, Leo was finding the night a strain, and in a hurry for it to be over. He went into the dining room and surveyed a dead turkey, a loin of unidentifiable meat beside an untouched pile of stodgy yellow rice and a mound of fruit, then helped himself to a sticky pastry. But, oh, splendid! There was some European nougat and fudge cut in small pieces on silver plates, and behind that an open tin of English toffees in shiny, coloured wrappers. He stuffed the pockets of his trousers with toffees, spoiling the line of his tunic, then selected some creamy fudge. As he popped it into his mouth, a voice behind him said, "I was wondering where you were. Come and talk to these chaps. They have had the most extraordinary meeting with this chap Gandhi. He was half naked they say, and sat on the floor." Leo turned and the speaker said, "Oh, sorry old chap, thought you were someone else."

By midnight, Kapasala's crew had exploited the Hendersons' entertainment to the full and were all ready to move on. To Leo's surprise, they stopped at the cornucopia table on their way out and left their anonymous contributions to the Great War. Leo followed them out and seated himself on the folded canvas hood of Kapasala's roadster. The car roared off, scattering sheets of gravel over dozing ponies. He hoped his tonga driver hadn't seen him go.

After less than a mile down the moonlit hill, the car screeched to a halt; its driver needed a pee. Leo took advantage of the stop to find out where they were going.

"Kapi's den, then maybe over to see some of his tame girls and boys, depends."

"Which do you prefer, Adonis?" asked the silver shoe girl, touching his knee.

"I like girls," laughed Leo. And he cocked his head in his own special way and gave her a lopsided grin.

The girl licked her upper lip with a pointed pink tongue. "My name is Lena, and you are mine tonight – I've told them."

Leo winked at her from his perch. Then the second son of the Rajah of Kapasala jumped back behind the wheel and fiddled in the dark to locate the new-fangled ignition. Leo wriggled backwards, intending to stage a fall off the back of the car as it lurched back to life. If they stopped to pick him up – well, so be it – if they didn't, he was free for the rest of the night.

The fall was harder than he had anticipated but the turban, or perhaps the lucky ruby, saved him from concussion. The white tunic made disappearing into nearby bushes a challenge, but he managed it in a manner which did credit to the Craven's mad genie's training.

"Kapi, stop!" the girl cried.

"Singsong's fallen overboard!" one of the goodfellows shouted

"Let him find his own way home," Kapasala said.

"He didn't want to lose his virginity," quipped the pasty-faced Anglo-Indian.

The rest was lost as Kapasala revved the engine and moved off again.

Leo waited until the car was well out of sight, checked the toffees were still safely stuffed in his trouser pockets and made his way back up the hill to the Henderson residence. He slipped behind various waiting vehicles and climbed aboard his tonga unseen. "I need a breather," he told the driver and settled back out of sight.

Leo very nearly fell asleep waiting for the woman wearing the Empress Emerald to leave. Two things kept him awake; what to do about his white tunic, and the gut-churning fear that the woman might have lost the necklace at a gaming table.

Chapter 12
Bombay, 1917

The papers were full of it: 'Priceless Emerald Stolen!' – 'Malabar Jewel Theft' – 'Daring Robbery'. Editors had gladly latched onto a bit of light entertainment; the war was currently offering only very glum headlines. Sir Lionel scanned the newspapers on his desk. His secretary, Arnold Mackay, tapped the *Bombay and District Morning Herald*. "That's the best version," he said.

The famous necklace, known as the Empress Emerald for its kindly likeness to our late lamented Queen, has been stolen from the Bombay residence of Mr and Mrs Ernest Wilson.

A distraught Mrs Wilson told Bombay police that in the few weeks she had been the proud owner of this very singular necklace (a wedding anniversary gift from her beloved husband) she had of course kept it in a safe. The adornment had been left in her room only a matter of moments between removal and placing in the domestic stronghold when it was taken. Its disappearance is proving a troublesome mystery for the police.

Mr and Mrs Wilson have a number of dogs on their property, including a bull mastiff, but none of the dogs raised an alarum as to an unwanted intruder. Only one member of the domestic staff was present in the residence at the time of this heinous crime. The other two native servants have been arrested by police but we can report that the two servants, who have long been in the employ of the Wilson family, are most anxious to establish their innocence.

"Who writes this stuff? Oh, never mind." Lionel slapped the paper down, picked up a slightly more serious periodical and made a show of reading the war news. "*Russians Decline to Fight*," he read aloud. "What's this?" He ran an eye over the front page column and turned to the editorial.

Ongoing negotiations with Bolshevik leaders were brought to a close yesterday when the otherwise oratorical Mr Trotsky made the following brief statement, "I just announce the war is over."

Despite allied efforts at numerous peace conferences, the new, and dare we say cowardly leaders of Russia refuse to continue fighting the Germans.

Military strategists say this will enable enemy troops to withdraw from what has hitherto been the Russian Front. These troops will undoubtedly be used to strengthen enemy lines in France . . .

Sir Lionel looked at his secretary. Mackay was reading a report on the Malabar Hill robbery with just a little too much personal interest.

"Blasted reporters," he said tapping the editorial, "they know more about the war than we do."

"They make up most of it."

"I wouldn't call this fiction?"

"The robbery or the Bolsheviks?"

"Russians – *declining to fight*."

"Sir Lionel, my job is filing, not speculating on international political issues."

"Arnold, you underestimate yourself."

His secretary responded with a venomous look. Sir Lionel put down his newspaper and began sorting through his post, standing at an angle to the window overlooking the street. The news reports, of both kinds, had thoroughly unsettled him, and now he was nervous about how much his secretary suspected regarding Leo. *It's time*, he thought, then said, "Arnold, go down to the travel bureau and see what's sailing next week. Single passage, second class – no, first class – for one passenger. I'm only interested in Southampton, not Le Havre or Marseille."

"For you, sir?"

"Not for me, no."

As Sir Lionel watched his secretary scurry out of the door as fast as his stumpy legs could carry him, he felt his stomach lurch. A number of passenger vessels sailing from the subcontinent had been targeted by the German submarines in the past year. There was a very real risk the boy's ship could go down. Perhaps that was why Arnold Mackay was so eager to run the errand.

Sir Lionel accompanied Leo to the ship. There was a fresh October breeze blowing off the sea. Standing apart from anxious passengers and hopeful coolies, Sir Lionel handed the boy three buff envelopes and two brown-paper packets. He then ran through a litany of instructions. Leo was to pick up the keys to a small flat near Westminster from a Mrs Smithers, who lived near Waterloo Station; he was to buy cold weather gear on arrival; he was to take these dispatches in person to the India Office in Whitehall. They then ran through which packet was to be delivered to whom.

"On no account allow yourself to be separated from these documents. And don't mention what you are delivering to anyone, now *or* in the future. Is that clear?"

Leo opened his new attaché case and slipped the packets and envelopes inside.

"If the ship is hit, Leo," Sir Lionel continued in a grave voice, "destroy them as fast as possible. If there's a severe storm, strap them inside your shirt. Arnold gave you an oilskin pouch, didn't he?"

Sir Lionel tried to be cool and factual, but the danger to the ship had hooked into his consciousness. There was indeed information of great importance contained in the missives he'd given the boy, but he knew he was really sending Leo away on suspicion of theft. But what a theft! On the other hand, sooner or later the boy was going to be caught and it was better it didn't happen in Bombay. Leo had to go, and they could not wait for the war to be over.

Leo himself, however, seemed unperturbed about the risk. He was trying to be calm and serious, but Sir Lionel could see the fellow was as excited as a schoolboy. The moment had come for him to hand over two more envelopes.

"Now listen, these are for you. Only for you, and I don't want you to open them until this evening. It might be wiser to wait until you have dined."

Leo reached out a hand for the two unaddressed, white vellum envelopes. One was fat, the other thin. As he started to put them in his inside jacket pocket, Sir Lionel caught a glint of red and gold. Leo was wearing a damned great ruby ring.

"How did you get that?" he blurted. "No, don't tell me, I don't want to know." The boy was a magpie. An incorrigible magpie.

"It's to protect me, sir. I have great faith in the protective power of the ruby."

"Yes, well it's big enough to protect the whole ship."

"I hope so, sir."

Sir Lionel laughed and pulled the boy into an unconventional, uncharacteristic embrace. Leo, who lacked self-consciousness hugged back.

"Well, that's enough," said his patron. "Off you go. I'll be in touch as arranged."

Lionel Pinecoffin turned on his heel and strode away through the crowd, a drowning man in a sea of unspoken words.

Leo picked up his attaché case, kicked at a coolie who tried to pull it from his hand, and walked up the gang-plank alone. He turned once to look back at his city. A woman in the crowd, a tall, thin woman in unfashionable clothes, raised her hand and waved at him. Leo gasped. She was shouting something. He tried to make out what she was saying but it was impossible. Then she began pushing her way through the crowd towards the gangplank. Leo thought she was crying. He gulped, unsure what to do, then turned back to face the deck and hurried to find his cabin.

A man, who had been standing in the shadow of the harbour buildings, also raised a hand, an involuntary action. He watched the retreating figure, its height now exceeding his own, until it had disappeared among the other passengers on board, then he also pushed his way through the crowds – but in an opposite direction – summoned a tonga and returned to his little perfumed palace on Malabar Hill.

The Empress Emerald

Sir Lionel headed straight for the Taj Mahal Hotel. Sitting in a private booth in the elaborate bar, he ordered a large whisky then pulled out his handkerchief and blew his nose. His vision was blurred. He blew again and looked up to see who was in the bar. His nose prickled and he couldn't seem to swallow. "Oh, God Almighty," he muttered to himself, furious at his weakness. He hadn't blubbed since the week after Hermione left. But that had been in the privacy of their bedroom. The thought of Hermione took him over the top. He got up and went to the gentlemen's washroom to splash cold water on his hot face.

The attendant, who missed nothing, handed him a lemon-scented towel and lowered his eyes. Sir Lionel handed him two coins and returned to his whisky. He downed it in two goes and stared at the rows of bottles behind the bar, wondering what to do for the rest of the day. He couldn't face going back to his office: the poison dwarf would have a field day. Perhaps he should have sent *him* with the confidential reports on the Home Rule connections. But then Leo, in his unprincipled way, was far more trustworthy than the devious little chap he called his private secretary. No, Arnold was safer kept on a tight leash at his side.

Leo did not obey his instructions. As soon as he was shown to his narrow cabin, he locked the door, removed his jacket and pulled out the two envelopes. Which first: the fat one or the thin one? The fat one – it might be money.

It was money. He counted a thousand pounds in large English bank notes. There was also a card with the name and address of a City bank. Leo sat back against the wall of the cabin and whistled. So much! Why?

He slipped his thumb under the seal of the thin envelope, opening it with a jagged tear. It was empty. No it wasn't. There was a very thin piece of officially-stamped paper. He pulled it out and unfolded it. It was his birth certificate.

PART 2

ENGLAND, RUSSIA, SPAIN, INDIA
1918 - 1929

Chapter 13
Cornwall, 1918

A roll of thick, white mist curled around the many-cornered house, sidled up the chimneys and settled down to await the sun. Below, between high willow herb and tall rushes, the old river barely moved. A late-night water-rat cut his way home through the shallows. An early-rising trout snapped a fly. Along the waterside, never-quiet ducks pattered and chattered. Coots gathered food among the reeds. A heron speared an unwary amphibian for breakfast. Morning had come to the final turn in a Tamar River valley.

Davina awoke to the silent call of Hans Andersen swans. She buried into the feather down of her white pillow and pulled a blanket up around her ears. She was poor Elise, alone in her prison garret. High above circled her white-clad brothers.

She sighed and stretched her arms into the air. Today she would illustrate Andersen's tale in river-coloured water-colours. But first she had to finish all the different fruits in Rossetti's *Goblin Market.* "Currants and gooseberries, Bright-fire-like barberries . . ." Davina recited. Rolling onto her stomach, she poked around under her bed at a pile of books. The large, pink volume of Andersen's Fairy Tales was just out of reach. She shifted and pulled, and out came two leather-bound tomes. The first was her beloved *Morte D'Arthur*. The other was a mud-coloured volume embossed with the image of a damsel in steeple hat and floating veil. From her precarious position balanced over the side of her bed, Davina contemplated the image, thinking about all the pretty ladies who were changed into hags or locked in turrets; so many sad and tragic tales. Guinevere and Lancelot, Tristan and Iseult: such love, such sorrow. Groping further into the dust balls, Davina located a variety of poetry books and selected her new copy of Rossetti's *Goblin Market*. That at least had a satisfactory ending. She read again the goblins' cries as they trotted down the glen to tempt Laura to sin. There was a moral in the tale, and morality, although she wasn't altogether sure exactly what it was. Her mother called it Victorian twaddle. Her mother had no time for sentiment.

The door opened and her ancient nanny, Morrigan, entered. The woman hobbled across to the window and yanked the curtains back. Davina shuffled back under her blankets.

"You not dressed yet? I'm not coming up those stairs again. You'll have to sort yourself if you're not out of that bed this minute."

"I'll sort myself, Morry. I can, you know. I'm a big girl now."

"So you say, but you don't act it. When I was your age . . ."

Davina poked a freckled nose over the sheet. "What? Tell me, when you were my age, what?"

The old woman in the yellowing starched collar and cuffs, who cared for Davina when she was staying in the Cornish house, sniffed, "None of your business." She hooked the book of fairy tales with her foot then bent down to pick it up. "All this nonsense. Time you're finding a husband, not reading children's stories no more."

"Oh don't you start!" Davina burrowed back into the bed. "Can I have porridge, with honey and cream for breakfast?"

"No, you cannot! Toast's already made and getting cold and that's your look out. Now then, look sharp or I'll feed it to your precious birds." Morrigan's Cornish accent caught on the letter *r* in birds, making them sound unpleasant. She lumbered around the room, pushing in drawers, tugging at the curtains, making a display of her aching knees. "And I'll thank you to be a bit more considerate when you come home next Christmas. If you do. No more sleeping up here on the top floor. Not when I'm down there in the kitchen being cook, skivvy and lady's maid, and me with my roomatics."

"Yes, all right. I'll get up now, promise." Davina swung her tanned legs out of bed.

"Is there any news of Matthew?"

"Lor', I don't know. Why have you put your stockings in your petticoat drawer again? Fancy going all the way to Bombay, wherever that is, in wartime."

"Bombay is on the west coast of India, where the imperial sun never sets. Mr Parry Jones taught me that, years ago." Davina leaned over her washstand, swished cold water over her face then tickled her neck with a threadbare flannel.

"Your brother's looking for trouble if you ask me. Sooner he's back the better."

"Won't be long now. That's why I asked."

"Don't make sense to me, it don't, gallivanting across the globe. What's wrong with staying where you belong, anyway? If people stayed where they belonged, there wouldn't be no wars, I'll tell you that for free." Morrigan pulled a clean blouse from Davina's wardrobe and held it out to her, "This do you?"

Davina held out a hand for the blouse, saying, "I saw him yesterday, Mr Parry Jones. He said he missed me. Said it had been a 'real education' coming here to teach me when I was little." She mimicked his Welsh accent, 'a *real ed-u-cation*'. For himself, naturally; it's our library he liked . . . Do you think he missed the money when I went to school?"

"Ah, don't you fret about Parry Jones. He's none of your business."

"But he was my teacher; why shouldn't I be interested in him?"

Morrigan, who was folding a discarded sweater, ignored the question. "Mind you, I dare say they needed the extra pennies. His Mary won't be coming here to skivvy much longer, neither, not in her condition . . ."

Davina was only half-listening. "I always wanted Mary for a friend."

"You can't be friends with servants. Didn't you make no friends in that fancy school you've just left?"

Davina sighed, "Not really. Not a proper friend." Then Morrigan's words penetrated, "Why won't Mary be coming any more, we need her?"

"You telling me? I can't be up and down, up and down no more, not with my ole roomatics. That skirt belong in a wardrobe, or is it on the floor resting like I should be?" Morrigan, who had been handed down in Davina Dymond's mother's family from generation to generation, inspected a crumpled linen skirt.

Davina waved a hand, "I don't want it anymore. It's too long, too old-fashioned."

"Well, wear it while you're here then when you'm gone up to Bristol or London or wherever it is you're going for the winter, I'll give it to someone that needs it."

Davina pulled her thick blonde hair up off the back of her neck over the collar of the clean cotton blouse. "Why is Mary still called Mary Peach, she's my age? It's a baby name."

"Blessed if I know, but she was as pretty and soft as a fresh peach when she was a baby."

"Was I like that?"

"No, course you weren't. You were bald as a coot and the rest of you was like a pudding. You're never going to wear them fancy shoes here in all this mud." The crotchety old lady caught the look on Davina's face and sat down on the faded, over-stuffed window-seat pulling the girl to her. "You was pale and silky and smelling of sweet violets and warm custard."

"Custard, ugh!" Davina slipped out of the woman's hands. "Move over, let me sit down so I can button my shoes." Changing her tone as she did so, she said, "*Please* can I have warm porridge with honey and cream for breakfast?"

"No you can't. Nobody eats porridge in August." Morrigan made for the stairs.

"You'd give it Matthew if he asked."

"Prob'ly I would. But then he's not here to ask, is he? Away in vurin parts eating Lor' knows what concoctions . . ." Her voice drifted out of hearing as she turned onto the first floor landing.

Davina half-listened to the mumbling and felt a twinge of conscience; she didn't really need to be up in the top room of the old Tudor tower – but it was so romantic, and she could see right across the river. She looked down at her new beige button-topped shoes and realized Morrigan was perfectly right, they would be ruined by the Cornish mud – and she wasn't going to spend the day indoors, no matter how much it rained. In a week's time she would be in Bristol and that would be the last of her freedom – possibly forever – because after that, her mother planned to spend the winter in London, war or no war. Davina couldn't decide if she was afraid, angry or excited. Nor could she decide if she was happy about being what Morrigan called 'a proper grown-up'. Sighing at her confused emotions, she found a sturdier pair of shoes and bent down to tie the laces. A shaft of sunlight shimmered on the golden hair of her arms. "Swansdown!" she gasped, and jumped up to open a window and call to her white-winged swan brothers.

Chapter 14
London, 1918

The room had begun to tilt. Not dramatically – the bottles and decanters were still on the tables – but the room was definitely listing. The new maid, Jessie, passed her with a tray of empty glasses and over-full ashtrays. Her pinafore was stained with wine, as if she had been shot in the stomach. "Happens every evening, but I can't change tonight, I've got nothing left," she confided.

"Have they spilled wine on you before?"

"Every night since the Armistice. Honestly, miss, I'm dead on me feet."

"You mean all these people have been celebrating like this for a whole week?" Davina asked. But the girl had gone, chivvied by an ex-officer's pinch.

So that was why the house seemed so, so . . . She searched for a word: debauched. Her mother would be furious. They had hardly used the house for the past four years and her mother was due within a week, there would have to be a major clean-up.

Davina examined her surroundings; she hadn't been here since she had left boarding school, but now that she was on the marriage market this was to be her new home – until she was claimed by a suitable suitor or returned to Cornwall as a lifelong spinster. The city of Bristol, where her father had his sherry-importing business, had proved inadequate to her mother's idea of matchmaking – so London, she had been informed, was her best hope. Especially now there were so few men left. Her mother didn't beat about the bush.

The room tilted again. Davina grabbed the door jamb. This was a lesson; from now on she would fill a glass with water and pretend it was gin. She turned to go down to the kitchen just as Jessie was admitting two strangers, complete strangers. One of them was definitely not English. He had the swarthy look of dark Cornish stock. But this was no Cornishman, the clothes were too elegant. He was removing an opera cape; rather over-dressed for a week-old drinking session, she thought.

An older man separated himself from a group conversing in the hall and turned to greet them. The two Englishmen then left the foreigner standing on his own and went up to the drawing room. Nobody seemed to notice. Having no wish to embarrass herself talking to a total stranger, Davina sneaked down through the kitchen and into the scullery, kicked off her shoes and sat on the floor. The tiles were cold and reviving. A rancid odour of ageing dishcloths hung in the air, but it was preferable to the stale tobacco smoke and sweat upstairs.

Davina wriggled up her narrow skirt and hugged her knees. If this was her brother's London, she would be happier being a spinster back by the river in Tamstock. What a disappointment. What a dilemma: this, or a winter of boring hunt balls and all the same old faces in Cornwall. They would be old faces too: very few of the local boys had got through the war. There had been a bizarre, tasteless row about the height of Tamstock's new war memorial; every week or so, they had to change the structure to accommodate more names. In the end, the project had been postponed altogether – to see who did and did not come home. The whole thing had been highly embarrassing for everyone except her father. He couldn't see what all the fuss was about, but then his son, who had been called up in the final months, had come home, wounded but in one piece – not counting his game leg. Davina rested her head on her knees and sighed a deep, world-weary sigh.

Leo Kazan took stock of his surroundings, smiled a crooked smile at nobody in particular and sauntered in the direction of the piano. Someone with a good voice was singing something he didn't recognise. It didn't bother him, he was used to being *disconnected*. He paused at a makeshift bar and poured himself a large scotch and soda. The singing had reached the melancholy stage. It was a pleasant tune, nevertheless, whatever it was.

The voyage from India had taught him how to steer through what he had come to think of as these *disconnections*. There was a lot he didn't know about the British; little things that confused him. He didn't know the difference between popular songs and war ditties; he didn't know some people called 'luncheon' 'dinner', that 'tiffin' was called 'tea', or that some people had tea, to eat, for supper. He wasn't familiar with the names of music-hall 'turns' and couldn't name boys' comics. Added to which, he was nothing like the rough public school toffs in the first class smoking-room or the less-educated commercial travellers, who sniggered at smutty jokes and gambled away their sales commissions at his card tables. He had, and was quick to recognise it, much more in common with the few Anglo-Indian and Eurasian boys he'd met on the second class deck: sons of craftsmen and modest tradesmen who had chosen to make their homes in India and married native girls. They had been good company. Finding a suitable candidate to befriend and perhaps emulate, however, had been a problem. 'Not too solitary to attract attention' Sir Lionel had warned him, unnecessarily, 'nor too chummy to invite interest'. In effect, he'd followed his old orphanage code: sociable and jovial when necessary, and keep to yourself when not. For the first two weeks he had been extremely sociable and jovial: he had entertained at table and smoked mediocre cigars with chinless wonders on deck. But it had been tiresome, and too easy to beat them at cards. Fortunately, once his gaming success became known they left him alone.

Sir Lionel would be satisfied with his progress so far, though. He had made contact with the relevant men in the India Office and would be starting a training course for them soon; he had settled into the mews flat arranged for him; he had spent wisely on a new winter wardrobe. Everything as he had been advised – except this particular party had not been on Sir Lionel's itinerary. This was part of his own private arrangements. He needed to make contact with a young Hatton Garden jewel dealer, who, despite the war, was still trading uncut precious gems. Sir Lionel knew nothing about any of this, or so he hoped.

Leo surveyed his surroundings more carefully: expensive furniture, tasteful decoration, not a style he was familiar with, but he liked the pastel shades on the walls and the absence of the flowery soft furnishings so popular in the Bombay civil lines.

"A very pleasant house," he said nodding to a fellow guest, "I wonder who lives here." The fellow guest shrugged his shoulders and lurched off with Leo's chosen Scotch bottle.

"Oh, Miss Davina, there you are. Whatever you doing down here?" Morrigan, looking fragile and furious like an angry wasp, entered the cold scullery, "You'll catch your death! Get up this minute."

Davina struggled to her feet and followed the elderly woman into the kitchen. "I didn't know you were in town, Morry."

"Your mother's idea, as if I want to gad about at my age. Anyways, never mind that, Jessie said you were here, and I am that glad you can't believe. Now, you got to make them stop. It's not good for any of them. We're all worn out down 'ere. A week they've been at it. I told your brother, I said you'll get a sclerosis of the liver with all that wine, but he doesn't listen to me. 'Don't nanny me, Nanny', he says." Morrigan had obviously had no chance to vent her feelings on anyone for quite a while.

"Morry, if Matthew won't listen to you, he most certainly won't pay any attention to me. I only arrived this afternoon and I haven't even seen him to talk to properly." Davina chuckled, "I thought the house was in a bit of a pickle."

"Bit of a pickle! It's a wonder *they* aren't all pickled – and bottled. It has *got to* stop before some real damage is done. What's your mother going to say when she gets here? I'll get the sack, I will. Then what's to become of me? I don't want to stay here in this God-forsaken city your mother loves so much and there's no room at my sister's place, and . . ."

"No, of course not. Calm down, Morry. Let me find Jessie and we'll start to remove the bottles and decanters. Tell her to say we have run out of drink and not to serve any more of anything."

"I'm not going back up they steps, Miss Davina. Not until all those hoity-toity, spoilt . . . Not until they've gone. I will not be laughed at, not at my age."

"Have they made fun of you, Morry?"

The Cornishwoman sniffed, and disappeared through the service door that led to the back staircase. Davina sighed. Matthew was ten years older than her, but she always felt the elder. She didn't really like him, not like some girls who worshipped their big brothers. He teased her for being 'mousy'. She wasn't mousy, just quieter than him. Now, with a new, unfair responsibility on her shoulders, she decided that she didn't like being in London, either; she didn't want to be with Matthew – and glory, glory, how was she going to sort this out before her mother arrived?

Reluctantly, Davina put a foot on the first step of the service stairs. It had gone rather quiet above. Perhaps the party was dying a natural death. But that was not the case. In the library they had set up a séance and were sitting in silence, sweaty fingers on upturned sticky tumblers, all eyes closed. A disparate group of partygoers were conjuring spirits less tangible than those that had led to their communal trance. In the drawing room, a half-naked woman in slinky silk was lisping a love song. Men still in uniform lounged around, trying to keep her in focus. In the sitting room, couples smooched while four earnest young men re-established European borders.

Davina turned to look for Jessie and came face to face with the foreigner. He was leaning against a wall, watching her. Close up, he seemed much younger than the man with the cape. He cocked his head to one side and Davina was instantly reminded of a blackbird listening for worms on the lawn at home, or perhaps a beady-eyed magpie looking for richer pickings. A couple pushed past him, he was much taller than they were. He was in fact tall and large, and . . . sleek, that was the word: 'sleek'. Not handsome, but sleek. Nationality: Spanish, Italian, Portuguese?

"You appear to know as few people here as I," he said. Was there an accent?

"Well, yes. My brother is here, of course, otherwise I wouldn't be here." The stranger made her nervous. She looked around for a means of escape. "And you?"

"Oh, I was invited by a third party, I fear. Without wishing to seem rude, who is our host?"

"My brother Matthew, I suppose."

"Oh dear, how embarrassing." His eyes twinkled.

He isn't embarrassed at all, thought Davina.

"So you are my hostess?"

"No, not at all," Davina laughed, relaxing her shoulders and smiling. "I don't know anyone!"

"Good, then stay and talk to me." There was a pause, then he added, "Your hair glints in this light like spun gold."

And Jessie and old Morrigan could have flown to the moon. Davina located a bottle of French wine and two glasses and they found a vacant sofa. They sat and chatted, but apart from the fact that he said his name was Leo, Davina didn't discover anything personal about him – not why he was in London, or how old he was or what nationality. None of the things she really wanted to know. Then, when they left the house to go to a restaurant because they were both starving hungry, she had a sudden stomach-cramping fear; suppose he was a Bosnian, someone from the Balkans, or a Turk come to spy, or for sabotage.

"Tell me about London."

"Can't, only been here a few times. I know the shops my mother likes, that's all."

"You do not live here then?"

"Heavens, no. There is – was – a war on, you know?" Davina looked up from her plate of veal in cream sauce. "I wonder where they get this divine food? We have been living on bits of cheese and potatoes."

"Divine? Well, if you like bland flavours, I suppose. It's very English, I'll grant you that. Where do you live, normally?"

"I was away at school, but I came home to Cornwall for summer vacations, and for Christmas I went to Bristol. I prefer Cornwall but my mother hates it. She was born there but she says it's boring. The house in Cornwall is her house. Father owns the house in Bristol. In the city. I quite like it there. My father's business is in Bristol. He's got some agents in an office here in London, as well, but he prefers being there. Bristol. Anyway he's almost never at Crimphele – that's our house in Cornwall. It's been in my mother's family for generations. I like Cornwall best. It rains a lot but in summer it's lovely. What's your family home like?"

Leo poured her another glass of wine, and Davina, aware that she was getting no response to her question, filled the silence with a description of summer mornings in Cornwall: how the morning mist floated up from the slow River Tamar and enveloped the ivy-covered, stone walls of Crimphele like a fairy tale castle.

Leo eventually said, "A fairy tale castle? Can't say I know anything about those. I do know about mists and damp places, though, that's for certain. I've been living in Bombay."

"Bombay!" Davina grabbed this first bit of private information and reached for more. "So you're Indian?"

"No. No, not Indian." Leo sipped his wine and dabbed his mouth with a small, stiff table-napkin. "Do you know anything about Bombay?"

"Yes, in fact my brother was there earlier this year. He sells our family sherry – well, it's not our sherry of course, it's from Spain . . . That must be why you were invited to his party. Were you on the same ship or something?" Davina sensed a mystery and didn't know how to ask the relevant questions or react. Embarrassed, she stopped talking and finished her meal.

As she put down her knife and fork she tried again, more quietly, "Do tell me, why are you here, in London, now?" She got no answer because the waiter came to their table to collect their plates.

Davina picked up her glass and tried not to slurp her wine; she was more than slightly dizzy and out-of-control. She knew she should be more circumspect, she was telling this foreigner far too much and he could very well be a spy. He said he wasn't Indian, but he was definitely foreign, despite his perfect English, or perhaps because of it. Nobody she knew spoke like him, not even her mother's falsest posh friends. But it was impossible. He wanted to know everything and was telling her nothing, and she really couldn't cope with silences. When the waiter left, she said, "My mother's latest idea – awful idea – is that she can get me presented at court. I tell her I'm too old now, but that won't stop her. She's a terrible snob. You do know about debs?"

"No, tell me."

"Oh, no, I am much too tipsy and much too tired."

There was another pause while the waiter returned with their dessert. Davina scooped up a spoonful of real ice cream. "Wonderful," she sighed.

The foreigner laughed and tipped the last of the wine into her glass.

"No, no, no! I shan't be able to walk home."

"Then I shall call a taxi."

"You'll be lucky. The London taxi is an endangered species."

"Then I shall carry you."

"Hah, after what I've eaten!"

Leo paid the bill and the restaurant owner ushered them into the street, evidently glad to see them go.

A Siberian wind was blowing down the narrow street. Davina was pulled into the surprising warmth of Leo's opera cape. It was, she decided, the single most romantic thing that had ever happened to her in her whole life. There was no taxi, and Leo only managed to carry her for a few yards because she squirmed and squealed so much he said it looked as if he were abducting her and put her gently back on the pavement. Davina grinned and said, "I am really stupid sometimes. Pick me up again. I want to be abducted."

The front door was wide open, although the party appeared to be over. Davina suggested Leo have a cup of cocoa before he set off in the cold again. He shuddered; she wasn't sure if it was the mention of cocoa or the cold, and declined graciously, then asked her if she would be free the next day for afternoon tea. He kissed her goodbye and was gone.

Davina closed the door, leaned against it and slid down onto the chequered tile floor. Now she was home she could feel her feet; they were in agony, satin dance shoes were not made for London streets. Carrying her shoes as if they were Cinderella's glass slippers, Davina climbed the stairs to her bedroom. Exhausted from the long walk, dizzy on wine and emotion, she was certain she wouldn't sleep a wink. She washed her face and cleaned her teeth, taking care not to touch her precious, kissed lips, then fell onto her bed, wrapped herself in the feather-filled eiderdown and slept like a fairy tale princess until Jessie pulled back her curtains the next day, saying it was nearly lunchtime and did she want vegetable consommé or oxtail?

Chapter 15
London, 1918

Davina was dressed for afternoon tea and waiting behind the St Anne's Terrace drawing room bay window by two-thirty. She sat with her handbag, coat and a dinky navy blue hat at the ready until Leo arrived at five. They went to the nearby Chocolate Sundae Tea Room and ordered cakes and a pot of tea for two.

Once their order had been taken, Davina said, "Busy day?"

"Busy, busy and productive, too. I spent the morning in Hatton Garden with diamond dealers."

Davina looked up from pouring tea, her eyes as wide as the saucers beneath their cups. "Diamond dealers? Gosh!" If her mother only knew she was taking afternoon tea with a diamond dealer. But Mother probably wouldn't like the 'dealer' bit. Horse dealers, card dealers: the connotations weren't quite right. Still, diamonds were diamonds. "Gosh," she said again. "Diamonds."

After much probing, Davina finally got Leo to tell her how and why he had come to London. As he related his story, she converted it into the conversation she would have with her mother. This man had risked his life, like her brother Matthew, on a sea voyage all the way from India (*before* the war had even been declared *over)* to sell *some* of his mother's family diamonds.

"My father, Sir Lionel –"

"Sir Lionel – so your father is English?"

There was a minute pause. Leo looked away from her and said, "Yes. From the West Country."

"Oh, that explains it – why you're so . . . you're a Celt like us."

Leo looked at her then looked away again.

Davina laughed and touched his arm, saying, "Another coincidence."

Leo turned back to her, beaming, his eyes glinting with pleasure.

Davina sighed. She'd been afraid he really was Indian – and there was no way to manoeuvre that around her mother. She touched Leo's hand, "Sorry, what were you saying?"

Leo recounted how his father had *begged* him to get a good price for some uncut diamonds; it was *so* difficult maintaining their social status on a reduced income during a war. And, this year, he regretted to admit, his mother had lost a *little* too much at the gaming tables in the hill station during the hot weather months.

Davina stopped her interpretation, or fabrication, of Leo and his life story and started to really listen. She wanted to know about India. He told her about the snow-topped mountains that cooled the blood just by looking at them. And yes, there were man-eating tigers and beautiful but mortal leopards. He himself had saved the Viceroy's wife from a man-eating leopard when he was only twelve. He described the incident in detail. Then he explained how leopards sneaked into villages and the outskirts of big cities like Bombay to steal babies during the night, and they wouldn't hesitate to attack an armed adult if they were hungry. They were far more dangerous than tigers. No, cobras were no problem, you just had to stamp the ground and they'd wriggle away. And pythons? He'd kept a ten-foot python as a pet when he was a child.

Leo spun a special web of exciting events and exotic places then said, "Look, I'm awfully sorry about this, but I have another appointment this evening. Do you mind if I escort you home? I know it's still early but I have to dine with our family lawyer on the other side of the City."

Davina's tummy dipped. She swallowed an 'oh' of disappointment and said, "Of course not. I quite understand."

"Will you be free to see me tomorrow afternoon?"

Tomorrow and the rest of her life. Davina allowed Leo to help her into her coat, shivering inwardly as he squeezed her shoulders before opening the door to the street.

Once back home, she hugged herself with joy and anticipation. She had so much to tell. But who would listen? Certainly not brother Matthew. The only person available was old Morrigan.

The elderly Cornishwoman listened to the very end of Davina's breathless account of her new life and said, "You be careful, my girl – fancy words and fancy ways – it'll be a broken heart or something more serious, or I don't know about vuriners!"

"He's not foreign, not like that, Morry. His father is English."

"Some English is vurin. Them that came working in the tin mines from up-country when I was a girl. Smooth-talkers, the lot of them."

"He's hardly a tin miner, Morry. Come on!"

"Exactly. That's what I'm saying."

Davina looked at her elderly nanny and wondered if perhaps she was losing her reason. She was, after all, very old. Cross that the woman had spoiled her new happiness,

Davina turned to go up to her room. But the old woman reached out and waved a gnarled finger at her.

"Vurin or English or no, he's a man and you're a maid, and I know more about the girls in this family than your ma would want me to tell. Just be warned. Fancy words and fancy ways never done no girl no favours."

The following afternoon, Davina and Leo crossed the Thames and wandered down the left bank, re-crossed the river and stopped at another tearoom near the Houses of Parliament. They ordered a pot of tea, a cream horn and a jam doughnut. Davina poured the tea and they tucked in. As there was no way to eat her cream horn elegantly, Davina didn't try. She licked at the cone like an ice-cream and made fun of her own lack of dignity. Leo bit into his doughnut and jam squirted onto his white collar. They giggled like school children. Then, just as Davina bit into her puff pastry, Leo tipped her hand so her nose was smothered in cream. The girl hooted with laughter and people turned to watch. Leo, ignoring everyone, leaned across to lick the cream off her nose. Over his shoulder, Davina caught the eye of an outraged matron in tweeds at the next table. She spluttered and slapped her white napkin up to her face.

Davina was hiding behind the napkin trying to pull herself together when there was an almighty crack, a scream and then a moment of absolute silence. A teaspoon rattled into a saucer. The world stopped turning. Two waitresses bearing heavy metal trays stood frozen in their steps.

A man in an army greatcoat got up from his chair. He was holding a gun.

"Shut up. All of you. Shut up!" He fired a shot at the ceiling and plaster fell on the tweedy matron. A small girl started to cry. Her mother put her hand over her mouth and pulled her onto her lap. The tweed lady whimpered.

"You pathetic, fat cows!" the gunman shouted at the women. "Shut up!" he screamed, pointing the gun at the child. The tearoom stopped breathing.

"Shut up! Do y'hear? Shut up!" He took a step toward the mother and child. There was a noise behind him. He spun round. The barrel of the gun panned the room. It came to a halt at the tweed lady.

"What have you got to cry about, grandma? Stuffing your face. Look at you! Great fat COW!" He went up to her and stuffed a piece of bread into her mouth. "Suck on that and shut yer face!"

Inside the coat he was skin thin, his wispy hair glistened with sweat in the steamy hot tea-room. He kept the gun in front of him, his finger on the trigger. Nobody moved. Then one of the waitresses dropped her heavy tray. Hot tea scalded her legs. She screamed out in pain.

"That's it!" shouted the man. "Scream, scream. That's what you should be doing. All of you." He panned the room again. "You sit here guzzling while we're out there, dying. Dying to save your fat arses. You bastards! You lazy, food-stuffing fuckers, you don't give a shit about us."

The street door swung open, the bell mechanism above it sending out a grotesque 'ding-dong'. A woman with two small children in school uniform entered. As the man's attention was diverted, a number of people scrambled down under their tables. The woman and children stood transfixed in the doorway. The gunman turned back to face the tearoom and fired two shots at a row of copper kettles on a shelf.

Davina and Leo were seated at a small round table near the back of the room. Leo slowly, very slowly edged his chair from the table. Davina turned to him, asking with her eyes what he was doing. A bullet ripped past her head and lodged in the wall behind them.

"Look at me, when I'm talking to you," cried the gunman pointing the gun straight at Davina. "Yes, you, Miss. Look at me. I've been saving your fucking life for four years. Look at me, God damn you!" Davina was too scared to react. "All of you. Look at me when I'm talking to you."

The gunman turned round to face the door. Leo grabbed Davina, pulled her off her chair and under the table. She cracked her head on the tiled floor and stuffed her hand in her mouth to stop herself crying out.

"So," said the man with the gun, advancing on a table of elderly ladies, "you don't like nasty bangs, do you? Well don't worry my hearties, you can die in quiet, too. Shall I go into the kitchen and turn on the gas? Let you try it for yourselves?"

The women at the table watched in horrified fascination as he waved his gun shakily at their faces, selected the eldest, then stepped back and took aim. There was utter silence, women and gunman trapped in a terrifying tableau. People under tables peeked out, white-faced, investigating the deathly hush.

Then it was over, but not all over. "Right then my fat friends, ready when you are." The armed soldier turned from the elderly women and waved the gun around like a boy with a water pistol. Everyone froze again, terrified of what might come next. The gunman smiled, laughed, then looked down under the tables and screamed in a high-pitched voice, "Get up you cowards! Get up and face the bloody guns. You can't hide down there. Get up like we have to. There's men dying in mud and you hide under bleedin' tables and drinking fucking tea."

He fired. The bullet struck a thick metal teapot and bounced off. As if on cue, the swing doors to the kitchen opened and two policemen emerged, holding brass trays in front of them like shields. They looked ridiculous.

"Ha, the porkies!" laughed the gunman. "Come to take me back? Not bloody likely!" He fired twice, straight at them.

The bullets bounced off the trays. The policemen gasped then, as one, they dropped their shields and scooted back through the swing doors.

The soldier started after them but tripped over a foot sticking out from under a small table. Yelling filthy abuse, he got to his feet, grabbed an old man sitting at the nearest table, and pulled him in front of him as a human shield. The man's wife jumped up. "No! Please, no! His heart!" The gunman ignored her and started to run, dragging his hostage towards the swing doors of the kitchen.

Leo peered out, watching the gunman's back then, turning to Davina, mouthed the words, "Follow me."

Keeping to the floor, as low as possible, they began to swarm through the jungle of table legs, chairs and trembling tea drinkers.

The pensioner in the gunman's grip twisted and turned and crashed into a table, trying to get away. The gunman pulled his trigger. Thick bright blood spurted from the old man's shoulder across a white damask table top. It splashed the shirts of the two men sitting at the table, staining their clothes like doughnut jam. Someone screamed. Someone called, "Get an ambulance!"

Leo, checking to see Davina was still with him, began to crawl along the side wall in the direction of the main entrance. The gunman turned back to the tea-room, fired another shot at random then made a dash for the swing doors. Leo pulled Davina to her feet and pushed her in front of him as they got to the door. It was blocked by the terrified mother and children. Reaching around them, Leo yanked the door open and pushed them all outside. A cheery 'ding-dong' betrayed their escape, but they fell through the doorway into a semi-circle of police.

The street had been cordoned off, and already a crowd of onlookers was at the barriers, like spectators at a dogfight.

Before Leo and Davina could reach the barriers, though, there was a warning shout, and from behind the tea-room's cosy façade more shots were fired.

The two policemen who had entered through the kitchen now came charging down the narrow tradesman's alley and into the open, pursued by the gunman. The crowd stepped back, leaving an arena for the performance. As the thin soldier in the greatcoat turned into the open space, a police sergeant took aim and fired. The soldier's body leapt into the air then fell back into the pretty mullioned window. Squares of leaded glass tumbled out in slow motion one after another as the body jerked and finally slumped over the windowsill. Ignoring the glass, the two policemen threw themselves on the body, pulled it onto the pavement, rolled it onto its front and clamped the mad, dead soldier in handcuffs.

The police sergeant looked into the tea-room from the outside and said, "All over, folks. It's all right, it's all over now."

Davina began to tremble with shock and the cold. Leo took her hand and, side-stepping police and spectators, pulled her back into the café.

"Which is yours?" he asked, tugging garments off a coat stand.

"The blue one."

"Put it on." He held the coat for her. "Now, drink some sweet tea."

"Are you crazy?"

"Do as you are told, you need sugar."

Davina collapsed in a chair and started to sob. "There's blood."

"Ssshh. Just a drink a little and we'll go."

"My hat . . ."

"Forget your hat."

"I hate London. I want to go home," Davina sobbed.

"Ssh, I'll get you home now, don't cry."

But it wasn't that easy. Crowds of people had appeared from nowhere. Policemen were everywhere, some taking statements, some marshalling the onlookers.

"Excuse me sir, madam, excuse me, dear people. Sir, would you be so kind?" A newspaper reporter panted up to Leo like an eager mongrel anxious to ingratiate itself in the hope of food. "You were inside. What a terrible experience. How did it start exactly?"

Leo replied in an incomprehensible foreign language. The reporter's face fell. "Ah, you're not from here, sir. P'raps not, then." He turned in search of other witnesses.

Leo steered Davina forward. When they finally reached the street corner, traffic had come to a standstill. There was a line of three buses but none were going near St Anne's Terrace. All the taxis were occupied. Not being Londoners, neither Leo nor Davina thought of using the Underground.

"We'll have to walk," Leo said in a brusque, matter-of-fact tone, although Davina could see he was starting to wobble a little, too. "I think my flat is closer, we'll go there."

Davina said nothing and let herself be led away.

The mews flat was dark and cold, the coldness that goes with places left unoccupied too long. Leo filled a battered kettle in the tiny kitchenette and struck a match to light the gas. Mrs Smithers, who came in to 'do' for him, had stocked his cupboard with English food and drink. He opened the tea caddy and spooned what the English called tea into a Brown Betty teapot.

Davina collapsed on his uncomfortable two-seater sofa in the small, square sitting room. Neither of them spoke. Leo poured the tea English style and handed a cup to Davina. Bits of cream floated on the surface of the thick brown liquid. She looked at it and put it on the floor. Leo looked at his cup:

blue and white willow pattern, it stirred a memory; he cocked his head and smiled a crooked smile.

Davina didn't notice. She was gazing up at a rather dusty imitation chandelier. "I'm a Dymond, you know. A white Dymond. My brother is a black Dymond. Celtic dark. Old Spanish blood they say."

"What?" Leo looked at Davina huddled round her cup, mumbling.

"Nothing. Just that I'm a Dymond – with a 'y'."

"Is that your family name?"

"I told you at my brother's party."

"Oh, yes. Sorry."

"Davina Dymond. It's ridiculous. I'm a white Dymond. From my mother's side. They aren't Dymonds, of course, they're Fulfords. They're all very fair."

"Diamonds aren't white."

"Aren't they? What colour are they then?"

Leo looked at her: she was bunched up on the sofa, her knees tucked underneath her like a beaten animal. She was harmless, and very pretty. He liked the way her wavy gold hair seemed to move as she spoke. "What did you say?"

"Diamonds. What colour are they?"

Leo got to his feet. "Stay there a minute and I'll show you." He went into the kitchen.

Among the food Mrs Smithers assumed Leo needed, among the packets of biscuits and pots of potted meat, behind a tin of Oxo cubes and a packet of custard powder were two shabby old biscuit tins and three new Indian brass containers. One container contained rice; one contained marine salt crystals; the third contained brightly coloured boiled sweets. Leo had brought them all the way from Bombay in his trunk. He pushed the biscuit tins to the very back of the cupboard, took out the brass containers and unscrewed them. The one containing sweets he returned to the musty cupboard. He took the other two into the sitting room and put them on the small dining table.

Davina looked up, sleepily. "Are you going to do a conjuring trick to make me happy again?"

"Yes. Come and sit here." Leo indicated a chair.

"Can't move. Too sleepy."

"Oh, no," he pulled her up off the sofa, "you mustn't go to sleep. Do you feel sick?"

"No, just sleepy. Why?"

"Basic first aid."

Davina let herself be moved to the table. "You know the strangest things, Leo."

"Yes, I do. Watch." He took a small key from a jacket pocket and opened a nondescript bureau standing against a wall. From its inside shelves he pulled some sheets of heavy vellum writing paper and a small set of scales. He put them on the table in front of the girl. Then he put on the table a bedside lamp with no shade, three glass plates and a pair of tweezers. After that, he closed the sitting-room curtains, switched on the electric light and plugged in the shadeless lamp.

Davina shrugged off her coat and sat down. "All right, I'm ready for the show," she said.

Opening the two brass containers, Leo said, "What do you see?"

"Don't know."

"Lick a finger and taste." He demonstrated, licking a finger and putting it into the pot of rough, unrefined rice. A few grains stuck to his finger.

"Is it rice?" she said.

"Well done. Do you have rice in England?"

"Of course we do. Rice pudding. Children have to eat gallons of it. Didn't your nanny or your mother ever make you eat rice pudding?"

"Yes. Now, what's in this pot?"

"Salt?"

"Correct and incorrect." Leo shook a small measure of rough salt onto a plate. With the tweezers he selected a large crystal. "Not salt, Davina, not salt."

"Is that a diamond?"

"This is a polished diamond. Big enough for a solitaire ring or it could be cut into smaller stones."

"Gosh. So what's in the rice?"

"Diamonds as well. Look." He sprinkled some of the rice he had brought from Bombay onto the second plate and selected a tiny pebble. "This is a stone from the ground. Rice has to be washed, there's always grit and stones in it. But this," he held a fragment of what looked like dusty quartz up to the light, "this is a very precious bit of grit."

Davina squinted at the object in the lamplight.

"You see," Leo said, "true diamonds do not start life as white. Let me show you. First you have to find them, and they are dirty and dusty, then, before you clean them or cut them, you have to see if they are flawed and how much they weigh."

He selected one tiny stone with his tweezers and weighed it. "Diamonds are measured in carats, which I am sure you know. A carat is one-fifth of a gram." He held the stone up to the light again. "This is one is octahedral." He placed it on the third glass plate and held the plate over the lamp. "This helps to judge the clarity, even the tiny ones have to be examined for impurities. As with all things of value: purity is the essence."

Leo selected another stone and held it over a sheet of white paper. "This is what is called *glace*. You see the colour almost matches the paper. But it's only white because it's on white, if I move it next to your eyes it will become blue." He held the gem up to her eyes then put it back on the paper and picked out a much bigger stone. It was an irregular lump of dirty grey. He weighed it.

"Thirty grams: quite a whopper – but inferior. In Africa this is called *mackbar*. I like the name, *mackbar* – it sounds like what it is – inferior. Now, come round here and look at these three stones. They are quite different in size and value and yet all three are magic. They can only be damaged by each other; it takes a diamond to scratch a diamond. Did you know that?

"These are the truest elements of our Earth. They were formed below the deepest layers of the Earth's crust, maybe a hundred million years ago. It has taken volcanic eruptions to bring them to the surface and perhaps millions of years of rain to wash them out into the common dirt. And now here they are in London, ready and waiting to be shaped and polished to make women prettier and men richer – or poorer, of course."

Leo smiled at the lovely blonde girl at his side and slowly put an arm round her waist. "Can you see their beauty? I think they are truly marvellous, even in their natural state." He watched the girl closely. The stones had no effect on her. "Davina, Davina," he whispered into her hair, "look at them. This is as close as you may ever come to the stars."

Davina looked at him guiltily. "Am I so easy to read?"

For a moment neither spoke, then Davina whispered, "If these are your stars, how can I ever figure in your universe?"

"Do you want to?" Leo looked into her eyes. "Do you really, really want to?"

"Oh, yes, yes."

"Why?"

Davina gave a tiny shrug, "Because you are brave and clever, and strong and kind. And I've never met anyone like you, ever." She smiled and held out a hand for him to hold.

Leo smiled back but continued pouring rice and tiny pebbles back into a brass pot. Gathering up his paraphernalia, he said, "I should take you home."

"No! Not yet!" Davina crossed the room and knelt by the low sideboard. "Do you have anything stronger than that awful tea?" She looked inside. "Yes, look; gin, whisky, rum, green cordial and . . . oh, yuk, what's this?" She held up a jar of mouldy cherries. "This has been in here for years." Davina put the grey-furred cherries back inside the sideboard and looked up at Leo. "Get some glasses, I am going to make a large gin and something, and prepare myself to face the world again. What do you want?"

Leo laughed. "I'll have some of that scotch. It's all right, I've already tasted it."

Davina pulled out the bottles, talking nineteen to the dozen. "He was quite mad, of course. But it did scare me. You are such a hero, Leo. I think you must be more than a diamond merchant. That's what I am going to tell Mother; you're a merchant, not a dealer, sounds much better . . ."

The flood gate of relief had opened. There was no lemonade or tonic, so she swigged back a glass of neat gin and coughed. "Oh dear, better put some water with it. You haven't got any lemons I suppose? Do you know I haven't seen a lemon since . . . Oh, I can't remember when."

Leo sat on the sofa watching her. She handed him a huge measure of whisky and snuggled down beside him. They drank their over-strong drinks without talking for a few minutes, but then Davina broke the silence.

"I'm going to recite a poem," she said, "and I want you to tell me what it means, and then, if you still want to, you can call a cab and send me home."

She went to stand by the fireplace, gulped some more gin and curtseyed. "A little recitation by Davina Dymond." She lowered her head, suddenly embarrassed by her girlish behaviour. "Two verses from 'Sing Song' by Christina Rossetti.

> *"An emerald is as green as grass;*
> *A ruby red as blood;*
> *A sapphire shines as blue as heaven;*
> *A flint lies in the mud.*
>
> *"A diamond is a brilliant stone,*
> *To catch the world's desire;*
> *An opal holds a fiery spark;*
> *But a flint holds fire.*

"So what does it mean?"

"It means you are the loveliest girl I have ever met. Please come here."

Davina did as she was asked and Leo kissed her.

The kissing didn't stop. Her lips and tongue were moist and warm; her skin smelt like springtime. His hands moved across her back, shifting her into a better position on the small sofa. Davina struggled for breath.

Leo gently pulled away the high cotton frill of her blouse and kissed her neck. "You smell wonderful."

"It's only rosewater."

"Relax," he said, opening the top buttons of her high-necked blouse.

The girl did not protest, so he continued with the little pearl buttons until he could nestle into her freckled chest, lick the hollow between her breasts. He ran a hand down over her ribs, over her hip, went down to her knee and then back to her chin. He ran a finger over her wet lips and kissed her again with his tongue. Davina made no attempt to resist. He opened the remaining buttons and kissed her breasts above the silky liberty bodice.

She put her arms up around his neck and sighed, "To think I nearly wore a woollen vest because it's November."

The words brought Leo to a halt. He moved apart from her. "Oh, heavens, I am sorry," he said. He got up. "Please, you must go home."

Davina clutched her arms across her body. Tears came into her eyes. "You don't want me?"

"Of course I do! That's the problem." Leo scanned the room for an escape. "Where's your coat? No, oh no, don't cry, please don't cry. It's just the shock of what happened this afternoon. You aren't thinking straight, and I am taking advantage. I can't take advantage of a girl who's a . . . look, you'll be better tomorrow." He snatched up her coat and held it out to her.

She made him wait with his arms stretched out whilst she buttoned her blouse, keeping her head down, away from his concerned gaze. Then, for the second time that day, Davina turned her back to him and put her arms into her coat sleeves. As she did so she leaned back against him and he closed his arms around her.

"Please don't send me away," she said.

He kissed the back of her head, took her hand and led her into his bedroom.

As he closed the heavy curtains, Leo mentally disappeared into a stuffy, incense-scented room across the ocean. Except that now it was different. Now he was the instigator and teacher; his hands led, his lips warmed and wetted. This girl was so round and soft: so unlike the bony women and girls in Bombay. He loved the way her hair fell loose over her shoulders. He nuzzled into her neck again: rosewater.

He was a small boy running his fingers through velvet rose petals in a basket. *"Shall we make rosewater, Leo? Don't the petals feel nice? Softer than velvet."*

They put some of the petals in bowls. With the rest they made rosewater.

Davina was cocooned by Leo's gentleness, the tone of his voice. As his body moved into her she felt a sharp pain, but it dissolved, and as they moved together she drifted across water to a place far beyond London, until he brought her to a shouting, gasping, back-arching halt. Then, as he began to move again, this time more urgently, she found herself among the tall rushes of her old river. She came back to consciousness as his act of love terminated in a pumping spasm and collapse.

He licked the sweat from between her breasts, touched her nipples with sticky fingers and rolled away to the other side of the bed. While he slept, Davina traced the fine black hair that covered his chest and came to a point between his ribs.

For the next five afternoons, Davina was initiated into the gentle, slow, sensuous art of love-making. For her, each afternoon was a new heaven on earth.

For Leo, each afternoon was time given for no reward save the pleasure of lying with Davina. He realised he had never done anything voluntarily that was not in some way an investment calculated on long-term gain. But here was this lovely girl, who could offer him no advantage or benefit for his future except her presence, and he never wanted to be apart from her again.

Chapter 16
London, 1918

On the morning of the 15th December, a dark day of driving rain and grimy sleet, Leo was summoned to an anonymous office off Sloane Square. A grey man in City uniform pinstripe kept him standing beside his desk and cross-examined him like a schoolmaster. Now and again the grey man consulted a sheaf of papers. It was evident to Leo he knew the answers to his questions; he only needed confirmation. Behaving like a schoolboy, Leo became taciturn and said no more than was required. Eventually, the civil servant placed the papers on his blotter and covered them with a book, but not before Leo had glimpsed Sir Lionel's handwriting.

Leo was to go to Russia. It would be similar to what he had been doing in Bombay, except this time he would be entirely on his own and his reports would be coded. They had yet to agree on transmission. Leo was astonished, then angry; and then his time with Sir Lionel slotted into place. *So this is what it had all been leading up to.* Memories, snatches of conversation charged around Leo's head.

The grey man took his silence for acquiescence, gathered some of the papers from the desk and left the room. Leo sat down uninvited. Before he had time to decide how or what he thought, another man entered the office. He was altogether larger and more portly, but otherwise another grey man in black jacket and pinstripe.

"Mr Kazan, our very own Kim! Have you read it? Tremendous story! My name's John Shepherd."

Leo jumped up, annoyed at being caught off guard. The civil servant proffered a smooth hand. Older, more genial and more senior, calculated Leo, but he still fell into the category of 'grey men': civil servants who moved pieces of paper from desk to filing cabinet, and all had the beige-grey pallor of office-dwellers. The nearest they had ever been to the outside world was opening an atlas.

Mr Shepherd seated himself behind the plain desk and, smiling good-humouredly, gestured to Leo to resume his seat.

"Well, I am pleased to tell you that you have passed muster with my colleague so we can go ahead with your training and placement. Not very orthodox but then these are hardly orthodox times." He took some paper and a fountain pen from a drawer and wrote down an address in Canterbury. "Present yourself at this house tomorrow evening before seven at the latest. They are expecting you. During the next few weeks we want you to learn to drive and pick up a few of our special skills. You will also have a Russian tutor."

Leo's heart fell: *Sidney Tamchian and verbs all over again.* "But I've already started a training course for the India Office, sir."

"Yes, I know. But that's all been changed. We need you more than they do."

Leo clenched a fist. His life was being settled among people who gave him no say – again.

"Once you are ready," continued the civil servant, "you'll be sent to enrol in Saint Petersburg or possibly Moscow, depends what's happening and who's where."

"Enrol, sir?"

"Yes. You are going to be among students. You will need to study something."

"Study!" Leo was horrified. "What must I study?"

"Whatever you like to start with – geology for instance – then switch to whichever faculty has the greatest number of Indians. Russians have been sponsoring Indian students for a good while now. Some chaps are genuine, of course, good students – eager to learn and all that, but they're told that all forms of monarchy are evil and independence is a virtue, and then they become proper little Reds. Russia has always been interested in our family jewels; she'll use any means to get them now – raw materials are going to be a priority now the rouble is devaluing. Dropping by the day. That doesn't seem to be stopping their politics, though, unfortunately. There's a civil war going on, as no doubt you know. Which leads me back to why we want you to see what's going on – in relation to India ostensibly, but any extra titbits will be of great value."

Leo watched John Shepherd stand up and go to his window while he was speaking. The view, however, appeared to displease him. "Have to say," he continued, "I wouldn't mind being off out of London myself – even to join a bunch of over-excited students in a foreign land." He returned to his chair and lowered his bulk behind the desk. "Sorry, thinking out loud. Regarding your studies, I'd start with Philosophy. That leads to anything and everything. You could try Russian Literature as well. Good stuff if you have a morbid turn of mind. Take advantage, not many young men your age able to study these days. You can always go back to Bombay and teach; this business can't last very long. None of these Bolshevik types have got any idea about leadership, except that chap Lenin. Personally, I give them another year. A bad harvest and they'll be done for."

Leo stared at him, trying to gather his thoughts, but before he could speak, the civil servant reached into a drawer and withdrew a buff envelope, saying, "You'll need these papers. Name: 'Leonard Kapadia'. Nationality: 'Indian'. All the rest corresponds to you. You'll have to fill in 'religion' yourself. You know more about that than we do, I expect. Now, we'd like you to sign this document to say you accept our terms. This is a formal arrangement, albeit, we hope, of limited duration."

Leo looked at the fake papers: a new identity but more or less the real him. As to religion, except for the Malabar Hill lark, he always batted for the Christians – some things couldn't be faked. He examined the document for small print. It was straightforward. It meant nothing. Learning to drive would be useful. He signed.

"Good, well done." John Shepherd countersigned the document. "You must be one of our youngest recruits. Speaking of which, I have to make a particular request." He looked Leo in the eye then quickly looked away. "We would like you to make a commitment *not* to make contact with your er – *family*."

"Family?" Leo cocked his head to his right shoulder.

"Yes, I understand that lately you . . ."

Leo stared at him, unblinking, daring him to make eye contact again.

". . . that you have rather adopted Sir Lionel Pinecoffin. Ha, ha, ha. Jolly decent sort, Lionel. Same school, you know, lot younger of course. Won all the cross-countries . . . It wouldn't do, though."

Leo dropped his gaze, touched a fancy new cufflink.

The grey man said, "Fine, fine. No need to worry about that flat you're in, we've got all that arranged. Get yourself packed and keep your tickets for expenses in Canterbury – but get rid of anything tell-tale like that before you leave

England. You don't have anything personal to wind up, do you? Obviously you can't take personal belongings. Leave them where they are: quite safe in the flat. No mementos, souvenirs, personal effects we'd want anybody to see. Nature of the game. We'll kit you out with suitable clothes – socks, boots, the lot. You *won't* take anything compromising, will you?"

A very green, very valuable emerald flashed before Leo's inner eye. "No, nothing I would want anybody to see. What about money, sir?"

"Don't worry about that. You'll be well remunerated. Paid into your bank account here. My colleagues in Canterbury will go through all those details with you. Anything else?"

Yes, Leo had a very important question. "Why, sir?"

"Why Petersburg? Or why you? I can give you answers to both. Petersburg is where Indian agitators are drumming up support for some sort of Russian alliance for their silly Home Rule ideas – riding on the success of Trotsky and his damn Bolsheviks. The sharp ones – on both sides, and this is the important bit – know damned well they can't manage on their own; they both need trade, industry, financial and governmental support of one sort or another. Not just us concerned, either; it's got all the little rajahs in their Princely States wetting their knickers – afraid they might have to give up all their lands and luxury if Communist ideas take hold. Not without reason. I'm told that mischief-maker Kapasala, the one they set you to flush out in Bombay, may be playing a key role somewhere along the way, or he's being used by someone more important. Keep your eyes peeled for anything to do with that little set up. You know about gems; follow it up if you can – get to the source. We want the organisers.

"The India Office has put in another request as well. They want anything on Hindu-Moslem relations. This Moslem

League is growing by the minute. They may be looking for sponsors on their own. Not too far-fetched to suspect they may be planning a government take-over in Delhi. They've got a lot of advantages already with the extended franchise. We want to know who's mixing with whom, as usual, but we also need details about financial agreements and plans for just about anything. They'll explain in Canterbury. As far as I am concerned, we need to take advantage of any chance to upset friendships. Divide and rule, as the great man said."

John Shepherd drummed his fingers on the desk exactly like his school fellow in Bombay then leaned forward, as if about to impart a very great secret. "There's also another dimension you need to be aware of. Now you have signed the document, I can tell you we'll be sending British troops into Russia: an Intervention Force to stop and destroy the Reds, nip this Soviet nonsense in the bud while they're busy fighting amongst themselves. They'll explain all this in Canterbury, as I said. But mostly, as far as you are concerned Mr Kazan, we want to know anything and everything to do with the Russo-Hind student connection. We do not, repeat, do not want these student types stirring up coolies, getting it into their heads that they can do to us what they've done to the Tsar."

As if realising he was getting too agitated, John Shepherd eased his collar and sat back in his chair. Drumming on the desk again with his right hand, he said, "And, as to you, young man, it's because a very highly thought of Indian Political Officer," he tapped the letter on the desk, "tells us *you* are the one for the job. That answer your question?"

"Yes, sir, thank you."

"Right then," John Shepherd rose from his seat, "Let's get you started. We'll be keeping an eye on you to start with, after that you are on your own."

"The same men, sir?"

John Shepherd frowned, "Same men?"

"Who have been keeping an eye on me. You've been keeping an eye on me since I arrived, sir. Two men wearing the same overcoats. Taking it in turns outside my flat. You might suggest they change their outfits now and again."

John Shepherd got to his feet, laughing a little too heartily, "Ha, ha. Well done, well spotted. Pretty girl, they tell us. Country stock, just right for you I should think – but nothing in a billet-doux. In fact, no letters whatsoever, understood? She'll have to be dropped I'm afraid."

Leo was led to the door. They shook hands. John Shepherd held Leo's hand for just a second more than necessary. "Your situation with Lionel Pinecoffin wasn't personal. You know that, don't you? All in the past. Over and done with. Anything goes wrong in Russia you are, as I said earlier, on your own. We are just as likely not even going to hear about it. Understand?"

Leo nodded, but said nothing more than, "Thank you, sir."

"Well, off you go. Happy Christmas."

Leo nodded and slowly descended the draughty staircase. He didn't hear the door close until he had reached the next landing.

Instead of going straight back to his flat, Leo wandered down various unknown streets and eventually went down some steps to the river embankment. His pace was slow, but his mind was racing. Pausing at the railings, he stared across the dark water of the river seeing nothing but the contents of two biscuit tins. What was he to do with them? The uncut stones could be stitched into his clothes, but the tins, one in particular, were a problem. He needed somewhere safe to store – hide – them. Somewhere as safe as the Bank of England.

The answer didn't come to him until he was emptying the

little bureau in the mews. He had a bank account now, as Sir Lionel had instructed. Banks, he believed, had safe-deposit boxes. Safe as the Bank of England. When he filled out the documentation this time, though, where he had to state the name and address of his next of kin, he would put his spinster aunt's name: Miss Davina Dymond, 3, St Anne's Terrace, London. If anything happened to him, she should have the contents of the safe-deposit box.

At five p.m. of that same day, a motorcycle messenger delivered a letter to number 3, St Anne's Terrace. It was addressed to Miss Davina Dymond. It said:

> *I regret I cannot see you this afternoon as arranged.*
> *I have to go out of town.*
> *I may be away for some time.*
> *I shall think of you often.*
>> *Yours,*
> > *Leo Kazan*

Chapter 17
Bristol, England, 1919

Matthew Dymond settled back into his chair, lit a cigar and looked at the Spaniard seated next to him in the lounge bar of the Bristol hotel. "My father has asked me to sort out the new arrangement for your dry sherry and your *amontillado*: price per barrel and per bottle, we'll look at all the options. Then we need to discuss shipment. Now this bloody war is over, we assume your shipping rates will become more lenient – stands to reason. My father sends his regards by the way."

Matthew drank from his tankard, put it back on the low table in front of them and tried to ease his game leg into a more comfortable position. The Spaniard watched him; he watched everything. His father had warned him, "Don't underestimate the playboy, Latin style; this one doesn't miss a beat".

"Your father is ill? I hope not. Such a strong gentleman."

"Strong physically, strong mentally when it comes to business, not so strong when it comes to his little girl," Matthew replied with rancour.

"Your sister is ill?"

"My sister is flaming pregnant!" The words blurted out before he could stop them. "Family scandal – eighteen and unmarried – and all *my* fault for not looking after her. She should be able to look after herself, I told them. Mollycoddled country bumpkin. You'd have thought she'd have known ..."

Matthew stopped, but it was too late, and that was the war's fault as well. He would never have spoken to a business associate about such personal matters before. He had lost his temper forever the day a bomb blew him out of a trench and into a hell of hospitals and nosy specialists. He had also lost most of his right leg, which, as far he was concerned, was far worse than keeping or losing his temper. And everybody said he was lucky! Lucky to be an invalid; lucky to be at his father's beck and call; lucky to be stuck in a hotel in Bristol negotiating wine shipments when he could have been living his own life, making his own decisions, not tied to his family's apron strings.

"Tell me about your sister."

"I hardly think you would be interested, Mr García. This is a family matter."

"On the contrary, I am always interested in family matters. I have three sisters. You could say I am an expert. One is married, but without boys – she is a widow; two live with my mother. They are not married. They are," he searched for a word, "plain."

"Well, my sister is not plain – obviously."

"She is good-looking, like you?"

Matthew shot the Spaniard a sharp glance. "No!" he tried to laugh it off. "I am a black Dymond from my father's side. Davina is mousy."

"Mousy? Like a mouse?"

"Like a country mouse, absolutely: fair, quiet, gentle. Does water colours, visits the poor and needy."

"But not so quiet, it appears."

"Hmm, and that's the grand mystery. They've got her shut up in her room until she tells them who."

"Who is the father?"

"Blessed if I know. Came to one of my parties, apparently. Must have done because she didn't go anywhere without me for over a blasted month. I took her everywhere, we went to the theatre, met my friends for supper, et-bloody-cetera. She hung around me like a flaming puppy. Ruined my fun while she was having a bit of her own, that's what gets me."

"So?"

"So? Excuse me for asking, but why the interest? Morbid curiosity?"

The Spaniard, who Matthew thought looked more like a patrician Frenchman than a Dago, leaned back in his chair and said – as Matthew was to tell his London pals later – with all the bloody calm and matter-of-factness you can get in a Latin, "Mr Dymond, please convey to your father, that apart from exporting sherry I am in the market for a wife."

Matthew spluttered into his beer, "What?"

"Simply that: a wife would be convenient."

God all bloody mighty, thought Matthew, *I need a brandy.*

Fred Dymond glowered across his office desk at his son. "What d'you mean *'convenient'*? Convenient to get into our business? Convenient to get higher prices? Convenient to do a bit of blackmail?" His Cornish accent thickened as he roared the questions. Then he stopped, looked at Matthew and said more quietly and more slowly, "Mind you he's got a tasty bit of business himself. Family must be worth a fortune. They've got everything: vineyards, *bodegas*, bottling plant. Old family too, that'll keep your mother sweet. We could do worse. Gawd'n'bennet, we could be stuck with the brat. Tell him I'll talk to him tomorrow evening. Tell him to come here to the house. We don't need anyone listening in on this deal."

"You mean you are ready to marry her off? Just like that?" Celia Dymond snapped her manicured fingers before the varnish was quite dry. "Damn you."

For spoiling her nails or exiling their daughter? After twenty-five years, Fred still couldn't tell what his wife was thinking or feeling. Then she added in her own special accusing tone, "You might have told me before. I need time to prepare myself to meet this . . . What's his name? Really Frederick, it is rather precipitate."

"'Course it's bloody pre-ci-pi-tate; she's three months gone! You got any better suggestions?"

Celia Dymond returned to her nails. Fred went back into his dressing room and put on a stiff white shirt.

"Have you told her?" called his wife from their bedroom.

"That's your job."

"Mine! I hardly think so."

"Well you should think so. If you'd been around to tell her how to look after herself we wouldn't be in this situation. Got to be said, Celia, you've left her to grow up on her own. In that gert barn of a house every school holiday and you off with your fancy friends somewhere else. You should have looked after her better."

"That's not fair. I always made arrangements for her."

The stocky Cornishman came back into the bedroom fiddling with a collar-stud. "Fasten this, will you?"

"Can't, they're not dry," Celia held up her freshly-painted fingers. "Anyway, Morrigan was always with her."

"Your Morrigan is old enough to be Methuselah's mother. What she remember about courting? If she ever did." Fred Dymond's face grew redder, his jowls now trapped beneath his chin as his stumpy fingers tried to twist a collar-stud into place. "Oh, fuck it!"

"Frederick: language!"

"Frederick: language! Gawd, fuck a duck and tup the cow, it weren't like this in my mother's house."

"Don't you start on about your sainted mother. She drank tea out of a saucer; she could barely read or write . . ."

But the usual barbs missed their mark. Fred was crossing the landing in search of help. He tapped on Davina's door and went into her bedroom.

Davina was sitting at her dressing table fully dressed, hair brushed, nails buffed but not polished; one of her beloved poetry books lay open at a Bronte poem.

"Davy, do this for me, my 'eart."

They exchanged places and Davina screwed down the studs over her father's black tie. Fred watched her in the mirror. "You all ready then? Best bib and tucker." He tried to see what she had been reading, maudlin stuff by the look of it. Her face was white as a sheet. Involuntarily, he sought a bulge in her straight dress. "I got a bit of news for you," he said.

Her father's Cornish accent was very pronounced; Davina knew that meant he was under stress. All her fault, of course. She wanted to hug him, tell him she was sorry. She wanted to be hugged and told not to worry, it would all be all right. But it wasn't going to be all right because it was all wrong.

She had tried to cry on Morrigan's shoulder but received no compassion there. Had she been raped at gunpoint she would probably have received the same comment: *I warned you, fancy ways. You can't trust vuriners.*

Her mother had just been furious. First, because she had ruined their Christmas with her miserable face then, when she refused breakfast all through January, Celia Dymond had guessed and challenged her. After that, her elegant mother had withdrawn into a tight-lipped silence. Barely a word had been exchanged since. They were together for more than a month as mother and daughter for the first time in years and the act of transgression separated them more physically than all the miles between London, Bristol and Cornwall had ever done.

"Daddy, please don't make me come to this dinner. Please."

Poor maid, thought Fred, *she ought to be told before they came face to face.* He would leave aside the business angle; just tell her he wanted her to meet a valued associate. He'd tell the bloody Spaniard to do his own proposing.

Fred moved over to the window seat and said, "Come and sit here, my dove. Sit with your old dad a moment."

They dined on venison at the Limes Park Hotel near the famous suspension bridge. Being a Saturday evening, there was a Palm Court Orchestra and people danced before and after dining. Fred began to relax a little when he saw that the venue met with his wife's approval. As did the young man.

"Well," she said *sotto voce* as the Spaniard conversed with Matthew, "he's tall, fine-boned, close-shaven, quite fair really: not even as dark as your family. He might even pass for an Englishman if it weren't for the cut of his evening clothes. He barely looks foreign. Yes, I think he'll do nicely, and your Davina should be more than grateful."

Fred picked up the 'your Davina' and sighed. It was true, Davina was still his little girl, despite everything, and he wasn't as happy about the arrangement as he'd expected to be. He looked at Davina now. She'd pushed the ripe meat to the side of her plate and had hardly touched anything else. He wondered what his mother would have said and done. *She* had been a tartar, no mistake, but she'd loved them all. A tin miner's widow coping on less than five bob a week, she'd raised five out of seven, and all the boys had done well for themselves. He still missed her. Missed her common sense, her bad language and sense of humour. Celia Fulford had been a prize, of course, what with that old house, aristocratic ancestors and all. Called herself a good Catholic and went to Mass every Sunday but she was no mother: no maternal instinct and no humour.

When the men went to take coffee in the lounge, Davina and her mother went up the ornate staircase to powder their noses in the ladies' room. As soon as they reached the pink refuge, Celia checked to see they were alone then went straight to the wall-length mirror. Davina sat on a chair and tried to relax.

"Shame about the name," Celia said. "Alfonso – it's a touch too Gilbert and Sullivan. But you heard what he was saying about his family home. Four storeys built round an open patio. Carriage and horses still kept on the premises. Obviously, you'll accept darling. Quite a catch, under the circumstances."

Davina eased her hairpins and waited on her pink chair, saying nothing. Then the word clicked into place. "Accept?"

"I thought your father had told you. He told me he'd explained why we're here."

Davina replayed her father's little speech. Thought about the way her father, mother and brother had been behaving: about what they had *not* said. *So this was what it was all about.* If she wasn't able to marry the father of the child, she had, as her father had said, 'better settle for someone else quick like'. Very 'quick like'! A matter of three hours between suggestion and conclusion. *Well, no, darling parents*, she would most definitely refuse.

"Naturally it's your choice. But I think you should remember you are not twenty-one yet. And I for one am not going to sit out six months in some dreary little *pension* in Belgium, or wherever it is that girls of your sort go." Celia turned from the mirror and tapped her daughter on the chin.

"You *have* examined the usual options, haven't you? Under other circumstances France might be an option, but I don't think poor old France will be much fun for another year or two. Pity, it would have been a good excuse to go down to Nice and enjoy some decent weather."

Davina stared at her mother. "But . . ."

"Shall we join our menfolk, as your dear old Granny would say. Now that would have been the perfect solution: you could have gone to her." Celia Dymond sighed. "People are never around when you need them." She snapped shut her little beaded bag and patted her hair one final time. "I look quite ash-blonde in subdued lighting. The Spaniard, I might say, is actually quite dishy – in an angular sort of way." She opened the ladies' room door. "Come on, it's hardly lamb to the slaughter. You could do a lot, lot worse."

As they went down to join the gentlemen, Davina counted the stairs, trying to get her nerves and anger under control. There were nineteen. Not enough.

The men were waiting in the doorway of the palm court. Matthew greeted his mother then headed off for the bar. Her father took his wife's arm and led her onto the dance floor.

Alfonso Ignacio Jose María García del Moral Lopez-Rey took Davina's right hand and bowed over it just close enough to touch it with his lips without actually doing so. "Shall we dance?"

He led her between ailing aspidistras onto the chessboard dance floor, a hand barely touched a vertebra and they began to waltz in a circle. There was one palm in the centre of the floor, its poor leaves bitten back like chewed fingernails. Staid couples waltzed around it, bored beyond words.

"You like dancing? You dance well," Alfonso stated in his clipped English.

"I used to enjoy dancing."

"I may call you Davina?"

"Of course."

"I like your name. It is from the name David?"

"I suppose so."

He was tall and thin, a head taller than she was. Not ugly, but his features were not pleasing in the kind, warm way she had thought a prospective husband should look. Not remotely like Leo.

Her parents were dancing in silence: her father's hand held an inch from her mother's back. The Spaniard's right hand, however, guided her firmly. His left hand was smooth and cool, but he kept his body separate from her, independent of her, as if trying to keep her face in focus.

Davina tried to focus on the dowdy lady playing the violin.

"You dance well. I am pleased you dance well. You also have self-discipline. This is clear also from your conduct at the dinner table. My sisters make a fuss over food they do not like." He smiled and Davina's stomach clenched. "You are also good-looking – in an unsophisticated way. Your youth is an advantage. My mother will be pleased. You will be . . ." he searched for words and smiled again, "no threat to her."

"Good, I am so pleased," Davina replied, but the sarcasm was lost on him.

"We will go to a quiet place now. I would like to speak with you."

"Oh, no, really, I am so enjoying this dance."

"I wish to talk with you."

"Oh, yes, I know. Might we talk while we dance?"

"If you wish."

They danced on in silence. The orchestra came to the end of a nameless melody: people stood and clapped. Her parents left the dance floor, ignoring them. The orchestra took a lifetime to rearrange music stands and scores, sip water and wipe their fingers. There was no alternative; they would have to sit down. Davina led the way to a low table in the furthest corner. Her heart was beating so fast she feared he would hear it. Alfonso held a chair out for her then sat down beside her, folding one long elegant leg over another, smoothing the crease in his immaculately-pressed trousers. Davina waited, hardly daring to breathe for fear she might scream at the tension.

"Davina I will tell you immediately. I would like to be married with you."

Davina breathed out. "You know of my – situation?"

"Yes."

She wanted to ask him why? Why did he want to marry a pregnant girl he didn't know? But she didn't because she was too embarrassed. And afraid of the answer. Afraid of what her father had arranged. Fred Dymond had a formidable reputation as a businessman. The possibility that the engagement was Alfonso's idea never occurred to her.

"I am honest," Alfonso said, "when I tell you that you will like my home. Your father is pleased with the arrangement."

"Arrangement? It is all arranged, then?"

"Not without you, clearly." Alfonso reached for her hand and gave it a very gentle squeeze, "I am not a monster, Davina. Not a Bluebeard. You will be happy with me and my family."

"Well, if it is all arranged, what can I say?"

The orchestra struck up something a little more lively and they returned to the dance floor.

"You may visit England as often as you wish," Alfonso said as he whirled her round. "My ships bring sherry every month now, so you can return to be with your mamá."

"Oh, good, that will be so nice." Davina was seething.

"So we are agreed?"

"Arranged, agreed, engaged. *Veni, vidi, vici.* What else can I say?"

"Excellent, you know your Latin. That will help."

The Spaniard laughed drily, pulled her closer to him and traced a vertebra with his thumb. Her pelvis responded: she was appalled. He had no right to do that. And her body had no right to respond. He was a complete stranger. All that about his house and *bodega* could be a pack of lies. She had not said 'yes', but she had been waltzed into an arranged marriage.

Chapter 18
London, 1919

Davina and her mother returned to London. Celia Dymond now had an excuse for a shopping spree and spent every day buying new clothes – mostly for herself. Davina mooned around the house and eventually found herself in the tiny room allotted to Morrigan, who had stayed in London for the winter.

"Well, you can't say as I didn't warn you." Morrigan sat back in her old tapestry chair and folded her arms. Davina stared into her meagre fire. It was the first time she had ever been in Morrigan's London room. It was in the attic, at the very top of the house. She remembered how the old lady had complained about her sleeping in a turret in Crimphele. The sudden memory of Tamstock, of tranquil, misty Cornwall gave her a start. If she went to Spain she might never see the swans or hear the gentle river again.

"What's to do, then?" asked the elderly woman.

Davina hunched her shoulders. "I shall have to go."

"You considered the alternatives?"

"That's what Mother said. Are there any?"

"Dear Lord, 'course there are. But I don't expect your mother helped you any along that line."

Davina looked up. "Tell me. What are the alternatives?"

"Well, it's too late for a back street job. Anyway you're too precious for that. There's gin and a hot bath . . . or you could stay here. Have the cheel here, with me to look after you. Or we could go back down to Tamstock and pop it in with Mary Peach's little one."

Davina shot her a glance, "Mary Peach has had a baby?"

Martha Morrigan looked at the girl from the corner of a rheumy eye. "Aye, Missy, you're not the first – girl's fall for an 'andsome face, it happens all the time."

Davina waited, not knowing how to respond. Morrigan was staring at her, twisting a thin circle of gold around a gnarled finger. Davina had never noticed that she wore a wedding ring before.

Morrigan caught her gaze and raised her left hand. "Just realised, have you? Ah, yes, I been married, and had a cheel. The right way round, I might add. 'Cept they can't be trusted, any of them. Billy Morrigan left me with a sick baby and no pay packet to go off for the rich mining in Africa."

"Morry, what happened to your baby? I didn't know you had a baby."

"'Course you didn't. My baby died the week it was left with the other poor little bastards in a cold, stinking cottage with no running water, so I could come and work for your mother's mother . . ."

Davina shuddered. Baby farms – she'd read about them. Her thoughts drifted into the stories, until she heard Morrigan say, ". . . Mary's married the father in Tamstock church, and there's cheek for you. Mind you, church or no church, if I know anything, she'll regret it. There again, what choice has she got?" There was a pause, then Morrigan added quietly, "But that won't be happening to you, will it? Don't even know where he is, do you?"

Davina closed her eyes at the pain of the jibe and shook her head slowly.

"Thought not." Morrigan blew her nose with an embroidered handkerchief that didn't belong to her then said. "So there you are. Only this don't help you much, do it?"

Davina shook her head, "Not really, Morry, no."

"You going to go on like this, girl? Mooning about, letting your ma and pa ship you off God-knows-where with God-knows-who without a bleat?" Morrigan slapped her hands down on the hard wooden arms of her chair and looked up accusingly at Davina. She was angry, spitting out words. "That's the way, with your lot. You've always got someone to sort your troubles for you. I'm telling you, my fair lady," she wagged a misshapen index finger in the air, "you don't come as no surprise to me. Oh, no. You're none of you any better than you should be. But you sleep sound in your beds, all of you. You have fancy jam pots and a wench in the scullery to wash your dirty linen. Well I'll tell you – have the brat and farm it out. You can pay. And the likes of us need the money. We spend a lifetime up and down stairs and eating humble pie then when you're done with us, when we're too old to be useful, kick us out on the street. They pension off the poor ol' mine ponies in a pasture, but the likes of us is out in the street with no food and water. Like me."

Davina was lost. Morrigan was rambling. The old woman leaned out of her rocker and pushed viciously at a slow coal with a sharp poker. A blue flame licked the air and died in the act. Davina sat exactly where she was, watching the woman who had always been in her family home and realised that all her life she had taken the woman's complaints in jest. She had ignored the woman's aches and pains and moaning as 'just Morry's way'. And it was all genuine. The woman was a real person who had once had a baby, and it had died. And she'd had to live with strangers all her life.

Davina felt her childhood lurch into the fireplace. A flicker of dusty coal smoke and it was gone. She got to her feet. Saying nothing, she crossed to the woman who had been her nanny and kissed her on the forehead, wanting to say something but finding no words. She opened the door to leave, but turned back as Martha Morrigan spoke.

"There's one thing I always say – my mother said it and it's as true as true: what you worrit about you draw on yourself double. Think on it. You got to survive girl. For your cheel's sake, you got to do your best for yourself. Make your own decision and take the best path for your journey. You can't come back and start again. You can't never come back and start over. You just got to move forward best way possible."

"Thank you, Morry," Davina whispered.

Davina counted the narrow service stairs down to the kitchen. She picked up a tumbler from the draining-board and filled it with water, but before she began to drink she tipped the water into the sink and went up to the drawing room.

Kneeling on the floor, Davina pulled all the bottles out of the drinks cabinet. There was no gin and the decanters were all completely empty. She sat back on the floor. So that was that. *No alternatives, mother dear.*

Davina placed her hands on her growing belly, smiled ruefully to herself and said aloud, "Well, little one, you are safe. And you always will be. We'll make a life together in Spain with strangers – because *I* shall never ever leave you with anyone."

Chapter 19
London, 1919

Alfonso was named after his father, maternal grandfather and Saint Ignatius Loyola, the Jesuit. He was tall and always immaculately turned out; the sort of gentleman who never wore brown. He had a long, thin neck and a long, thin face, and a sharp-beaked nose. As he leaned across her to put the wedding ring on the third finger of her right hand, the Spanish way, Davina caught the gesture – a vulture reaching out for a tasty morsel of carrion. She shuddered. He smiled into her eyes and confused her.

Outside the register office, icy confetti fell from the sky. The March wind ruffled Celia Dymond's furs. Davina, in a dove-grey cashmere coat with a high collar, smiled obligingly for the photograph. They lunched in an anonymous restaurant. There were no speeches. Nobody tried to be jolly. Matthew drank too much. Her parents said goodbye. Nothing was said about when they would meet again. Fred Dymond gave his lovely daughter a brief, tight hug; there were tears in his eyes. Then he grabbed his elegant wife by the elbow and steered her into the everyday London streets.

Alfonso paid the bill and escorted his new wife to their hotel: he had not requested a suite. Then he left her alone. That afternoon was the first time Alfonso absented himself without explanation. But that evening he did return to dine with her, and take her to bed.

It was the first occasion on which they had been together for any length of time unaccompanied. It was easier than Davina had anticipated. Alfonso made conversation during the meal, informing her in greater detail about his family home and his family business. She was not required to participate or make conversation above a nod or a smile. After the coffee, he went to the lounge – or somewhere else – to smoke a cigar, and she went up to their room.

When he arrived, Davina was propped up in the large bed, her hair loose across the pillows behind her. She placed her poetry anthology face down on the gold satin eiderdown.

Alfonso sat on the side of the bed. "You have beautiful hair. My sisters will be very jealous. You will not cut it to be fashionable." It was an order, not a request. He curled his fingers into the tresses and bent to kiss her. He smelt of tobacco and brandy, his mouth was dry. "Mmmm," he murmured, "now we shall see."

He then disappeared into the bathroom and Davina, who had forced herself into a passive state, was almost asleep when he emerged in burgundy silk pyjamas. Alfonso lit a cigarette and went across to sit in the bay window. "Please, get out of bed," he said. "I want to examine my acquisition."

Davina did as she was told. The floor was cold despite the thick carpet.

Alfonso lounged back in his chair, "Please, remove your . . ." He gestured with a hand. "Now, come here please."

Davina moved toward him.

"Stop. I can see you well there. You are trembling. Are you cold or excited?"

"Cold."

"Of course, not excited. Not yet. Please, turn around."

Davina turned slowly.

"Your body is getting thick."

Davina stared at him, seeing only a blur of a shape among her tears.

"Your body is very white. What do you call it here – lard?"

Davina reached behind her for her nightgown and started to get back into the high bed.

"Wait, please." Alfonso stubbed out his cigarette and opened the fly of his pyjamas. He went up to his new English wife and rubbed his penis across her bottom. "Get into the bed, I am ready," he said.

Davina pulled back the eiderdown and her poetry book tumbled to the floor. She looked at it then lay back on the spotless sheet. Alfonso kicked the book under the bed and sat beside her as he had done earlier, but now he put his hand between her legs.

"You are dry." He pushed her legs apart and licked her fanny, then, keeping her legs up, he pushed himself into her.

Davina gasped; it hurt.

"My God," he laughed, "I have married a pregnant virgin!"

It did not take long, a few thrusts and it was all over. Davina lay absolutely still, crying silently, fearing she would she lose her baby.

Alfonso rolled on his back and said, "I thought a woman with a full belly would know more how to please a man." He got up, adjusted his pyjamas and went over to the table for his cigarettes. "Montaigne said a woman should drop her shame with her underclothes." He settled himself against his pillows. "Drop her shame with her petticoat – that is the word – petticoat. That is what Montaigne said, I believe."

"Montaigne? Is he French?" Davina asked, pulling down her nightgown clumsily.

"He was French. A wise man for a French."

"I don't think my mother would allow me to read French writers."

"She sounds like a good Catholic mother."

"She is. She's Roman Catholic."

"*Vaya!* That will help you with my dear mother. Be sure to go to Mass as soon as we arrive."

"No, I can't do that. I was confirmed by the Church of England when I was at school. Mother was furious. When all the girls in my year were preparing for confirmation I went with them. I didn't think I was doing anything wrong. My father's family aren't Catholic. We were confirmed by the Bishop of Exeter."

"Bah, one church, another church! They're all the same – bishops and candles, saints and relics." Alfonso stubbed his cigarette into the ashtray on the bedside table and rolled over as if to sleep muttering, "A pregnant virgin. *Mi madre estará contentísima . . .*"

Davina surreptitiously pulled the sheet up to her neck. She would wait until Alfonso was asleep then she would go to the bathroom and wash herself.

"A pregnant virgin . . ." Suddenly Alfonso was wide awake and staring down at her in the lamplight. "But my mother will never know. She will never know. Do you understand?" He pulled back the sheet and blankets and spread his long-fingered hand over her belly, "No one will ever know. And if you ever tell the child, I shall kill you – both of you."

Davina watched his nails dig into her flesh.

His head twisted round to look her straight in the eye. "This is not a threat, English lady, this is a promise."

The crossing to Cadiz was stormy. Davina felt the end of the world was upon her. Once the sickness had abated, however, Alfonso became solicitous and charming. He arranged for her to have camomile tea and chatted to her in their cabin. He was clearly pleased to be returning to Spain, and once they docked in Cadiz to make the transfer to El Puerto de Santa María he was in high spirits, joking with the lighter-men; exchanging news with other well-dressed young men on the quayside. If this was his natural temperament on home territory, Davina thought, perhaps she might come to like him.

Standing on the deck of the sailing vessel crossing to El Puerto, Davina noticed the way Alfonso's fine hair blew in the wind. He caught her looking at him and put an arm around her shoulders.

"I should have become a sailor," he said.

"Why didn't you?"

"Duty and obligation. I am now the only man in the family. I have to run the business, keep my mother happy and all the rest."

"Do you not like your business?"

"Yes, I like it. My grandfather made a success with the sherry. I am proud to follow him and my father. And I want my son to feel the same."

Davina wanted to say, *"But what about the boy who is not your son?"* She didn't.

Alfonso looked at her, "The wind brings the colour to your face. After the baby you must become more stylish. I shall . . . mould you."

Davina watched seagulls circling and swooping around a fishing boat, her thoughts elsewhere. "If I were a boy I'd probably go to sea, too. I love the fresh air. I love the way water ripples in the wind. I can watch water for hours."

Alfonso laughed and hugged her to him. "You are still a child."

Davina went cold with apprehension. Alfonso was much older than she was; he had his own successful business and an air of command about everything he did. But he could also be charming one minute and tyrannical the next.

Perhaps, if she did as he requested, he would always be nice to her like this.

A car collected them from the quay in El Puerto de Santa María and they were driven in stately silence up from the coast and over the long, white hills to Jerez. Up here it was colder and a knife-edged wind cut right into the interior of the vehicle. Davina, wrapped in her voluminous grey cashmere wedding coat, shivered and hugged her arms across her body, staring out at her new country. The landscape was wide, wider than she had ever seen in her life. Open rolling hills with nothing but occasional stubby bushes and marching rows of round olive trees. There were no streams, nothing green and not even a hint of springtime.

As they neared the town, they passed between rough, tumbledown dwellings where chickens scratched in the dirt road. There were no pavements, no street lights. A skinny mule tied to a post skittered around at the approach of the car. A mangy dog ran across the road in front of them to snap at its heels. Then they were behind a herd of goats, the nannies' udders scraping the dust. A rickety old man, stubbled like the hide of his dirty herd, ambled up after them, occasionally poking a long stick at a straggler, but making no attempt to move them off the road for the car to pass. Taking advantage of the slow progress, barefoot urchins appeared from nowhere and started to run around the car calling out for coins, then shouting abuse as they received none. A black-haired, square-set woman with a fair-haired toddler clamped to her hip emerged from the doorway of a neater, whitewashed, single-storey dwelling and yelled something sharp at the children. The calling immediately ceased. Davina turned to watch her through the back window as they crawled up the hill. The woman stared after the car. Alfonso lit a cigarette and said nothing.

Eventually, they reached the town and bumped down a cobbled boulevard lined with Alice in Wonderland orange trees. On their left was an imposing church.

"*La parroquia de Santo Domingo. 'Parroquia'* means 'parish' in English," Alfonso said, wafting a gloved hand at his window. "My mother's weekday church. On Sundays she goes to the cathedral. Mass every evening, and twice on Sundays." He opened the window and tossed his cigarette through the church railings. "Personally, I can't stand piety."

The car turned a corner into a street of tall grey buildings that appeared to grow out of one another. In this street there was no green, save the painted railings of high, narrow balconies. To Davina the street appeared austere, grim, closed in.

The driver stopped the car outside two vast doors, blackened with age and reinforced with iron. Davina was instantly reminded of an illustration in one of her big picture books: Bluebeard's castle. As if by some sinister magic, the door swung open. Alfonso ushered her into a fern-infested patio. It smelt dank and uninviting. Davina looked up and around her. The patio was open to the sky. On all four sides above and around her, there were windows. She sensed watching eyes and lowered her gaze.

The driver unloaded their luggage and tipped his hat. Alfonso nodded in response, saying nothing. A maid appeared from a side door and grabbed two of their cases. Allowing them to pass before her, she lugged the cases unaided up the steep staircase to another vast, bolted door of varnished wood and oiled hinges.

Alfonso rapped twice. The door jerked open and Davina was immediately pulled inside a narrow corridor with windows opening onto the patio below. Two large women like huge brown hens set upon her, pecking at her clothes, tugging at her gloves, removing her hat. Davina clasped her hands to her head to protect herself. Claws scrabbled at her hair, beaks squawked over its wheat and barley waves.

Alfonso pushed past them and disappeared behind thick, brown velvet curtains. Then, before she could either focus or speak, Davina was shoved further along the corridor by the two women, nudged around a corner then down another corridor and into a heavily curtained room. She could see nothing in the gloom, and stood trembling with shock and confusion. Tears welled in her eyes. It was precisely in this moment of weakness that she first met her mother-in-law.

As her eyes became accustomed to the dark, Davina saw a fine-boned, grey-haired woman seated in a high wing-backed chair. Two grubby Pekinese snuffled at her feet.

Doña Mercedes spoke to her daughters, "Where's Alfonso?"

"I'll get him!" cried one.

"No, sister, I'll go!"

The plump brown sisters heaved themselves simultaneously into a narrow door-frame becoming jammed in the process. As they huffed and puffed, Alfonso appeared in another doorway to their right. Seeing that their darling brother had arrived, the sisters subsided in a mutual sigh of relief and returned to normal human dimensions. Davina, no longer afraid of what she could not see, was suddenly amused by the ridiculous women. Her smile met with disapproval. Alfonso scowled at her then swung into the room and kissed his mother on the cheek.

"Here we are, Mother," he said in English. "Here is my wife Davina Dymond, who has a variety of other names and none to be ashamed of, but I haven't troubled to learn them." He signalled to Davina with a wave of his arm. "My mother, Doña Mercedes. You may call her 'Doña Mercedes'. Unless she says otherwise, which I doubt. She has no English, by the way. *Now* you can smile – at her."

Davina stepped forward to be introduced and politely offered her hand. Doña Mercedes looked at the hand, pursed her lips and nodded.

"And here are Esperanza and Gloria," continued Alfonso. "Hope and Glory. My dear older, unmarried sisters. My eldest sister Mari Fe – that is Mary Faith – who has actually been married but unfortunately, as I informed you, lost her husband and son, will no doubt be here as soon as word reaches her."

Alfonso arranged himself in a chair. "Well, this is cosy," he said. "Your dogs haven't moved, Madre, have you had them stuffed?" He then shifted into Spanish.

Davina could not understand what was being said but it was clear to her that Doña Mercedes was not prepared to stand to greet her newly arrived daughter-in-law. And Alfonso was afraid of his mother.

Esperanza and Gloria clucked on either side of her. They pecked at her sleeves for attention then started to argue across her.

"They can't decide whether to call you 'sister' or 'sister-in-law'," Alfonso explained then turned to the two brown women and said something that included her name.

"Dabina, Dabina," echoed the two fat spinsters, giggling.

"*Basta ya!*" stated Doña Mercedes. The matriarch nodded her dismissal.

Alfonso got to his feet but was signalled to remain. He hovered for a moment, then reached inside his jacket for his silver cigarette case and tapped a tube of tobacco onto his initials.

Davina waited to be told what to do as he lit the cigarette, but Esperanza and Gloria pushed her into the corridor, cackling non-stop and taking it in turns to give her another little shove until they reached a glass-panelled door.

Alfonso stayed where he could see which room Davina – they – were to have. As soon as they had arrived, he'd checked to see if any of his belongings had been shifted from his old room: they had not. It had been a tremendous relief. His bureau looked untouched. Not that it really mattered: he never risked leaving anything personal of importance in the house.

His mother waited until he turned back into her sitting-room then said, "Sit."

Alfonso sat.

"Tell me."

Alfonso related a version of his extended visit to England, glossing over the date and details of the marriage. "And she is – no doubt you noticed – already expecting a child."

His mother gazed at him between half-closed eyes. "What do you want me to say? That I am thrilled for you? My only son, my last surviving male child, has married without consulting me – has told me nothing beyond the contents of a brief letter. What do you expect me to say?"

Alfonso drew on his cigarette and got up to locate an ashtray.

Speaking to his back, his mother continued, "Except, of course, it *is* high time. And very convenient for you, no? Convenient to be finally, legally married. A legitimate child will be a blessing." Doña Mercedes sighed, "But marriage to a foreigner of unknown provenance – that is not so convenient."

"She is young and so far speaks no Spanish. That should make her manageable for you." Alfonso avoided looking at his mother. "All you need do is make it plain that you are not going to accept dowager status in your own home. I may choose to purchase a house for us later, but for now, with your permission, I would prefer to stay here." He waited for some response from his mother. Getting none, he continued,

"All things considered it is not so bad for you. Better than having some uppity local girl strutting around the house, wanting to decorate rooms and buy new furniture."

"Local girl?" Doña Mercedes' tone was venomous.

Alfonso gave a dry, embarrassed laugh. "No, quite." He paused then said, "Even so, that would never do, would it? The house must stay as it was before Father died. No changing things for change's sake. Just make it plain from the start that she need not concern herself with household matters."

"And how am I to do that? She cannot even speak my language."

"She'll learn fast enough, she's young."

"Young and lacking in style; immature, I would say. Too nice for her own good, is she? Is that what suits your plan? So she won't put up any opposition to your lifestyle? You are the one who doesn't want changes Alfonso, not me." For a few moments there was silence then the woman spoke again. "Bring her to my room before dinner. I shall give her something from my jewel box, it is her due. Now you had better go to her, or your stupid sisters will exhaust her with their nonsense."

Alfonso stood, stooped to kiss his mother on the cheek and left. He took the corridor that bordered the right-hand quadrant of the patio below, dipped into his old bachelor room, collected his hat and gloves and went straight down to the street, saying not a word to his wife or anybody else.

Some hours later Davina stood in the doorway to her mother-in-law's room. There was a bed with a carved walnut headboard, a vast wardrobe, a round table covered in lace, and a pink, damask-covered armchair with a matching footstool. What seemed like hundreds of miniature paintings in silver frames were arranged in groups on three walls, on the fourth wall, arranged around the dressing table mirror were a dozen or so plaster cherubs. The cherubs rather spoiled the effect, but otherwise it was very much how she had imagined Miss Havisham's room in *Great Expectations* – without the cobwebs and the wedding cake, of course.

Doña Mercedes sat at her crowded dressing table. Before her was a large, fancy jewel casket. Alfonso pushed Davina gently into the room and remained slouching against the door jamb. Davina went to stand beside the woman. She could smell her hair, it was not pleasant. At this distance, she could see where powder was clogged in the wrinkles around the mouth. Alfonso continued to lean against the door jamb.

Doña Mercedes said something and Alfonso touched Davina's shoulder. "Mother has something to give you. It is a normal tradition."

Doña Mercedes ceremoniously opened the casket. The lid was lined with faded purple velvet, parts of which had moulted, leaving bald patches. The woman then ran a finger across a shelf littered with mismatched earrings and dull rings. She lifted out this shelf and placed it carefully on the stained white lace runner. The next layer in the casket held a jumble of necklaces – some bright with precious stones, some muted and sedate with coral or pearls. This layer was removed and set beside the top shelf. In the base of the casket there were more oddments of jewellery.

"I shall give her the earrings *my* mother-in-law gave me." Doña Mercedes selected a pair of pearl earrings from a section of the first layer. "What else do you want her to have? Nothing from here, mind!" Doña Mercedes waved a long twisted forefinger over the bottom of the casket and hastily reinserted the second layer. She looked up at her son, "Well?"

"Whatever you like, Mother. She doesn't wear much jewellery anyway."

"Will she appreciate something of value?"

"Her mother will."

"Ah, yes," Doña Mercedes turned to her son with a quizzical look, "her mother. It did occur to me. Is she beautiful?"

"Yes."

"And is this mother also glamorous and a socialite?"

"Absolutely."

"But you chose the . . ." She looked at Davina's soft hands, her smooth features, her rounded figure, "the innocent daughter."

Alfonso's lips widened into what was neither smile nor grimace and shrugged his shoulders. "I told you in my letter. It is a good family, and they have a successful business. The father is a good type. There is only one son and he is a fool."

"You should have informed me of that before today, I would have bought the child something modern that she — and her mother — might appreciate." Doña Mercedes spread some glass beads and a tarnished silver locket on the stained white lace runner of her dressing table. "So she brings you a good business. We had better make it *our* business to keep her happy then, and raise her son appropriately. In the meantime, she'll have to make do with what I give her."

Doña Mercedes looked up at Davina and said something, waving her right hand over the dressing table as if offering her all the wealth of ancient Egypt. Then she said something else and Davina turned to her husband for translation.

"She says take your pick from either of those two trays. She keeps the valuable stuff in the bottom of the box, don't expect any of that."

Davina was too embarrassed to speak and bit her lips in confusion. She had the distinct feeling she was being insulted. "I would like only what is the tradition, thank you."

Alfonso told his mother what Davina had said and the woman picked up the pearl earrings and handed them to her. She then tapped Davina's arm and selected a strand of dingy pearls, rattling off something to her son.

"She says she wore that necklace with the earrings. The clasp is broken, but I'm to get it fixed."

Doña Mercedes held the broken pearl necklace in the palm of her hand and proffered it to Davina with a sigh. The woman was upset with her son; the sigh was one of disappointment. It seemed to Davina that her mother-in-law begrudged the gift; she felt she was taking something she should not have and the woman was angry. She had no idea what to do.

"Take it," Alfonso hissed, "it's for you."

The pearl necklace slipped from the palm of Doña Mercedes' hand and fell to the floor. Davina instinctively bent to pick it up. By the time she had reached under the dressing table, the woman was on her feet with the closed casket in her hands. Davina went down on her hands and knees to reach a pearl that had separated itself from the strand and rolled into a crack in the marble tiles. The floor was very dusty.

Neither mother nor son stooped to help. She felt them watching her. It was all too humiliating. Tears rolled onto her cheeks and she stayed with her head lowered so they should not see her cry. Doña Mercedes eventually stepped around her to give her more space. As Davina pulled herself up with the help of the dressing table stool, her head swam.

Staying in that position, waiting for her head to clear, Davina watched her mother-in-law place her precious casket into a niche in the wall beside the bed. She pushed it as far back as it would go, then closed a plain wooden door over the hole and locked it with a key from the many on the chain at her belt.

Davina got to her feet and dusted her knees, desperately trying to control her tears. Alfonso looked at her and raised an eyebrow. "An emotional ritual I see. One has to be a woman to appreciate these things, I suppose." He put an arm around her shoulders and continuing in English, said, "My wife is lost for words, Mother. I shall say 'thank you' on her behalf." He blew his mother a kiss and steered Davina out of the room.

They stopped at the door to the room they were expected to share. Davina said, "Your mother is angry with me. Please, take these back to her."

"She's not angry with *you*. She's angry that you are young and she isn't. And I told her your mother was beautiful."

"Is she?"

"Is she what? Which she are we talking about now?"

"My mother."

"*Por Dios!* Women!"

Alfonso strode past her and disappeared into his own bachelor room. A few minutes later Davina heard a door slam and feet running down the stairs. She went to the corridor windows and looked down. Alfonso was crossing the patio. He did not return for dinner. And that was her first night in her husband's family home.

Davina thought she heard Alfonso return well after everybody was in bed. He did not come to her room. For which she was grateful.

Chapter 20
Petrograd, 1919

Leo suppressed an expression of awe and appreciation. The room was magnificent; a high ceiling decorated with intricate plaster blooms, a chandelier that would take a week to clean, soft blue velvet drapes. It was far grander than anything he had seen in British India or London, and exactly what he wanted for himself – one day.

"Leonard, good to see you again. Come and join us by the fire. We're burning books to keep warm."

Leo followed Oleg Lenz across the elegant salon. Six young men were lounging around a bright fire in a large ornate grate. They were indeed burning books. Leo sat down, but his eyes strayed to the paintings on the wall: still-life rosy apples on plates and slaughtered hares, various non-Russian-looking country landscapes, plus one large canvas crowded with coloured blotches and stripes that looked like nothing at all.

"That's next to go," laughed Oleg following Leo's line of sight, "bourgeois pretentionism."

Leo didn't think such a word existed in Russian or in any other language but grinned good-naturedly. "Hideous, whatever it is."

"Drink, Leonard? Vodka, German wine, French wine? Or here's something for you to try – absinthe. Your countrymen are taking only water, but I suspect you go for something more adventurous." Oleg was sorting through a fine array of liquors in an even finer drinks cabinet.

"Absinthe, excellent. That'll do me." Leo watched while Oleg opened a decorated bottle and selected a brandy glass. "No, a tall glass is better – you serve it with water."

"So, our new foreign friend knows about Parisian absinthe as well, does he?" Oleg Lenz's eyes assessed Leo, not unkindly. "I thought you were from Bombay – this stuff comes direct from the City of Light."

Leo shrugged, "You can get it in London, too – perhaps. You can get *anything* there. I think I had it on a steam liner."

"I wouldn't advertise any of that, if I were you." Boris Shulgin muttered, tamping down an ivory pipe, evidently not his own. "Viktor, get our exotic visitor a glass of water."

"A jug would be better, Viktor, please, and a tall glass as well, if you are going to the kitchen – if you don't mind."

Viktor Grekov was the group's general dogsbody. When they weren't bossing him about they ignored him, but Leo was careful and very polite with him, and everyone else. It had been a part of his Canterbury training, what there was of it. It had also been part of his orphanage survival kit.

"So, Leonard, how do you like our new HQ? Not quite so cramped as my old rooms, is it? Didn't expect it to be so blasted cold, though," Oleg sidled up to the fire, kicking legs out of his way to get nearer the hearth.

Leo inclined his head then settled in a chair, noting that the two Sikhs from Delhi, who were often part of Oleg's get-togethers, looked ill-at ease, and that they'd been joined by a dark-skinned southern Indian he didn't know. He caught Ajit Singh's eye and nodded towards the newcomer, hoping to be introduced. When that failed, he said, "There's a storm blowing outside. Is it always this cold in April?" Nobody replied to this either so he prattled on, "Whose is it – this apartment?"

"Whose *was* it? Solyev's," Oleg said, turning his other cheek to the blaze.

"He's renting all this to you – wow."

"Not quite. Local branch of the Cheka came for him yesterday. Viktor and Yuri were here for a tutorial when it happened."

Fat Yuri said, "Scared the living daylights out of me – afraid they'd think I was his son or something and drag me off with him."

Oleg laughed, "So we thought we'd move in – shame to waste glamorous surroundings, and his stupid novels are keeping us warm nicely."

It was one of Oleg's various affectations to begin every statement with 'so'. Oleg's affectations would have made him at home in any salon in any city; he was a most unlikely ardent communist. Leo could just see him lounging about with Davina Dymond's brother. He stopped himself. That short chapter was closed. Not to be revisited. He said, "Solyev? Doesn't he teach European philosophy? Ah – I see – he *did*. But why have they taken him as well?"

"He was teaching Milton and Adam Smith. Free will, free trade – all that stuff."

"Doesn't mean he believed it, I mean, aren't literature and philosophy students supposed to study and think about different –"

"Not anymore." Boris Shulgin had finally got his pipe going.

Leo opened his palms in submission, tried to look uninterested, then made another attempt. "What about his family? What happens to his wife and children? Place like this means he must have a family."

"Wife's father is a White: land-owner class."

"Ah." End of subject.

Viktor brought in a tray with a cut-glass jug of water and a tall glass. Leo was delighted; he could top up the cloudy absinthe and keep a relatively clear head while his companions got legless on vodka and expensive imported brandy. He busied himself with his drink and listened to his companions make desultory conversation. There was a lull, followed by a thump on the door.

Another member of Oleg's coterie entered waving an envelope. "This has come for you, Oleg. I brought it straight over. Knew you'd want to know immediately."

Oleg ripped it open with a manicured finger and read the contents rapidly. "He's got it! My father's got the post. Moscow, here I come!" He waved the letter at the group around the fire. "Anyone want to join me?"

Leo waited for the congratulations to die down, allowing himself to fall into the edges of the conversation then gradually disappear from it, the better to hear about 'the post in Moscow'. After a few minutes he looked up, aware someone was watching him. It was Viktor Grekov. Colourless, shapeless, ageless Victor: a pasty face below dull brown straight hair. "You'll be off to Moscow too, then," Leo said brightly.

Hearing him speak, Oleg turned, "What about you, Leonard? Want to come with us?"

Leo looked at the Sikhs and intercepted anxious glances. "Don't see how I can. I'm supposed to be here to study Russian literature." Why wasn't he inviting the boys from Delhi?

"Literature! What use is literature to anyone! You'll learn far more useful things in Moscow with me." Oleg was being serious. "With my father where he is now, I can probably even get you a paid job. Train you up for your own revolution, assuming you want to release your country from the yoke of colonialism."

"That's it, Leonard. Come with us," Fat Yuri was saying, "Moscow is where it's all happening now. Petrograd is dead and we, the younger generation, are taking the law into our own hands. Moscow is the place to be, not surrounded by all this . . ." he waved an arm, indicating the ornaments and ruffles of the Solyev apartment. "Come and learn how to start a new nation; run a country without the strangle-hold of the old oppressors."

"I think we'll need a bit of help for that in our country. Do you have any idea how big India is?" Leo grinned and took a sip of absinthe, watching Patel and Singh over the rim of his glass.

Yuri was glowing pink with excitement, "There are plenty of others already involved, I thought that's what you were doing here, learning the ropes for student agitation like these two. The Hind group in my faculty are all red hot to get the British out. You should talk to Veejay Whatsisname. Imagine, you could be the Indian Troika. Go back to your cities and –"

"And get put straight into jail. No, it'll take slightly more than three – or four – of us to unseat the British Raj." Leo joked, smiling at the southern Indian newcomer, trying to get a response one way or another.

"Careful, Leonard, we don't want the Cheka thinking you're belittling our great leaders." Boris's lugubrious voice cut through the banter.

"No, quite," Leo went quiet, genuinely disturbed. There was no such thing as an idle threat anymore.

"Do come with us," Oleg said, "at least for a while. You could pick up some useful contacts. You speak English and – what else? All sorts of people might be interested in you. How did you learn Russian so well, by the way?"

"His father's Russian," colourless Victor said.

"Is he now? I didn't know that," Oleg leaned forward.

Leo laughed, "Neither did I! I thought I was a poor little half-caste orphanage boy. What's this post in Moscow your father has secured?"

Oleg grinned with satisfaction. "My father's been selected as one of the new Sovnarkom – the People's Commissars. There are only ten men on the Sovnarkom and each has been named by Lenin himself." He tossed back his drink. "Once I get there he'll find me something to do –"

"Lenin!"

"No, stupid, my father. Then I'll find something for my friends. That's how it works."

"And how could I be of any use?" Leo also leaned forward in his chair, looking eager.

Oleg peered at him as if they were the only two people in the room. "Come here tomorrow at ten." Then he turned to Victor, "Another drink all round, Viktor, let's celebrate. Open another bottle of brandy."

Moscow was nothing like Petrograd, and not at all to Leo's taste. It was grey, cold, austere, and he hadn't slept through the night since he arrived. For sure there were carnival gilded onion-rooftops, and the Kremlin was suitably imposing, but this part of the city, where Oleg's pals had moved into what had been other people's homes, was dismal. And he was bored. Oleg kept himself entertained, inventing meetings and lunch-time obligations, sending Fat Yuri to find restaurants and diners that still had enough food for clients. Boris read books all day. The only person who appeared to have anything useful to do was Viktor Grekov. Oleg returned from his meetings with reams of scribbled notes, which he dumped on the nearest surface. Viktor then read them, every word, and then disappeared for hours, presumably to report to someone who was reporting to someone else. It gave Leo a brief respite. Viktor watched his every move.

By May, Leo had had enough. He had made no useful contacts, found no useful leads; he loathed the climate, and the food, what there was of it, was worse. It was time to move on.

"I've had a letter from Bombay," he said, breezing into Oleg's new office in what had been an insurance broker's suite. "I've got to go back and present an application for my grant to be renewed."

"You don't need a grant. Stay and I'll get you a job." Oleg had promised him that a dozen times.

"How did you get a grant to come to Communist Russia, anyway?" Boris asked. "Bit odd now I think of it. Why would British India pay for you to come here? They're fighting with the Whites against us. Doesn't make sense."

Leo shrugged, "The exchange programme has been working for years, started well before the war and your revolution. Actually, I don't know if any of you have thought about this, but I might be more useful to you there."

"In Bombay? What could you do for us there?" Oleg said, exchanging looks with Viktor Grekov.

"You tell me. I assume Russia still needs our raw materials the way it did before – and rice and tea. You drink gallons of black tea here. Or can you get all that from China?"

"Viktor says your father is in Calcutta," Boris drawled looking up from his book.

Leo swallowed and turned to the dirty window. *Where was this coming and from, and why? Was it even true?* And did he care one way or another?

He turned back to the young men around Oleg's fancy new desk, his face a mask. "I've never been to Calcutta. Who is this chap, anyway? This figment of Viktor's fairy tale?"

Boris looked at Oleg. Oleg exchanged glances with Viktor again then said – as if he'd been given permission, "Ex-diplomat, apparently."

"Diplomat!" Leo scoffed, but the word burned through a flimsy sheet of paper in a carefully filed manila folder, now stored in an English bank safety deposit box. "Pity no one told me this when I was an orphanage boy. No, nice idea, but if I do have a father, which I suppose I must – somewhere – alive or dead . . . But hey, no – not that sort of father, not a nice idea at all. Diplomats were land-owner class. I don't want to be sent off to a labour camp! Can we not talk about this, all right?" He kept his tone bright and breezy, but his stomach had turned over.

"Probably better," Oleg said, "they'll have you in the Lubyanka jail as fast as you can say his name. Doesn't do to be connected to gentry. My pa's been burning family papers like billy-o. That's our new job, by the way: 'Department of Family Histories' we're calling it. We'll be checking up on wives and relations. Like Solyev's wife; land-owner class, White Russian, obvious source of opposition to the state – straight into jail then off to a chilly gulag, or into a grave if they try to make a run for it. Viktor's getting really good at it, sniffing through documents, winkling out traitors to our Soviet state."

"Here and abroad," Viktor added.

Going down the stairs some minutes later, Leo stopped at the second landing and listened. Someone was following him. He turned as if to go back up and met fat Yuri face-to-face.

"You going back up?" Yuri said.

"Forgot to give Oleg my address."

"You know what? If I were you I wouldn't even . . . no, nothing. Safe journey, Leonard."

Leo dithered. Go back and face them again or . . . or what? This was his first mission for London, and he'd made a pig's ear of it. He'd got very little to tell the grey men in Whitehall and, like as not, he wouldn't get back into Moscow again safely. But did he really mind? Did he care what Mr Shepherd would say? Did he care that he'd failed Lionel Pinecoffin? Did he care that a nasty little bunch of school bullies had nailed him as belonging to a man who'd never made any attempt to find him, help him, treat him as a proper son? No, actually. No, he didn't. But he hated failing himself on his first proper assignment.

He descended the final few stairs and was in the entrance hall when something made him look up through the stair well. Viktor Grekov was leaning over the banister above, smoking a cigarette. Watching or waiting – or what?

The tap on his door came late that night, as he feared it might. Leo took a deep breath: friend or foe? Or were they one and the same? He kicked his packed case further under his bed and shoved his small pistol into his dressing gown pocket.

It was Viktor. Leo opened the door and let him in. A nondescript young, but not so young man, a bundle in clothes – neither fat nor thin, neither good-looking nor ugly. A face to fail to see in a crowd: a face to overlook at your peril.

Viktor crossed the small room and sat on the bed. "So? As our friend Oleg would say."

Leo opened a bottle of vodka, saying nothing, and handed Viktor a glass. There was a lull, each waiting for the other to make the first move. The visitor won.

Leo said, "*Sooo*, what can I do for you, Viktor? I doubt this is a social call. What is it you want?"

Viktor looked into his tiny glass, avoiding eye contact. "While Oleg's been prancing about I've been doing something useful. There's plenty to be done. We have a desperate shortage of skilled manpower in Russia. I'm not saying anything critical you understand, but the Great War and now our civil war is – well, too many men have been killed. There's virtually a missing generation here in Moscow alone. Not so bad for us, means we can move into useful posts faster, climb the ladder more rapidly, but there is shortage of labour, and that cannot be denied. We need people – clever, valuable people, urgently. Engineers, for example."

"Engineers! If that's why you're here, to get me into a factory, forget it. I'm studying Literature, for heaven's sake."

"It was your suggestion, Leonard – working for us in Bombay."

"Was it!"

"Yes. We want you to help us recruit a workforce."

"Ah, help like that. Not impossible." Leo gave a good-natured shrug. "You'll have to offer us – them and me – decent conditions, though, especially if you need men to actually work through winter here, they'll get ill in this climate, for sure."

"That can be arranged. Could you do it? Find skilled workers to come here?"

"I suppose so. I could advertise in newspapers, put the word about – a few words here and there with a contact address."

"As you say, it'll have to be somewhat low key. We don't need London knowing our situation here, not at the moment."

"Will I be paid for this with real money, or are you expecting it as a favour?"

Viktor raised an eyebrow, "As a favour? In return for what, Leonard?"

Leo tried to back-track; he'd made a stupid remark because he had at that exact moment realised Professor Solyev had been arrested while Viktor was at his home, and it hadn't been for a tutorial. Viktor had denounced him. Viktor had led the secret police right to the door. Viktor hadn't been studying anything in Petrograd; he was a bloody police agent, or a spy, or both.

Keeping his expression open, Leo lounged back in the room's single chair and said, "You'll need to pay the workers travel expenses up front."

Viktor nodded, "We can come to an agreement."

"Why don't you ask Patel or Singh? Or that other chap in Petrograd? They might have contacts already. Wasn't Patel studying Chemistry?"

"They have their roles already."

"Which are . . .?" Leo waited for an explanation. There was silence. "And, what happens if I change my mind, go back to Bombay and don't do anything at all, what will you do then, Viktor?"

"It might be better for you that way."

"Better? Why?"

"Because I was an orphanage boy as well, and I don't trust you. Is that bottle empty?"

Leo poured more vodka into Viktor's glass, saying, "It's you who has the interesting post in Moscow, isn't it? Not Oleg."

"Correct."

"What exactly is Oleg doing?"

"What I tell him."

"In the Department of Family Histories? That's genuine?"

"Perfectly genuine. There are thousands of files to examine, hundreds of thousands of family-related documents to sift through. That's how I found your unwanted papa. It's quite a family history, if you ever care to ask."

Leo desperately wanted to ask; and he desperately didn't want to know.

Leo was followed from Moscow to Kronstad. He was watched boarding his ship for Rotterdam. He thought he was being watched as he boarded the Dutch ferry to England, but reasoned that if this was the case and they'd bothered to trace him thus far, they would also see him getting on the steam liner for India, see he had a passage home that way.

Knowing he was being followed was disturbing, but knowing he was returning to London as a 'useful young man' with contacts in Petrograd and Moscow, and more useful connections to come, made it worth the risk. The sense of success was too good to lose. And so what if he was being trailed? It would give him a chance to play 'hare and hounds' the way they'd shown him in Canterbury. Then he remembered the limp, life-less game on the walls of the Petrograd professor's apartment and stopped feeling so smug.

Chapter 21
Jerez, 1919

Somewhere across a harvested cornfield a lark rose and fell, leaving its short song hanging in the early morning air. A mile away, the memory of bird song interrupted a valerian-induced sleep and Davina opened her eyes. The room that had become hers alone had no window save that of the glass door opening onto the corridor. She looked around at the austere, white walls. It was like a convent cell. There had been adornments in the room but one by one she had removed them. A plaster-cast bleeding heart had been popped into a bottom drawer; a chipped Jesus, arms extended to a dusty multitude, had been hidden at the back of her musty wardrobe. The rosary placed for easy access on her bedside table was now hanging with her long necklaces over the side of her dressing table: just another set of beads among glass baubles. Apart from the large wooden crucifix that hung precariously over the bed and which Davina did not dare touch, the only remaining adornment was a small picture of a gaudy Mary in bright virgin blue. The Madonna, wide-eyed in her innocence and motherly love, gazed down at the plump, rosy-cheeked babe cradled in her left arm.

Davina traced the shape of a tiny foot kicking inside her, and wondered for the millionth time where Leo was, and how he would react to knowing about their baby. She was doing her best to accept her father's arrangement, but she could never, never get Leo out of her thoughts. The baby kicked again and she smiled to herself, hoping he or she would make her happy again.

She reached for a small towel she kept under her pillow and wiped her brow, then dabbed at the sweat between her swollen breasts. The room was more stifling than usual. She tried to roll into a more comfortable position, but it was so hot, so very, very hot, and having the door closed only made her feel worse.

Davina had learned why windows and doors had to be kept closed during the day, but hated the way the shutters were bolted against the sun and then the curtains drawn to hide all trace of the outside world. The house became blind inside and out. Except for the early evening hours when Hope and Glory were obliged to sit on their respective narrow balconies and make an attempt at embroidery. Stabbing at their linen squares, they would stare down at the street below and fill their silly heads with ideas for gossip. They rarely saw any 'suitable' young men, which was the object of the exercise. Doña Mercedes still maintained a room on the ground floor where a daughter might sit safely behind black iron bars and converse with a prospective *novio*, who naturally could not be admitted to the house until an official engagement was announced. But the sisters, Davina believed, were content in their spinsterhood. For all their silliness, they knew they had never been beauties and were never likely to marry.

The eldest daughter, Mari Fe, had been married, though, to bring a lesser sherry firm into her father's business. Within a year, her father had died and then her husband; her sickly child was born posthumously under her mother's roof then it, too, expired. Mari Fe had had enough strength of character to insist on returning to her marital home. She visited her mother every day, as was expected, but was free to return to the peace and quiet of her own house each evening. Davina envied her, but recognised that in having her own home she would have to share it with Alfonso – unaccompanied. She didn't know which was the better alternative, her mother-in-law and the silly sisters, or her husband on his own.

Davina sometimes told herself she was living through a chapter in an extraordinary novel and eventually there would be a happy ending. But everything was different, every single thing from the time of meals to her choice of clothing was a challenge to be overcome, and no matter how she tried to fit in, to accept her circumstances, the more she learned, the more alien she felt.

She had quickly adapted to the petty rituals of her new abode, though. Having a good ear, she picked up enough vocabulary to make herself understood when she was obliged or permitted to speak. Her sisters-in-law never stopped asking questions, but these questions, which were either attention-seeking or pathetic attempts to ingratiate themselves, required no complicated answers. More often than not, a smile would suffice. Esperanza and Gloria repeated themselves constantly and argued incessantly. It was tiresome, but Davina used it to her advantage. It enabled her to live within herself, which was the only way she could survive. And, as Morrigan had told her, she had to survive and be strong for her baby.

Days merged into weeks, and the weeks into a suffocating summer. In the morning the house was cleaned; rugs and washing were taken to the roof; dust was disturbed from one place and shifted to another. A cook with a face like a melon clattered about the primitive kitchen, abusing the maid-of-all-work and concocting evil stews out of dried beans or chickpeas. Occasionally, she served up a piece of unidentifiable leather and called it beef or mutton. Her salads were to be approached with caution. During one interminable supper, Davina had watched a weevil-like creature weave its way round the crystal bowl, in and out of the limp lettuce, under and over the soggy tomatoes. Its progress fascinated and revolted her. No one else noticed it, the salad was eaten and the bowl left clean.

When it became too hot for the sisters to continue their balcony watches, they all sat in Doña Mercedes' darkened sitting room. The matriarch did nothing, except watch her daughters ruin their eyesight crocheting ochre-coloured circles or stitching shapeless baby garments. The three sisters shared titbits of gossip. A random comment could be spun into a fine thread of dubious facts and used to stitch a patchwork of conjecture. As the weeks dragged on and her Spanish improved, Davina came to realise their gossip was not as harmless as she had supposed. When the mood was upon them, they could cut a saint to the quick. Nobody was safe – except Alfonso, who was never mentioned.

Alfonso kept a strict daily routine. Monday to Friday at nine a.m. he ate a bread roll for breakfast then took his coffee and newspaper to his room. He left the house at ten to go to his office. He would return at half-past two to change his shirt and have lunch with the family at three. At five he went down to the town *casino*, which was essentially a gentleman's club, then back to his office for an hour or two. He did not return home for the evening meal and despite the fact that they did not share a room Davina knew he almost never got in until well past midnight. She slept badly, and Alfonso made no attempt to come in quietly. Here was a very juicy morsel for the sisters' afternoon dissection sessions, but nobody ever mentioned it.

The labour pains started one afternoon in mid-August.

Doña Mercedes and the two sisters had retired for their siesta; Alfonso had left the house. Davina was trying to read by the dim light in her room. She stayed seated in her chair and waited for the pain to lessen. The spasm passed and left her breathless. Then her bones began to disconnect. Her head was heavy, hanging like that of a wooden puppet over a body that was no longer hers. Sweat trickled down her neck and between her aching breasts. She got up clumsily, crossed out of her room and opened a patio window. It was a cardinal sin but she had to breathe.

Davina hung over the window sill and stared down at the patio ferns and began to see her river moving between rushes. Ducks chattered, a swan paddled by. The next pain came; she gripped the window frame then she staggered back into her room to the bed. From a sitting position she swung her legs up and crouched sideways over the stiff pillows. Her head swooned. Was it possible to faint lying down? Now she and the bed were soaking wet with sweat and broken waters. But still she did not call out.

She must have slept a while before the next contraction gripped her. Holding her abdomen she tried to lift herself; the walls were closing in on her, trying to suffocate her. A caul of humidity was strangling her – she had to escape and she could not move. Now she wanted to call out but no words came, only a desperate scream.

The next time she looked up there were faces at the bottom of her bed. Angels. Angels with brown hair: facial hair.

"Mother sent us," said one.

"Are you all right, sister?" asked another.

"No, I'm bloody not!" Davina screamed in English. "Get out!"

Sometime later, they ushered a small woman into the

room and closed the door behind her. The woman spoke to her. She was incomprehensible; her Andalusian accent slurring over words and eating the endings before Davina could grasp them. But her hands were kind and she went about her business with a comforting certainty. Davina was terrified. And the pains went on and on, through the night and into the next morning. By the time the tiny, wrinkled creature that was her daughter was placed on her breast, she was too exhausted to feel anything. And then there was an urgent, crushing, physical sense of what she could only assume was motherly love. Davina felt her mouth form the same silly smile as on the plaster Madonna's face and was content.

Then they came back again, the faces around the bed. Someone was mopping her brow with tepid water. The baby was taken from her arms and passed around.

"A girl," someone said.

Davina put out her arms to take the child back. The nurse turned to the woman standing in the doorway.

Doña Mercedes nodded her assent. Davina heard her say, "Let her feed it for a week or two, it won't do any harm. Don't tell anyone."

"Of course not, Señora, I am always discreet," the midwife replied.

"Doesn't matter anyway, she doesn't have any friends and no one invites her anywhere. It's the hair – too blonde. Decent women don't approve; they assume she's a . . . you catch my meaning?"

Davina met the midwife's glance. The kindly woman, her face weary from a long, sleepless night, gently smoothed the wet, mousy strands from Davina's eyes. *She feels sorry for me,* Davina thought.

"She doesn't have much of a figure to lose," Doña Mercedes continued. "She can feed the child for a week or two. Now, you stay with her, everybody else, leave. I shall send someone to clean up the mess."

Davina gazed down at her baby. Tears welled in her eyes. The floodgates of relief, of physical and emotional exhaustion, broke; she sobbed, heart-rending, shattering sobs. She cried for Leo and for herself, for all the things she had tried to forget: for her home by a slow, old river; for her father calling her 'Davy'; for her books and her poems; for mist and rain and fresh air. For a world that had ended one cold London morning a lifetime ago.

"The child will be named Maria de la Inmaculada, Mercedes, Josefina and something else. I could ask the priest to include Davina in the list but I doubt he'd allow it. Women in Spain are not normally named for David. She will be baptised on Friday. If you are well enough, you may accompany us." Alfonso began pacing around the stuffy room. "It has a certain irony about it, don't you think? Inmaculada – do you think the old witch knows?"

"Inmaculada? I don't understand."

"Maria of the Immaculate Conception."

"Oh. But I don't like . . . I want . . ."

"Want and don't like are not relevant."

"But it's such a long name. I –"

"Call her Inma – or Marina, that's a short form of Maria de la Inmaculada, and everyone else can either call her by the full list – or Inma or Arturo or Gabriel or Pilarina – do what you like when you are on your own. But Mother has decided on the girl's name and you can't change the baptism."

"But . . ."

"Davina, you live in Spain. This family is Spanish. We do what is done in Spain. Although, I admit that normally a girl is named for her mother."

"Mari-Fe wasn't named for your mother."

"Her older sister was. She died when she was three or four – before I was born."

"Oh. I'm sorry. That's so sad. I didn't know."

"There's a lot you don't know – but none of it is relevant right at this moment. Look, my mother is naming the girl for the Virgin and for herself. You should be honoured. What is your problem?"

Davina wanted to say that her problem was that she did not like the names and didn't have one iota of belief in any Virgin. And she hated his blasted mother. She said nothing, because she had in that instant decided that *she* would always call her daughter Marina and only ever speak to her in English. Maria Inmaculada could, as he said, be shortened to Marina, which was a nice enough name. She also didn't want to aggravate Alfonso any further: she had never seen him quite so discomposed.

Davina sighed and said, "All right. I can get up now. I feel perfectly well."

Alfonso nodded in approval and turned to leave. With his back to her, he said softly, kindly, "She is your child: you may call her the name you like in private. I do not oppose it. At the baptism my mother will name her, and my sisters will be Godmothers. Mercedes is also a good name for a girl born in Jerez. She is our patron saint. It will make your daughter more Spanish. Do you follow me?" He turned around and smiled at her. "You feel better, that is good. I should like you to be well as soon as possible."

For a moment Davina thought he was genuinely concerned about her.

Chapter 22
Petrograd, 1920

Leo leaned back on the grimy pillow. It smelled of stale human sweat and winter dampness. The whole building reeked, but this tiny room was the worst place he'd ever had to sleep. The miniscule dormer window was nailed shut, meaning every inch of the closet-sized attic accommodation stank to high heaven from all the cabbages being cooked on kerosene on the floors below. What had once been a single family's private home, then a student lodging house, was now a slum. The cubby-hole Sidney Tamchian had given him in Bombay was a palace compared to this.

Leo stretched his long limbs, wondering why he'd let himself be talked into returning and whether the up and coming Viktor Grekov knew he was back. The name Leonard Kapadia would be on a list in Moscow, and here as well, like as not. He rubbed his chin and turned to wondering if the blade he'd hidden under the washbasin was still there. A rough nail caught on his cheek, he nibbled at it. His wash-bag, scissors and safety razor had all been stolen during his first week back on Russian soil. The thief, who had almost certainly been after his soap, must have celebrated all night at finding real shaving cream as well. Soap was an unobtainable luxury. Food was an unobtainable luxury. His stomach rumbled and he let himself drift back into the daydream where he was politely deported for being an alien, thus freeing him of his new task of identifying 'Commonwealth communist connections, please': his personal CCCP.

Leo hadn't seen or heard of Viktor since he'd been back in Petrograd, but he was certain Viktor would know he was here. One genuine but gentlemanly run in with Viktor Grekov and he could tell Mr Shepherd and his flock of boy scouts that his student days were over, and thank heavens for that.

He'd said it would be more difficult for him this time: told Shepherd that lectures were being cancelled for good on a daily basis before they even went to Moscow in the spring. Returning to Petrograd with a supposedly renewed grant, was just plain dangerous. But he hadn't bargained for just how thoroughly unpleasant it would be as well. Living standards hadn't declined, they'd plummeted. Surviving on a daily basis in what was now a country in a full-scale 'Communist civil war' was proving horrendous for a number of combined reasons.

The previous year had been tricky, but getting messages back to Britain now was *very* dangerous. Everyone was under suspicion. Oleg's Department of Family Histories was evidently doing a sterling job. Even the most innocent of people feared betrayal – because their parents were Christians or their parents were Jews; because an uncle was or had been a White, or a Menshevik, or simply because they had a supply of beans in their cellar. Everything everyone did was under surveillance. Little old ladies denounced their neighbours for a mere break in routine.

Leo dragged himself from his foul-smelling litter. He had to attend another supposedly secret rally of White supporters: Mr Shepherd also wanted to know who to help.

The Empress Emerald

For secret police they were hopelessly un-secret. One grabbed him by an arm as he came out of the main door. "Papers," he demanded. Leo handed them Kapadia's passport. They took him to a police station and grilled him about his identity. He responded in Marathi, vaguely, then, foolishly, in English, feigning only very basic Russian.

What the Cheka police said between themselves curdled his blood: he was to be conscripted despite his papers showing he was a foreigner; he was being sent to Murmansk to fight with the Reds. He listened carefully, but played the soppy foreigner, fielding questions back in bad grammar, agonising over whether Viktor had actually traced him in London. If that came out, he'd get no nearer to the Bolshevik front line than the next ditch.

Eventually, one of the bully boys left the windowless room they had taken him to. When he didn't return after a few minutes, the other left as well. Leo took in his surroundings: pea green walls, brown floor, small table, damaged in places, two upright chairs, badly scratched. They hadn't touched him, though. The Cheka, notorious for their appalling cruelty, hadn't touched him. Why?

Viktor came in. It was almost a relief.

"Leonard! Sorry about this." For a featureless, characterless person, Viktor was nearly effusive. "Good job I was in Petrograd."

Leo jumped to his feet, "Viktor! Am I glad to see *you!*" Then he remembered to stumble over his Russian, not wanting the goons to feel they'd been duped. "What you have want you me for myself in this place?"

Viktor smiled. "To be honest, I was waiting for you. Left a message that if you did return – with a new grant to study Russian Literature during a civil war – that I should be the first to know. Naturally, I've had to appraise my department as to why I wanted to return to Petrograd. I told them it was to meet an old *friend* . . ."

So you're more than a mere police agent now, Viktor, but who and what are you exactly? Leo let his thoughts stray then came back to the moment, but stayed silent.

" . . . Come, I know somewhere where we can get real beer and ham from real pigs. You've realised your old faculty has been disbanded, I assume."

Viktor's arm ushered Leo from the room and they were out on the street. Leo looked back, trying to identify the building. It was an ordinary block of flats. There was nothing to identify it ever again, not a street number or, when he looked, the name of the street.

They sat at a table in what had once been a prosperous German-style beer-cellar.

"You should have let me know you were coming," Viktor raised his tankard. "You should have stayed in Moscow. I can find you a real post now."

"Up and coming – I knew you were the successful one – told you, didn't I?" Leo grinned. "And I told you I'd be more use getting you workers from Bombay. They arrived safely, I suppose. I haven't heard a word from your colleague in factory recruitment."

"It is all well. A few men came. Not many, unfortunately."

"Sorry about that. I tried. But what could I have done in Moscow anyway? I haven't finished my dissertation on folk tales and fairy stories yet."

"Fairy stories: you're good at those, aren't you, Leonard?"

Leo cocked his head to one side and gave a cheeky one-dimpled grin, feeling a cold chill run up then down his spine. Were Viktor's gloves about to come off?

"They are a great indicator of cultural values. I met this really interesting German studying Philology called Propp here a couple of years ago, he was –"

"Philology," Viktor scoffed, dismissing the topic. "Look, stop wasting words, I have something to say. I have a small proposition."

"Another business proposition? Your communism is rife with them." Leo caught himself in time. It didn't do to be flippant, as the sober-minded Boris had warned him. "Is this for a new venture?"

"Yes and no. Not in the capitalist sense, no, obviously."

"Fire away." Leo swigged his lager, nearly choking on his own words.

Viktor looked into his beer mug, avoiding eye contact, as was his custom. "Before I begin, you should bear in mind that you now owe me a favour."

"I owe *you* a favour?"

Viktor raised an eyebrow, "For getting you out of a Cheka arrest in one piece and saving you from a Red Army unit. For getting you out of Petrograd, safely, as only I can. For having provided you with an income during the last year. I assume you have collected payment from your Bombay bank."

Leo bridled; London knew all about the recruitment task, but it was an uncomfortable reminder. "I'm damned sure I have no idea why the police wanted me." Then he rushed on, pretending incomprehension, "I've come all the way here to collate your ruddy folk tales and listen to your best professors and all you can do is arrest me! Getting here from India takes weeks, means an expensive sea voyage to England then a ferry to Holland or Finland . . ."

"Why don't you come overland? Logical route is via Persia."

"Overland! I never considered it. No, I prefer sea-voyages. All that time sitting in one place on a train – I'd go mad."

Viktor held up a hand, "Your choice. As to travel expenses, that will all be taken into account. We shall discuss money and come to an agreement. You can fret about your personal travel arrangements once we decide whether or not you may ever return to Russia again."

A waitress appeared at the table to re-fill their tankards from a frothing jug. When she had gone, Leo said, "I didn't know places like this still existed."

"They don't. Doors are closed to normal clients."

They drank from their tankards. After a few moments Leo said, "All right, suppose I just go back to Bombay and get a boring job as a teacher once and for all. Will that suit you?"

"No, because now I need you."

"And if I go, regardless. What could you do?"

"Find you, and kill you."

"Bloody hell!" The words spurted out in English. "As the English say," Leo added, hastily. "That's a bit extreme! Why?"

"Let's say because what we discuss today is *nobody's* business except ours. And because, as I told you before, I was an orphanage boy as well. I know what normal orphanage boys are like, and you aren't one of them."

"So why get me out of Cheka detention?"

"I told you. I was waiting for you. I need you."

"For your personal advancement . . . You never were a student with us, were you Viktor?"

"Correct. Do we continue, or shall I take you back where I found you?"

"I could make a run for it."

"You might get across the street."

Leo sighed. "Go on, tell me what you want. What's this all about?"

"Diamonds."

"Diamonds!" Leo was genuinely surprised.

Then he wasn't. There was no such thing as a coincidence. Viktor was aware of the alluvial diamond scheme, if he hadn't been involved in it himself. He'd been in Petrograd because that was where the Russo-Hind student exchange programme was running.

Leo smiled, though, saying, "Diamonds I will discuss, and happily. But what the hell does a good communist comrade like you want diamonds for? You could loot anywhere in the city and find a dozen jewels a day if you wanted, especially here in old St Petersburg."

"Not industrial diamonds for precision tools and machinery."

"And for making weapons, I suppose." Leo narrowed his eyes. "This will have to be a strictly capitalist arrangement, comrade. *If* I *can* supply them, who will be doing the buying? This has to be a good old cash purchase deal, all right? I can't risk going back to India, finding what you need, bringing them all the way back or paying shipping costs then not getting paid myself."

"You'll be paid. Directly by me."

"Because there's more to it than that."

"You will submit expense sheets and report on anyone who approaches you to make personal transactions."

"What you call 'profiteering'?"

"It is a major crime in Communist Russia."

"I can't do that, Viktor. I couldn't possibly denounce someone who's basically doing what I'll be doing myself, trying to get enough money to live on."

There was a silence. Viktor finished his beer and wiped his mouth with a carefully ironed, clean white handkerchief.

"But if I don't," Leo sighed, "you'll find me and . . ."

"I shan't need to find you, Leonard. I'll know where you are."

"When I'm on Russian soil."

"When you are in India, as well. You provided us with contacts in Bombay, didn't you? A very convenient arrangement and all thanks to you."

Leo struggled not to respond, cursing Shepherd, but cursing himself doubly for falling into the trap. Viktor, on the other hand, was showing signs of animation. His mouth moved into a semblance of a smile.

"We now know so much more about . . . all sorts of people: superannuated diplomats, consuls and ex-consuls, and everyone once attached to the Bombay, Calcutta and Delhi trade missions."

Leo forced himself to relax. "Can I ask a personal question?" Viktor shrugged. "How old are you?"

"Considerably older than you. Older than I look."

Viktor looked anything between twenty and sixty. Leo examined his interlocutor's features: an old face, a peasant's face; the sort of face that aged prematurely with a prospect-less future, except this member of the peasantry was involved in changing his entire country's destiny. And he, Leo Kazan, with all the fast chat and quick thinking in the Indian sub-continent had come up against a lump of solid rock. A sensation far worse than when the Cheka brutes had man-handled him earlier because this time he recognised that he was trapped between the gentlemen in London playing their out-dated version of the old Great Game and this new man, Viktor Grekov, and what he represented.

"Were you in India," Leo said, quietly, "a few years ago?"

Viktor looked him in the eye for the first time, "Does it matter?"

"No, I suppose not."

Viktor put enough money on the table to pay for an eight course meal then handed Leo a card and got up to leave. Pulling on his gloves, he said, "Come to this address at ten tomorrow morning. You'll need an internal visa and travel documents; my secretary has them ready but they require your signature."

Before seven the next morning, Leo reached under his bed to check his boots were still chained to the leg. They were. He got up, splashed used icy water over his dark jowls, dressed hastily for the room was freezing cold and stuffed his few belongings into his leather case with a relatively glad heart. After a sleepless night of trying to find a convincing way to keep London satisfied and agree to Viktor's scheme just sufficiently to enable him to come and go, and make lucrative diamond deals on his own behalf, he was exhausted. Keeping in with Viktor had major advantages, but he also wanted very much to stay out of Viktor's sights – starting now, because he was going to chance returning straight to London. From there, as before, he would take ship for Bombay. If Viktor's eyes did follow him all the way there, or if he had men on the ground there already, he could confuse them through the London underground.

Whatever happened, his student days were finally over, and this was the last time he was ever going to rough it anywhere. Industrial diamonds would provide a tasty little income; an excellent, strictly capitalist enterprise he could shape and make his very own. It would provide him with a decent income. Decent enough to provide for a girl he couldn't seem to forget. If he returned to Russia it would be as a respectable married businessman, not a guileless student to be played with or bossed about.

Before going to Viktor's office, Leo walked into the cavernous, eerily quiet railway station and stood before the destinations board. There was a weekly train across Russia from Petrograd to Moscow, then on to Kazan and the East. One day he would go to Kazan. But not yet. *Not yet, Leo. You will go, but not yet.* Leo sighed at words he'd heard in a previous lifetime: something else he couldn't seem to forget.

A month later, on a beautiful sunny day, with London plane trees creating speckled shadows across the pavements, Leo took a purposeful walk. A blackbird in a garden chink-chinked a warning as he strode down the street. He stopped at Number 3, St Anne's Terrace and looked up at the bay windows. A bourgeois home. It was all so tidy, so civilised. A world away from Bombay's heaving streets, two worlds away from the Petrograd tenement.

He went up the scrubbed steps, lifted the brass lion-head knocker and rapped politely three times for luck. A maid answered.

"Miss Davina Dymond, please. Is she at home?"

"No sir."

"Can you tell me when she will be back?"

"No sir."

"Well . . ." Leo's felt his stomach turn over with foreboding, "may I leave a message?"

"We won't see her, sir. She's in Spain. She lives there now."

"In Spain?"

The maid gave him an embarrassed smile, "She got married, sir. To a Spanish gentleman."

"I see. Well, thank you. Good day."

Leo felt the maid's eyes on him as he descended the steps. Why did everyone watch him leave? John Shepherd had done it again after a rather heated discussion that morning. He straightened his shoulders and quickened his pace. But now the maid had been joined by someone else. Leo willed himself not to turn round but, feigning interest in a garden rose, he caught sight of a tallish woman in blue-grey suit. She had walked out of the house onto the top step to get a better look at him.

Leo turned the corner and the blackbird set up another round of warning chink-chinks. "Don't worry little bird," he said, "I'm going back where I belong – I think."

Chapter 23
Bombay, 1924

Millicent Cleaver found Leo again quite by chance. She had not been looking for him. She was in her preferred haberdasher's buying ribbon and lace for a camisole that she was making, when someone very like her darling Leo walked in behind her and passed straight into the back room. He was much thinner than when she had last seen him, but that had been five long years ago; he was bound to have changed.

The girl who was serving her, Kitty, Jack Cartmel's daughter, followed the young man with her eyes and flushed scarlet.

"Do you have a beau, Kitty?" Millicent asked gently.

The girl scrunched up her pretty face and pushed back her dark hair, "I think so, Miss Cleaver."

"Good. I'm very pleased for you. And what is his name?"

"Will that be all, Miss Cleaver?" Kitty's mother edged the girl down the counter none too gently, adjusting her green and gold sari more tightly as she moved.

Millicent could feel the antagonism but she still had to ask, "So your pretty daughter is walking out. How quickly they grow up, Mrs Cartmel."

Mrs Cartmel pursed her lips and wrapped Millicent's purchases, "Too quickly."

"He looks a very – um – grown up sort of young man."

Mrs Cartmel fixed Millicent with a sharp look, "That is precisely what worries me. In here five minutes and taking charge of Kitty as if . . ." The woman bit her tongue and cut the string on Millicent's small package.

Millicent was about to say something else but thought better of it. Kitty's Maratha mother was evidently not pleased about her daughter's young man. "Thank you, Mrs Cartmel. This is all I need today." But she couldn't resist prying for more details. "I have to say, he looks a very well set up young man."

"Too well set up to my liking. Here one day, then gone for weeks at a time. Kitty says he's told her he'll be away for months before they can marry."

"Marry? But he must have an important job if it takes him away . . . abroad, is it?"

"London."

"Goodness. Your Kitty will be marrying well. Your husband must be pleased."

"Oh *he* is. They get on like father and son – better."

"Oh, I am glad. A proper family at last! Oh, I am so glad, so very pleased." Then she caught Mrs Cartmel's looking at her as if she were a mad spinster and coughed, patting her chest, embarrassed at her slip.

"Do you know him?" Kitty's mother asked suspiciously.

"Oh, I doubt it. How could I possibly know him? No. Must be going, can't chat here all day. Goodbye."

As Millicent left, the door-bell tinkled happily. She gave a little sigh of relief and something she could not name. Trotting contentedly down the alley leading to the main commercial district, she made her way back to her new rooms near Victoria Terminus. When she arrived in her comfy little rented rooms, she took the lace and ribbon from the brown paper parcel and laid them across her work table. Her new occupation as a music teacher left her little time for herself, but once she had stitched the lace and ribbon on her new camisole she thought she might take up knitting or . . . embroidery . . . or something creative in that line. Something that required the frequent purchase of silken or woollen yarn, cotton thread or colourful ribbons.

Chapter 24
Moscow, 1926

The small room, part of an apartment created out of what had once been an elegant drawing room perhaps, was dominated by a tall, conical and very stylised bronze samovar. It stood on its own table among as much beautiful furniture as could be shoved into the reduced space. The small, beige man, who had invited Leo to take tea with him after he left his workbench in the optical instrument factory, pushed aside the glass *podstakinniki* cups he had set out and put a crescent-shaped leather box on the table. From its shape Leo knew its contents. He raised a hand and covered the box before the man could open it.

"I think you are mistaken, or you have been misinformed, sir. I am an industrial-diamond supplier. I do not deal in precious gems."

"But you know people who do."

It wasn't a question. Leo was at once curious to know what had led the man to take such a risk – inviting him to his rooms then begging him to sell his wife's baubles – and just as anxious to get away. Doing business like this in the centre of Moscow was very unwise. But all he said was, "Please, don't put me in an embarrassing position. I cannot help you."

The man's mouth twitched. He was amused, or irritated. Either way, it mattered not. Leo had to keep his private business very, very private when he was in Moscow. Miserable, hated Moscow. He shook his head. "Sorry."

"Perhaps you will be," the factory craftsman said, and pushing Leo's large, soft paw aside he unclipped the clasp and opened the box.

Leo blanked his features, but his heart raced. Diamonds and rubies – it was beautiful. He thought of old Mr Craven, how he would have loved such a setting, how he would have put on his special examining glasses and lingered over the gems. He shrugged. "You can't sell it, of course. I understand. What use is a necklace to a woman without soap?"

The workshop foreman smiled, "Well put. Forgive me – I do not know your full name."

"Leonard Kapadia. My friends call me Leo."

"Your friends – wherever they are."

"We are all Russians now, or soon will be."

"But you are from –"

"The warm south. Fertile lands under the sun."

"Ah, the sun, we enjoyed the sun here too, many years ago. It no longer shines. There has been a decree."

Leo nodded and closed the lid of the box. Then the man said, "But *your* true home is India, is it not?" making Leo look up.

Where had he got his information? Not, he thought, from the fat-faced pudding who arranged his factory's purchase of precision tool parts. "I was born in India."

"And that is your home, where you return?"

"It is where I come from," Leo said thinking: *If this is a trap, let it be stated I am no Soviet Russian and not subject to their miserable existence.* Not that it would make any difference; he'd simply disappear. "This is a beautiful apartment," he said.

"It was a beautiful house. My beautiful house."

"I see." Leo sighed. "You have a large family. That is a blessing for you. Is one allowed to say 'blessing' these days, I forget?"

"Probably not, and no, I do not have a large family – anymore. Let me explain, it may interest you. My father worked with Ivan Khlebnikov, you will have heard of the jewellery firm Khlebnikov. He then set up on his own and developed his craft into a very successful business."

"And you learned the craft *and* the business."

"I did. Now I must work with machines, *comrade*, in a factory."

"But you still have a number of – shall we call them 'embarrassing possessions'?"

Tears gathered in the man's eyes. For a moment he could not speak then he said, "The garrotte is being tightened. They follow my daughter everywhere. I fear for her . . . any excuse and they will . . . I have two sisters. They married foreigners, fortunately." He handed Leo a small, embossed calling card. On the one side it had the printed name and address of a Mrs Laban in Vienna. On the other, in tiny Roman script, was the name and address of a Mrs Rosenthal in Hamburg. "I have a cousin who worked with us, now also in Vienna. His sons have moved all the way to the Mediterranean, to Gibraltar, I think. We are 'dispersed' as they say."

"It could be for the best."

"I try to think so."

Leo read both sides of the card and cocked his head to one side, questioningly.

The man responded by removing the necklace from its box. "Please, take this to wherever is convenient. You can travel, I cannot. Your occupation provides valid travel passes." He paused and looked at the necklace glinting in the low light. "We can remove the stones from the setting; you could put them in with your industrial stones and –"

Leo raised both his hands. "No! *That* would be a real crime." A thought occurred to him. "Mr Goldman, if your family have been involved in jewellery-making for so many years, can you tell me anything about a large, pigeon-egg pendant emerald that's called the Empress Emerald? It was said to belong to –"

"Catherine the Great. That's what people usually say when they inflate a price."

Leo was disappointed in the man's attitude. "It is an antique setting; there are pearls and diamonds together, which modern designers avoid. I think it might have been made for the Empress Victoria."

"Or in her honour. Is there no hallmark on the setting?"

"No, which suggests it may have been made in India, I suppose, not London."

"The only thing I know about London jewellers is that I should have joined them thirty years ago, when I had the chance."

Leo sipped his scalding tea, pondering on the wonderful emerald pendant in his favourite biscuit tin, now safely stowed under floorboards in a Bombay haberdashery store. It was time to sell it, but how? He really couldn't bear to part with it.

"The emerald itself, is it of particular value?" Chaim Goldman asked bluntly.

"Must be, it's huge and flawless, as far as I can see."

"Fifteen years ago I'd have said 'bring it to me'. Obviously, I can't do that now. If it's yours to sell, you could take it to . . . Sorry, I can't help. I was hoping you would help me."

Leo sighed, genuinely sorry. "It's not that easy – I am watched – they follow me, sometimes even attend my transactions. There are informers everywhere. There's a man here in Moscow, he . . . No matter. The fact is that I am no freer to do as I please than you, and that's that." What he was saying was true – in part. "I could never promise anything, and I can't say when I'll be in Germany or Vienna again. Not this winter – I was planning to return to Bombay – I am married, you see."

The Russian jeweller's hand dropped the necklace onto the lace tablecloth. His arm slumped to his side then his face suddenly changed from its melancholy expression and he beamed, "It shall be an anniversary gift, for your wife! I also have something very special . . . *very* special. I cannot sell it, and I cannot keep it. When you find a buyer for your emerald you could offer them this as well. It was for my daughter Sarah, but who is left for her to marry in our religion?" Rising from the table, the ex-jeweller, now a factory workman, hurried through a door into a chilly corridor.

Leo followed him, saying, "Whatever it is, it will have to be smuggled out of Russia and – even assuming I can make a sale elsewhere – how will I ever pay you?"

"What can I do with money here, now, *comrade*? It is not the money that motivates me, Mr Kapadia. Besides, I doubt you will ever get their true worth. No, what I ask is that you take all that you can to my sisters. They will pay you your travel expenses, and far more if they can. Wait here – no, come with me to the lavatory. I keep everything in the cistern, but I can't go on like this. Every time there's a knock at the door I panic. And my daughter . . . it is as I said. They will get her and do what they want with her sooner or later. Someone has reported me, I'm sure of it. There have been men loitering in the street all week."

"In uniform?"

"Some."

Leo shook his head in despair, "You should have told me that before."

"Then you wouldn't have come. You're safe enough. You can say I was giving you tea."

Leo blew out through his cheeks. "It's not that simple. I've just explained: you're not the only one who has to watch who's walking behind you."

"But you have a travel pass. I will never be allowed to travel again unless it is to a salt mine."

Gradually, over these gruelling, ever-unpleasant years in the Soviet Union, Leo had met other small men with large fortunes. He now had a network of useful contacts and a healthy, growing account in an Amsterdam bank, and he barely slept two hours together any night he was on Soviet soil. He never opened a door without wondering if there were uniforms, or men in long coats and low caps waiting for him outside.

In the past two years he'd successfully ignored pleas such as this to take beautiful items to 'safety'. He ran far too many risks for his Imperial British Majesty's government, with Viktor Grekov too often on his heels, to risk open peddling on the side in the Soviet Union. So far, he had avoided doing what Viktor had asked – denounce someone for so-called 'profiteering' – in return for allowing him to work, and he didn't want to have to do it now. But it would be necessary if Viktor's eyes watched him leave through this front door.

The man who had invited him home opened the door to a lavatory then stood on the wooden seat cover and pulled a waterproof pouch from the cistern above. Carefully, he stepped down and opened the pouch in the confined space. He extracted a ring, a perfect pink diamond in a pink gold setting, and displayed it on the palm of his hand.

Leo put his own hand to his mouth. It was exquisite. He wanted it for himself – for his pretty wife, Kitty. "I'll buy it off you," he said.

"I will exchange it," Goldman replied.

"For a lifetime's supply of the finest Darjeeling?"

"For my daughter."

"Your daughter!"

"Sarah. Take her with you. Find a way to get her to Austria, to her aunt, or to my other sister in Hamburg. Either: just get her away from here. Please! They will come for me – and what will happen to Sarah then? I was foolish. I thought it wouldn't last, this regime. I thought I could sit it out, wait until it was all over. But it isn't going to be over, is it? And there's more . . ." the man's voice was barely a whisper. He edged round Leo's large frame and stepped back into the corridor.

"You've been selling privately?" Leo's voice was icy.

"Buying. I've been buying family jewels and keepsakes. At first . . ." Chaim Goldman returned to the sitting room and stirred the tea leaves in the pot on the samovar. "I didn't think the regime would last, you see. Thought it might be a year – two years – five – then we'd go back to normal. My family held tight through pogroms before the revolution; we have survived all manner of tests and tragedies. And we have, in our way, helped people in the past survive their own disasters by buying their valuables, providing them with cash to move away or stay in their homes." He shrugged. "I started by helping my neighbours – ready money for basic commodities – thinking I could sell on, sooner or later. Then it was 'later', then 'much later'. Now there's no point. But I can't keep our precious stock here, not anymore, and I won't let those brutes have it when they take me . . ." His voice rose, there was an element of panic and Leo caught it. "Or the satisfaction of finding their proof. No, let them send me to a labour camp, kill me faster or slower, but they shan't have anything of beauty in return. And that includes my Sarah."

Leo swore under his breath. "Mr Goldman, I fear you are very naive."

The man's eyes glistened, "We can say you are her young man. You can walk out with her. Get on a train, or take a river cruise to Astrakhan then get to Turkey, and . . . Please, I beg you. Get her away from here. Here, take the ring. You must! It's a wonder. It cannot go to those dogs! Take it – and my Sarah – please!"

Leo went to a high window. Standing at angle, as he'd been advised during a very different sort of diamond affair, he glanced out. There were uniforms outside – two standing in the street, a black car parked nearby. He tried to see whether his own particular bloodhound was among them and checked through another window. He wasn't. "Is there a back entrance?" he asked.

His bloodhound was in the back alley with a uniform. They were smoking, sharing a joke. "Ha-bloody-ha," Leo snorted in English. Returning to the s, he said, "Do you still have an attic?"

"It is an apartment now. It's occupied – a widow. She suffers with her nerves, her –"

"No matter – I'll get a message to you in the next few days. Tell your daughter to be ready to leave. She is to pack nothing, but bring whatever food she can get hold of, all right?"

Grabbing his attaché case, Leo bounded up an elegant, winding staircase two at a time and burst through the top flat door. Ignoring the terrified woman clutching a shawl to her breasts, he danced around the compartmented room, looking for a sky light.

The Empress Emerald

A chair, a table, and up on the roof. He shoved the case out first. The tiles were like a children's slide and it nearly hurtled to the street below, but he caught it by the handle just in time and set it more safely on its side. Then, a large man on an unhealthy diet, Leo clasped the window frame and struggled up after it. Grasping the freezing bricks of a long-cold chimney, he cast about him, wondering how the hell he had ever found rooftops fun. It was ten years since his escapade over the roofs and fences of the houses on Malabar Hill – and all that for an emerald. But it was altogether a different game now.

He laughed inwardly at his own absurdities, and checked the pink diamond ring tucked into his inside jacket pocket. If he fell four storeys down to the street it might pierce his heart on impact. A suitable irony. If the case fell, they'd know exactly where to find him.

A shot rang out. If he couldn't see them, surely they couldn't see him, could they? Another shot pinged off stone. Leo was astonished. Uniforms on surveillance didn't waste ammunition. Slowly, awkwardly, he rolled onto his stomach and tried to peer into the street below. A uniform was coming out of the building.

He waited. How long before they found the widow's skylight? How long before he'd freeze into a gargoyle? He looked at his watch, calculating how long before it was completely dark. His mind wandered back to Malabar Hill. That had been a hoot: up and over roofs and garden fences, staying out of reach of snarling, snapping dogs. No chance of getting from one building to another there – not with those huge gardens. But here, yes. He could probably get to the end of Goldman's street if he moved from chimney to chimney. If he was careful. He had to be careful: the pink diamond would fetch more than a fortune. He could retire and set lovely Kitty, darling little Kitty, up in a mansion with a staff to rival the Viceroy's. He wouldn't give Kitty the ring, he'd use it. The way he'd never quite managed to use the emerald necklace.

Leo peered down at the street again. He couldn't see anyone, but that didn't mean they couldn't see him. Hitching up his heavy overcoat, he tucked his wide trousers into his socks, double-knotting his shoe laces while he was at it. Little by little, on hands and knees, shuffling his case in front of him, he made his way across the steep, wet roof until he hoped he'd gained the next house, or set of apartments as it would be now. A few minutes later, he noted a flatter roof below. If he tied the case to his back with his belt and risked a drainpipe, he might be able to reach it. He pulled off his belt and fastened it through the handle of the leather case then round his doubled-up overcoat as best he could. If they got him now they might shoot straight into the case. It was a very minor comfort. And then, bingo! Shiva and Ganesh and all the sainted Christian saints had come to his rescue. There was another sky-light just a few yards on, and it was open!

Open – on a late September evening in Moscow – why? It was a trap. He edged back the way he'd come and tried to get behind a chimney stack. He waited for a full half-hour then crawled back to the open sky-light and peered in. Four very drunk old ladies were sitting around an empty bottle of vodka and a mah-jong board. They were creating enough cigar smoke to fill a Marseilles brothel.

"Evening, ladies. Do excuse me." Leo pushed the window frame up as far as he could and dropped inelegantly into their midst, up-ending an ashtray and disturbing various Chinese wind and flower tiles in the process. The women goggled, speechless.

Then he was round the table, through the door and haring down back stairs – attaché case banging the back of his legs black and blue – down to what had once been the mansion's back yard.

"Yes!" A rickety old wheelbarrow, and sacks of coal and, oh, disgusting mouldy potatoes. "Wonderful!"

Half an hour later, a lumbering old peasant robed in smelly sacks trundled a wheelbarrow down a busy city street, across the open square in front of the tall portals of Kazansky station, and into the ticket hall.

Leaving the empty barrow against a wall, the peasant nipped into the gents' waiting room. Divesting himself of the smelly rags and the paunch created by his attaché case, Leo was tempted to abandon his overcoat as well, it stank of sour roots and was slimy black in places, but didn't, not least because a man without a coat at this time of year would attract attention.

Soon, he was in the station buffet and slowly supping hot root vegetable broth. There were at least two hours to kill before he could risk returning to his own building to collect his belongings. Leo kept his head down. At least it was warm here, and he'd have time to examine his dilemma and think up a way to get a message back to his minders. But to say what? That he was going absent without leave with a jeweller's daughter? Was he really intending to help the fatherless Sarah? For surely the pistol shot had been for a once-wealthy Jewish Soviet traitor. The buffet door opened. His personal bloodhound wandered in.

A woman in a green woollen headscarf entered behind him and sat at a nearby table. Sighing, she kicked off her right shoe to examine a hole in her stocking. She had good legs.

A hand tapped his shoulder from behind.

It was Viktor Grekov.

It wasn't Viktor Grekov, but someone very like him. Broad forehead and piggy eyes like Viktor, but heavier, more muscular. One of Stalin's new GPU men. The Cheka had been disbanded and replaced with a larger, even more brutal force. Viktor was one of their main men, and more.

"Mr Kapadia, come with me, please." It wasn't a request.

Leo felt his gut loosen, but he got up, and pulled on his overcoat as if unconcerned. Lifting his attaché case, he tried to calculate whether swinging it backwards would catch the brute on the chin, but his mind had moved into a fog. Across the buffet, the bloodhound scraped back his chair. Leo straightened his back and led the way out.

As the door closed behind them, a train pulled in and dozens of doors opened. Babushkas and bundles were dropped alike onto the platform. There was a piercing, whistling scream and the train let off steam, engulfing everyone in a white cloud. Leo leaped sideways, pushed through a milling family group and climbed into a carriage. He was in luck: the carriage opened into a corridor. Swinging around passengers, shoving his way through cardboard cases and leather valises, he reached the dining car and wandered through slowly, apparently looking for a friend. Then he was out, and hastening further down the long train until he reached the sleeping compartments. Should he risk climbing into a bunk and staying there, or get off? They wouldn't be expecting him to get off. He dropped down onto the platform and looked back to see if anyone was following. His eyes caught the destination board above the carriage: Kazan. It was the weekly train across Russia from west to east. He jumped back on.

Kumar Dev, future graduate assistant at the Kazan University School of Oriental Languages, loitered in a corridor until the train moved off, then made his way back to the dining car.

They had had the Kumar Dev persona planned for some time, he and his new boss in Whitehall, a flamboyant Old

Etonian named Sir Gerald Travers-Deveraux. But only as an emergency exit. One of Sir Gerald's scribes had created a letter of introduction in Russian for a university principal or head of faculty. Choice of faculty had been left to Leo, who had hoped it would never come to this. Returning to academia was not appealing. But needs must – the letter was in his case, along with his emergency shaving kit, a bar of black market soap, a set of clean underclothes and a copy of *Kim* by Rudyard Kipling for his coded messages to Mr Shepherd's dowdy sheep.

Bribing the carriage attendant was cheap at the price. He was soon in an unoccupied compartment and in an upper bunk, in what had once been first class accommodation. All curtains had been removed, which made it easier to see who might come in or pass along the corridor. Fully dressed, his case at his feet, Leo settled back in his smelly overcoat. There was no heating, for which he was grateful, he could keep on his coat and the chill would keep him alert. He couldn't risk falling asleep.

Back-lit by the tiny light over the doorway, it was hard to see who it was. But it was a woman's voice.

"Let me up, comrade. I have nowhere to sleep . . . I'll keep you warm, if you like."

Before Leo could react, the woman was pulling herself up into his narrow litter. Blondish hair, sharpish features, any age between twenty and thirty.

"Take your shoes off," he said.

The woman eased off her shoes and lay back next to him. It was a tight squeeze.

"You've still got your coat on," she said. "Aren't you hot? Take it off comrade. I know how to keep a man warmer than an old coat."

Leo grinned, but stayed exactly as he was.

"Suit yourself." She rolled onto her side and eased her bottom into his groin. The thick overcoat softened her effect.

For a while the regular rhythm of the wheels on rail tracks lulled Leo into a half-waking doze. The girl beside him was very still; he adjusted the blanket over her and dozed again. The train crossed a set of points jerking him back to consciousness. A sulphurous yellow dawn lit the compartment. He pushed himself up to see where they might be and noticed a stockinged foot sticking out of the blanket. There was a hole over the big toe of the right foot.

The woman smiled up at him and began to pull at his tie, "Take your coat off comrade. I know the best way to start the day."

Leo sat up and edged himself into a position with his legs over the side of the bunk. "Sorry, I need the lavatory."

She was waiting for him in the corridor when he came out. Putting an arm up around his neck she thrust her body into his open coat. Her left hand crawled inside his jacket twisting his shirt buttons. She ground her hips between his legs. Despite himself, Leo responded. He relaxed and leaned down to kiss her. She was small; the top of her head barely reached his shoulder.

Her right hand dropped from his neck. She shifted position then began stroking the outside of his leg. There was a sharp pain. He let her go and she jumped to one side. There was a syringe in his thigh. He dashed it away, breaking the needle. As he bent to pull the end out of the thick material of his worsted trousers, the woman aimed a tiny pistol at him.

Leo stared at the broken needle, wondering how deeply it had penetrated the skin; then he looked up, straight into the barrel of the gun. "What the hell . . .?"

The woman's mouth gave a twitch of satisfaction. Her eyes never left his forehead.

"What's in the syringe?" Leo asked in a voice that sounded far calmer than he felt.

"You'll find out."

"Why?"

"Orders. Move down the corridor."

"But why . . . last night, you were . . ." Leo didn't bother to finish the question; she'd been stalling for time, waiting for one of the two men in the station buffet to find her – him – them. If he'd removed his clothes as she'd wanted, she could have shoved the needle in deep – and probably unnoticed – while he thrust away at her like any normal red-blooded male. He felt slightly, very slightly relieved. That she was doing this now suggested she was the only one on the train.

So – she was on her own, and small. But small pistols killed tall men just as fast. Leo backed away from her and bumped into the carriage attendant carrying a pile of unused blankets. Turning to see who it was he caught the attendant's eye. The man winked. That was how she'd found him.

"Sweetheart," Leo said, spinning round again and pulling the woman into a clinch. "Don't get so cross." Holding her close to him, cradling her head against his chest with a large hand and trapping the pistol hand against her body, he winked back at the attendant.

As soon as the attendant had gone, Leo repeated, "What's in the syringe?"

"You'll find out." Struggling in his arms, then suddenly dipping down to the floor, the woman succeeded in freeing herself. She raised the pistol first to his throat then against the spot behind his ear called the medulla oblongata – the guaranteed killing point. She had been trained well. "Move backwards until I tell you to stop," she said.

Leo did as he was told. She wanted him next to a door before she shot him. If he was lucky he could open the door before she fired and jump.

"Stop," she said.

Leo felt behind his back for the door handle while saying "How long before the stuff takes effect?"

"We'll see."

"So it's not immediately fatal? Always look on the bright side." Leo was trying to stay breezy, masking the noise of the handle turning. In all the danger and tension of the moment he heard a woman's voice from the distant past: *"Always look for the good things, Leo."* There was *nothing* good in falling into the middle of a Russian forest from a moving train with a dose of poison in your thigh and a Siberian winter on its way. And even if the injection wasn't lethal, snow and wolves would . . . "It's something that'll cause joints, muscles to seize up, isn't it?" he said. "Prevent me from walking . . . You want me incapacitated, helpless . . . Ah, yes, so you can deliver me back to . . ." Leo was amazed at how rational and calm he was. "Who is it you're working for?"

As he released the door handle a violent inrush of ice-cold air knocked him off balance. Grabbing the door jamb to stop himself falling out, he craned his neck away from the gun and swung outside the moving train then hurtled back using surprise and his large frame to crush the woman against the corridor wall. Flattening her against the wooden panelling, Leo lifted her arms so high she was on tiptoe then squeezed her pistol hand until the weapon dropped to the floor. With a neat, lucky, back kick he sent it swivelling out into the snow. The woman started her downward wriggling again, but this time he held on tight.

Step by step, holding her two hands above her head in one of his, he waltzed the agent – or whoever she was – around, so it was she who had her back to the open door. This way *she* would fall and he wouldn't have to hurt her. Wolves and sub-zero temperatures were her look out now.

"Who are you working for?" he demanded, wanting his fears confirmed.

"You'll find out," she hissed.

Outside the carriage, Russia streaked alongside them, an open maw of wilderness. "Who?" Leo repeated, leaning her out into the air.

"Who do you think, traitor?" she gasped, dipping down low then surging up with an extended leg to kick him in the groin. "Your sort are scum, we don't want you in our country. He told us you were no good."

Leo side-stepped without loosening his hold, knowing he should simply let go. She would sprawl backwards into whatever lay along the rail track below; with luck the fall might only injure her. He had been raised in a country where to hurt even the most pestilent of creatures was a sin. Keeping her at arms' length he pulled her back into the carriage to face him.

She began to scream. A piercing female wail. Leo grabbed her behind the neck and twisted her chin the way he'd been shown and never dreamt he'd ever have to do. But he couldn't do it. He couldn't break a woman's neck.

Checking that no one was coming to investigate the noise first, Leo gently dropped the woman with a hole in her stocking from the speeding train.

After a struggle in which he nearly fell from the train himself, Leo managed to close the door. Shaking from head to foot, he shuffled back towards his berth and struggled back into the bunk. His case was still there. Pushing down his trousers, he tried to examine how far the needle had penetrated his thigh. It was only a graze; there wasn't even a proper puncture point – that he could see. *I should find the syringe, take it back to London for analysis*, he thought and willed himself not to pass out.

When the carriage attendant came in to help turn the bunks back to seats, Leo was wrapped in his thick coat and the blanket as well, but trembling, shaking like the proverbial leaf, too weary to move.

"Rough night was it, comrade?" the attendant joked.

Leo couldn't speak. But whether it was due to the content of the syringe or from the horror of what he'd just done, he couldn't tell.

PART 3

SPAIN, THE NETHERLANDS, ENGLAND, GIBRALTAR, INDIA
1929 - 1936

Chapter 25
Jerez, Spain, 1929

Propelled by hope in the stout form of Esperanza, Marina thrust her sturdy, white-stockinged legs out before her, leaning forward to impel herself even higher. With her long, wavy, jet black hair streaming out like a banner, she took the swing as high as it would go, then tucked her legs under her and bent forward for the return trajectory. "Look, Mamá, look!"

Davina, sitting on the park bench below, smiled an uncomfortable smile. "You be careful. You'd better come down now."

"Oh, no, sister!" Gloria cried, bustling into the path of the swing. "It's my turn to push."

Davina jumped to her feet and grabbed Gloria out of danger. "For heaven's sake, there'll be an accident! Marina, come down immediately. That is enough."

"You can push her tomorrow," Esperanza said, pulling her brown sister away from the swing.

"That's not fair. We agreed."

The two sisters fell to squabbling. Marina slowed her movements and gradually returned to earth. She looked at her mother on the wooden bench and grinned.

"They are fighting again."

"Over nothing, as usual," Davina replied, taking hold of a rope and bringing the swing to a halt. She let go and stood back. "Off you come, now."

"My nuns at school tell children not to fight. But *Tia* Esperanza says she and her sisters never went to school. So that's why they do it." Marina reluctantly brought the swing into its final, gentle arc but stayed on the seat. Gloria made a grab for her niece and the swing jerked round dangerously. Marina called out, "Mamá!"

"Stop it! Stop it both of you! She'll fall off," screamed Davina in fluent Spanish.

The middle-aged spinster looked shamefaced. "I only wanted to have my turn. It *was* my turn to push."

"For heaven's sake," said Davina, "the girl is not an object for ownership; she's a child."

"Yes, you are right," sighed Esperanza, folding her arms over her ample bosom and shaking her head in exaggerated commiseration. "Just one little girl."

"Yes, sister-in-law," added Gloria, picking up her sister's thread, "one little girl, that we all must share."

"Such a pity for our brother, he would so like to have a boy. A man needs a son. He cannot take a girl to the bullfights, or buy her a fine white horse, or show her the fine gold pens on the desk in his office and tell her the desk will one day be hers."

In her annoyance, Davina caught hold of the swing rope herself.

"Mamá!" screamed Marina as once more she nearly fell to the hard earth beneath her.

"Sister-in-law!" cried Gloria. "Take care. Our niece is not a boy, but she is very precious to us."

Davina grabbed her daughter's hand and marched out of the children's playground. Her head raced with resentment and angry retorts – all the things she wanted to say, but never dared. Was there nowhere she could go to get away from these women? They were insufferable. Would no one rescue her from their incessant taunts? Ten years of their vicious stupidity. Ten years of doing what she was expected to do. Ten years of marriage to a husband who didn't care for her or about her. A decade of suffocating summers and bone-chilling winters in a cheerless mausoleum. And the utter, utter loneliness of it all. If it weren't for Marina, she would most definitely have left by now. But where could she go? She had a little money of her own, but she also had a child to take care of. She couldn't just pack up and return to England, though God knows that was what she desired above all things. But she couldn't, because her mother wouldn't have her.

They turned the corner of the street and Marina's hand slipped from hers. "You're hurting me, Mamá," Davina stopped and looked at her daughter.

"I'm sorry, sweetheart. It's just that they make me so cross."

They can't help it," said Marina sagely. "Can we get an ice-cream?"

Davina purchased two vanilla ice-creams from a street vendor and they sat on a bench. Marina licked at hers, watching two scruffy lads playing marbles in the dust, then she looked up and caught her mother's eye. She smiled her wide, guileless smile and Davina bent to kiss her forehead. And that was another thing she couldn't fathom. Her own feelings for her daughter were so strong it seemed incomprehensible that her own mother could be so cold. She had not written one single letter, nor sent a birthday card, not even a Christmas card. Her father came once a year, but he spent more time in the *bodega* and Alfonso's office than he did with his daughter and granddaughter. He always said his wife would join him for the next visit – but she never did. And he had never once hinted that Davina should return with him for a holiday, which for sure was her mother's dictum. She had been an exile for ten years now. Had she not paid for her crime?

Davina sighed, "Finished? We'd better get back before your aunts start telling tales."

"They're worse than children," replied Marina.

Mother and daughter set off, back to Doña Mercedes' mansion. *How nice it would be*, thought Davina, *if we were really on our way home – to our own apartment, or one of those lovely new houses they are building on the Seville road.* She took Marina's hand gently in hers. "I'm sorry about your play-time – I lost my temper, didn't I? What would your nuns at school say about that?"

"Oh, they'd say it was very wrong, but they do it all the time. Most of them are very bad-tempered. Like Grandma. Anyway, I think I'm getting a bit old for the swing. I've been to the top. Can I learn to tap-dance?"

"Tap-dance! Wherever did you get that idea from?"

Marina chatted on about her school friends, their hobbies and pastimes. Davina half-listened and then got lost in her own train of thought. It had become a bad habit, but she spent her days living through scenes and conversations in her head – to the point that her mind would go off on its own track even when she had someone to talk to.

How lovely if they could be a normal family; father, mother, daughter – and perhaps one day a son. Just them, no mother-in-law, no sisters-in-law – Hope and Glory were so irritating. But you couldn't hate them, not with real hate.

The Empress Emerald

They simply made a difficult situation ten times worse.

And so it went on, until one afternoon, in the autumn of 1932, Davina learned quite by chance that two men had entered Esperanza and Gloria's lives.

The first was a little man wearing a jacket two sizes too small and shoes five sizes too big. The second was a dashing Rudolf Valentino. The sisters had discovered Hollywood.

Davina also noted that, either because she had finally accepted that her daughters would never marry, or because she had simply given up caring, Doña Mercedes ignored their increasing visits to the town centre, where, Davina discovered, Esperanza and Gloria had been watching a building being converted into a cinema.

The new cinema evidently satisfied their wildest imaginings and they returned from each trip bursting to tell her about how sheiks of Araby delivered *them* from marauding hordes; how a poker-faced bachelor defied runaway trains to save *them*; and the sad-happy tramp called Charlot lived out tragedies more profound than they could ever fabricate. And Mary Pickford and Clara Bow, she learned, were women with stories more scandalous than any snippet of gossip they might acquire.

What delighted Davina most about this fascination with the screen was that they lost interest in her, and so, to encourage and consolidate this blessed new-found pastime, she bought them magazines about the lives of film stars. Each issue gave them interesting foreign women to scrutinise, envy and criticise.

Curiously, the more the sisters left Davina in peace, the more time Alfonso spent at home. He no longer stayed out until the early hours on weekdays, only troubling to sleep with her if they had been to an unavoidable dinner party or concert on a Saturday night. Now, he returned for the evening meal during the week and often took Davina with him for a stroll before supper. They would encounter other local businessmen and their wives and exchange comments on the weather and recent or forthcoming events. There were more invitations to dine, more concerts: Davina was now expected to accompany Alfonso to a number of social events and chit-chat about nothing to other local burgers' wives. And then Alfonso started going to church on Sundays.

Davina could not say precisely when she first realised her husband had lost his swagger; it had been a gradual process. His hair had gone quite grey, and with it he had acquired a more staid personality. It also became increasingly evident that Alfonso was a worried man. His newspapers featured reports on labour unions wresting power from their employers in Barcelona and Madrid. The dangers of syndicalism were anxiously discussed in the *casino*. There were serious labour disputes going on with the men who transported sherry to the railway station and down to the coast. A group of wagon-drivers had started a trade union – and now the men working in the sherry bottling plants were demanding improved conditions, too.

There was a lot of scandal-mongering, mostly focused on how communists were planning to annihilate the middle-class. People said the Republicans were going to secularise education and sack priests. There were increasingly violent incidents involving agricultural labourers in the south and factory workers in the north. Davina assumed Alfonso simply felt safer at home during long, dark winter evenings.

That winter had been particularly dull and cheerless for all, so as the days lengthened and lightened, and the year shifted forward into the short Andalusian spring, everyone began preparing for the big fiestas in April and May. One bright afternoon in late March, Davina took her daughter to collect a frock from a new dressmaker living on the Cádiz side of town. Coming out of the dressmaker's house into the daylight, carrying her cumbersome cardboard dress box, Marina caught sight of Alfonso walking along the opposite side of the street.

"Papá, Papá!" called Marina. Alfonso didn't hear her. "Papá, Papá," she insisted, running awkwardly with the box in her arms across the dusty road. "Papá!" she screeched.

"Marina, be careful!" Davina called.

Alfonso turned. He was embarrassed, annoyed. "She's making a fool of herself," he complained, crossing to Davina's pavement and looking about him to see who was watching.

Davina couldn't see why he was so angry. "She meant no harm."

Alfonso stopped what he was about to say. Then his attitude changed from one extreme to the other. "*Vaya*, I didn't realize how pretty our Marina has become." He stood back and surveyed the girl with mock seriousness, "Raven's wing black hair and eyes as green as rare emeralds. *Vaya, vaya, vaya.*"

Marina gazed up at him with undisguised affection.

"But, *cariño*, what are you doing here?"

"We've been to fetch my dress for the *feria*. Look, it's soooo beautiful." Marina struggled to open the lid of the box an inch or two.

"Not now, *cariño*. I'm busy."

"Later on then, I'll put it on for you before dinner."

"Well . . ."

"After dinner, before I go to bed. Please!"

"Not tonight, darling."

"But Papá I look beautiful, like a film star. You have to see me. Please!"

"I'll try. I have to sort out some business. I'll try to get home before you go to bed – if I can. Now go straight home with Mamá.”

Davina had stayed where she was, watching the scene. She saw her daughter's excitement evaporate as she turned away from the man she thought of as 'Papá'.

Alfonso looked across and met Davina's eye. He seemed to see her, too, as if for the first time after a long absence. He smiled. “You've lost your roundness and acquired a certain style, my dear.”

Davina blushed despite herself and pushed her gold-blonde hair, so despised by his mother, off her face as it moved in the breeze. “Come home with us, Alfonso,” she said. “See Marina parade in her dress.”

Alfonso nodded, “As soon as I can, I promise. Then I shall take my new wife out for dinner. Just the two of us. You won't mind will you, *cariño*?” he added, touching Marina under the chin.

Marina beamed, “No.”

Alfonso tipped his hat and left them. But he had not taken two paces across the street, when a swarthy workman ambling home came alongside him. He acknowledged Alfonso with a gesture of the hand; “*Buenas tardes, señor*,” he said. Then he looked across the street at Davina and Marina. He raised a bushy eyebrow and gave a slow knowing nod. “*Hasta luego, señor*,” he said knowingly, then sauntered off down the hill toward the area where the poorer labourers and gipsies lived.

Davina saw immediately that this workman had literally stopped Alfonso in his tracks. He was clearly at a loss, wondering what to do. She waited for him to say something.

When he spoke he was brusque, not angry, but clearly giving an order. He waved a hand urgently, “Get Marina home. You shouldn't be out and about on your own around here. It's not safe in this area.”

“Oh,” said Davina, looking around her. “I didn't think

about that. Can you take us?"

"No, not now, I'm sorry – I – I have things to do." He leaned forward as if to kiss Marina on the cheek, but didn't, instead he pushed in her the small of the back. "Off you go home now. Quick as you can. And not a word to your grandmother. She worries."

They went their separate ways. *She worries,* thought Davina. *About what?* Doña Mercedes knew where they were. All this so-called trouble with the new unions: Alfonso was exaggerating. Who on earth would be interested in them?"

"Where's Papá going?" asked Marina.

"To see a man about a dog." It was what her father had always said when she asked him where he was going. In her mind's eye, Davina caught a glimpse of her father winking at her and disappearing out of the back door of the Bristol house. She sighed: she never stopped missing him. Then she turned to look at her daughter, who was as stubborn as her grandfather and as dark as a black Dymond. "Come along," she said, "Papá is right, we shouldn't be dawdling in this area."

"Why?"

"Because there are people in the street who do not like . . ."

She was going to say 'us' and what she meant was 'them' – the García del Moral clan. Alfonso's increasing involvement in right-wing politics was viewed very negatively by his workforce – and his new *paterfamilias* persona convinced very few; even the family cook had developed a scornful attitude. Davina quickened her pace, but Marina dragged behind.

"Come on now. Do as you're asked, please."

Marina hung back then ran to catch up. Struggling with her dress box, she said, "He doesn't like dogs."

"What?"

"You said he's gone to see a man about a dog. But he hasn't."

"How do you know that?"

"Because he doesn't like dogs."

"He might do. He didn't like those stupid Pekinese your grandmother used to have. But they were disgusting creatures."

"Well, I've told him I don't want one of those. Every birthday and Christmas, I tell him I want a puppy, and he always says they smell and make a mess. He doesn't like dogs."

Davina didn't reply. Marina was just a growing child looking for an argument. But as they walked briskly back towards the town centre she thought, *who knows what he likes? He never really talks to us. He makes comments about this and that, shouts at his sisters, fawns over his mother and reads the newspaper. That's all we know about him. We've spent more time together during the last winter than ever before and all he ever talks about is his blasted fascist Falange party. He's certainly never said a word about Marina nagging him for a puppy.*

Nearing the centre of town, Marina said, "Let's look in the shoe shops for a pair to match the dress while we've got it with us."

As Davina was taken from shop to shop, the incident in the Cádiz road area slipped from her mind. It wasn't until they had reached the uninviting portals of her mother-in-law's mansion and she was crossing the patio that a thought struck her, *if it isn't safe for us to be in that area of town, what is Alfonso doing there?*

The following afternoon at around six o'clock, Davina said to the women gathered in Doña Mercedes sitting room, "I'm just going to pay the dress-maker. I shan't be long." And she was off down the stairs and through the patio before Marina had a chance to say she was coming, too.

She saw Alfonso before reaching the area where the dress-maker lived. He was some distance in front of her, which was better, as long as he didn't take one of the narrow side-streets. She just managed to keep him in view. Where the taller Jerez town-houses stopped, he crossed an unmade road and headed down the hill in the direction of the coast. Some way down, he stopped under a wide chestnut tree, and Davina watched in amazement as he loosened his tie then took off his jacket. It was a warm afternoon but that was no excuse for a gentleman to remove his jacket outdoors. Alfonso swung the jacket over his shoulder and carried on at a jaunty pace, like a man without a care in the world.

I've been here before, thought Davina. *We came up here in the car from El Puerto. This is where we saw the mule and the herd of goats on my first day.* She followed as best she could, her heart pounding in her chest. If he saw her, she would say she was looking for the dress-maker's house and she'd somehow got lost. The excuse was ready, but in her heart of hearts she knew he wasn't going to see her. His mind was fixed on wherever he was going. The man in front of her was a very different man to the Alfonso she knew.

Davina paused at the chestnut tree to get her breath back. She wouldn't go any further; she suddenly didn't want to know any more. Alfonso was entitled to his own life. She swept her hair off her face and swallowed hard. Just a second to calm herself and she'd go home. But even so, she couldn't help gazing at the man going down the hill.

At a bend in the rough road ahead, there was a single-storey, white-washed dwelling surrounded by a rickety, painted fence. Chickens scratched in its yard. From where she stood, she could see a kid goat playing with a brindled puppy outside the gate. Alfonso stooped to scratch the puppy's neck and shooed the kid back into the yard, then he went up the short path to the low doorway and opened the front door without knocking. The brindled puppy scampered up behind him and began to whine as the door was closed on it. Then the door was pushed ajar and the puppy disappeared inside.

Davina stood frozen to the spot beneath the tree, her heart racing. She couldn't move. There was the sound of bells in the distance: a mule team was labouring up the hill. She mustn't be seen skulking under a tree in this neighbourhood. She tried to gather her wits, but then the door of the little house opened again. She grabbed the bark of the tree for support. He would see her for sure.

But it wasn't Alfonso. A short, square-set woman with a tiny baby in her arms came out and paced around the small yard. The baby was screaming the way only very young babies scream and the woman was rocking it. She hoisted the tiny creature onto her shoulder, patted its back and started to sing. Then a small, pretty woman with tumbled black hair came to the doorway. Laughing, she called, "Mami, come in. Let him hold her. See if Fonsie can stop her squealing!"

Fonsie! The crying baby was Alfonso's daughter! Alfonso's daughter . . . Davina felt herself go hot and cold. She was jealous! The thought crowded her mind: jealous. He had another woman, had always had another woman. And he was happy with her. And he held their baby. He had never once picked up Marina, held her in his arms.

But then, Marina was not his daughter.

Chapter 26
Bombay, 1932

It was the morning of Diwali and the excitement in the street was palpable. Everyone was hanging brightly coloured bunting, and setting out their earthenware candle bowls. Mothers hung brightly coloured shawls and festoons from balconies and doorways, while small children raced between their legs or skipped about in the street, narrowly escaping carts and tonga wheels to pick up titbits of fallen decorations, squabbling and shrieking with excitement over nothing at all. Millicent Cleaver rarely ventured out during the week leading up to Diwali; gangs of youths chasing each other with coloured flour bombs terrified her. But something on this day sent her into the street to buy odds and ends. Later, when asked, she couldn't explain it to anyone – but she had simply had to get out and get to the streets near the Cartmel's haberdashery.

A crowd had gathered around a shoe store in an adjoining lane. Millie thought it was a British shop, but she couldn't quite remember. Something had been painted on the window; everyone was commenting on it, but she couldn't see what it was. Then a man – a boy really – appeared to come out of the shop with a tar-topped torch. He started to run, and the crowd turned as one to follow him. Then more men appeared from another lane to her left, with more lit torches.

J. G. Harlond

Millie clutched her bag to her chest. It was the middle of the day; there was no need for torches, even on the eve of Diwali. She was being pushed along, hustled and harried by the crowd; everyone was following the torch-bearers. Suddenly the mass came to a halt: a policeman had stepped into their path and tried to challenge the torch-bearers. He was knocked to the ground. A cheer went up and the crowd surged on.

Pulled and pushed down the street in a heaving mass of angry, exhilarated people, Millie began to weep with fear.

Panic stricken, desperate to get out, get away, she gradually manoeuvred her brittle body through to the edge of the crowd, and at the junction of an alley dashed into a doorway for shelter. It was the alley leading to the Cartmels' shop. If she was careful, she might be able to get there and claim sanctuary.

Before her, the crowd swelled in numbers. More and more people were joining, and all of them angry and excited, but she couldn't see why. There was a smashing of glass somewhere ahead. Grown men whooped like schoolboys. Flames leaped from a tinder dry wooden shop front further down the street. Millie hugged herself, wanting to move but scared to venture out of her niche until the turmoil had died down or they had moved on. Cowering back against the closed doorway, she waited, heart racing, eyes streaming.

The crowd surged forward again. Another, louder, cheer resonated through the stifling confines of the shopping lane, then the monster turned and the torch-bearers headed back towards her. Millie screamed. They turned into the Cartmels' alley. They were going to torch the Cartmels' shop. "No!" she cried, pointlessly.

The alley was too narrow for so many people, but the spectacle of another English establishment going up in flames was too good to miss. The crowd heaved itself into the mouth of the alley, blocking any exit – blocking any attempt at rescue.

Then Millie caught a glimpse of what looked like Kitty Cartmel in western skirt and blouse rushing towards the alley with a toddler in her arms. Her daughter, Ellie – Leo's daughter. Millie scrambled forward, "I think it's your shop!" she shouted, trying to make herself heard.

Kitty stared at her, white-faced, "My parents . . . I have to get them out!"

"No, stay here, don't go. You can't do anything. You'll be killed."

Kitty moved towards danger nevertheless. Millie grabbed her arm. "Stop!" As she spoke she pulled the child from Kitty's arms, "Let me have Ellie. Leave her here with me, don't take her! Don't go! They'll kill you – they've gone mad."

Her words were wasted. Kitty was elbowing her way through the crowd, screaming, "Let me through!"

Little Ellie cried out, "Mama!" and struggled to be free as her mother was swallowed up out of sight.

Millie Cleaver held the child to herself with a strength she didn't know she possessed, and stayed where she was. "Shush, there's a good girl. Mummy will be back in a minute. There's a good girl. You stay here with Aunty Millie. Mummy will be back soon."

Chapter 27
Amsterdam, 1932

The metallic heels of the red shoes tapped sharply over the uneven Amsterdam cobbles. The woman walked purposefully, avoiding the deeper puddles but never deviating from her way. Leo, walking behind, was delighted by the red shoes. They were so smart and bright in the drab afternoon. The shoes clicked down the street and he followed. They were going his way. Tall buildings held the two forms in a labyrinth of early afternoon lights and admitted a third. Another man. A man in a grey gabardine, collar turned up, hands deep in pockets. By turning round, as if naturally curious to see who else was out on such a filthy afternoon, Leo registered his presence as they passed a modern shop window. The man's hands were thrust too deep in his gabardine pockets – it wasn't that cold. Wet and nasty, but not November winter cold.

Leo stiffened. The hair on the back of his neck prickled. He moved his left arm across his body, checking the small bag tucked safely into his inner jacket pocket. There was nothing else of value on him. This chap wasn't a petty thief, anyway. Perhaps he was over-reacting. His visit to Levi had rattled him. He had gone expecting to conclude a deal for the cutting and polishing of stones, which would then be traded by the Jew in Antwerp. The elderly Jew had turned him down. Precious stones were losing their value by the hour, he'd said. Sensible people were hiding their wealth in Swiss bank vaults these days, not parading it in public.

"If you are so interested in the diamond trade, join the legitimate dealers in the *Diamantclub*," the old man said. Leo had been trying to join the international *diamantaires* on the Pelikanstraat in Antwerp for years, but he'd never been accepted. He lacked the 'necessary credentials'.

Leo was annoyed, more so because he knew the old man was right. It was time to shift his focus. But to what? The industrial diamond business with Moscow and Leningrad had been lucrative but it had always lacked élan. During his stay in Kazan he'd managed to create a new network of contacts rather like the jeweller in Moscow. Buying things they couldn't sell at knock down prices, then passing them off in London had been amusing, but it had channelled his energy away from what Sir Gerald was expecting from him. It had kept him out of Viktor Grekov's clutches, though, *and* he still had the wonderful pink diamond ring and the ruby necklace. The rubies, a pretty gift for his daughter's coming of age or for Kitty, for their wedding anniversary. The ring he'd sell – one day. Young Mr Craven would take it, get a good price . . .

Leo took a deep breath, he still felt very badly about not going back for the daughter called Sarah. But it was a risk he couldn't afford to take. Viktor had come close to unmasking him that time. Unmasking him for what, though, a jewel thief, an intelligence gatherer . . . ? Who, or what, was the real Leo Kazan these days? His existence as a person, his identity, or the lack of it, had been brought into question the night his daughter was born. That had changed everything. Holding Ellie for the first time . . . it had changed him. Knowing there was an adorable little girl waiting at home for him . . .

Which was why he was now in Amsterdam looking for a private arrangement that might lead him into something more exciting and lucrative than pretending he knew far more than he did in tedious private language tutorials, or peddling stones for industrial instruments. Not that he intended doing much business in the Netherlands: the guilder was in free-fall, same as the German mark.

Leo stopped in his tracks, aware he'd let himself become distracted: a sure sign of tiredness. He set off again, quickening his pace. Once back in his rented room, he'd get packed and get out: back to Dover, pass through debriefing in Canterbury then a passage home to Bombay. It was time for a complete break; his nerves were on edge. He turned round, making no attempt to disguise the action. The man in the grey gabardine was still behind him. Why?

The woman in the red shoes turned left to cross a narrow pedestrian bridge. The same bridge he needed to cross. The gabardine man stopped to read a menu on a restaurant wall. Leo decided to follow the red shoes.

A schoolgirl in convent brown was crossing the bridge in the opposite direction. She had a satchel on her back. It would be easy to stop her, ask her for directions, grab the satchel straps and use her as a shield – if necessary. But Leo stepped to one side to let her pass, unhindered.

The red shoes tapped over the wooden planks, then turned left again. Leo followed, as did the man behind him. They were now walking down an otherwise empty street. Half way down, they all turned up a side street, walked another block and came out alongside another canal. They crossed another, wider bridge, each now looking over the low wall at the green-black length of silent inland water then back in the direction they were going. They turned left again and started down the other side of the canal. The buildings were taller, more elaborate and elegant here. Wide stone steps led up to the heavy doors of respectable burgers' houses. Some houses were divided into apartments. Apartments with long rooms and high windows, where lonely people or nosy people with binoculars peered out, hoping for a glimpse of someone else's life. A delivery boy on a heavy bicycle overtook them, whistling cheerily in defiance of the weather.

Just before the steps to number 105, the woman in the red shoes stepped into the shelter of a book-seller's doorway and rested her body on the narrow window sill, extending her legs before her. Opening the cheap bag she carried over her left shoulder, she extracted a pack of cigarettes. Leo watched her until he had to pass and then ostentatiously averted his eyes. She was just a tart after all.

As he ascended the five steps to the front door of 105, he saw the man draw level with the woman, then watched him light her cigarette. As he opened the door above, the man stepped into the middle of the empty street and bent down to tie a shoelace. The hem of his long mackintosh fell into a dirty puddle. Because of the weight in a pocket.

Leo moved fast to close the door behind him, but it was too late; a smart red shoe prevented it.

"Can I help you?" he said in English. "Oh, so sorry, do you live in this building, too? How charming."

The woman smiled what should have been a winning smile. She had pink skin and under the thick mascara her eyelashes were white. The white-blonde hair was natural. She reminded Leo of undercooked French lamb.

The woman said, "Charming, as you say." She brushed herself up against the door jamb.

Another of Viktor's nasty Soviet sex-kittens? Leo wanted to laugh but an appalling memory flooded into his mind and he froze.

"Do you think I could come up for a moment?" the woman continued. "For to get warm. It is a horrible afternoon. And you are all on your own, are you not?" She ran her tongue over her upper lip.

Leo watched her with stony eyes. "I'm sorry, that won't be

convenient." Because, even if he were tempted, which he most definitely wasn't, not with this scraggy cat, he never under any circumstances played at home.

The woman shrugged her shoulders then pushed her way into the gloomy hallway.

Leo selected the key for his rented apartment and ignored her. As he did so, two very strong arms locked around him and the keys dropped to the floor with a clang. The woman searched his pockets and removed his small pistol.

She signalled the stairs with the gun, "Go up. Or do you want to call for help?" She stuck the gun dramatically into his neck, "You can try, if you want. But we have three guns, you have no gun."

Leo led them up the flight of steps to his landing and stood by his door. The woman extracted a key from her shoulder bag, opened the door and stood back for the men to enter.

The man in the gabardine raincoat pushed Leo through the doorway.

Fool, fool, fool! Leo was furious with himself. It had been so obvious from the start.

The woman with a copy of his key and a foreign accent switched on the electric light and pushed the door closed with the slightly muddy toe of her court shoes. Then, standing square and intimidating in front of Leo, she said, "Now, listen, we do not want to hurt you. That is not our intention. We need only your co-operation. You must give us all your documents, papers, letters, that sort of thing. And then you must come with us. We do not want to hurt you, but we can and we will if necessary. Do you understand?"

He had two other guns in the apartment. Leo's mind raced through possibilities of how he could get them. Then his eyes focused on the state of his lodgings. The sofa had been gutted. Through the open bedroom door he could see his clothes strewn everywhere, the mattress skewed across the bed.

The Empress Emerald

The man in the raincoat said, "Bit of a mess, isn't it?" and looked questioningly at the blonde. She met his eyes then turned away without blinking. Then the man looked at his watch and said, "Hey, we've got time for a cuppa." He was English. His accent was London English. He pushed Leo into the kitchenette.

The apartment had been ransacked. *They haven't found what they were looking for and expect me to help them find it,* thought Leo. *What are they after? What documents?* Did they think he was a complete idiot who left interesting items lying around for any little streetwalker to lay her hands on?

They might, of course, have followed him all the way from Leningrad or Kazan. Or maybe they'd picked up his trail while he was with the Labans in Vienna, or the Rosenthals in Hamburg. If they had anything to do with the German fiscal police they might, justifiably, be suspicious.

What did they think he'd got? Photographs of people talking to people they shouldn't even know? Precision machine tools the West hadn't yet invented? Soviet code books? Pilfered documents? The names of men in India and Britain organizing funds for starving Soviet peasants? Family jewels to be sold to raise cash for destitute White Russians or beleaguered Jews? What were they after? And for whom?

Leo said, "There's no money here."

"Wrong," said the woman. "There is a Thomas Cook traveller's cheque worth twenty pounds sterling." She extracted the paper from her shoulder bag and held it out to him. Take it."

Leo took it then looked at it as if he had never seen a traveller's cheque in his life. He nearly laughed; what the hell was going on?

"Right, then," said the Londoner, shrugging off his wet raincoat. "Let's make ourselves at home for ten minutes. I'm

John, she's Mary and there's the kettle. No funny business lighting the gas, sir, if you please. You've got no reason to hurt us."

Leo filled the kettle, lit the gas and spooned loose tea from an upturned caddy into the teapot. They had emptied the tea caddy but not the sugar bowl. The salt jar was also intact. So they weren't after the Rosenthal stones. Or they were and they wanted to make him jumpy. Or they wanted to see what else he might have smuggled out of Germany. Or they were amateurs acting on their own.

The woman called Mary, but more probably Marie or Marietta, had now disappeared into the bedroom. It sounded as if she were banging empty drawers. In the kitchen the man stood legs apart, arms folded across his chest, with his back to the door. The 'sir' clicked into place. Well, well, well, a London bobby. Leo went through the motions of making the tea, his mind racing backward and forward over the past few days, then weeks and months. What had he acquired that these two might want?

The woman came into the kitchen and placed a bundle of dog-eared, well-travelled letters on the green gingham table-cloth.

Letters. *Never put anything in writing; never keep anything personal with you – no mementos, souvenirs, personal effects . . .* Rules were made for reasons. *Fool, fool, fool!*

"Well?" she said.

Leo cocked his head on one side and gave her a half grin, wondering how best to deal with this new friend or foe. London Johnny could have sold his limited skills to any number of firms, and she was clearly his boss. But whose outfit?

"Now, this isn't very clever, Mr Kazan, I'm sure you were advised against it. Keeping letters – tut, tut, tut . . ." John said, turning the bundle of envelopes over with a podgy hand.

"They're love letters," said Mary. She didn't sneer; she didn't need to. Her statement was sufficient. She was almost certainly Russian. A modern Russian. Product of a Leninist high school and a Stalinist finishing school on some snowy Ural alp.

"Oh, dear," said John. "I hope this doesn't complicate things." His patronising, nasal voice made Leo want to smack him very hard across the mouth.

"They are from his wife."

"Blimey."

Leo said nothing. He stood watching the kettle, waiting for it to boil, every sense trained on the woman's movements. She had gone back to the bedroom.

John opened and closed the drawers of the kitchen dresser. He ran a hand behind the water heater. Plaster flaked off the wall and clung to his cuffs. He tried to brush it off but it clung to his fingers. It was a good moment. Leo calculated the moves to get out of the kitchenette then out of the building. He didn't move. Even if he set fire to the tea towel hanging by the sink, he was still in a very weak position regarding the speed of bullets. As if picking up his thoughts, John picked up the tea towel and made a fuss of wiping his sleeve with it. Mary came back into the kitchen area and tapped her watch.

John said, "Kettle's just boiled."

"No time."

"Ah, well, time and tide wait for no man, or so they say." John buttoned up his mackintosh and slapped his hands over the bulging pockets. "Time to go. The lady's right, we'll miss the tide."

"Tide?" asked Leo.

"The tide, Mr Kazan. We are off to the seaside. And just in case you don't fancy our little excursion, remember that apart from this little chap," he waggled a pistol in his right hand,

"I've also got these." He flipped a pair of handcuffs from his left-hand pocket, grinning. "Shall we tell him where he's going?"

"No!" Mary replied sharply. "You talk too much. Shut your mouth." She stuffed the letters in her shoulder bag.

"I need to use the lavatory," Leo said.

"Yeah, yeah," John replied.

"Go," said Mary.

Leo went to the bathroom and stood looking into the toilet. *Amateurs*, he decided. *But no less dangerous for that.* He closed the wooden seat, stood on it, then pushed up a cuff and inserted a hand into the cistern above. They had got guns, he hadn't. He located a flat, square-shaped package covered in oil-cloth. They said they wanted him 'to help them' then didn't ask one damn question. He wiped the waterproof cloth with his fingers and checked its sealing. Not that the packet needed to be dry; pearls were created in water and diamonds didn't melt anything – except a silly girl's heart. His wife had no time for them. She liked red, red rubies, clever girl. He stepped down, wiped the seat with a sleeve and pulled the flush. Then he popped the damp package down the front of his underpants and jiggled until it was in a tolerable position.

Now what? If these two goons hadn't raided his rooms, they knew who had. So run or play along? Was there an option? Yes. Find out what the options were first.

Leo returned to the demolished kitchen and sat down at the table. "Look," he said, making eye contact first with Marie-Marietta, then London Johnny, "this is all rather confusing, not to say unpleasant. You have turned my temporary home upside-down. The place is a complete shambles. Tell me what you are looking for and I can tell you where it is. Then you can leave, and I can try and tidy up before my landlady arrives and faints on the doorstep. My wife is always accusing me of untidiness, but this really isn't fair."

There was an exchange of glances. John said, "Tell him."

The woman looked straight at Leo then focused on a point behind him. "At two o'clock the day before yesterday, there was an explosion in or outside your father-in-law's shop. It happened during a street demonstration. Your wife and her parents were killed."

Leo looked at the two people and then said slowly and clearly, "That is not true."

"I regret it is."

"And my daughter?"

"I didn't know you had a daughter," said Mary, too fast.

"No, you know absolutely nothing about me. You have just been given orders and you are making a total fuck-up of carrying them out. My wife and family live in the centre of Bombay. How do you know what happened there *at two o'clock the day before yesterday*?"

"The building was destroyed. Completely. There was rioting in the street. Many people have been killed and injured."

There was silence. Eventually Leo said, "What do you want?"

"You, and any documents of any description in your possession," Mary tapped her shoulder bag. "If you have anything else, please tell us. It will be worse for you if you do not."

"This is nonsense!" cried Leo. "Absurd. How the hell do you get information from Bombay that fast? Who the hell are you?"

"If you have a warmer coat than that mackintosh, sir, you'd best put it on," John said, quietly. "It'll be arctic out on the water."

Leo could not move. John took his arm and gently pulled him to his feet then directed him into the bedroom. Leo silently moved over to the wardrobe. The key was in the door but the door was hanging like a broken limb from one hinge. His heavy winter coat was on the floor. They hadn't slit open the lining. He picked it up and put it on, remembering the short domestic story that came with it. The last time he had seen Ellie, she had been sitting in her high-chair, waving a spoon in the air. He had kissed her fluffy head and she had smeared egg yolk over his shirt and the lapel of his jacket. He'd rushed into their bedroom to change. Kitty had laughed at him. He'd been cross and left in a hurry, forgetting this thick winter coat. Then he'd turned around at the bottom of the stairs, dashed back up, grabbed the coat and left again – without saying a proper goodbye.

But it wasn't true. Couldn't be true. When he got back to Bombay . . .

"Can I take that suitcase?" Leo pointed to the top of the wardrobe. "I really don't understand why you have wrecked this room and left a suitcase like that untouched?" he added with scorn.

Mary looked at her partner. John shrugged and said, "Just some old pictures on blocks of wood. Let him have them; they're no use to us. Here," he pulled a chair round to the wardrobe to stand on.

"I can reach," said Leo, who towered over the inner-city-bred English Johnny.

"Open it," demanded Mary.

Leo placed the leather case on the bed and opened it. There was a cotton draw-string bag inside containing exactly what John had described: pictures of the Madonna and child painted onto thin blocks of wood. Some were chipped and very old. Leo had rescued them from various churches during his recent travels in Russia. The churches had been converted into warehouses or children's nurseries. In one, he had found some women burning icons and bibles for warmth. Leo ran a hand over the bag.

"Here," said Mary. She scooped underwear from the floor, picked up a shirt from the disrupted drawers. Leo packed them around the bag. John threw in a jersey and some socks.

"That's enough," Mary said.

Leo snapped the locks of the suitcase and was escorted by his unpredictable kidnappers down the stairs, Mary in the lead and John, with a gun in his right hand, keeping as close as possible behind him. Once out on the street again, they walked back past the bookshop and turned onto the Princengracht. They had a car parked alongside the canal. John motioned to Leo to get into the front passenger seat. Mary sat in the back, immediately behind him. She tapped his shoulder with his pistol but said nothing.

As John reversed from the parking space, another car pulled out further down the row. Leo peered round, trying to identify a face, but could see nothing clearly. The vehicle followed them onto the new road between Amsterdam and Den Haag. John appeared not to notice it. Leo could not decide if this was because he knew who was in it or because he really was a complete amateur. The car followed them through the evening rain, all the way to the North Sea harbour of Scheveningen. Were Viktor's hounds dogging his tracks here as well? Leo lay back against his seat: he had been very slack, very stupid, and he was paying for it.

The quayside was strangely deserted, unless they had missed the tide – or they were too early? There was a man sitting on a bollard, he signalled to them as they drove up. John parked where the man pointed and they all got out. Leo was marched at gunpoint to an evil-smelling fishing trawler. He looked around for their followers – his followers – but apart from a handful of genuine-looking fishermen and a couple of scrawny dogs scavenging among abandoned fish crates, there was no one.

So they were shipping him off somewhere: north or south?

Or were they going to ferry him west, across the North Sea? If they intended to kill him, they were going a long way about it, unless they planned to dump him at sea, which on a foul night was a fairly safe way of disposing of any trouble-maker.

A fisherman climbed aboard the trawler and alerted the skipper. A huge Dutchman in sea boots and jersey appeared on deck and said, "Come, come, I am expecting you." He stepped forward and held out a hand to Mary. She ignored it and hoisted her skirt up to climb over the gunwale. John poked Leo in the back and said, "Now you, sir." Then he followed them aboard. The skipper directed them to a poky cabin and went about his business.

John pushed Leo down the ladder. The awkward suitcase banged against each step and bruised his legs. The woman squeezed into the cabin after them. There was an element of humour about the whole manoeuvre: Leo wanted to laugh at the silliness – because he was frightened.

John put his hand on Leo's shoulder and said, "Skipper will drop you off, when he sees fit."

"Where?"

John gave his habitual shrug and went up on deck to light a cigarette. Under other circumstances Leo could easily have grabbed the woman and used her to get away. But he didn't, because his brain was not functioning at its usual speed. He looked at her and said, "Is it true?"

She lowered her eyes, "Yes. I am sorry for your loss."

Leo said, "Whose side are you on?"

"I think you must ask yourself the same thing." She closed the low door and Leo heard a key turn in the lock.

Keeping his head down to avoid cracking it open, Leo looked around him: an oil lamp hanging above, a thermos flask on a tiny table, and a snug-looking bunk. He took off his overcoat and sat down on the bunk. Above him, feet ran to and fro. A good few years had passed since he had last made a trip on a smelly fishing boat. Then he grinned and ran a hand over the lining of his coat: he never travelled without sharp little scissors, and a needle and thread.

He must have slept for some time, because when the door opened it took him a good second or two to register where he was. They were still rolling with the sea. Had they reached their location? They weren't about to put him ashore.

The skipper stood over him, his right hand raised directly over Leo's chest. He had something in his huge right fist.

Leo rolled over and fell to the floor but there was no space – he was lying on the Dutchman's boots. They were of a similar build, but the Dutchman had all the advantages: he was on his feet – he was obviously stronger – and he had a weapon in his right hand. Trying to escape was pointless. His only chance lay in dialogue.

"Aagh," Leo moaned in mock agony. "I forgot how narrow bunks are."

The Dutchman was off-guard – he had a knife and wasn't using it . . .

He bent and helped Leo to his feet with his left hand, saying nothing. Leo sat back on the bunk, rubbing his side. The big man looked down at him, grunted something in Dutch and dropped what was in his right hand on the bed. Then the door was shut and locked once more.

Leo put his hand on the package. Kitty's letters. He put his hand on them and knew it was true.

These letters were the sum of his marriage. He had married a kind-hearted, pretty girl, but hadn't stayed at home to love her. For all the years of their marriage, they had been together for perhaps a matter of months. His daughter had been born while he was away. And now she had died while he was away. While he was doing dirty work for the British government. Where were the British during this street demonstration? For the past twenty years, he'd been running around helping them to keep their precious Raj in one piece, and where were they when his family were threatened? His father-in-law was an ex-soldier who had fought for his country with his native shire regiment during the Great War. Why had they done nothing to save him? Or his mother-in-law: a tiny Maratha woman who had no argument with anyone, except on occasion, him? Why would Bombay 'demonstrators' want to kill her? And Kitty and little Ellie . . . why them?

Anger kept him awake for the next hour or so, until, exhausted, he rolled onto his side and hugged the letters to his chest. Kitty: gentle, good-humoured, innocent Kitty. He should have been there with them – not chasing after fat bellied Marxists – or lining his own pockets for the fun of it. The woman was right: whose side was he on?

For the rest of that long, dark night Leo wallowed in self-pity, sleeping in snatches and waking to the injustice of his existence. Just when he wanted to go home, and for the first time in his life had a proper loving home to go to – it was taken from him. Let them dump him at sea. The game was up.

Chapter 28
England, 1932

The Dutch boat landed him at Lowestoft and left on the same tide. He booked himself into a boarding house and stayed in his room until the landlady asked him if he needed a doctor. On the third day, he asked her to buy him a razor, and a pad of writing paper with two eraser-topped pencils. Then he tidied himself up, converted the traveller's cheque into cash at the nearest bank, paid the landlady and purchased a train ticket to London.

Leo went straight to Whitehall. He was tempted to go in through the main entrance and straight up the fancy staircase to the India Office departments, throw open the door to his section and demand an explanation. But histrionics would get him nowhere with civil servants.

Going up the back stairs to the third floor, he realised he had only ever used the tradesmen's entrance, which put his so-called job in perspective. He provided a service; he was a handy extra, not even a pawn in the Game of State.

The third floor corridor was alive with people: men and women trotting to and fro with sheaves of paper, a harassed tea-lady carrying a huge tray, a post-boy pushing a trolley. Two southern Indians in snow-white cotton and thick, black rubber-soled shoes were conferring in whispers outside a closed door.

Leo knocked and entered his usual office. There had been

changes. A nondescript female secretary with a smart, new typewriter now occupied the ante-room where he normally wrote up his reports in long hand.

The secretary said, "Yes, how may I help you?" in a tone suggesting she would do nothing of the sort.

Leo looked around him, took in the pile of correspondence beside her typewriter and gave her a beaming smile. "Hello, you are new here. Leo Kazan to see Sir Gerald."

She was impervious to charm. "Wait here. Sir Gerald is in Downing Street."

Leo raised his eyebrows, "Good for him! He deserves it."

She didn't catch on. "I'll tell Mr Howard. He's here." She opened the door of the main office and said, "Mr Howard, Mr Kazan is here. Do you want to see him or shall I tell him to come back later?"

Leo, riled by her tone, entered the office before Mr Howard, whoever he was, had a chance to speak. There were now two desks instead of one. A ferrety little man was sitting at the smaller of the two. He was wearing a brown suit. *Times are changing*, thought Leo.

"Mr Kazan, a pleasure to meet you. My name's Howard, Jim Howard." The ferrety man got to his feet behind his desk.

They shook hands over the desk and Leo, out of custom, removed his hat and coat and hung them on the stand behind the door. Howard resumed his seat and observed him with what looked to Leo like a mixture of curiosity and trepidation.

"Take a pew," he said finally, indicating an upright chair in front of his untidy desk.

Leo settled himself on the wooden chair, adjusted the crease in his trousers, touched each of his garnet cufflinks and cocked his head to one side, waiting for Howard to open the debriefing.

"Would you like a cup of tea, Mr Kazan?"

Leo declined the tea. He was curious to see how this little man, corporal made up to captain perhaps during the Great War, was going to cope with international intelligence gathering. Howard spent a few moments making a space on his cluttered desk for a new block of lined writing paper. Once he had that in place, he began to fiddle about with a fountain pen and blotter. Leo was irritated by the effective clerk charade and simply handed over the list he had compiled during his stay in Lowestoft. It contained the names of members of the Indian National Congress who were active Marxists.

The ferrety man was clearly uncertain what to do. He looked at the list, then looked at Leo and said, "Yes, yes. Perhaps you had better explain it to me. That way I can make sure Sir Gerald gets all pertinent details."

He's playing for time, thought Leo. *He's a bumped-up clerk, nothing more.* He made a mental note of the contents of Howard's desk while the man's whining voice recited the names. Sticking out from under the blotter was another list of names. Leo leaned over the desk and picked it up, giving Howard a quizzical look. Jim Howard stopped reciting and said, "Ah, yes, that came in yesterday, from Delhi, I believe."

"Why don't we check to see if they match?" Leo was becoming angry.

"Well, we've got Pran Seth and Narandra Dev Prakasa on both lists. I know Prakasa from somewhere else. Where? I think he's been in the limelight for some time. Sir Gerald says these are mostly Hindus and a few Sikhs. Yes, yes, this list came in from Delhi."

"Did it? Should you be telling me that?" Leo watched the clerk squirm. "Never mind – you don't have Daniel Gopi and Mahesh Lakh. They're on my list and not the Delhi one."

"Gopi and Lakh?"

"They are teaching. Lakh is a mathematician in Moscow – it's a good name for an Indian mathematician. Gopi is an expert on Katha Kali. He's been in Kazan."

"Sorry," said Jim Howard, "I don't claim to know any of the languages. I'm just here as a sort of general assistant to Sir Gerald during the crisis. They're very busy with this new Government of India Bill. I used to be in Transport actually. Not a lot I don't know about trams."

Leo smiled, he'd scented blood. "What would you like me to tell you about Gopi and Lakh? They are influential in academic circles; we'll need to watch their political contacts. I know Gopi has arranged a limited amount of finance for a campaign in Delhi linked to the INC. He's very popular with students – quite a character, gets invited to all sorts of events." Leo extracted another neatly folded sheet of paper from his jacket pocket and handed it to Howard. "This is a brief outline of the financial links in the chain."

"Oh, good, good. Now that will be useful."

"I should hope so, it took months to achieve. Do you want me to explain it to you – or to Sir Gerald?"

"Oh, well, yes, um . . ." Howard pressed the nib of his pen onto his pink blotting paper and stared at the shape of the blot.

Oh, Lord, thought Leo, *he's out of his depth. Whatever were they thinking of putting a tram man in the India Office?* He suddenly felt sorry for the small man who had to work for the larger than life Sir Gerald and didn't know a turban from a tea-cosy. *No games with this one*, he decided, *he'll burst into tears.*

As if rejecting Leo's sympathy, Jim Howard waved the Delhi list and said, "We do know about a lot of these people already, you see. Not that you've been wasting your time, don't get me wrong. It's that they've come into the open, so to speak. They've actually set up a separate party and . . . come into the open. While you've been in Russia – it is Russia you do, isn't it?"

Leo nodded and said nothing. Even timid animals snapped back when cornered.

"Yes, well, we now have the Congress Socialist Party, no less. On their way to taking over Gandhi's 'self-governing, independent India', they say. I wonder what the little chap thinks about that when he's at his spinning wheel – eh?"

If it was an attempt at humour, Leo was not amused.

"I'll chase up that tea, shall I?" Howard was out from behind his desk and through the door in a trice. Leaving it open behind him, he stopped in the ante-room and Leo distinctly heard him take a deep breath then say, "Joyce, get us a cuppa, will you?"

"I am Sir Gerald's secretary, Mr Howard."

Leo then heard Jim Howard open the corridor door and leave, presumably to get his own tea. He sat back and waited, wondering if the new India Bill warranted so many changes. What were they afraid of now – what was afoot? He leaned back in his chair listening to the tap-tap-tap of the typewriter and gazing at a filing cabinet.

Sir Gerald, who called his network of informers 'intelligencers', kept their files under lock and key in this filing cabinet. Leo got up, edged the internal door closed and opened a middle drawer. Quickly, he flicked through names, glancing at odd details until he came to K. His file was thicker than most. And in personal terms it was a corker. Leo smiled: he had apparently spent fifteen years in and out of Russia, first as a student then as a merchant peddling industrial diamonds, more recently as a language assistant in a university. Skimming through the file, it seemed to Leo he had actually spent his life picking up titbits here and there, keeping a check on who moved where and when, taking advantage of open windows to obtain little gems of information. It hadn't, in the long run, been all that dangerous after he'd survived the first experience in Petrograd and the dreadful incidents in Moscow and on the train. But if Viktor Grekov had ever succeeded in having his suspicions confirmed and found out who he was really working for, it would have been *very* awkward. Then his stomach did an almighty somersault. *The shop, Kitty and her family, had they been targeted because he'd refused to help or co-operate with Viktor?*

Years ago Viktor had told him he had contacts in Bombay; he had more now, thanks to Leo's own efforts to find workers for Soviet factories, not to mention the unseen but no doubt still loyal members of the alluvial diamond supply outfit.

Shoving the fear and doubt to the back of his mind, Leo hastily flicked back through sheets of paper and came to what he was looking for, the stuff about his young life. There was a report on the orphanage . . . and a press cutting about the abduction of a Russian child on a train from Goa. Leo lifted all the pre-1930 papers from the drawer, folded them neatly in half and slipped them into his inside his jacket.

When Jim Howard returned to the office with a tea tray, Leo was sitting in his chair staring out of the window at a young sparrow on the windowsill. "Poor creature," he said, nodding at the window, "seems afraid of heights, or it hasn't got the strength to get back to its nest. Put some water in a saucer for it. The mother bird will come back for it sooner or later to feed it, or the father." Jim Howard looked at him as if he was mad. "I am Indian," Leo said, "we cannot abide cruelty to innocent creatures."

"Ah, yes, I think I knew that. Religious belief, isn't it? Actually, come to think of it, there was a bird on the windowsill this morning. Must be the same one. Learning to fly, I expect. Poor little devil needed a parachute."

"Still does." Leo shook himself mentally.

"Tea? With milk or without?"

"I never touch tea in England. Can we get on with my report? I have other things to do today. We were comparing lists."

"Yes, yes, the lists." Jim Howard reluctantly set his tea aside. Leo folded his arms and waited for him to speak again.

Jim Howard finally got the hint. "I was telling you about the Congress socialists, wasn't I? Well, listen to this . . ." He extracted a typed sheet from his overflowing in-tray. "Where was it? Oh, yes, here: 'Independence must mean the establishment of an Independent State'. Nothing new there, they've been banging on about that since before you started, haven't they? But now we have a new twist for the old tale: 'wherein all power is transferred to the producing masses'. 'Producing masses'! They couldn't make a decent cup of tea between them when I was out there before the war. And then, get this! Blah blah, blah, ah – here: 'and such objective involves refusal to compromise at any stage with British Imperialism'. What do you think of that, Mr Kazan? Refusal to co-operate and we're all breaking our backs trying to make life better for them with this new Bill, which will become an Act as sure as my aunt's name is Clara Jane." Jim Howard looked at Leo for a reaction and got none.

Leo didn't move a muscle, but the final phrase in the document, spoken with ignorant sarcasm, flooded his mind: *'refusal to compromise at any stage with British Imperialism'*. It made sense. It made perfect sense. It had taken his homeland three centuries – and him personally, three decades – to realise it, but it was neither too late, nor too early to stop compromising. It was time to start making one's own decisions. Time to sort out the muddles, clarify the origins and accept the consequences. And well past the time to stop playing piggy-in-the-middle.

Leo looked at his interlocutor, produced a rue smile and nodded.

The pen pusher in the brown suit grinned back in gratitude. "You do know of Sir Gerald's plans, don't you?" Then, realising he had made a gaffe, he added hastily in a more formal tone, "Sterling work, Kazan. Links confirmed. Patience rewarded, eh? Now we can keep an eye on the blighters *in situ*."

"Not me, Mr Howard."

"No, no, not you. You have done your bit. And you're blown – as they say. You should have told us about Viktor Grekov."

"Grekov? I did. Shepherd knew all about him. What's he got to do with anything now?"

"Head of the Moscow GPU. Not sure what it stands for, but they make the old secret Cheka outfit look like boy scouts, apparently. That's what Sir Gerald says. Sorry about the travel arrangements. Sir Gerald wanted you to be seen to be removed from the scene. If you see what I mean? Exciting stuff, I must say. Mind if I smoke?"

The man kept a packet of Players in a drawer – not in a silver case in his jacket. The clerk's hands shook as he lit a match.

Leo cocked his head on one side. "Am I being dismissed?"

"Dismissed! Good heavens, no!" Sir Gerald's loud voice boomed as he strode into the room all brandy fumes and bonhomie.

Leo jumped to his feet and they shook hands like old colleagues. Jim Howard hastily stubbed his cigarette on the outside window-sill and flicked it into the courtyard below. The sparrow fell from the ledge.

Sir Gerald dropped his briefcase on his side of the room and balanced himself on the edge of Jim Howard's desk. Leo was not asked to resume his seat.

"Call it 'resting', like the actors. There'll be other work for India hands and Russian speakers like you for sure – anon. That girl Marietta, the one in Amsterdam – Bulgarian, by the way – she tells us, as do many others, that Joe Stalin has his sights on the Balkans. Makes sense – access to warm sea ports, that's what they've always been after, isn't it? And if they do get any power in India, God help us!" He shook his mane of thick brown hair like an indignant horse. "If that happens, you'll be back in demand pretty damn quick. Trouble with India is that too many fools still see Soviet Russia as their great deliverer from the North. But you've done enough in this context for now, Leo. We think it's time you lay low for a while."

Jim Howard picked up Leo's list and the financial links report and held them out to his boss. Sir Gerald glanced at the sheets of paper and said, "Excellent. Well done. All double-checked, no dropping any innocent fellow travellers in the mire, I hope."

"Time will tell," replied Leo.

"Time, time, time! It's always a ruddy race against time. Going back to what I was saying, we may need to bring you in if there are any further developments between strange bedfellows. I've just been called in to update members of the Cabinet regarding princely states in the Punjab. Most petty rajahs there want nothing to do with the Muslim League or Congress, for obvious reasons of personal finance. Socialism in any form is anathema to them, as you well know. So leave us your new address. Make sure we know where to find you – whether you're in England or elsewhere."

"I've booked a passage on the *Viceroy*," said Leo. "This Friday. I wasn't intending to stay. And I was not intending to continue."

"At your old address? No, naturally."

"I was not intending to continue with my work, Sir Gerald – for you."

Sir Gerald raised his eyebrows, put on surprised face. *He's relieved*, thought Leo. *I've saved him a bit of unpleasantness.*

"Fine, fine. Well, if you and my splendid aide-de-camp here have finished, our little lady next door has a nice, fat envelope ready for you." Sir Gerald moved to his feet, placed a hand under Leo's elbow and directed him into the secretary's office. Keeping a hand on the door handle behind him, he said, "We'll be in touch."

Leo suddenly remembered another matter. "About my wife, sir . . ."

"Yes, all very sad. Terrible business. But it was a bit naughty, getting married and not telling us first. Families do have to be vetted. We've always been tolerant with you, you know, but there are limits."

"Sir Lionel was at the wedding. I assumed it had been minuted."

"Mm, well, I'm afraid Lionel rather lost his grip. Not the only thing to have slipped by as 'not relevant'. As I was saying –"

"Marietta, your Bulgarian woman, said my wife and her family – have been killed in rioting."

"Oh, God, yes, that's right. These disturbances are getting very nasty in some areas. Her father was ex-Hampshire Regiment. We did get that bit of information. He should have put his wife's name on the shop. English names are being used for target practice these days. Fact is, we're not too popular. Anyway, all things Indian from now on: Dominion status. They say the Act will be through by November, implemented early next year. Things should quieten down then."

Leo was on the verge of physical violence. He wanted to

shout, "Tell me, you stupid bastard, tell me what you know, or shut your mouth!" He swallowed hard and stared at a crack in the wall plaster, trying to erase any emotion from his features. He was just about to speak when the secretary quietly offered him a buff envelope.

"Sign for it, please," she said, "in my accounts book."

Leo went up to her desk and signed his name against a set of digits and the date.

"Pinecoffin, too, you know," said Sir Gerald opening the outer door onto the corridor.

Leo turned, "In the rioting?"

"No, natural causes. He was getting on, and that climate was no good to him. Pity you weren't at the funeral. Your father was there to represent you, of course."

"I think you are mistaken, Sir Gerald."

"Hardly, the chap got a three-column obit in *The Telegraph* and two in *The Times*."

"No, sir, about my father. I went to a British orphanage school."

"Well, where else would they have sent you? British education, logical choice. My parents sent me back to Blighty when I was seven and I bet you can decline Latin as well as any of us. Gallic wars are the Gallic wars in any school. Well, can't stand here chatting, seeing the P.M. first thing tomorrow and got a bit of homework to do." Sir Gerald clapped Leo on the back and strode back into his office.

The secretary sat down and began to rattle away at her typewriter.

Sir Gerald did not wait at the door to watch Leo walk down the corridor the way his associate John Shepherd always did. After a few paces Leo paused, then quietly wandered back and opened the door again. "I think I left my brolly," he said.

The secretary stared straight through him.

"Could you have look?" Leo insisted, although he could hear Sir Gerald's half of the conversation perfectly well behind the closed middle door. The secretary got up and opened it.

Sir Gerald was saying, ". . . not any more he isn't. Red hot as we speak. He's reached saturation point with his Russia job and I'm not entirely convinced Grekov didn't recruit him, you know."

Leo heard Howard mutter something like, "That's treason."

"We'll see. He may go very *pro patria* in India now, though . . ."

The secretary must have warned them he'd returned for there was a sudden silence. She returned to her desk saying meaningfully, "There is nothing belonging to you here, Mr Kazan. Good day."

Leo got on the first bus that passed, but it became so crowded he jumped off on the station side of Waterloo Bridge. Taxis were pulling into the station, delivering passengers on the first stage of their journeys south-west. Sir Lionel had used this station. He used to say . . . what? Something about a cup of tea and a Bath bun at Waterloo — or was it Paddington? He'd forgotten. Dodging people who had somewhere to go, Leo crossed the road and went down the steps to the embankment. Cold and damp seeped under his skin. He knew he should keep moving, but suddenly he was drained of energy, could go no further. He sat on an elaborate wrought-iron bench and pulled the collar of his overcoat up around his ears. For a matter of moments his mind was empty: he could have been anywhere. His brain had simply closed down.

Slowly, very slowly, he came back to consciousness and began to register his surroundings. Dolphins curled up lamp-posts on dry land. Cats were eating bread tossed for pigeons. A seagull landed on the paving stones and strode towards them with felonious intent. Nothing was where it should be, as it should be. Leo looked around, trying to locate something that made sense, and realised how close he was to Dickens' villainous waters. But even the river looked wrong for its element, it was solid, unmoving.

He turned his attention to the grey sky lurking above the city on the other side of the river. Gradually, his surroundings took shape and he remembered he had been here before. Perhaps not the same bench, but very close. The girl at the Armistice party – fifteen, sixteen years ago. That nasty incident in the tea shop. And the embarrassing moment on her doorstep. He'd tried to forget that, thought he'd succeeded. And now, when he should be mourning his wife, his daughter, his mentor – an entire existence for God's sake – he was thinking about a soft, fair-haired girl, whose only meaning to his life was that she had made him realise sex could be more than a series of gymnastic exercises.

He must have been born without a soul. Kitty had said that once, perhaps twice. But he loved, had loved, Kitty, for her gentle ways, her kindness and honesty. She had never, ever tried to be anything other than what she was. Was that because her parents thought she was so wonderful that she had never had to *try* to please? They were good, honest people. Perhaps that is why he had wanted to marry Kitty, to share in the security of their home. *In which case, Lord, tell me why I spent more time away than with them?*

Leo stood up, ready to move on, ready to erase sentiment through action. And as he did so, the certainty that he had been on this spot before overwhelmed him. The girl at the Armistice party – the one he had dropped because he'd been sent to do a man's job in a dangerous place when he was still a boy. The dalliance he had discarded because he had suddenly become important. Except – and it was now abundantly clear – he wasn't, and never had been, important. Useful – Viktor's word – useful, but having no intrinsic value. Like the industrial diamonds.

That English girl had been a sort of Kitty, fair instead of dark, but very similar, the same innocence. Perhaps she had been his first love and he'd never realised it.

Love. Why couldn't he cry for Kitty and Ellie? He got up and leaned over the railings, staring down at the sludgy Thames. A steady drizzle rolled in from the west and disturbed the water. He shuddered: no wonder Lionel Pinecoffin had stayed on in Bombay.

Retracing his steps, he set off across the bridge in the direction of the City, wondering if Lionel's sons had arranged a memorial service at Westminster or somewhere in the West Country, because they wouldn't have been able to attend his funeral. He swallowed hard. Sir Lionel Pinecoffin had been more than a father to him and he had missed his funeral as well.

'Your father was there to represent you, of course.'

"What bloody father?" Leo shouted to the wind. "Where has he been all my life?" Viktor Grekov had claimed to know all about him and Leo had deliberately ignored him. Why? "And why, Sir Establishment Gerald, are you telling me this, now?"

A woman carrying a shopping basket scuttled past him, nearly losing her groceries in the passing traffic. Leo looked about him. He must have been thinking aloud. There were strange people on the streets these days, and he was one of them – talking to himself like the madman in the café all those years ago. He inadvertently caught the eye of a bag lady crouched in the lee of the wall. The toothless crone screeched with laughter, pointing at him. A wave of nausea sent him rushing for the parapet of the bridge.

Why had Lionel never explained his birth – and why had he always put off asking? Well, it didn't matter now. Mark it as 'not relevant'. He was never going back to Bombay. End of a story never begun. He would start again from scratch.

Purposefully, Leo unfolded the sheets of paper and the press cuttings about a lost child and a priceless emerald that he'd taken from the file in Sir Gerald's office and tore them into tiny pieces, scattering them in the air like wedding confetti.

Then he reached into his jacket pocket and extracted the envelope containing his passage to India. He pulled the ticket out and held it up to the wind and rain.

The old crone was suddenly up on her doddery feet. "He's going to jump!" she screeched. "He's throwing his money away, Lord luv'im, throwing his dosh away! Catch it, catch it quick!"

The paper ticket fluttered upwards for a moment then hovered over the Thames. The old crone screeched again: it was blowing her way. She watched it drift across to her and drop down into a puddle right at her feet. Then she cursed him, "Damn you – this ain't no tenner, no fiver, nor an IOU, niver – I've had a few of them in my day. Nah, this ain't worth having." She pushed the ticket with her foot deeper into the puddle and hobbled back to her niche, out of the rain and traffic fumes.

Leo watched her and turned away. He had taken perhaps ten paces when a thought struck him. "Bugger!" he shouted in English. Then he rushed back, shouting a stream of filthy abuse in English and street Marathi.

"'Ere, you!" shouted the crone as if she understood every word. "Mind yer language."

Leo stopped in his tracks, "Sorry," he said. "No offence meant."

"And none taken, but you'd better watch yerself, sonny.

You'll get picked up by the peelers, you will."

Leo bent over and retrieved the limp, muddied ticket from the puddle. "I have to get back you, see. It's my biscuit tins. I'd forgotten all about them."

The old lady stared up at him, "You're barmy as what I am. Barmy! Potty as a public lav." She huddled into herself, muttering, "Too many strange buggers on the street these days, yer aren't safe in broad daylight no more."

Leo smiled and handed her a real fiver, then hastened on his way. His precious biscuit tins, wrapped in green and gold sari material pinched from a washing line expressly for the purpose, were buried under the floorboards of his late mother-in-law's outside kitchen. Had they survived the rioting? For sure the shop had been looted. He had to get back as soon as possible. Amongst other, lesser treasures, the round tin contained the exquisite Empress Emerald.

Chapter 29
Gibraltar, 1935

The P & O ship *Viceroy of India* passed Trafalgar as the sun appeared over the horizon and was piloted into Gibraltar's North Harbour as late-rising passengers finished breakfast. Leo Kazan was up on deck early, arms akimbo over the rails, watching for the twin Pillars of Hercules. A pretty blonde joined him and snuggled up against his left arm.

"This sort of morning in November only happens after Finisterre and before Port Said," Leo commented.

The girl murmured assent, rubbing her cheek like a cat against his grey tweed arm on the polished rail. "Lovely."

"I'm like that rock."

The girl giggled. "What, big and surrounded by water?"

"No, silly, Gibraltar is not a true island. It's linked to Spain – to Europe – by a narrow isthmus."

"Fancy," said the blonde.

Leo looked down at her peroxide parting. She wasn't a natural blonde. She wouldn't do. He shook her off, made his excuses, then strode down the deck feeling cross and embarrassed with himself.

Once the ship was safely anchored in the deep sweep of the bay, Leo took the lighter that ferried passengers to the quayside. Over the years, he had done business with various jewellers in Main Street. On Bombay-Tilbury-bound trips, he had sold them interesting items: rare black pearls, lapis lazuli, rings with unusual settings. On an outward-bound trip a few years before, one establishment had commissioned uncut rubies. Old Mr Craven's hill tribesmen had served him well then. Cheating nobody, he had made a small fortune. Americans on world trips still had plenty of money in their pockets by Gibraltar. The Wall Street crash of '29 had destroyed many companies and private investors in the USA, but there were still enough wealthy travellers to keep the luxury goods business afloat on Gibraltar.

Leo had also, over the years, developed a special relationship with the Indian merchants on the Rock. Many sold fabrics and curios that could be found in any Indian street bazaar; some used this as a cover for more lucrative business in hashish and opium. But regardless of trade, they all retained a strong interest in their homeland and, in particular, the progress of the Home Rule movement. Most ships to and from the Indian sub-continent put in at Gibraltar and their network of contacts covered the length and breadth of the Raj. Back in 1921, a Hindu on Main Street had tipped him off about the boycott arranged for the Prince of Wales' visit to Bombay. He had taken it seriously and tried to get a message to Sir Lionel, but it had either not arrived or made no impression. To the Raj's appalled embarrassment, the Prince of Wales had been driven through deserted streets and there had not been a native flag-waver to be seen: all shops were shut and everyone stayed at home for the day.

Patwardan of the Empire Store had a brother who was arrested during the 1930 Salt Law disturbances at Dandi. It had been Patwardan who had told Leo about the proposed march on the Dharasana Salt Works. Leo had passed that on, and much, much more – while keeping his nose to the INC-Marxist trail. One way and another, as his file showed, he had spent the past sixteen years sniffing around like a trained spaniel. But not any longer. Leo was furious with himself; he had been telling tales on his homeland, trying to win favour with his teachers – but it was all over now. It was time he got involved. Time he did something useful, as Viktor Grekov might say. High time he established his independence – and did what he could to obtain independence for his country.

He watched a seabird swoop for a fish. Its wings barely touched the water and it was away with its morning catch. No, thought Leo to himself, his retriever days were over and done with forever. Better to be like that bird, dive and catch for sport or sustenance, the prize was your own. Except that today's transaction wasn't for himself, either, it was for the Rosenthal widow. The pearls secreted in his Amsterdam cistern would be his final European obligation. Once these were safely delivered to the Laban brothers, he could sail out of the Mediterranean a free man.

Sitting in the bows of the *Viceroy* lighter, Leo turned the well-travelled waterproof package over in his jacket pocket. But if he sold this on, for his own benefit, not the widow's, and added to the sum using funds tucked away in his various bank accounts, he could probably buy a decent-sized mansion on Malabar Hill and retire to dabble in whatever took his fancy. He looked around at the women in the boat: well-heeled, well-fed and comforted by their money, which protect them from all evil. Perhaps the widow Rosenthal had been one such as these, but now her home had been stripped, her bank accounts frozen and her dignity destroyed. He couldn't harm her further. There'd also been something about her, the way she'd carried herself, the way she'd poured tea from her one remaining silver teapot that had reminded him of . . . He couldn't name it, but her manner of dress – the high necked blouse, the long grey skirt – something had touched a chord. He would do as he had agreed; take her most treasured possessions to a shop in Gibraltar to be sold by her cousins. The money would be placed in a safe account until the time she, or any of her remaining family, could get out of Hitler's Germany.

Once they reached the quay, Leo waited for everyone to step onto dry land, then joined the queue for transport up to the commercial area. A row of dusty, black taxis and smart horse-drawn gharries were lined up, ready to take passengers on sightseeing tours of the Rock, but the drivers were more interested in two men brawling in the street than customers.

"What is going on?" he heard an elegant American woman ask.

"I have no idea, Madeleine. You're taller than me, can't you see?" her dumpy companion replied.

"Oh, yes. Oh, honestly, would you believe it? Some men are fighting."

"Latin types, hot-blooded," said the elegant woman's companion, nodding at this regrettable fact of life.

"No, they're not Latinos, at least not many, I don't think. Gibraltar is part of England, remember."

"Oh, save me! More blimey-limeys. Well they can keep their squabbles for another day – I am *not* walking up those streets." The smaller woman opened the catch of her capacious alligator handbag and extracted a metal whistle, pushed up her fluffy mauve coat sleeves and blew a long, sharp blast.

Leo looked around, it was as if a film director had said 'freeze', except now everyone's faces were turned toward a steep, narrow street from whence came a regular clip, clip, clip of hobnailed boots. As the noise increased, a British bobby, his face beetroot red under his domed helmet, rushed onto the scene and slithered to a halt.

"What's going on here then?" demanded the policeman.

No one spoke. The taxi drivers shrugged and opened their car doors; the gharry drivers were suddenly bustling fares into seats, tucking rugs over the elderly, jerking reins.

"Pure Buster Keaton," said the elegant American.

The smaller of the two said, "We going round this dingbat island or we stopping here all day? Hey, we was here first," she snarled, elbowing her way in front of a dowdy memsahib and daughter. "Blow your own whistle, lady, this horse-cab's for us!"

Leo watched the scene, laughing to himself, then realised the dowdy memsahib had taken the last gharry and only an aged donkey, head drooping to the dust, was left for hire. A shifty-looking lad with a checked cap over his eyes pointed at the poor little beast with the stub of his cigarette.

"No, thank you," said Leo. "Shanks's pony for me. It's not so far."

"Suit yerself." The youth shrugged and turned away to look for another customer.

Leo set off on foot, up the steep hill. He had barely gone fifty yards when he came alongside the American women's gharry. The small woman and the driver were in hot dispute about the price of their tour.

"Can I help at all?" Leo asked, doffing his hat.

"Only if you know the going rate for doin' this lump of rock."

"Actually, no I don't. But if you would allow me to accompany you as far as Main Street, I will more than gladly pay your total fare."

The woman's jaw dropped. "Nah, get your own."

"That won't be necessary, Mr . . . We can easily afford the fare. Beryl just likes to haggle. It's her peasant blood." The taller woman smiled a welcome. Her companion made a show of securing the vast reptilian bag on her lap.

Leo spoke to the driver and climbed into the seat facing the elegant American. Looking into her eyes, he said, "Leo Kazan. I am very pleased to meet you."

"Madeleine Marshall," replied the woman offering a gloved hand. The gloves were the exact grey of her eyes. *Attention to detail*, observed Leo to himself, *a pleasant change from shapeless Soviet girls and off-the-peg blondes.*

"I apologise for my paid companion here," said Madeleine Marshall. "Her name is Beryl; she is from Brooklyn, and her familiarity is sheer contempt. Shake the gentleman's hand, Beryl."

Beryl hissed at her and didn't move. Leo swallowed a smile and indicated the ships anchored out in the blue-water bay as they appeared in a gap between tall whitewashed walls. "You are also on the *Viceroy*?" he said.

"Yes."

"We are going all the way around the world," informed the irrepressible Beryl. "New York to Liverpool – Liverpool, what a dump. London, nice shops, I like the palace with the funny soldiers. Does the king actually live there?" Leo nodded, but had no time to get a word in. "Now it's India; the ship's okay. The soup's always cold but I told the waiter – he said he'd fix it. Then Calcutta to China. China! We bin there already, China Town, Los Angeles. There's enough Chinks there – who wants to see any more? Then Australia – kangaroo, didgeridoo, what's to do in a country of criminals and poisonous spiders? And *finally* home sweet home, Belvedere Park, Santa Monica, California, hallelujah."

"What a splendid trip," said Leo. "And today we are all in Gibraltar. Perhaps you would both care to have lunch with me at the new Rock Hotel, or dinner on board – at least once before you get back to Belvedere Park, Santa Monica, California."

Madeleine looked at him, "Not lunch," she answered, "dinner. One has more time to be leisurely over dinner."

Beryl rolled her eyes.

Sitting with his back to the driver, Leo noticed the little grey donkey that had been parked on the quay labouring up the steep bends behind them. Its owner was poking it with a short stick as he ambled along behind it. A man in an unnecessary mackintosh was perched uncomfortably astride the narrow beast, his feet nearly touching the ground. When Leo alighted the gharry at the top of Main Street, the donkey was just breasting the hill behind them.

He signalled farewell to the lovely Madeleine Marshall and winked at Beryl, slipped a very generous pound note into the gharry driver's hand and crossed the street to a shop that bore the sign 'Laban Bros. Gold and Silver bought and sold'. Then he had second thoughts. He waited for a moment until the gharry had trotted off, and walked to the end of the street to admire the portals of the Governor's residence. Within a minute or so, the little, grey donkey tottered past, empty.

Leo walked back down to the shop and spent a few moments perusing velvet lined shelves of rings, bracelets, elaborate silver pocket-watches and ladies' gold wrist-watches, but he saw no one reflected in the spotless panes of glass save himself. He tapped his pocket and sniffed *a la* Beryl. Someone with training? Or was he being overly cautious? One of Sir Gerald's lackeys? One of Viktor's? Or someone with a German National Socialist fiscal interest? Or no one at all? If the first – so what? If the second, serious deviation was called for. If the third? He consulted his own watch; there was time to spare, and better safe than sorry, as Matron used to say.

Making a fuss about tying a shoelace, he gave the donkey-rider time to get his bearings, then he led him off down the busy shopping street.

J. G. Harlond

Johnstone's Temperance Hotel: three floors, plus attic windows. Perfect. He banged his trouser pockets as if searching for a key. Then with a hop and a skip he was up the steps, past reception, and up the first flight of stairs. He turned down a green-carpeted corridor and popped into an open doorway. A bed had been stripped, the windows were wide open and the occupant was out for the morning – a long-term resident, judging from the open wardrobe door and the contents of a dish on the dressing table. Jet brooch and earrings, an enamel hatpin and – oh, pretty, a flower brooch set with amethyst petals and aquamarine leaves. He popped it into his top pocket. And what might be in the bottom of the wardrobe?

An outside shutter rattled, a breeze moved one of the windows, the door swayed on its hinges. "Damnation." Leo shot back behind the door just as the chambermaid pushed her bed-linen trolley into the room. She was singing a Spanish *copla* and took her time about unfolding a sheet. As she shook the starched linen over the bed, Leo nipped out of the bedroom. There was no one to be seen, so he strolled down the ill-lit corridor, peering at door numbers, then turned up another flight of stairs, along another dim corridor, then down the back service stairs to the ground floor, past the kitchen and into a mulligatawny dining room. A spotty young waiter asked him if he would like to reserve a table, which he did, to oblige him: table for two, by the bay window and would he be a good chap and rustle up a cup of coffee. A shilling piece sealed the deal. Then he was seated near the window of the coffee lounge, opening a day old copy of the *Daily Sketch* and watching the mackintosh man trying to persuade an officious Spanish receptionist he had not entered the hotel simply to make use of its 'sanitation facilities'.

The Empress Emerald

The mackintosh man was obliged to leave the premises. Clearly rattled, he took up a very conspicuous position across the street and opened a packet of Navy Cut. Leo drank his disgusting chicory coffee and examined him from behind the net curtains: not unlike Amsterdam John – English, small fry, pink around the gills, and the cigarettes were a clincher. Nothing to fear on Widow Rosenthal's behalf, but if Sir Gerald was still interested in his movements he was happy to provide some action. He folded the paper, replaced it on its rack and walked out onto the hotel entrance steps then, as if remembering something, he slapped his forehead dramatically with the heel of his hand. Giving the mackintosh man time to stub out his cigarette, he headed back toward the dining room, where he had indeed remembered there was a door with the word 'Gentlemen' in well-polished brass lettering.

Once the mackintosh man had followed him into the gents, and the officious receptionist had dashed in behind to prevent '*un abuso*' of the hotel's sanitation facilities by a non-resident, Leo simply squeezed past them, exited the dining area, nodded to the girl on the reception desk and sauntered back onto Main Street.

At the Laban brothers' shop, he made arrangements for the sale of the diamonds and pearls in Mrs Rosenthal's package, then spent some time discussing Hitler and the situation in Germany with the owners. He was playing for time, trying to decide whether he could part with the pink diamond and the ruby necklace.

"Our father's family left Russia because of the pogroms, Mr Kazan. You know about this, you helped our uncle in Moscow, we know about this, and what you tried to do for Sarah. We came to Gibraltar years ago, sent by our father, but he stayed in Hamburg." Jacob Laban sighed. "Where should we go next? Gibraltar isn't so safe anymore. If there's another war it will be one of the first places to be occupied. We just want a home, a peaceful home, to be a family together. We don't make trouble for no one; we just run our business, a legitimate business. An honest business."

As Aaron Laban held the door open for Leo, he said, "Home is where the heart is, but our hearts yearn for a home Mr Kazan, they yearn."

Leo nodded, "I understand that very well. But I have no answers. Sometimes it seems that whatever you do — wherever you go — it's wrong."

Aaron Laban looked up into Leo's eyes, "But you are not one of ours," he said.

"No, but I have no proper home."

The two brothers began to discuss Leo as if he was not there.

"But he's not one of us," insisted Aaron, " although his family might have been once."

"I think not, brother. His eyes are wrong. I've seen those eyes before. A long time ago, when we were very small, but I've seen them. They aren't so very slanty but they are the green eyes of the Steppes. Green seas of grass, brother. Those are the eyes of a Tartar khan."

Leo coughed. "Erm, there's something else. I nearly forgot." He stepped back into the shop. "I have these, they belong — belonged - to your uncle in Moscow, I believe." Reaching into his inside jacket pocket, Leo pulled out the valuable necklace and the even more valuable ring. "If I leave these with you, could you arrange for their sale — or get them back to Mr Goldman's daughter?"

The two brothers goggled at the necklace then at the ring. "You nearly forgot these?" Aaron asked, astounded.

"It's a pink diamond," Leo said. "Genuine."

"You want a document, a receipt? What is all this?"

"It's a long story. I can't explain. But these belong to Sarah Goldman. They are for her. Except, if she's still in Moscow . . ."

Aaron Laban raised a hand. "It shall be."

"You are a good man, sir," said his brother, "to return such gems – a very good man."

Leo shook his head, "No, that is not true. I only had to . . . it's that . . ." he sighed. "I must go."

They shook hands and Leo walked out into the street. Jacob closed the door and turned the 'open' sign to 'closed'.

That evening, back on board the *Viceroy*, Leo sat down to write a brief note on plain paper to Mrs Rosenthal. It would be posted in Marseilles.

My dear Aunt,

I was received warmly by your cousins, who send their best wishes. They are delighted you are safe and well. They strongly recommend you join them. They say the Mediterranean has a pleasant climate. I also find it warm and peaceful. Personally, I support their idea. From what I have seen of Europe these last few months, an extended Med. cruise seems just the thing. The atmosphere in London was also very chilly. I do not recommend it, even for a short break. Going north, of course, is now out of the question.

Mother's belongings are all being taken care of, nothing to worry about there. The cousins say you can write to them at the address you gave me, but they will be neither surprised, nor in the least inconvenienced should you drop in on them without warning.

I wish you all the very best, and once again encourage you to come south before the unpleasant weather you are currently experiencing worsens.

Best wishes, L

He got up and stared at the grey circle of his porthole. Then he stretched his arms above his head, flexed his shoulder muscles and loosened the tightness that had crept up around his neck. Feeling slightly more relaxed for having completed a promised task, Leo turned briskly to the narrow desk and put the letter case into a drawer. Then he put on his evening jacket, straightened his cuffs and stepped out of his cabin to dine with the lovely, if perhaps not so youthful, Madeleine Marshall. A wealthy widow or a widow and no longer so wealthy? Or gay divorcee? Whichever, she would keep his mind occupied for one evening and prevent him from being pestered by the bottled-blonde mistake of the previous evening. In fact, this Madeleine could prove the ideal solution: a congenial companion without painful or embarrassing emotional involvement. And Beryl made him laugh. Perhaps he'd give her the amethyst flower brooch. It would match her hair and coat.

As Leo sat at their table and made small talk, he mentally patted himself on the back. This way, he could be alone but not a loner for the next three weeks – as he preferred. Although, perhaps the less time he had to himself on this voyage, the better.

"Keep yourself busy boy, that's the ticket," Sir Lionel said from somewhere in his past.

Chapter 30
Bombay, 1935

As soon as they docked in Bombay, Leo booked himself into a modest hotel on Marine Drive under the guise of a commercial traveller. His new cabin trunk, crammed with clothes and items he had purchased on the assumption that he was never returning to London, was carried up to his room by a couple of voluble porters, who were very taken aback when Leo addressed them in their own tongue.

"And," he said, "I want this room watched. Watched, not investigated, understand? Because if I return one afternoon to find one item out of place, one wrinkle in a sock . . . then you can be sure, best beloved, that this yellow scarf, which is always in my pocket waiting – this pretty yellow scarf will be round both your necks and your eyeballs will be bouncing across the floor before you can say 'Kali'."

Their dark faces blanched to the colour of their cotton pyjamas. They looked at his shoes and made *namasté* ten times; they vowed on the souls of their departed mothers they would be on guard day and night, that no one would enter, not even over their dead bodies, and they backed out of his room with their foreheads touching praying fingers but their eyes firmly fixed on a sliver of yellow silk poking out of the black-haired sahib's jacket pocket.

For two days Leo wandered around the old colonial city, looking at it from a new pair of eyes; seeing it as a native, not a minion of the Raj. As he took a tour of his city, he tried out new versions of his old personae: as a well-heeled Indian jewel dealer, as the coolie that he had often played. On the first day he took a modern taxi up to Breach Candy in the morning, then a tonga to Malabar Hill in the afternoon. In the evening, he strolled along Chowpatty seafront and ate at an expensive restaurant. The next day he broke his fast at an anonymous street stall then spent the day wandering around his childhood bazaar and wherever his sandals took him. On the evening of that second day Leo came to the conclusion that he was the same – but different. And that he should leave it to time to take him in the direction he should go. He would let the great Wheel of Life turn, let destiny decide the way.

On the third day, Leo Kazan, international jewel merchant once more, left his hotel after breakfast bearing a cheap but larger than average leather briefcase: the sort used by commercial travellers, the sort large enough to hold two biscuit tins. He passed through the hotel doors, took a quick turn and disappeared up a side alley into India. Then he spent an hour in some rooms rented by a pretty girl named Mumtaz and reappeared, still carrying the large briefcase, in a scruffy grey kurta and what was now called a congress cap. Tossing a generous handful of coins at some street urchins, he headed for the Churchgate commercial district with the urchins in his wake.

The alley where his father-in-law had established his haberdashery was intact, the main street utterly alive. Tongas squeezed between barrow boys, ancients on bicycles wobbled between basket-bearing coolies, beggars crouched in doorways and dogs wound their thin frames round bony legs. A few people in western dress marched purposefully from one purchase to another, taking care to make eye-contact with no one. It was as if nothing had happened. So it wasn't true. Leo's heart lifted, he skipped a step round a bevy of nuns, forgot himself and doffed his congress cap like an English gent. The street was alive, Kitty and Ellie were alive – nothing had happened.

And then he was staring at a blackened framework where the shop should have been. He looked up at what had been the first floor, where he and Kitty had come to live while they looked for their own house in a decent suburb – until Kitty told him she was happier with her parents while he was away. How quickly he had settled into their lifestyle. It had been so pleasant to come home to a warm welcome and people round a table for meals – to be part of a real family.

All that remained was an ugly hole. Leo stepped down into the debris. The premises had been thoroughly looted, except for a box leaking black ribbon and the empty, broken cash register. His stomach took a turn and dive, thinking about what must have happened. But he took a deep breath, stepped into the small premises and walked through the remains of the partition wall into what had been his mother-in-law's domain. Then his stomach involuntarily lurched again – this time with relief. The wooden boarded floor, swept twice each day and scattered with pellets each evening to keep the cockroaches and vermin at bay, was still intact. Some of the boards had been chewed by fire, but not consumed.

He pushed at a board with a sandaled foot. It wouldn't budge. That was good. Very good. He beckoned to the urchins. "Take what you can find for your mothers and sisters," he said, throwing a handful of coins across the cinders and soot of the outer shop floor.

The boys instantly started pulling at rubble, exclaiming over charred ribbons and squabbling over metal buttons found under the cash register. Once they were sufficiently distracted, Leo crouched down and prised at the third floorboard with his manicured finger nails. Nothing, it wouldn't move. The wood had swollen with the heat of the fire. A knife – he was in the kitchen area, there had to be a knife. The urchins would be round him any moment, ruining his plan, if he didn't hurry. He pulled open the black teak food dispenser. Nothing. Looters had taken the lot. Frustration made him clumsy, he fell back on his haunches – and caught sight of a fork.

A fight broke out among the boys – excellent. He shoved the prongs down between the boards. The prongs bent backwards, the wood did not shift. Sweat dropped into the dust. *Bugger, bugger*, then the Marathi abuse and, finally, the fat end of the fork moved the swollen plank up and he was able to get the fingers of his left hand under it. Using the toes of his left foot to hold it up, his right hand squeezed into the space below and he touched his cloth-covered treasure trove.

Leo looked up and leaned back, distracted by an angry male voice. A local policeman, hands on hips, was shouting at the boys. With a lunge that tore skin from the back of his hand, Leo tugged at the dusty green material and pulled the receptacles to safety. In a flash, the briefcase was opened, closed, and the floorboard stamped into place.

He stood in what had been the partition doorway and yelled, "Little vultures! Be off with you," in chi-chi English, kicking at emaciated backsides. "Thank you, officer. Thank you, thank you," he said, wobbling his head like a simpleton with each phrase. "It is a crime that such creatures take advantage. Why are they not in school for the benefit of Mother India? Now please to be telling me, sir, how it is that this shop that buys my wares and sells so nice handkerchiefs and the suchlike is no longer? And please, what has happened to the also so nice family who live above, if indeed, not upon the very premises. Such a pretty baby they have, just like my own sister's girl child, Uma . . ."

The policeman confirmed what Sir Gerald had so happily thrown in his face. The shop had been targeted because it was owned by an Englishman. Rioters had torched it after a rally organised by textile workers. The firemen had recovered three adult bodies. The street had been chock-a-block with angry, shouting demonstrators; the army had to be called in so the firemen could reach the shop; shots were fired to calm the hysteria. Some hotheads had been injured. The family could not escape because of the crush in the street, and look – there is no back exit. So they had been asphyxiated and then burnt to death. Very sad. No one had mentioned a child.

The sign on the door of the Oriental Curiosity Shop said 'closed', which, despite the fact that it was now late evening, surprised Leo. He peered through one of the mullioned windows. The shop was in darkness but there appeared to be a light on in the back room. He gripped the greasy, badly cured leather handle of his commercial traveller's briefcase and walked round to the side alley that led to the labyrinth wherein had dwelled Old Mr Craven and a mad Pathan genie. No urchin now led him higgledy-piggledy round the houses; he knew the route by heart. He turned left at a street pump, left again under a decrepit gallery, and was at once in the alley leading to the Oriental Curiosity back entrance. A rim of light around the door suggested someone was on the premises. He tapped three times with his sore knuckles.

"Yes?" said a weary voice in English.

"It's Leo."

Bolts were dragged open, the door opened a few inches and a weaselly face peered at door handle height through the crack. It was Arnold Mackay. "What you want?" he demanded.

"Arnold, it's Leo."

"I can see that. What you want?"

"I was just passing. Thought I'd pop in. I've got something that might interest Clive."

"Not anymore, it won't." The small man gazed up at Leo in the shadows of the alleyway; the light was poor, but he must have noted the grey rings under Leo's eyes because he said, "You look different." Then he sighed, "Oh all right . . . you'd better come in." He opened the door the minimum space and hid behind it, forcing Leo to edge in sideways.

Once inside, the door was shut, locked and bolted behind him. Leo looked down at Mackay's small figure. He looked even smaller now because he was hunched under a thick woollen shawl. "Are you ill, Arnold?" he asked. The weather was cool, but by no means cold.

Arnold Mackay ignored Leo's concern. "Clive's not here."

"No, well in that case . . ."

"Come through." Picking up some matches from a work bench, Arnold lit a brass oil lamp and carried it into the main shop. He put it on the counter.

The wall-mounted figure of Ganesh the elephant god scowled down at them, the brass cobra reared out of the gloom, a glass eye of the perpetually arched mongoose winked in the meagre light. It all looked the same. But not the same. Leo shuddered. Arnold Mackay climbed onto the balding velvet chair provided for long-stay customers and folded his short arms.

Leo stepped behind the counter out of habit and put the briefcase carefully on its shiny surface. The contents rattled against each other; he smoothed his hand over the thick leather as if to calm them.

"What's in there?" The small man threw his woollen mantle back and extracted a cigarette from an engraved silver case.

"Clive might be interested. Why is the shop so dark? Don't they leave lights on in the evening anymore?"

"*They* don't, anymore. And *I* don't either. No need to court danger."

"Arnold, you are speaking in riddles."

A series of perfect smoke rings hovered in the dusty air.

"Clive's gone."

"Gone?" There was a brief silence. "You mean . . .? When? How?"

Arnold inhaled a lungful of nicotine then said slowly, "After his father passed on – nearly a hundred, the old devil – Clive just seemed to run out of steam. No one to tell him what to do. The old man was a bully, remember?"

"I remember."

"Well, Clive sort of, I don't know, lost direction. Happened this time last week. Keeled over where you're standing now."

Leo shifted in spite of himself. He pushed the cut-glass ashtray always kept on the counter closer to Arnold to cover his discomfort. "What happened, though? Was he ill?"

"Must have been – it was a heart attack. I don't think he was eating properly, and he was scared to death they'd torch this place as well. Sorry," Arnold flicked ash into the ashtray and looked at Leo. "Didn't mean to . . ."

"No, no, of course not. Difficult times."

"Difficult! Difficult!" Arnold Mackay snapped. "I'll say difficult. He left all this," he waved his cigarette at the contents of the shop, "the shop and every blasted thing in it, to me."

Disappointment punched Leo between the ribs and winded him. He swallowed hard and brought an imaginary curtain down over his features. He had always thought, assumed, the Cravens would pass the shop over to him. What did this bloody-minded, little man feel for its glorious contents? How would he ever find the curios and artefacts, the gems and golden goblets, to stock it? How would he convince dithering clients to choose the more expensive item? The stuffed animals would rot before he found them a caring home. Then he realised Arnold was angry because he didn't want the shop. "What will you do? Sell it?"

"I served Lionel well, you know. He said it was because I lacked imagination. He trusted me with everything. Said I was naturally secretive. Good qualities for my job. I never pictured myself outside the routine. Sir Lionel kept me on as his P.A. after he retired because he needed me. I was part of *his* routine. Old men like stability. But now I've lost the lot. Every blessed thing I – we – worked for. My job's gone, my employer's gone and my best – only – friend has died. And left me this flaming emporium. I'm not interested in business. And the accounts – those account books read like fiction. And, to top it all – on top of all this . . . mess, their bank balance is into the negative." He stubbed his half-smoked cigarette severely into the ashtray. "Who the hell will buy this now? I can't sell it and I can't keep it. The British in India are a doomed race. Everyone who can is getting out before Congress comes into power and nationalises everything we've created. And that means this shop, lock stock and barrel, will be taken from me, just like that." Arnold tried to snap his stubby fingers. "Even if I wanted it, I can't keep it."

"That's scare-mongering talk," retorted Leo, who was very surprised by Arnold's information and secretly thought there was another set of accounts in Old Mr Craven's rooms. Guarded by the immortal Pathan, no doubt. "The steamer was rife with it. Box-wallah shop owners, importers and exporters giving each other the willies. There is no evidence that is going to happen. Hell, I've just been in London – Dominium Status doesn't mean they can nationalise anything; it's only giving us more provincial autonomy. It doesn't give us anything like the right or power to make our own decisions."

"Us! Our!" Arnold's head shot up. "Us? Whose side you on now? Those murdering coolies have just killed your wife and her family and you say 'us'! Jesus Christ, Leo, you're a cold-blooded bastard if ever there was one."

Leo opened and closed the drawers under the counter, mumbling, "Forget it. It wasn't what I meant. I'm not thinking straight these days," anxious to avoid a scene with Arnold, not least because the small man clearly wasn't thinking straight, either. "Look, there's no reason to think British-owned properties will ever be confiscated, now or in the future."

"Well, that may be so. But financially this emporium is . . ." Arnold, still shaken by Leo's lapse, searched for a word on the walls around him, "moribund. The cash register is not going to ring out when jolly mems buy their Christmas gifts anymore; no more jolly Raj boys with hot polo winnings to spend. And if the communists in Congress and the lefties in England get their way, there'll be no more jolly rajahs, either."

Leo laughed out loud.

"You can laugh, but it's no joke. What's a man like me going to do? No job now Lionel's gone – and now this."

"Well," said Leo, feeling a little more relaxed, "I suggest we shut up shop here for the night and get ourselves an evening meal. We might see things in a more positive light in brighter surroundings. You're not the only one reassessing the future, you know."

"No, sorry – got a bit carried away. Shame about your wife and that. Nasty business. I'd like to get my hands on the organisers of these so-called rallies, inciting good people to cause havoc."

"That's one of life's little ironies," said Leo, picking up his bag so as not to jostle its contents. "I have more than likely rubbed shoulders with the very chaps who were there winding things up. Very likely I've sat in their dens, smoking their pipes, sharing their bhang, and you know, I never for once took it seriously. I just listened to the gossip the way I was told to, got the information back to those that wanted it – the way Lionel trained me, and that was that. Now it seems quite different."

Leo looked around at the contents of the shop he loved so much. Something else that had acquired true value by being taken from him. He said, "Just when I want to come back and make a proper life here, I can't. I can't even nail the bastards that caused Kitty and Ellie to die. I've been given my cards. I am no longer needed by our great and good Imperial government. What d'you say to that, Arnold?"

Arnold looked sideways at Leo, started to say something and then must have thought better of it. "What you got there?" he said nodding at the counter.

Happy to change the subject, Leo opened the catch of the smelly leather briefcase. "I'll show you. It's another little irony." He moved the lamp closer to the bag and carefully removed, one by one, three cloth-wrapped wooden blocks. He laid each one flat on the counter. Then, slowly and gently, he began to unwind white sheet material torn from a rented bed from around the ancient paintings.

Arnold did not speak until the last one was revealed. "They're Russian icons, aren't they?"

"Mmm," Leo traced his fingers around the gold leaf halo of a Virgin.

"Are they valuable?"

"That's what I wanted Clive to tell me. I don't think they'd get much at the moment. Probably only of interest to émigrés, and they don't have much money these days, from what I've seen."

"Have you only got these Madonnas?"

"No, I've got more. I found the first one in Kazan."

There was a silence. Then Arnold said, "Kazan?"

"Russian city on the Volga. Where I probably come from."

"Do you know that, for sure?"

"No I don't. But I think *you* do. It's my father's name, according to my birth certificate. I think you, and Sir Lionel and Lady Hermione, and the Cravens, father and son, and half of Bombay city know – knew – an awful lot more about my life than I do."

Arnold lit another cigarette, saying nothing.

"I did something clever and very stupid in London. I found some papers that would have explained my sad little childhood – then I tore them up and scattered them to the bloody wind."

"Best thing you could have done." Arnold's voice was matter-of-fact.

"No. It's like everything I've ever done, a mistake. A spur of the moment, stupid error. And exactly what Lionel wanted. He betrayed me from the start. And he betrayed me at the end. Always letting – making – me think I mattered. You've all known about my real family, who I am, and you've all acted against me – in your own best interests. God Almighty, why do think I've turned to Home Rule?"

"No, Leo, it's difficult, but it isn't like that." Arnold braced a hand against the counter. Then spread out his other small, square hand, as if measuring how far he should go. "Lionel knew – perhaps – but he never confided in me. And, if there had been a conspiracy, believe me, I would have known about it. I always keep – kept – an ear close to the ground. No choice when you're my height." He smiled, slipped his woollen shawl off the back of his chair, and carefully folded it into a neat square.

Leo thought the conversation was over, but then Arnold started again. "I feel better now. Funny old world. I never thought you'd be the one to help me through a bad patch. I've never trusted you further than I can spit, and I don't spit."

Leo let his shoulders relax and gave a dimpled half-grin. He started to wind the cotton sheet material back around an oriental-looking Madonna. Her angular child looked hungry. "I found this one in a church where they were burning bibles to keep warm," he said. "It had been converted into a nursery for factory workers' babies. They'd pulled down all the screens, the altars and everything. Place was like a barn. The little ones were freezing to death. I nearly stepped on this one," he said, indicating the icon. "She was next for the bonfire."

"Have you got any saints? Or is it just the mother and child figures that caught your fancy?"

"I didn't notice any saints. I don't know anything about saints." Leo looked at Arnold, "What happened to your parents?"

"Cholera. I was five or six – don't remember much. They brought me down from the Hills to see a special doctor because I was so small and got ill. They died and I lived. That's why I was sent to the BABO."

"Were you at the orphanage as well? I didn't know that." Leo wrapped the second Virgin and placed her carefully in the bag. "I remember my first day there. I remember exactly what happened the day my mother left me, and I was much younger than you were."

"She wasn't your mother."

Leo kept on winding, "I thought you said you didn't know anything."

"I don't know about your real parents. I do know about Millicent Cleaver."

Leo stopped. Millicent. *"Millicent!"* shouted an impatient voice in his head, *"Put the kettle on."* "Is she still . . .?"

"Oh, very much so. Very sprightly. I'll tell you over supper. Not something to be rushed. Finish what you are doing and let's get out of here."

Leo placed the mother and child icons carefully in his briefcase and said, "My hotel does a decent meal, we can eat there."

"Good, let's go. These things," Arnold indicated the mongoose and cobra, "give me the creeps."

As they were leaving through the back door, Leo said, "What about setting up shop elsewhere?"

"Like where?" replied Arnold, turning the key.

"It crossed my mind a couple of weeks ago that Gibraltar might be a good place for a business. Pleasant climate, British but not England. You've got the steamers dropping off rich American tourists on round-the-world trips, all anxious to buy cute little curios to show the folks back home."

"I thought there weren't any rich Americans anymore."

"Ah, there's a new brand. They start on the stage in New York and then the movie industry picks them up and makes them filthy rich just as fast as you can say *'Ziegfeld Follies'*."

Unable to sleep after what Arnold had told him - tossing, turning, wide awake - Leo felt himself being pulled down thought paths he didn't want to tread. He would not stay. Returning to Bombay had been foolish. Thinking he could find a new personality or become a new, better person was ridiculous. And he would not visit Millicent Cleaver, who had looked after him when he was a baby but was not his mother. It was too late.

J. G. Harlond

Sleep crept in. He was conscious of his limbs sinking into the mattress – sleep, finally, sleep. And then a little round face framed in a mop of black hair was looking up at him, her plump caterpillar arms reaching up: "*Daddy, Daddy . . .*"

Leo struggled out of bed, tugged back the curtains and leaned out of the open window gulping for air. A few minutes later he pulled on his worn cotton kurta and his down at heel sandals, pushed the coins on the bedside table into a pocket and stumbled out into the night. He walked, going nowhere, down to the seafront, onto the sand and along the beach.

The tide sucked at his feet. The chilly sand squeezed between his toes and told him he was awake, alive. But if he turned toward the ocean – and he did – and he walked into the water – and he did – then if he went in a little deeper, a little further, soon, soon he would be floating and safe and not awake or alive anymore. Pushing against the heavy waves, he waded in right up to his chest, then suddenly he stepped onto nothing. His head went under. He was swallowing the sea – gallons of salt water – and going down, and down and down . . . and then he wasn't. He was struggling. Kicking. Kicking up – up – up, up to the surface, beating at the waves, gasping, retching, stumbling back onto dry land.

Leo sat on the sand, his back up against the sea wall, and put his head between his knees. And he cried. He cried from the shock of going under, from fright, for his cowardice, for his mother who wasn't his mother, for a pretty woman who had been his wife, for a black-haired baby with big, green eyes. Leo cried until his body heaved and rolled sideways, until he was sprawled on the beach like flotsam thrown up by a storm.

He must have cried himself to sleep, for he awoke shivering with cold. A pi dog was sniffing around him. "Scavenger," he said, "nobody wants you either."

The skeletal mongrel came up to his hand, licked it, then hopped away on three legs; the fourth dragged a pattern in the moonlit sand.

"Oh, God!" shouted Leo. "Stop! Enough! That is enough! I give in. You don't have to make me feel bad for anyone or anything anymore! I'm sorry for all the things I should and should not have done. I am sorry! Please, no more, please."

Leo waited for an answer. He waited until his exhausted instinct for survival asserted itself once more and he knew he would have to get warm and dry or risk pneumonia. He got to his feet, pushed his hair back off his face and turned toward the steps that led up to the city. His sandals had gone. He would have to walk back to civilisation barefoot.

A sadhu holy man and an elderly beggar were perched together on the back of a park bench like two old vultures. Leo passed them and, despite his near-death experience, wished them a pleasant evening in Hindi out of respect and habit.

"Stop and speak with us," said the sadhu.

"Speak with us," echoed the beggar.

"What must I say?"

"What is in your heart, sahib," said the beggar.

"I am no sahib. Look at me." Leo almost wanted to laugh.

"I see a sahib." The beggar held out a gnarled claw, palm upwards.

"What must I say?" Leo repeated, ignoring the empty hand.

"What is in your soul," said the sadhu.

"My heart and soul are empty of words, masters."

"Then go, find new emords, and God be with you," the sadhu replied.

"And with you." Leo started across the promenade on his way back to the hotel, then stopped and looked back. "Which god, masters?" he asked.

"Shiva, Vishnu, Allah . . ." said the sadhu.

"Jesus Christ and the Buddha . . ." added the beggar.

"They are all of the One Being," affirmed the sadhu.

"God is merciful, sahib." said the beggar, holding out black talons, palm upwards.

"God is not!" retorted Leo. "Tell me, wise men, you who have nothing left to lose – how can God be merciful if he takes the lives of the innocent?"

"No one is innocent," answered the sadhu.

"Except the little children," added the beggar.

"It is a sadness, but each man comes with a part to play that involves deception. Then, when he has played his part and deceived his fellows then he goes," the sadhu said.

"Some are taken by cholera, some by typhus, some by birth itself," rambled the beggar, "God gives, God takes, regardless of age or status."

"God gives, God takes, according to His divine plan," said the sadhu.

"Why?" shouted Leo. "I was told at school that God is love and God is good and that we are created in his image. Why then should he take an innocent child?"

"The white Christian says this. But it is not my belief," the sadhu replied. "The white Christian *says* Christ is benevolent because *he* wishes to be seen as benevolent. Have they, best beloved, created *you* in this image of deceitful benevolence?" The sadhu stuck out his head and long nose, and fixed Leo with a stern look.

Leo said nothing, for now he was engaged in thought. It was his upbringing that was to blame for this torment. He was not British, but he had been reared by people who had imposed their ideas upon him. "And when shall we be rid of this hypocrisy?" he asked.

"When the sun has come and gone. When the battle's lost and won." The bald-headed sadhu burst into a gale of laughter. He flapped his bony arms up and down, "Aiii, the white bard," he cackled, "the Swan of Avon always has the last word. We shall lose, my son, they have got Jesus Christ *and* Shakespeare on their side."

"It is," said the beggar who inhabited another world, "that we are each nothing more than a grain of rice. Gandhiji says one grain is nothing, but a whole bowl of rice, when it is full and ready, it swells. Only as many grains together shall we be both many and one, and strong, and part of the great Unity."

Leo dropped the only damp coin that remained in his pocket into the beggar's open hand.

"God be with you, sahib."

"And with you, masters," Leo replied, then ambled across the silent waterfront.

Now and again he stopped to look at the lights of the ships from the western world or the dip and spread of phosphorescent wings. This is what he had come for, the solace of the sea and the flicker of candle-white waves.

As he reached the front door of the hotel, some boys scuttled past him with brooms, mops and buckets. A policeman on a bicycle pedalled by, half asleep. An empty bus coughed to life. Morning had come to Bombay. Its citizens were climbing down from feather beds or up from the earthen floors of make-do shacks, ready to start once again the daily scramble for justice or survival.

"Poor, mad city – poor, confused country – what a mess we are in," Leo said to no one. "What an absurd life this is. Maybe the Mahatma is right - we should try passive resistance. Well, goodnight Mother India and good morning, and may all the gods be with you."

J. G. Harlond

Unconscious of his bedraggled appearance, Leo strolled through the open doors of his hotel and into the reception area. A coolie employed as a night watchman came to attention on his mat on the floor. He took one look at Leo, noting his torn clothes, his bare feet, his haggard face, then dashed to hide behind a potted palm. The Kali-worshipper had been out all night – to give sacrifice. Look at him – exhausted by his acts. "Aiiii," he moaned involuntarily, "aiiii."

Later that morning, Leo stepped from around the night watchman's palm tree, the very image of a very Anglo-Indian: his face closely shaved and swathed in aromatic balsam, his clothes impeccable save perhaps for the rather artistic sprig of yellow peeping from his lapel pocket. Unaware of the commotion he had caused among the servants below stairs, Leo strode up to the reception desk. He wanted to settle his bill before breakfast, enjoy his repast in comfort, and move on.

He was stopped in his tracks by an envelope resting against a brass bell, with his name printed clearly upon it in neat, schoolroom, blue-black lettering. Trying to ignore it, he paid his bill and walked towards the breakfast room, but just as he reached his table the receptionist came running up behind him, waving the envelope. He had no choice but to accept it.

Leo propped the envelope against his sugar bowl and poured his tea. He smeared over-soft, acidy butter across his toast and spooned English marmalade made from Spanish oranges onto his plate. He stared at the envelope, trying to see inside without breaking the seal. Because breaking the seal would force him to make another decision. To go or not go? Because this letter, he knew for certain, was from

Millicent Cleaver. Arnold Mackay, who used to hate him and perhaps still did, had told her where to find him.

He waited until he had finished a slice of toast and wiped his hands on his damask napkin. Then he poured a second cup of tea and picked up a knife to slit open the envelope. He extracted a single small sheet of cream writing paper and held it in one hand. With the other, casually, as relaxed as he could muster, he picked up his cup of tea.

My dearest, dearest Leo,

Arnold has told me where you are staying. Do come to us as soon as you can. Ellie is safe with us here . . .

The cup rattled to the floor. Arnold had said not a word about Ellie. The words blurred. Leo started again. . .

We are at your father's house on Malabar Hill . . .

Leo stared at the paper as if it would bite. The woman who, according to Arnold, had said she had saved him but more likely abducted him on a train from Goa, and the man who had never made any attempt to claim him, now had his little daughter.

Chapter 31
Bombay, 1935

Two ibises stretched their beaks symmetrically to the sky; two peacocks fanned their tails in ostentatious array; above them, birds of paradise hopped among branches alive with all the leaves of Asia. The gates were a naturalist's dream in wrought iron. Behind them, up a short, gravel drive, was a rambling but surprisingly modest bungalow. The walls were painted white, the window frames green. Ivy and jasmine climbed to the roof and spilled out around corners, lilies opened their opulence for the touch of rain, bougainvillea and other garish blooms toppled over the garden walls. It was, thought Leo, exactly the sort of house he would like. Not too big, comfortable-looking, and set in a jungle of plants, except he would have a special rose garden, too.

As he stood there, trying to find the energy to face the scene ahead, a Siamese cat insinuated itself under the gate and paused to glare at him, annoyed that its moment of indignity had been observed. Then it arched its back, regained the poise of good breeding and trotted self-importantly down the hill. A dumpy house-boy came rushing out of the front door, apparently in pursuit of the cat, and stopped short when he saw Leo's tall profile behind the gate.

"Sir?" he said.

"I'm here to see Mr Kazan. He's expecting me." *And that,* thought Leo, *may or may not be true.*

The Empress Emerald

The boy pushed a hand between the curve of an iron branch and an ibis and held it flat for Leo's card. Then, without opening the gate, he rushed back inside and returned with the card on a silver salver. He opened the gate and led Leo round to the back of the house.

There was a terraced lawn, in the centre three people were playing French cricket. A large man dressed in an embroidered ivory silk kurta was holding the bat to his feet; a little girl with a mop of thick black hair was pretending to throw the ball but not releasing it, laughing and squealing at her cleverness each time the man moved the bat. A stick-like woman stood apart, her gaze fixed on the child.

The house-boy coughed. Before he could announce the visitor, however, Leo took the silver salver from him and signalled him to go. The boy remained where he was, but did not speak. Leo did the same.

The little girl jumped around her grandfather, trying to hit his legs with the tennis ball. He, in turn, made exaggerated groans as he twisted this way and that, daring her to get him – in Russian.

Millicent Cleaver saw him first. She gasped and put a hand to her mouth. Leonid Kazan looked up, and while his attention was drawn to Leo standing across the lawn, Ellie hit him sharply on the shin with her ball. "Ay!" It was a genuine yelp. He rubbed his leg then turned back to Leo, "*Milosti prosim. Pricojedin'ajtec.*"

"*Spasibo.*"

Staying in his own tongue, Leonid Kazan said, "She's too clever and too strong for her years." Then he stepped forward and looked hard at Leo without touching him. "You are like my brother. Like my father, as well. Welcome, welcome, my son." He clapped Leo on the back and pulled him into a bear hug.

J. G. Harlond

Eventually, he released Leo and turned to speak to Millicent Cleaver, whose face was as white as the jasmine and Japanese wisteria behind her. "What's the matter, woman?" Leonid Kazan shouted joyously in English. "Here he is! Here he is at last! Come on, smile, be a warm welcome."

Leonid turned back to his son and held out the cricket bat, "Now you are here, you can play. See if this little minx can get *you*."

Ellie, who had been watching what was going on above her head with a mixture of concern and excitement, dropped her ball and screamed out, "Daddy! Come and play. I'm winning!" She scampered across the lawn to retrieve the tennis ball.

Leo handed the tray he was still holding back to the house-boy and took the English cricket bat from his father. Millicent Cleaver watched him with eyes like saucers. He took up his position, holding the bat at his knees to protect his feet. Ellie held the ball, but now she had come over shy. She held the tennis ball between her plump little hands and stared at him, unmoving. Leo cocked his head on one side and winked at her.

"You've got eyes like my new grandpa," she said in English.

"Mm, and you've got eyes like me."

Ellie moved a step closer to him, still staring into his face. Then she dropped her ball, turned, and scampered into the safety of Millicent Cleaver's grey skirt. The woman bent down, whispered to her then gently prised the child's fingers open and turned her to face Leo, saying, "Go and say hello nicely, there's a good girl."

Ellie twisted back to hide in the long skirt. And Leo remembered doing exactly the same thing. The skin on the back of his neck prickled.

Slowly and gently, Millicent Cleaver turned Ellie back to face Leo then gave her a gentle nudge in his direction. "Be a good girl for Daddy," she whispered.

Ellie walked slowly across the immaculate lawn and stopped at Leo's feet. She took the bat from his hands and dropped it on the ground beside her. Then she extended the fingers of her right hand and said, "How do you do. I am pleased to meet you."

"Give him a kiss!" shouted Leonid in Russian. "Ask him what took him so long."

Not understanding what was being said, Ellie looked back at Millicent for reassurance. Smiling, Millicent shrugged, but she also gestured a hug. Ellie lifted her arms shyly. Leo swung her into the air and settled her in the crook of his left arm.

The child looked down at the adults around her and laughed out in delight, "He's like an elephant, Millie, a great big elephant."

Leo laughed too, but there were tears in his eyes.

Tea was laid out on the veranda. Millicent took charge of the silver tea-pot. Leo looked at the tea service, at the cups and saucers, looking for something familiar, something that might spark an early memory of his parents' home. There was nothing. Ellie sidled between his knees. He bent down and smelt her hair, kissing the top of her head.

"Well," said his father, stirring a third spoonful of sugar into his tea, "where shall we begin?"

Leo looked at him, lost for words. Millicent busied herself cutting cake. For a while they drank their tea, all focused on Ellie serving them slices of Victoria sponge like a society hostess. Eventually Leonid Kazan slapped the arm of his cane chair and said in English, "Now come along, Millicent. You start. We have a lot of years to cover. You must be our beginning."

Millicent looked at Leo then back at his father, "I – um – I . . . Where must I start?"

"Where you told me," Leonid was matter of fact.

"Oh, really, I don't think I can. It's so painful . . . I mean . . ."

Leo was torn between wanting to help her and wanting to see her suffer. In the end he said, "If it is all right with you, I think I would prefer to speak to each of you on my own. You seem to have settled . . . things . . . between you. But, all the same, can I get to know you on your own first, before . . ." *Before what?* Leo had no clear idea of what he wanted, expected or hoped for. In fact, for the first time in his life he was at a complete loss for words.

Millicent said, "That is a good idea, Leonid. If you still want me to go first, perhaps I could show Leo your wonderful roses. If that is all right?"

She led Leo away from the veranda and back across the lawn, then down some steps to the next terrace. It was laid out like a geometric maze, with triangles of pale green and mauve lavender, a paler green plant with wispy leaves Leo could not name and hundreds of roses of every hue arranged in triangles, squares and diamonds. Neither spoke. Millicent walked slowly among the prickly stems and Leo followed.

"Do you remember our roses, Leo?"

Leo looked at the full-blown head of a bright pink rose. He bent to sniff it avoiding Millicent's piercing gaze, then gently pulled its velvet petals into his hand. "We put the petals in bowls," he said quietly.

Millicent smiled. "My father hated them in the house. Said it made the place smell like a . . . He studied plants, you know. That is why he came to India. To study plants. He married my mother – she was a local girl, she came to work for him. Like Kitty's mother and father. Except Kitty was loved, and she always had her mother with her. My mother died when I was very young." Millicent paused, took a deep breath, "I've never told anyone this. It was difficult for me, you see. He didn't have much money. I wasn't pretty enough to get married. Some Anglo girls do find husbands, but I wasn't pretty you see, and my father did not socialise with people. He was always out looking for rare plants on his own. And then, of course, being a – what people called a "half-caste" - I didn't have good possibilities, so I became a governess."

Leo looked across a diamond-shaped stand of white roses at the aged spinster, trying to calculate how old she was, trying to imagine what it was like for her – for himself – to be an only, lonely child in a bare-walled bungalow. He remembered the roses, but the inside of the bungalow was a vague sensation of peeling paint and mosquito netting. He remembered her father, though, a mean-spirited crosspatch.

"I worked in three different households before I was twenty," Millicent continued. "Then I went to Goa. That was my last proper teaching job. It was not pleasant. I had to get away. I couldn't bear the shouting, the fights . . . I decided to leave and . . . I took a train back to Bombay." Millicent's voice died away.

Leo took a few steps closer to her to hear better, "How did you find me?"

"I didn't find you, Leo. It wasn't quite like that – I . . ." Millicent walked away from him, crossed to the edge of the terrace and looked out at the view. Below, there was a road and the rooftops of other bungalows and bigger houses, the tops of trees and the occasional white of a marble-tiled terrace.

Leo went to stand at her side. "You know, it doesn't really matter now what happened –"

"Oh, Leo, I'm so, so sorry."

"What for? You saved me." Leo put a hand on her thin shoulder.

Millicent raised a small handkerchief to hide her face, shaking her head. "I didn't."

The terrible doubt Arnold had planted was confirmed. Leo swallowed hard, stilling his hands and breathing deeply. He wanted to shout "You abducted me – stole me from my real mother!" but he lost his nerve and said, "You saved Ellie. How?"

"Oh, that was dreadful. There was a demonstration. It got out of hand. Cotton workers started it, the newspapers said. Everyone went mad. They had fire-bombs in bottles, the newspapers reported the next day. Your father-in-law stocked Nottingham lace and other English goods, remember? That was their excuse, I think, and because there was an English name on the shop. I was on my way to – there. The crowd was completely out of control. Trouble-makers organised it . . . I was . . . India won't get Home Rule that way, and it was such a terrible thing to happen. Your poor . . ." Millicent's stuttered account came to an end as she lifted her handkerchief to her eyes again.

"Arnold Mackay said they set fire to the shop. Someone else said it was an explosion – a bomb of some sort."

Millicent shook her head, biting her lips. "It was terrible."

"But Ellie would have been upstairs. How did you get her to safety?"

"No, she was with Kitty."

"Then how . . .?"

"I don't remember exactly. Kitty was coming back to the shop. I took Ellie, and Kitty went into the alley . . . As soon as the crowd moved on I tried to get in, but I'd got Ellie and I didn't want to risk her getting burned or being taken by someone else. I ran to the police station." Millicent started to weep in earnest, her bony shoulders shaking beneath the fine poplin of her white blouse.

Leo pulled the mother who was not his mother into a warm embrace. He swallowed hard again, trying to contain a lifetime's sadness and sense of loss. Millicent collapsed into his chest, sobbing, while Leo held her thin frame to him and stared out over her head at the view below. There was a house that looked vaguely familiar. A low roof and terraces like other properties, but this one struck a chord. *Was this where he had claimed the wonderful Empress Emerald*?

Gently, Leo pushed Millicent from him. "Enough," he said. "There is no point looking backwards. I've been doing just that and found only regret there. Let's go back to Ellie, she'll be missing you. Come along, I could do with another cup of tea, or a spot of something stronger."

Leonid Kazan, whom Leo now had to think of as his father, cocked his head on one side and gave Leo a questioning look over Ellie's mop of black hair. They were playing snap with children's playing cards. Leo responded with an identical gesture and they both burst out laughing.

"Do you have any vodka . . .?" Leo wasn't sure how to address him. Accepting the fact that the man was his father was one thing; feeling comfortable saying "Father" was another.

"See if you can beat your Millie now," Leonid ruffled Ellie's curls and handed his cards to Millicent. Looking at Leo and changing to Russian, he said, "Come into my den." As Leo followed him into the house, he continued in the same conversational tone, "Your grandfather, my father, was an explorer. Did you know that? No, of course you didn't. Well, he was. He explored Afghanistan, map-making. Got shot at quite often by the English and the locals in the process. They all thought he was spying, which I suppose, in a way, he was." He poured tumblers of neat vodka and rambled on, "Eventually he had to go back home, take over the estate. Eldest son, you see. Kazan is on the River Volga."

"Yes, I've been there."

"Have you!"

Leo nodded, knocked back his fire-liquid in one go and held his glass out for more. "Big industrial city now. Lenin studied Law there when he was still called Ulyanov, before he became Lenin. Is that ironic?"

"That our wealth and possessions may have influenced a murderer?" Leonid grimaced. "We provided for dozens of families, hundreds on our estate. It is on the east bank of the river."

"*Was.* The White Russians have all been defeated. Everything is communal property now. But what I don't understand is, if you have – had – the estate, why are you here in Bombay?"

"Second son, my boy, I had to find a profession. I became a diplomat." He laughed. "When they found out who my father was they sent me straight to the new consulate here in Bombay. Then I was moved to Delhi then Calcutta. But I came back often because – you see, I was always looking for you."

"But you didn't find me."

"I did and I didn't. I got very close to you, but I could never prove anything."

"How did you know I could speak Russian?"

Leonid looked up and laughed, "I told you, I got close – very close. Diplomats have access to all manner of information, even in back of beyond places like Malabar fishing villages."

Leo looked at his father, surprised yet not surprised. "It won't make much difference now, being first or second son, everyone's equal. Equal in everything and for everything, which means you've both lost the lot. Hasn't your brother explained this?"

"I haven't heard from him for years."

Leo shook his head; he knew what that meant.

"It's all been handed out free to our estate workers, hasn't it?" Leonid continued. "I expected as much. Expected, but not accepted. No, I cannot accept. This is why you have to go back. Find out what's happened. Find out how we can reclaim our inheritance. Fight for what belongs to you."

Leo looked at him blankly. "Me?"

"Yes, you are a Kazan of Kazan. You must go back and reclaim your Russian heritage."

"No!" The word came out before Leo had time to think about it. "I belong here. If I fight for anything it will be for Home Rule: self-government for India. I have joined the Congress Party."

"After what they've done to your wife?" There was a low menace in Leonid's voice.

"That's different. That was unforgiveable, but I can understand why it happened. It's complicated, hard to explain."

Leonid Kazan sighed, put down his glass and moved to the window, then sat down in a comfortable armchair, gesturing at the chair beside him for Leo to sit as well.

As Leo sat down, another doubt requiring clarification entered his mind. "I was born in India, wasn't I?"

"In Goa. I met your mother in Goa when I first came and was meeting people for trade missions. Your mother was with her family there. Her father is – was – a spice merchant, an exporter, but also an important importer. Portuguese, of course, originally – long ago. There was a famous Italian rogue in the family as well. Or so the old man told me."

Leo laughed, "India, Russia, Portugal, Italy; I'm a bit of a mix."

"And English. Don't forget the *Englishness* they put in you. I shan't. I shall never forgive the English for that, either."

"But you and Millicent . . . I thought you had sorted out your . . ."

"Differences? We have and we haven't. Besides, Millicent is no more English than my house-boy. She only sounds it. Like you. Although your Russian is good - you could be from Petersburg."

"Not called that nowadays. Saint Petersburg became Petrograd in 1914. Then it was changed to Leningrad. Place names change. People change."

"But their origin stays the same." Leonid Kazan looked hard at his son.

Leo pushed a hand through his thick black hair. He wanted to ask about the missing Goan woman of distant European descent who had married a young Russian consul.

His father picked up his thoughts, "I should take you to see your mother, except I'm not sure it would be a good idea, she is – delicate. One day, when the time is right. Go now, Ellie will be missing you." Leonid Kazan struggled out of his chair. "I will instruct you in your family history another time."

Leo got to his feet in something of a daze. This strange afternoon had given him his parents and his daughter, and the woman who had abducted him but whom he loved nonetheless. It had also confirmed where his future lay. The path he should take was clear now, and it wouldn't take him back to Russia. He might, on the other hand return to England, if obliged – on his own agenda.

Returning to the veranda, Leo seated himself in a cane chair and pulled Ellie onto his lap. She snuggled into his body and popped a thumb in her mouth. Millicent leaned across and gently withdrew it.

"I don't mind," Leo said.

"It will spoil her teeth."

"She has good enough teeth. We'll risk it. Indian children have a more natural upbringing."

"But Ellie isn't –"

"She is. She was born here. Like me. We are Indian, Millicent. And so are you."

For a while they sat in silence, Leo rocking his daughter on his lap, then he said, "How did you know about Ellie's Russian grandfather?"

"I've always known. Sir Lionel told me and confirmed what your mother said."

"My mother? When? What?"

"Sir Lionel told me about your father not long after . . . they took you in at the orphanage." Millicent paused and examined her hands. "His secretary found me. I was teaching at a school in Poona, but he told me I had to come back to Bombay. Sir Lionel arranged for me to have a small monthly income so I could stay in the city, in case they needed me, he said. His secretary, a very small man called Mackay, arranged it all and found me some rooms and a piano. I became a music teacher. I wasn't very good to start with, but I got better with practice – fortunately. My allowance stopped when poor Sir Lionel died."

Poor Sir Lionel! A lump of hard anger lodged itself in Leo's throat. They had all known, and they had all betrayed him. Sir Lionel had cheated him since before they had even met. Arnold Mackay had lied to him – or at least failed to tell him what he had a right to know – always. And the sleek, self-important Sir Gerald in London had been laughing up his sleeve for . . . how long? Leo started to reckon the years he had lost, the years he had given to people who had used him and – *betrayed* him. There was no other word.

Ellie shifted in his arms and snuggled her head under his chin. The movement brought Leo's negative thoughts to an abrupt halt. Whatever happened now, he had to provide for this little one. He needed a regular income and safe place for her to live. A safe place . . . In the short term, he had four bank accounts: two legitimate in London and Bombay, where his British stipend had been paid, and two others for his alternative income, plus his account in Amsterdam. He also had a small fortune in two biscuit tins: rubies, sapphires, diamonds and other gems, cut and uncut stones, rings and brooches, and the exquisite Empress Emerald. Those could be sold as funds were needed, to take care of Ellie's financial future. Except not the emerald pendant necklace, not unless there was no alternative.

Coldly, without making eye-contact, Leo said, "Millicent, tell me the full story from the beginning. Exactly how you found or acquired me, and why you sent me to the British orphanage. And why you have been paid to tell no one about it all these years."

Millicent Cleaver lowered her eyes. "I can tell you my part Leo, but, please, would you visit Reverend Johns before I do? Please?"

"At the orphanage?"

"Yes, he's still there. No longer working, of course, but he stayed on. He says he wouldn't be able to settle back in England."

Leo shook his head in bewilderment, "But what can he tell me?"

"About Sir Lionel. You ought to know, Leo, how he used you."

Leo gave a one-dimpled wry smile then said, "I don't need to be told that. I'll visit Reverend Johns, happily, he was a good man, but I don't need to, or wish to, discuss Sir Lionel with anyone. The boot is on the other foot now, you see.

Starting tomorrow morning, I shall be offering the Congress Party my undivided attention. My skills, honed in the service of Sir Lionel and his compatriots, will be employed exclusively for the Home Rule movement from now on."

"Oh, Leo, do you think that is wise?"

Leo raised a hand, "It's the first wise thing I've ever done."

"But they arrest people like that. Even the Mahatma has been in prison."

"Don't worry," Leo laughed, "I should be capable of staying one step ahead of the Raj's aging lackeys after all I've been through."

Ellie looked up at him. He kissed her forehead and gave her a hug, but his mind was already elsewhere. He wouldn't be working entirely exclusively for Indian nationalism; there was a small matter of revenge to attend to as well. Providing active nationalists with inside information about what was happening in London would hopefully undermine Sir Gerald *et al*, but the petit and pernicious Arnold Mackay deserved a similar, if not worse, revenge. He'd said he didn't want the Oriental Curiosity Shop, so he would not have it.

Dealing with Arnold, however, would be like handling a poisonous toad. He was going to have to be particularly devious, and not let himself get over-confident, because for sure that little man still had a direct line to the India Office in London, if not to Sir Gerald himself, plus a whole network of Bombay police and political officers, as well as Lionel's old local snoopers. Destroying Arnold Mackay would take time, but the outcome would be the sweeter for that.

PART 4

SPAIN, GIBRALTAR, INDIA, ENGLAND
1936 – 1940

Chapter 32
Jerez, Spain, 1936

Alfonso García del Moral Lopez-Rey straightened his collar, smoothed down his jacket and turned to examine his profile in the mirror. The uniform was not elegant. The material was somewhat coarse and quite inappropriate for the hot weather. The boots, however, made up for everything. Tall riding boots in conker-red leather. They were beautifully crafted and fitted perfectly. He gave himself another half turn in front of his dressing room mirror and jumped as his mother's figure appeared like a ghost behind him.

"May I come in?"

"Of course."

Doña Mercedes hobbled over to the dressing table beside the balcony window with the aid of her ebony stick and lowered herself into the chair with an involuntary groan. "You are going, then," she said.

"I told you."

"You are too old for the army." She examined a woman's silver-backed hairbrush. "Did you buy yourself in? To get away?"

"No."

"You are a liar, Alfonso. You have always been a liar."

"I am doing what I believe to be right. For our country."

"Grown men playing soldiers. You'll be shot."

"I am joining the cavalry." Alfonso indicated his uniform in exasperation.

"They'll shoot your horse."

"Oh, for the love of God, Mother! What is it you want?"

The old lady shook her head and picked up four hairpins one by one, the English woman's. "You're sleeping together. I didn't know." She bit back tears. "I came to say goodbye, that's all. A mother may bid her son farewell when he goes away."

Alfonso went to kneel by her chair in remorse, but his new boots wouldn't bend sufficiently at the ankle so he was obliged to bend over her. He kissed her powdered, scaly forehead. "I shall be fine. As you said, I am too old to be in the front line. Please, do not worry."

"Why?"

"Why what?"

"Why are you going, leaving me here alone with your stupid sisters and *la inglesa*?"

"Don't call her that. She's your daughter-in-law."

"Hah, according to English law. I've never seen your marriage papers. That black-haired young madam may be another bastard for all I know."

"Mother! Marina loves you."

"Marina!" Doña Mercedes scoffed, "That's what her mother calls her."

Alfonso ignored the jibe, turned his back and opened the top drawer of his tallboy.

"What about the business?" his mother continued. "You haven't told me anything."

"Álvarez and the Moreno boys know what to do. Álvarez knows more about the business than I do, and the Moreno boys are very sharp: their family has been working for us since last century. We can obviously trust *them*; we've been feeding, clothing and housing them for three generations."

"And you think that will keep the accounts straight and in our favour?"

"Yes. They wouldn't dare try to cheat us."

"Hmm. People are sometimes cleverer than you think. For all you know, they are Republicans just itching to get you out of the way and turn our business into one of their co-operatives. There's enough of that clan to keep the business running on their own!"

The thought had occurred to Alfonso, but he wasn't going to admit it. The Moreno brothers had been very congratulatory when he said he was joining Franco's rebels 'to keep the business safe'. But although they were younger than him, they had made no mention of wanting to join the fray. Nor had the chief foreman, Álvarez, whose son was a student in Seville. He was certain the boy had republican sympathies, as his mother had just suggested. Nevertheless, he said, "Everything is arranged and in safe hands, Mother."

"That's what you think. You shouldn't be going, leaving me, leaving the business. This war is going to cost us enough without you handing your inheritance on a plate to outsiders. What does she say?"

"If by 'she' you are referring to Davina, she understands."

"Ah, we are so lovey-dovey these days. What about the other one?"

Alfonso opened another drawer and selected four handkerchiefs. "That finished years ago."

"I know that. I'm not blind or deaf, yet. *La inglesa* found you out and threatened you with something serious – your pretty reputation, no doubt."

"How do you know . . .?"

Alfonso saw the little victory creep into her cheeks, her lips almost cracked into a smile. She gripped the edge of the chair to lever herself out. Alfonso bent to help her, but she pushed him away. He handed her the ebony stick. She looked up at him and traced a scar along his neck with the stick's silver and ivory handle. "You've been in the wars already, my son. Has it really ended with her or was that the gypsy bitch? I don't blame her. Have you taken care of the brats? I don't want that one coming round here expecting charity as well."

Alfonso refused to answer. He had settled an allowance on Maribel, the mother of three of his illegitimate children, but only 'during his lifetime'. It was an arrangement designed to keep him safe from her brothers, cousins and uncles. Alfonso had nightmares about that particular threat. He had made sure the Heredia clan understood the conditions.

As Doña Mercedes was about to leave his room, he said, "Please try to be nice to Davina. She has never said or done anything to harm you and she has put up with Esperanza and Gloria all these years."

"She hasn't given me a grandson."

"No, well . . ." Alfonso busied himself with his packing. "I have to go out now for an hour or so – I'll be back for an early supper. I have to report in at the new headquarters by ten tonight." But he spoke to no one. His mother was tapping her way down the marble-tiled gallery, wiping a forefinger along the window sills to check for dust.

Alfonso tugged at the hem of his jacket and gave an inadvertent shudder. His mother's mention of money made him check his wallet. Enough to get by; not too much to invite leeches. Joining the cavalry might ensure a better sort of companion, but they wouldn't all be out of the top drawer. His mother was right: the war was going to cost them serious money. Well, they could afford his absence for a few months.

It wouldn't take Franco's professional troops long to subdue a bunch of airy-fairy reds. A Republican government couldn't rule, by definition; it had only been voted in by illiterate peasants, who should never have been enfranchised in the first place. It wouldn't take them long to send that rabble running back to their hovels. Davina might get righteous over the poor needing education and hygiene, which, according to her, the city council could easily provide, but she didn't see the danger of letting the so-called poor take over. Let them get any power and everybody would be poor. Look at what was happening in Russia.

Alfonso patted his pistol in its holster, put on his cap and went into the corridor. He was intercepted by Esperanza, who was watering plants with a small brass watering-can. As she turned, water squirted out and stained his new boots.

"Careful!"

"Ooh, sister," she called, "come and see our brother! Ooh, you do look handsome. Those boots! Go and show Mother."

"She's seen me. Let me get past without ruining my uniform – I have to go out."

"Are you leaving already?"

"No, not yet, I told you this morning."

"Yes, Brother, but I've forgotten."

"Tonight, I'm leaving tonight. Have you seen Davina?"

"She went to her room for *siesta*. Shall I fetch her?"

"No, I shan't be long. Remind the cook about the early supper and tell Davina – after she has rested – that I didn't want to wake her and I'll be back about seven, if not before."

Alfonso left the house and stepped out into the leaden afternoon heat. October and it was still oppressively hot. The shops wouldn't open for another hour; the street was deserted. He set off in the direction of the Nationalist recruitment office. On his right was the main doorway of the parish church of Santo Domingo. A couple of decrepit widows garbed in black were asleep in the porch, wearied from a morning of fruitless begging. One opened an eye in her dried-fig features and pointed a stick finger at him.

"*Usted!*" she called out accusingly. "I see you!"

Her companion woke with a start and recited her plea for alms, "*Señor*, have pity on a poor widow."

Alfonso shuddered. He turned right again and headed down the wide street that led past the side of the church. One of the side doors was open. On impulse, he entered.

It was slightly darker but not significantly cooler inside the high, white stone building. His boots struck the paving stones and echoed around the nave. He genuflected in front of the altar and wandered around, looking for something with meaning. In one of the ornate chapel screens he spied a small figure of Saint Michael. He paused, looking at the angel with a sword. Then he manoeuvred his angular frame into a narrow pew, bent his head and tried to pray.

"Mary, mother of Jesus, help me in this time of . . ." what was he praying for? His own safety? Was that a real issue? For the longevity of his mother? She was ageing but hale. For his wife, who had become his real wife the day she discovered his mistress? For the woman his wife had become? Yes. If anything happened to him – which was highly unlikely – she might be in a difficult situation. When he came back on leave, he would put the house in her name. She and the girl deserved some security. His sisters had their income from the business, but he hadn't arranged any sort of income for Davina or her daughter. Their daughter. Only daughter.

And then Alfonso began to pray in earnest for a son. It wasn't too late. He had fathered three children, and Davina had borne a child. Why did God not grant them a baby together? When he came back – when he came back . . . He had to leave first. Maudlin nonsense.

Alfonso got to his feet and strode back into the glaring sun. Coming out into the bright light, he did not see a group of barefoot boys playing among the orange trees that lined the street. His leather-soled boots slipped on the cobbles and the inelegant move attracted their attention. The boys nudged each other, sniggered and fell into a parody of a formation behind him as he marched down the empty boulevard.

One of them said, "Look at his boots."

"Made for riding a mule!"

"Look at his hat."

"Made to keep his fat head from frying."

"Look at his posh breeches."

"Made for Franco's farts!"

"Look at the pistol in his holster."

"Because he hasn't got one in his pants!"

The comments became more obscene, the laughter more aggressive. Alfonso heard the taunts and walked faster.

"Hey, General, you don't need to run! We won't hurt you!"

"Much!"

With one accord the boys began to pelt him with fallen oranges. Alfonso was furious. He turned and started towards them, keeping an arm up to protect his face. The boys screamed in mock horror.

"Look out, the cavalry's charging!"

"Arm yourselves, lads. Defend yourselves to your dying breath!

Doubled with derisive laughter, the boys stooped to collect more missiles. In the dry circles of earth around the orange trees there were small, sharp stones. They threw these at random as Alfonso, tall and imposing in his smart new uniform, bore down on them. The smaller boys ran off, hiding in ones and twos behind tree trunks. A bigger boy, one of Maribel's Heredia clan, fitted a bigger stone into his catapult and took aim.

"Enough," shouted Alfonso. "Stop!" He put his arms out in front of him in a halting gesture and the sharp flint caught him right between the eyes. He dropped like a rock, face forward onto the hot cobblestones, and died in the instant.

Chapter 33
Jerez, 1936

A bolt had been drawn, a lock turned. Alfonso coming in, or going out? No, not Alfonso. Davina was wide awake. Not Alfonso and never again Alfonso.

Davina listened. Heavy rain drummed against the shutters. Rain to wash a thin trickle of blood off a hot, dry street. Rain to fill the water butts and flush out the drains. Rain to revive the rivers and feed the fields. Welcome rain in windblown blasts.

Their door was open, had she left it open? Had someone come in and left without waking her? Davina switched on her bedside light to see the time: four-thirty, her usual time to wake in the night. She switched off the harsh light and stretched a hand across Alfonso's side of the bed. She should have gone back to her old room. Why had she chosen to sleep in this room? She lay back and begged for sleep, but her mind reeled with all that had happened in the past three days and gave her no rest.

He had been waxed like a tailor's dummy and laid out for exhibition in the *capilla ardiente* – the funeral chapel. The whole town had come to gawp. A group of mawkish relatives had swamped the bereaved mother. All dignity destroyed, the stern matriarch had crumpled and sobbed through the brief funeral ceremony. Later, back in her house, she had sat silent beside the vast empty fireplace in the best salon, while visitors drank the family sherry and chatted about the weather and the price of fuel, and spoke not a word about politics or war.

After everyone had gone, Mari-Fe, the eldest daughter, called the doctor. He gave Doña Mercedes sedatives. Mari-Fe, another widow, helped her mother take the medicine then went home. The two spinster sisters gently, quietly, lovingly settled their bereaved mother in bed. Then immediately forgot about speaking in whispers and spent ten minutes arguing about who was to sit with her first. Eventually, bored with their squabbling, they ate supper together in silence and both went to bed.

Marina sat with her grandmother for a while, until it was evident the woman was too heavily drugged to wake, then she went to sit with her mother in the small parlour. As the clock struck the midnight hour, Marina gave her mother a long, tearful hug and went to her room.

Davina had almost told her. Almost said, "Do not mourn too deeply, child; he did no more for you than was expected of him." But she didn't. She was a real mother. Whatever else people might say of her, she always put her child first — would never abandon her. Never do what her own mother had, in effect, done to her. She would never leave Marina or do anything to unsettle her world.

Marina had held her hand all the time they were in the chapel, only letting go when the *bodega* foreman, Álvarez, and his son Pedro arrived to pay their respects. The girl and boy had stood side by side while the foreman spoke to Doña Mercedes, two healthy souls in a room of ritualised sentiment. Some minutes later they had briefly left the chapel together, close but not touching. She saw them leave, then re-enter just as serious as when they had left. Alfonso had clearly succeeded in putting a stop to their romance. A shame, they looked good together. She would speak to Marina: love should laugh at class. The foreman was a good man. His son would care for her daughter.

But if Marina got married and had her own home, what would she do? Where would she go? She would be free to leave Doña Mercedes' living mausoleum at last, but she'd have no money to take her anywhere. It would be unfair to impose on newly-weds. But if Marina did marry . . . that would mean no husband and no daughter, and possibly nowhere to live. And possibly, if not probably, no income apart from the pittance left in her English bank account. Had Alfonso provided for her in any way? She must go through his papers, find his will. If he had made a will, would there be anything for her or Marina, except perhaps a small allowance? Would there be any provision at all for either of them?

There had to be a copy of the will in the house somewhere. Doña Mercedes would have it among her papers in her bureau. It made sense. Alfonso wouldn't have left his will in the *bodega* office. And, under the circumstances, even if there was no formal testament, surely he had left instructions about what to do if anything happened to him.

Davina tossed this way and that. Slept for a while, then woke again, remembering that Alfonso had never said anything to her about the future. She knew in her heart he had left nothing to protect her or Marina. He had been as excited as a schoolboy about going off to war – at his age. It was absurd: someone had fixed it for him, one of his finger-in-every-pie friends. All he'd talked about was his uniform and Franco; the reality of civil war had never been mentioned. Not that he'd been killed in action.

Davina sighed, rolled onto her back and listened to the night. It was still raining, a steady hum interrupted by an irregular patter as water fell from the broken guttering and dropped onto the narrow balcony above the street. Lying still now, eyes closed, she saw steady rain breaking the surface of a slow river on a late summer morning long, long ago.

The Empress Emerald

Sleep would not return without a glass of hot milk. Reluctantly, Davina swung her legs into the cool room, pushed her feet into her slippers and pulled on a robe. She went to the window. The heavy wooden shutter opened onto blackness. Leaving it open to air the room, she lit a short candle to avoid putting on the glaring electric light and walked down the draughty corridor. Beyond their glass-paned door, the Ugly Sisters were snoring exactly as they lived each day, constantly interrupting each other, neither separate nor in unison. Passing the heavy velvet curtain that cordoned off Doña Mercedes' quarters, Davina paused. There was no sound. Perhaps she was dead, too.

The kitchen was still warm after the long summer heat, too warm for hot milk. She turned on the tap and held a glass under it while it gulped out metallic water. Then she ate a honey pastry from a fancy dish and headed back to her room down the right hand corridor. As she passed Marina's room, she peeked in. The girl was fast asleep, hunched under the counterpane. She went in, as she always had done, to tuck the covers under her chin. The candle flickered as she moved and flared up in a sudden draught, the bed was empty. A bolster had been stuffed under the covers. Davina sat on the bed. There was a white sheet of paper on the bedside table. She put the candle down and picked up the note.

Mamá,

I am sorry that I have to leave like this, but I know Grandmother will never permit me to marry Pedro. I do not want to leave you but Pedro is being sent to Córdoba, and then to help defend Madrid. I cannot live without him. I have to go with him. Father said he was not good enough for me but he was wrong, Pedro is good and kind and he will look after me, so please don't worry.

I am going away with the boy I love. I know you will understand. You left your family to come to Spain. You know what real love is like. Please forgive me for hurting you. Grandmother will probably be nasty to you because of me, I am sorry. Please understand there was no other way to do this.

I shall always be your loving daughter,

Marina XXX

How right and how wrong the child was: 'you left your family to come to Spain' – *but only because the boy I loved didn't want me.* Davina wrapped her arms across her body. Why did the only people she cared for leave her these notes? Then she remembered what Marina had said about Madrid. Pedro had joined the Republicans. He was going to fight. Marina would be a widow before she was a wife – if she weren't killed, too. Franco's Nationalists were dropping bombs on Madrid.

For the next few minutes Davina stayed where she was, unmoving. Then she came to an impulsive, emotional decision. She picked up the stub of candle, got up and went to her mother-in-law's quarters. Pushing back the heavy curtains, she stood and listened then stepped in. The door to the bedroom was open. The woman had rolled on her back and was now snoring louder than both daughters put together. Davina went straight to her dressing table and put down the candle. The key she needed was on the bunch in front of her, but which? It had to be one of the small ones. She flicked through them, keeping a watchful eye on the bed. There were three possibilities. Holding the bunch in her fist so it made no noise, she tried each in the lock of the wall-niche safe.

The third key turned. The lock seemed to click very loudly but the dragon slept on. Davina removed the jewel casket and then realised she had nothing to put the contents in. The whole casket would be too awkward to carry. She grabbed a shawl from the back of a chair and quietly tipped each shelf into the middle, then ran a finger over the base of the casket and extracted a final ring which she pushed onto one of her own fingers. She returned the box to the niche, re-locked the wooden door and replaced the keys on the dressing table. With the stolen treasure in one hand and what remained of the candle in the other, Davina moved out of the bedroom into the small sitting room.

Doña Mercedes' bureau was unlocked. Someone else had taken advantage of the sedatives; papers had been pulled out and put back untidily into their divisions, Mari-Fe, perhaps, anxious to know her situation or that of all three sisters. The Ugly Sisters themselves were too stupid to know what to look for. She opened a side drawer and gave a sudden "oh" of surprise. It was full of neatly stacked notes. She took all but the first two, stuffing them into her shawl bundle, then crumpled writing paper behind the remaining notes to act as padding. For a few more moments she read what she could of letters and the like, but there was nothing resembling a last will and testament or even a bank statement.

Back in her old room, Davina pulled out a travelling bag and rammed the shawl bundle down into the bottom. Then she pushed in random items of underclothes, took two dresses and a skirt from her wardrobe, emptied the contents of her dressing table drawers into the inside pockets, stuffed her robe on the top of everything and closed the leather straps. She pulled on her favourite old blue dress and a pair of sturdy shoes, then covered herself with the heavy waterproof cape her mother had bought for the crossing to Spain.

Picking up the bag and the candle, Davina moved quietly back into Alfonso's room. The flickering flame was barely enough to search for documents but she certainly couldn't risk putting on the electric light now. She put the candle on the dressing table by the balcony to get reflected light from the mirror and unlatched the tall windows to push the shutters open wide, although there was no moonlight in the downpour. Davina started with the top drawer of Alfonso's private bureau and found their English marriage licence, Marina's birth certificate and her own passport. It was out of date, but still proof of her British identity. The passport had been used three times: once for the drunken farce that had been her brother's wedding, twice for funerals. First, her mother's, then her father's. It had rained torrents the day her father was buried, too. She shivered at the memory as she slipped the birth certificate and passport into the inside pocket of her tapestry Gladstone bag. The rest of the drawers contained cardboard folders, titled and dated but in the gloom she couldn't see whether they were relevant to her or not. *I should have gone through all this years ago, she thought. Too late now.*

Turning around Davina noticed that there was nothing on top of Alfonso's tallboy: the box containing his shirt studs, cufflinks and tie-pins was missing. Strange. Quickly, starting at the top like an amateur, she riffled through the drawers. No cheque book, no bank book, no cash. There was nowhere else to look for legal papers or formal documents. So she was right. There was nothing for her or Marina.

At least she had her passport, though, and the housekeeping money from Doña Mercedes' bureau. Davina snapped the catch of her bag, closed the leather straps and left the room.

Just as she was about to open the door leading down to the patio, she remembered Marina's note. Leaving the bag on the top step, she dashed back to the girl's room, careless of making a noise now, she grabbed the letter and ran back to the bag, then she was off down the steps to the patio below and the heavy double doors to freedom.

It took what seemed a lifetime to slide all the bolts back, but finally she was standing outside the building on the rain-soaked street. Hood pulled up over her fair hair, bag hidden beneath her cape, Davina walked out into a damp, alien dawn.

She crossed the street and involuntarily looked up at their bedroom window. There was a faint glimmer of light; she had left the candle burning. And there, at street level, standing well back under the balcony of Alfonso's room, was a man. Davina turned and ran. The travelling bag banging against her legs slowed her down, but she kept up a steady pace until she was well past the church.

The sound of feet on the wet cobbles told Davina the man was following her. One of Alfonso's many enemies, no doubt.

He was getting closer. Davina's side ached. The bag was too heavy to go any faster. Now he was parallel across a narrow alley. She wasn't thinking, hadn't planned where she was going.

"Marina!" the man called.

Davina froze. It was Alfonso. She could see the man's outline in the street gaslight now – the height, the voice.

They stared at each other for a moment. It was not Alfonso – it had to be his son.

A boy who was not quite yet a man crossed towards her, saying, "I thought you were Marina. . . Where are you going?"

"I don't know." There were tears in her eyes. "You're Alfonso's son?"

"Yes."

"What do you want? I've got nothing for you. Nothing."

"The bastard hasn't left you anything, either? And his bitch mother has thrown you out!"

"No, no, not that. Not yet."

"And Marina?"

"She has gone."

"Gone?"

"With Pedro Álvarez."

"Ah, yes. They say he is a good person."

Davina nodded. She wanted to ask "how do you know Marina?" but suddenly she was too tired. It could wait. She said, "Yes, he's a good person."

"I'm called Sito. Come."

The young man, so physically like his father, took Davina's bag and escorted her across town to the Cádiz road, then down the hill to his mother's small, white, single-storey house. As they walked past the tree where Davina had once watched Alfonso holding his new baby, she turned and said, "Why were you at our house?"

"I needed to find . . . I wanted to know something and . . . I was told to look for something."

Davina nodded. She knew what he needed to know. "There's nothing for you. That I have seen."

Sito opened the rickety gate to the tiny house, "Didn't think there would be."

As they walked into the one main room, Alfonso's ex-mistress Maribel came out of a side room; her hair was wild and her eyes red from crying. Her mother, as if triggered by an alarm, rushed to the door and stopped in her tracks.

The square-set woman, aged beyond her years, looked at Davina and said, "So you have come. Nothing for you here, unless you've brought her," she nodded at her daughter, "your inheritance and pension." She moved out of the doorway and stood, hands on wide hips in the centre of the cramped room. She was wearing a vast white nightgown and looked like an avenging angel. "Well?" she demanded.

"Leave it, Gran," said the boy. "Leave her alone, she's never done anything to you." The gypsy sniffed and moved toward the hearth. She struck a match, revived a dead fire and prepared a pot of coffee. Davina watched her as if mesmerised.

Maribel said quietly, shyly, "Sit, please, señora." She pointed to a small upright chair by a pine table. Davina sat down. Another silence followed.

"I found her," said Alfonso's son to his grandmother.

Davina gave them a feeble smile. "I'm . . . if you all know about Marina, you know who I am."

"Why do you leave so soon, señora?" asked Maribel indicating the travelling bag on the tiled floor.

Davina couldn't begin to answer the question. She looked around her at the primitive conditions. Alfonso had never done anything for them, except possibly provide his mistress with this ill-built house and maybe a miserable income. "I'm sorry," she said. "You have less than I. What a mess we are in."

"We?" demanded the gypsy woman, sitting on a stool by the fire.

The old woman's tone, Marina's letter, the stress of the past few days, not to say the past eighteen years, all hit Davina at once. She put up a hand to hide her tears and sagged forward in her chair.

"*Dios mío*, not you as well," said the old lady. "He was a selfish bastard! What are you crying for?"

"Not him," said Davina, "for us."

"Well that won't put food in the pot. Here, take off that cape and make yourself comfortable. We'll sort ourselves out – us women together. Sito, get back up that hill and bring us some fresh bread. And not a word to anyone – absolutely no one, family included, understand?"

The young man nodded and opened the door to the street. An aged brindled lurcher bitch waiting outside the door jumped up at him. He bent down to scratch her behind the ears. Sito – Alfonsito. Alfonso's son, without doubt. He was in his early twenties, as tall as his father, better looking, without the sallow skin or hooked nose.

"How old is your son?" Davina asked, looking at Maribel.

"Nearly twenty."

"And the girl is just eighteen," added the grandmother. "A year older than yours."

"And your other child?"

"Died of the typhus two months ago," said the grandmother in a matter-of-fact tone.

"I'm sorry," said Davina. *What had Alfonso been doing two months ago? Was that why he'd decided to join Franco's troops at his age? Had he broken his promise – or never kept it?*

And then the image of the tiny baby crying in its grandmother's arms came to her mind, poor little soul. She hunted for a handkerchief, then used her sleeve to wipe away the tears.

As if to terminate any further expression of sentiment, the old lady said, "She was always sickly. One less mouth to feed."

Davina looked across at Maribel; the once-pretty woman tried to smile.

Without another word, the grandmother got up, went into her room and closed the door behind her. She reappeared some minutes later, dressed in the peasant woman's uniform of black. From a rough pine dresser she produced a jug of olive oil, a bowl of salt and a heavy bread-knife and put them all on a wooden board on the square table. Maribel didn't move.

Sito returned with two long loaves of delicious-smelling bread tucked into his coat. The lurcher bitch tried to squeeze into the house behind him. Laughing gently, he pushed her out, "No fresh bread for dogs. Out you go." The dog whined behind the door. "Haven't we got anything for her? She's hungry," he said.

"You wiped your plate clean last night," said his grandmother. "What d'you suggest? We haven't got enough for ourselves. You'll have to get rid of her."

Sito tugged the crust end off a loaf and threw it out of the door. His grandmother aimed a slap at his head but he dodged her and sat down.

"Here, have some bread before this fool gives it all to an animal," she said to Davina as she cut one of the long loaves in two and split the two halves into four with her hands. In complete silence she picked up each quarter and poured thick green olive oil onto the warm bread. Then she sprinkled salt over the oil and set the four rations out on the board. They ate without exchanging a word.

Eventually, after they had eaten and were drinking bitter, sugarless chicory coffee out of thick glass tumblers, the grandmother looked at her grandson and said, "What did you bring her here for?"

The boy responded with a shrug. "She was running away."

"Running away?"

Davina nodded.

"So you weren't good enough for her ladyship, either?"

"Gran!"

"No, I'm going to tell her and then we'll all be straight."

Isabel Heredia looked hard at Davina. It wasn't hate and it wasn't revenge: Davina knew it was what the woman felt she had to say.

"He married you, abroad, and brought you here because none of the 'nice girls' in town would have him after he'd flaunted this silly madam around with him in the street." She indicated Maribel with a square hand but never took her eyes off Davina's face. "When they were younger than this streak of bacon sitting here," she indicating Sito, "they – I mean my daughter and her *señorito* – would go around together in the town, arm in arm in plain light of day! We told her, we threatened her. Her uncles would have done for him if I'd let them. We told her he just wanted his way with a pretty girl and he'd ditch her the minute she was expecting. Which he did. But then he came sniffing around again, didn't he?" She looked at her daughter.

Maribel stared into her coffee, tears rolling down her cheeks.

"Oh, he loved her," the grandmother continued, "said he couldn't live without her, wanted to marry her but his mammy wouldn't let him." She took a slurp of coffee. "Sito, your sister should be listening to this, go and wake her up."

"No, Gran, let her sleep. She doesn't need your poison."

"It's not poison, boy, it's God's own truth. Your mother lost her good name and all her chances, and we haven't got anything to live on but what you can bring in because –"

"*Mami*, that's enough," begged Maribel.

"Well," continued her mother, still staring straight at Davina, determined to finish her tale, "after he'd been seen with his arms around a girl from this side of town, and half gypsy into the bargain, that was that as far as all the 'nice girls' were concerned. None of them was going to be second choice to his bit of *gitano* black stuff and everyone knowing it." The woman folded her arms, "And all this time, his precious mother was on at him about the family name and the family business or I'm the Queen of Sheba. So there you are. He needed a wife for the family name, he found you in foreign parts and you were the only one in town that didn't know about our Maribel. But what you are doing here, when you've got his widow's pension, a big house to live in and his daughter to marry off into money and look after you in your old age, defeats me."

"She's not his daughter."

Three faces turned to her. The old lady's mouth opened and shut. "What?"

"Marina, my daughter, is not his child. I was pregnant when I married him."

The old lady started to chuckle. Her double chins started to wobble. She placed her hands on her knees and laughed so loud her face turned red and Sito had to get her a cup of water to stop her choking. She drank the water and wiped her face with her skirt, settled herself back into her chair and looked at Alfonso's widow with new eyes. "You can stay," she said. "Whatever you need, count on Isabel Heredia."

"Thank you," replied Davina in a whisper. "Please, would you let me have a few moments on my own? I need to gather my thoughts and decide what to do next."

The laughter had woken Maribel's daughter. She put a tousled head around the door and said, "What's the matter?"

"Nothing's the matter, child," replied her grandmother, beckoning her into the room. "Come here and meet your new auntie.

Chapter 34
Jerez, 1936

Davina was woken about ten o'clock by a commotion in the main room. It sounded like Sito and he was saying, "She'll have to stay here now."

"Don't be stupid, she's mad. She'll set fire to this house, as well." It was a man's voice with a heavy Andalusian accent.

"She's not mad." This was the grandmother. "But you're right, she can't stay. We've got enough problems of our own without the Guardia coming here, poking around."

"I'll take her down to get a boat in El Puerto," said the man.

"No, too many people know her. They'll tell the police or the Guardia – you can't hide a face like hers, she's as English as English." It was Sito's voice, he sounded very like his father.

"She'll have to go back where she came from." It was the grandmother again. Another matriarch deciding her life for her and telling everyone what to do. Davina sat on the side of the hard, narrow bed, listening to what was being decided for her. The grandmother was giving the visitor his orders. "If what you say is true – she did set fire to the house –"

"I don't think she did, Gran." Sito mumbled something else that Davina couldn't catch.

"Don't interrupt — what do you know? You're soft, too soft. The sooner she leaves this house and this town, the better for all of us. Paco, you take her to Gibraltar."

Davina heard the man splutter, "What! Me? She's none of my business. Gibraltar's miles away."

"People do the journey every week, twice a week — to bring back tobacco, whisky, dried fish. Take beans and flour with you to sell. Take brandy and change it for some decent rum, I used to like a drop of rum."

"I'm not going anywhere — I've got work for the next month with the harvest. I'm not giving that up for anybody." Paco sounded determined but Davina wasn't sure he was going to win against Isabel Heredia.

"Gran," intervened Sito, "how's she going to get to Gibraltar? We haven't got a car and it'd take a week to walk it — even if she could — which she can't."

"You can take her. Paco will lend you two mules. Load them with panniers for regular business." It was an instruction, not a suggestion.

"All right, I'll take her — but I'll have to fill in papers when we go through the villages, the Guardia are everywhere these days."

"Then don't go through any villages."

"And what about *bandoleros*? There's a bunch of cut-throat outlaws on that road."

"They won't touch a boy and his mother."

"They will if she's got yellow hair and speaks with a funny accent."

"Then don't give her a reason to speak! We'll cover her hair and she's got that cape thing to cover the rest of her. Don't go anywhere people can get curious."

"We'll have to sleep in the open."

"So? It's not winter yet. It won't kill her. Do her good: she can find out what real life is like."

"Gran, you've got an answer for everything!"

"I was a widow before your mother was born, how d'you think we've survived this long?"

From across the room Paco said, "Getting the mules will be difficult. Juanito is using them for the grape harvest."

"Then hire a couple of others or some horses for God's sake! She can pay. Just don't say where the money has come from."

There was a silence. Doña Isabel had lost her patience and the men were trapped into an enterprise neither of them relished.

Davina got up, straightened her clothes and went to the door. Opening it quietly, she said, "I can't pay anyone anything I'm afraid. I don't have more than a few pesetas with me."

Isabel Heredia looked at her. "They say you stole the old lady's money and set fire to the house, and you and the girl have run away."

"Set fire to the house!"

The man called Paco said, "It's not burnt down, just the rooms over the street. The sisters were in the street running about like headless chickens. Then the fire brigade got there and asked them where their Ma was. Firemen had to carry the old lady out." He was laughing in spite of himself. "No one hurt . . ." He paused and was suddenly very serious, "Where's your girl? She wasn't in the house, was she?"

"No."

"But she's not with you?"

"No."

"Did you set fire to the house?" Doña Isabel demanded.

"No."

I didn't, thought Davina, *but it will give me extra time before the old lady or Mari-Fe discovers the housekeeping money and all the fancy jewels are gone. They might even think it was a real thief taking advantage of the family tragedy, or one of Alfonso's left-wing enemies or . . .* Her thoughts were interrupted.

Paco said, "Right, then, I'll see about those mules." He looked at Doña Isabel and raised his eyebrows. She nodded and indicated the door. He left without another word.

It wasn't a pair of mules to ride – it was a leggy youngster pulling a rough wooden cart. The cart stopped outside the Heredia doorway. Sito was up on the driving seat next to his uncle. Paco jumped down and picked up Davina's bag.

"D'you want this under the seat or in the back?"

"Under the seat, please."

"Right, then, up you go."

Davina was hoisted into the cart. There were no embarrassing farewells. As Sito picked up the reins ready to move off, his grandmother said, "Wait. What's in the back?"

The sides of the cart were rough-hewn wooden boards, and the back folded down on strong metal hinges. The cart itself was fully loaded and covered in hessian sacks weighted down with flat stones. Doña Isabel opened the back and lifted a sack. "Well, praise the Lord! We'll have some of these."

There were earthy smelling potatoes in wooden crates, a box of sickly looking turnips, yellow pumpkins in a woven basket, and the rest of the cart was jam packed with melons. There were a number of the grey-brown-green, knobbly rugby-football melons called toadskins and at least fifty glossy, bottle-green watermelons smooth and as large as footballs. Doña Isabel pulled out an empty sack and Paco stuffed in a few kilos of potatoes, two pumpkins and a few of the heavy, knobbly melons.

"Not those toadskins, they give me indigestion," said the matriarch.

Paco and Sito rearranged the cargo and closed the back board. Maribel came out of the house and handed her son a cotton bag. "Cheese, bread and chorizo," she said.

"Ha," said Paco, looking up at Davina, "you may get drenched and you'll have to sleep outdoors, but we Heredias won't let you go hungry!"

Sito winked at his grandmother, "Don't forget to feed my dog, Gran, she'll be whelping in a few days or so."

They set off for the first stage, into the night. The newly shod mule clipped down the streets but they attracted no attention, and within less than an hour they were out on the road to Medina Sidonia.

"How long will it take to get to Gibraltar?" Davina asked.

"Four, five days, I think."

"Five days!"

"There are a lot of hills between here and the coast, and this is a mule cart," said Alfonso's son. "Not one of your fancy cars. And she's young, only just trained. I promised not to work her too hard."

"What's her name?"

"Name? I don't know. Mule?"

Davina smiled a wry smile. The creature had an owner who didn't want to overwork her because she was so young, but she didn't have a name. Or perhaps she did and Sito was too embarrassed to tell. "I shall call her Liberty," she said.

"Call her what you like, just watch her back legs, she's got a temper like my Gran and a kick to match."

"It's true then, what they say about mules."

"Of course it is."

That first night, they travelled under a clear sky and a harvest moon until they were well away from Jerez. In the early hours of the morning, Sito moved the mule off the road onto a stony track that led to a small reservoir. They pulled into a clearing among almond trees to make camp for the night. The ground was too damp to sleep on and they were too weary to empty the cart to sleep in it, so they arranged Davina's waterproof cape like a groundsheet under it and stuffed sacks around the iron spokes of the wheels for warmth and protection from draughts. Using a long rope, Sito tied the mule to a tree and made a bed for himself along the narrow front seat.

Once she was wrapped in her cocoon, Davina poked a hole between the sacks and looked out at the sky and the black-shadowed countryside around her. What an adventure! Then she heard the first wolf. The mule became restless. Sito got up and tied her closer to the cart.

"Sito . . ."

"It's only a wolf, sounds a long way away. They won't come near us."

"No. All right, I was just worried about the mule."

"*Ai*, the English and their animals. Go to sleep, you must be tired."

"Goodnight."

"Goodnight."

"Sito."

"Now what?"

"Thank you."

"Goodnight, señora."

The next day they ate cheese and bread and watermelon for breakfast. They took it in turn to go down to the water to wash, then Davina spent a happy half hour or so collecting fallen almonds, which she tucked away in one of the empty sacks. It was a glorious morning. Sito moved the mule out into the clearing to graze and tied her to a tree stump. Liberty pulled at tussocks of grass and set larks and goldfinches bounding up around them. Then the boy set the cart to rights and began the task of sorting out the mule's harness. Davina collected the remains of their breakfast, climbed onto the running-board and stowed the food bag next to her carpet bag under their hard wooden seat. Suddenly Sito leapt up beside her as a group of wild boar grunted out of the trees around them. The mule snorted and shot to the length of her tether.

"That was lucky," said Sito. "You wouldn't want to be on the ground with them so close."

"Are they that dangerous?" laughed Davina, somewhat taken aback by their size and fearsome tusks. "I didn't know they were so big."

"Big and nasty. Don't you have them in England?"

"I think there used to be – like bears and wolves – but not anymore."

The group of tusked boar shuffled off and Sito jumped back down on the ground to reorganise the harness and unravel the long reins. "Are you happy to be going back?" he asked.

Davina looked around at her surroundings: clumps of low, scraggy bushes, peppery smelling herbs; in the distance tall pines marched across a grey-pink horizon. The sky over Spain always seemed so much bigger than over England. She tried to visualise a Cornish sunrise. "I think I am. I shall definitely be happy to be back in our old house at Tamstock. It's so lovely. All covered in ivy and surrounded by hundreds of roses – like something out of a fairy tale."

"What's a fairy tale?"

"Well, it's a story about a young girl or a young boy, who has to leave his or her family home and they go through a series of difficult or dangerous situations with nasty witches, ugly people or monsters before they can get back to safety. Sometimes they are captured and locked up in castles and they have to escape. Sometimes there is a peasant boy, or a clever animal that helps them. Then they become rich, or they marry the boy or girl of their dreams, and live happily ever after."

"Sounds like a lot of nonsense to me."

"No, not all of it, Sito. The difficult situations – I think they may once have come from true stories and got exaggerated in the re-telling. Or they are what my tutor, Mr Jones, called metaphors. They mean something else more serious, like fables."

Because they had been chatting and busy about their chores they hadn't heard the sound of low branches being pushed aside, but the mule's long ears were moving this way and that and she shifted about nervously as Sito tried to pull on her harness.

"Sshh," he said, "there's a good girl, back up, back up, good girl, there you go – nearly done." Then Sito picked up the sound, too. "I think the boar are coming back, señora. Get in the cart." He tried to buckle the bridle faster. "Quiet you silly . . ."

Then they heard something that wasn't an animal.

"If anybody comes near us, don't speak," Sito said quietly to Davina. "Put on that scarf Gran gave you. And your cape. Keep covered up – and don't say anything."

Davina scrambled around, pulling on the soggy cape, tying the cotton headscarf under her chin. Then, feeling very nervous, she went to stand by Sito. He put out an arm and pushed the hood of the cape over her head.

"Get back in the cart."

"Why? What's the matter?"

"I don't know. Stay quiet."

The cart rocked as Davina climbed up onto the seat. She felt very vulnerable sitting there with a half-harnessed mule in front of her and no one at her side.

"We shouldn't have come so far off the road," Sito grumbled.

"No, my good friend, it was not a good idea."

A short, heavy man with string tied around an oversized jacket wandered into the clearing. He moved very close to Sito and waved a very long, very sharp-looking blade under the boy's chin. "Look," he said, "I've got a knife, so no hasty moves, eh."

Sito buried his head in the mule's warm brown neck and closed his hand over a rein. She still wasn't strapped into the traces; she could easily run off. Davina could see he was scared.

The *bandolero* was apparently pleased with the easy effect of his words and turned to Davina with a swagger. "Good morning, *señorita*. Curro Gonzalez at your service." He doffed a greasy cap, bowed elaborately and took a step toward the running-board. "Have you anything in your cart to feed a hungry hunter this fine morning?"

Davina looked at him, her eyes like saucers. She looked at Sito for guidance but the boy kept his face hidden. Slowly, she shook her head.

"What was that you said: "Of course, my good friend. Here, please have some bread and cheese and some of our wine, too"?"

Davina shook her head again. The *bandolero* was delighted with her apprehension and came closer to press his advantage. "Why not invite me up into your cart to share your company, darling?"

"Leave her alone!" shouted Sito.

"Your boyfriend is jealous, darlin'." Curro Gonzalez, reached up, ready to swing himself into the cart with his free arm. "You just tell him to keep quiet while we have a little cuddle, eh? You got a pretty face and I've got a lot more in my pants to give a girl a good time than him down there." He leered at Davina. "And what is that, eh?" he asked, indicating with his knife the Gladstone bag stuffed under the seat.

"Sito!" Davina screamed, eyes were fixed on the blade.

Sito waited until the man had lifted a foot onto the running-board then charged. He grabbed the outlaw round his middle, the knife flew out onto the rough grass and both men fell backwards. Sito rolled over, trying to grab the knife. Suddenly, there was a second outlaw standing over him.

"The boy wants a fight, Curro. Let him have it!" He kicked the knife out of Sito's reach, then bent as if to help the boy to his feet and kicked him in the ribs. "That's just a start, boy. Here's another, and another."

Sito rolled onto his stomach and got a rope-soled boot in his head. His nose began to bleed and he started to cry with the pain.

"Just a start, boy. Now get up and do as you're told."

Sito tried to get to his feet, but the smaller man called Curro pushed him back to the ground and shoved the blade of the knife under his nose. "Don't play with us boy. Get that mule harnessed and we'll have your cart and leave you alone. Mess around and you're dead – and your girl is our pleasure for as long as she can still breathe. Now move."

Sito scrambled across the clearing to where the mule had bolted. She was stomping around, snorting, with the reins tangled round her legs. Out of the corner of her eye, Davina watched him try to reorganise the leathers and back the mule up to the traces.

Curro now had a foot on the running board again, preparing to get back into the cart. Sito yelled, "Leave her alone. She's my mother."

"What, the mule's your mother?" Curro scoffed. "Ah, you mean this little female? Take a look at his 'mother' Salvi. See if she's still tender enough to satisfy us."

Davina, shaking with fright, tried to climb over the seat to get among the crates and melons. The long cape wrapped itself round her legs and she fell as she caught a foot on the backrest. The men laughed.

"Hey," said the one called Salvi, "fancy leather shoes for a countrywoman." He advanced toward the cart waving and leered up over the side. Sito made a run at him, but Curro jumped down and tripped him up and sent him sprawling to the ground once more. But only for a moment. Sito, who had grown up in a rough area, rolled himself under the front of the cart, scrambled out of the rear and jumped onto the neck of the knife-bearing Curro.

Salvi folded his arms, laughed and left them to it. Then he noticed the mule and ran to grab her reins before she could run off. Liberty skittered round and dragged him off balance. Salvi made a lunge for her bridle to manoeuvre her back into the traces, but the mule was young and very unsettled by everything going on around her; she shifted her haunches from one side to the other and refused to back up. Holding on to the end of the long reins, he reached for the whip standing in its place on the running-board then struck the mule across her neck with a hard, harsh swipe. She squealed and lashed out with her hind legs, catching him in the chest with two metal-shod hooves. She kicked again. Salvi doubled over and fell to the ground in slow motion. The mule shot into the safety of the nearby trees.

Sito was still trying to get Curro's knife. He had the outlaw trapped against the side of the cart and was smashing the man's hand against the wood. Then he misjudged and cut himself on the blade. He fell back, grasping his right hand.

Davina lost her patience. She picked up one of the heavy, rugby football-shaped melons and bashed it down on the *bandolero*'s head. In the tussle for the knife, the knot in the string that held his jacket together had got caught between the rough planks in the side of the cart. As he struggled to extract it, Davina smashed the melon down on his head again.

"That is enough!" she cried. "I have had enough of you bloody Spaniards." Whack. The man's chin jabbed down against the metal frame of the cart and the melon split open. Davina grabbed another. "I have had enough of you men!" Whack, whack. "Enough!" Whack. "Enough!" Whack. "All of you!" Whack "Trying to run my life." Whack. "Making me do what I don't want." Her hands moved up and down like an enraged piston. "Who the hell do you think you are?" Whack. "Leave me alone!"

"Señora, señora!" cried Sito, reaching up with a bloodstained hand. "Stop! Stop! I think he's dead."

Davina halted, a toadskin melon in mid-air. The *bandolero* was completely still, his head was hooked at an unnatural angle over the side of the cart and his body was limp.

She sat back among the fruit and vegetables and burst into tears.

Chapter 35
Andalucía, Spain, 1936

It was growing dark by the time Sito and his father's widow were able to converse in normal tones again. They had spoken only essential words as the mule was finally harnessed and hitched to the cart. As they had turned to go back up the stony track, Davina had scrabbled among the fruit and vegetables and emptied the sack of almonds she had collected so happily earlier that day. They made no attempt to cover their tracks.

The two men, whom they both assumed to be fatally injured, if not already dead, lay where they had fallen in the pretty clearing by the reservoir.

The day moved into evening and as the sun dropped behind the warm, red hills Sito said, "We shall have to stop soon. I'm hungry and this animal is tired out."

"Yes."

"There is a small town up over there. You could find a room for the night."

"No. I was comfortable enough last night, until . . ."

Sito said no more. They pulled off the road, made a hasty fire, ate in virtual silence and settled down to rest as they had the previous evening. Next morning Davina was horrified to find she had slept soundly and felt tremendously well. She prepared a breakfast of cheese and bread while Sito coaxed a little fire to boil some chicory coffee.

"Today we might see the coast. Then it will get flatter and easier for your Liberty."

Davina patted the young mule and fed her some crusts. "Good," she said, "eat up and let's go."

"What about the coffee?"

"Sito, that is not coffee!"

"It is in our house."

"Yes, sorry."

The mule was also refreshed and set off at a cracking pace. Sito said, "You started to tell me about England. Would I like it there?"

"That depends what you like. Do you prefer the city or the country?"

"I don't know. Tell me about London."

Davina conjured London fogs and double-decker buses, theatres, shops, and tea and cakes in copper-kettle cafés. A chill ran through her and she said, "You know, I think I must be made of strong stuff – like my Granny Dymond. When I think about it, I have been in some horrible situations and come out unscathed, well, almost, and then I let other people make decisions for me. Isn't that stupid?"

"Have you killed anyone else?"

Sito's almost matter-of-fact question brought Davina to a halt. She wasn't sure whether to be shocked by its implications, or simply amazed at the absurdity of it all. She said, "Not that I know of. But I have seen someone killed, I think, although perhaps he survived. Do you think those two men – do you think . . ."

"What concerns you, señora? That they are dead, suffering, or that you – we – might be accused of murder? If it's the last, forget it. The police and Civil Guard are far too busy with petty criminals and General Franco's war to worry about those two. Tell me about what happened in London, or wherever it was, and please, forget them."

Davina started to tell Sito what had happened in the tea-room in London with Leo. She had just reached the point where the mad soldier had fired the first shot when Sito put a hand out to silence her. There was a woman sitting beside the road in front of them. She had a bundle in her arms and a basket on a long strap over her shoulder.

"Let her ride with us," said Davina.

"No."

"She's got a baby."

"She'll bring us trouble."

"Don't be mean. Ask her where she's going and how we can help her."

Reluctantly Sito stopped the mule and got down to speak to the woman, who was no more than a girl and looked so exhausted she could barely answer him.

"This is Cristina," Sito said as he helped the young mother up into the cart.

Davina smiled at the girl and patted the hard seat next to her, then took the child from her arms. The girl returned her smile gratefully. Her face was haggard and tear-stained, her breathing laboured as if she had bronchitis. The child was very tiny, only days old. It opened large dark blue eyes and surveyed Davina, but did not cry.

"Boy or girl?" asked Davina.

"Boy. Jesús," said the young mother. "They've taken his father."

"Who has taken his father?"

The girl shook her head and tears rolled down her grimy cheeks.

"Sshh," said Davina. "You don't need to tell us anything, just rest. I'll look after baby Jesus."

"Where's your mother?" demanded Sito. "Your family should be caring for you. Why are you on your own?"

Davina was appalled by his aggressive tone.

"They shot my mother, and my brother. Over there." The girl pointed west, into the middle distance.

Davina froze. Had the world gone mad? Who would shoot a mother and her son? "Why?" she asked.

"For our field and the well. Someone told the men in the uniforms about my father and my husband, because they want our field and well. I didn't see what happened, I was in bed and he . . ." she sobbed, looking down at her tiny infant. "One of them came into our room. He saw us – but he didn't tell them. They didn't touch the baby and me. We're alive but they took my ma and my brother and they shot them, and they took my husband and my father – they've . . ."

"But this is barbarous! Who are these people?"

"Señora," said Sito, 'don't ask. Don't get involved. Leave her alone."

"But . . ."

"There are too many sides and too many unsettled debts. It's happening all the time now. People who want to get revenge for something, or want something they can't get any other way, are telling the Civil Guard all sorts of vicious nonsense and lies, and the Guard tells – I don't know . . . If they think you're a red, or someone says you're a Republican you're lost, haven't got a chance. Don't get involved, this is nothing to do with you."

Davina stared ahead of her. *Nothing to do with her*? Her daughter had gone away, had followed a young Republican into the thick of the war. She was in real danger. And she herself was not at all sure whose side she should be on.

The cart rolled on and the girl fell asleep with the steady rhythm. At midday they stopped at a roadside water trough for the mule to drink. Sito filled their water containers from the fountain. Davina was as stiff as the board she was sitting on and very uncomfortable with the child in her arms, but it was now apparent that the mother was running a fever and needed a doctor. She had refused to tell them where she was going or where she wanted to go, or anything more about her husband, so they decided to continue on their way and leave her at the first convent or hospital they could find. Sito cleared a space for her among the potatoes and melons and they drove on, with Cristina lying asleep or sobbing to herself in the back of the cart. Davina gave the baby water and a crust of hard bread to suck on, and in this way they reached the coast.

It was dusk of the fourth day when they finally identified the Rock of Gibraltar rising out of a bed of low cloud, like a crouched lion.

There was a queue a mile long or more. People of all sorts, in all manners of attire, were waiting patiently to get into the British protectorate. Hundreds of Spanish civilians, Britons and hangers-on were camped out on a no-man's land that had once been a race-course. Members of the Spanish Civil Guard ambled by on tired horses. Davina found their apathy unnerving.

The girl, Cristina, roused herself to feed her silent child, then handed him back to Davina and settled down again in her uncomfortable litter. Sito unharnessed the mule, tied her to the shafts and disappeared to talk with peasants and Moroccans waiting to sell their merchandise across the barrier in Gibraltar the following day.

At some time during the interminable night, a local Spanish policeman shone a torch into Davina's face and demanded her papers. Sito emerged from under the wagon and spoke to him. He waved his identity card and said something about his wife and mother in the cart. His wife was suffering from the *gripe* – or maybe typhus; he thought his mother and the child might have it as well. The baby was feverish, he said with a sad countenance, they needed a doctor but he would have to sell their melons first to pay for it. The young policeman traced his torch over the cart. Davina coughed and spat over the running board.

"Take your *peste* to the English," the policeman said, and left them in peace.

Davina was fast asleep, her arms soldered into right angles around the baby, when Sito nudged her awake some time after dawn.

"She's worse," he said, nodding at the girl behind them in the cart.

Davina turned stiffly in her seat. The girl's breathing was irregular and she was murmuring as if in the grip of a high fever.

"We'll have to leave her here; they won't let us in if she's sick," insisted Sito. "Unless I leave you here, and you walk across the border by yourself."

"No. No I am not going to abandon her here – and what about this little innocent? What'll happen to him if his mother can't feed him?"

Sito reached into the back of the cart and shook the girl's shoulder, "Cristina, tell us, have you got any papers?"

"In my bag. All my documents."

"Good. Don't speak now unless you have to."

"Señora," Sito said, looking up at Davina, "it is up to you. I can take the girl back with me, leave her at La Linea or the nearest convent, if they'll have her, or you can get her into Gibraltar with you. The mule and I will be happy with a rest, a good meal and the road back home. What happens next is for you to decide."

Davina smiled. "Let's get to the front of the queue and see what's what. First of all, this girl needs a doctor; it's probably post-natal fever. After that, we might as well sell your wares. I think you deserve a little profit."

"But what are you going to do about her? Leave her here or in Gibraltar?"

"She'll be safer in Gibraltar than where she came from. Look, Sito," Davina sighed, "some things are just meant to be. I have lost a husband and gained his son, I have lost my daughter but gained another – what do you want me to say?"

Sito laughed. "I cannot believe I can love the woman that made my mother's life so miserable. But I do." Climbing back into the cart, Sito gave Davina a big hug and a kiss. The baby woke up and started to cry.

Chapter 36
Gibraltar, 1936

Leo noticed the woman in blue holding a baby on the front seat of a vegetable cart because she reminded him of a Madonna icon. The cart was one of many making its way up the steep incline of Gibraltar's Main Street. They were letting in another Exodus. Franco's Nationalist warships were bombarding Republican-held coastal towns and the Gibraltar racecourse had been converted into a refugee camp. The British were letting refugees onto the Rock, but it was a tight squeeze, and each day their numbers increased.

He noted that the woman didn't look very Spanish but didn't stop to watch the weary-looking new arrivals more closely because he was on his morning round, popping into diverse cafés and bars for a coffee or a glass of wine, a small cigar and the time of day, gathering little gems from people such as Vincenzo from Genoa, who served excellent espresso and had a brother in Abyssinia. Leo knew a man who was very interested in Abyssinia and Mussolini. Manolo had a limp and a family in nearby La Linea; he also kept a smoky little cave in the city walls and sold sharp, chilled *fino* in chipped tumblers. His brother was with the Republicans in Malaga, at least he had been until Nationalist troops moved in.

Albert from Brighton kept the newspaper kiosk outside the infirmary. His wife's cousin Fred was with the King's

Own Yorkshires garrisoned on the island. They, according to Albert, were in serious training for a 'spot of trouble'. He didn't know where – yet. Today, however, Albert was bubbling with indignation about domestic matters.

"Have you seen them? Hundreds coming in since the early hours! All these foreigners! I mean you used to know who was who on the Rock – us from England and the Spanish families that have been here for generations. But nowadays you don't know, you just don't know who you're talking to – gotta watch every word in case you criticise the wrong side. And who's in the right, I'd like to know? Killing your own countrymen! It isn't natural. Our Fred says even the officers in the garrison can't say for sure who they should be siding with. And in the meantime – look at 'em, they're letting in anyone and everyone. Could be a lot of subversives and villains, for all we know. Could be letting in whole cartloads of criminals! I dunno – the missus says we might as well go home. Find a nice little place on the seafront in Hove. She's right. It won't be long before them gunboats start firing on *us*. That's what our Fred says, anyway, and he oughta know, him being with the Yorkies. Mind you, sir," Albert leaned precariously out of his cubicle to impart a state secret, "our Fred says the Yorkies *are* taking it seriously." He nodded conspiratorially as one who knew what was what.

Leo handed over his coins and nodded back, "Good to know we're in safe hands, Albert."

"I should hope we are! Because when there's trouble, sir, one thing always leads to another. You mark my words. One thing always leads to another."

"Indeed, Albert, indeed. Well, cheerio, see you tomorrow."

Albert touched his forelock without thinking and Leo strolled off, scanning the front page of his paper. The bachelor King of England caught in the lens with a married

American woman called Wallis Simpson; '*Birmingham nail factory closing down – three hundred to lose jobs*'; '*Strawberry harvest beats all records in Kent*'. Not a word about the Spanish civil war, Home Rule for India, Hitler's Germany or the Italian invasion of Abyssinia. The British press suffered from collective xenophobia. He folded the broadsheet and tucked it under his arm.

On his way back up Main Street, Leo decided to call in on Vijay at the Red Fort Bazaar to enquire after his mother, a perennially ailing, white-garbed widow. Vijay's uncle was back in jail for being too actively in favour of Home Rule. Leo was particularly concerned about this: English officers in the Indian Police Force had an unpleasant way of getting information out of detainees. If they got a whisper of the name Kazan he would have to get himself off the British-administered Rock of Gibraltar as fast as possible, and that meant leaving unfinished shop business of a personal nature as well. It had always been a risk but now he was genuinely concerned.

Leo sighed. After seeing Vijay, there would be no alternative but to return to the new Oriental Curiosity Shop. Hopefully Arnold would have finished his morning's Morse practice. The tap, tap, tapping irritated him beyond measure.

"There's more Spanish coming in, Arnold, country-folk, whole families of them. Albert at the kiosk reckons there'll be no water left by the end of the week if they go on like this."

"Someone's got to take them," Arnold Mackay replied. "There but for grace of God, Leo. You wouldn't be so flippant if you were trying to escape cut-throat natives."

"It's not quite like that, Arnold. Do you ever read newspapers?"

"Not anymore, I'm done with foreign affairs and other people's wars."

"Are you? In that case," Leo said, running a finger around the rim of a black marble vase, "why are you learning Morse? And who is on the other end of the line?"

"I didn't say I wasn't interested in saving my skin – or yours – if push comes to shove." Arnold shifted round so Leo couldn't read his features, but carried on saying, "From what I'm hearing we're a prime target for attack here. One day you might be very grateful."

Leo looked at Arnold's back and raised an eyebrow, "Are you planning brave adventures?"

"No," Arnold replied swivelling back to face him, "I am not. I'm not interested in anything except putting enough in the bank to live on in my old age, and knowing it's safe."

For a moment Leo felt a pang of regret for what he was doing, but his thoughts were interrupted by Arnold pointing a stubby forefinger at a tray of exquisitely painted drinking glasses.

"She's not coming again today, either," he said. "We'll have to do the dusting ourselves, again. Now where are you going?"

Leo picked up his hat from the counter and made for the shop door. "Down to the harbour, the *Star* is due in and I've heard there's a party of younger Baroda princelings on it. I intend to invite them to our humble emporium. Hopefully Her Highness will be with them and she'll very likely spend a fortune if I can get her up here; she has a passion for the valuable and unusual I'm told."

What he didn't say was, "The old Maharaja of Baroda has been running with the hare *and* the hounds over Indian nationalism for years, and I'm in touch with two of the younger men in his party, who are prepared to sacrifice the independence and British protection of their Princely State for the greater good of Mother India." If Arnold knew anything about Baroda, though, he gave no sign. Leo waited for a reaction and when none came, slipped out of the door saying, "I'll check the small ads at the tobacconist on the way down, see if I can't get another Mrs Mop for you."

"For me!"

"It's your shop Arnold, it was all left to you, I'm just the sales rep." The door bell pinged open. Arnold huffed and began shifting sprays of dust from one object to another with his favourite feather duster. "That's it," laughed Leo, donning his trilby, "don't forget to poke your chicken feathers over the brass cobra as well, see if he still bites. Bye."

As the door pinged closed behind him, Leo squared his shoulders and smiled. While Arnold was focused on his Morse and dusting he wouldn't be ferreting about in the account book. The Cravens' shop accounts in Bombay had been a work of romantic fiction, but those of the New Oriental Curiosity Shop in Gibraltar had all the ingredients of a horror story. *Softly, softly, catchee monkey.*

Setting this thought aside, Leo strode downhill, greeting new acquaintances along the way; there was other important business afoot. He needed to find out what had been discussed at recent meetings between the Baroda representatives and members of the Cabinet and Foreign Office in London, then get the information back to Delhi as fast as possible.

Reaching the quayside, Leo made his way along the crowded docks as best he could, stopping now and again to see if he was being followed, waiting behind vehicles to see who overtook him, standing before windows to see who was reflected. It was an ingrained habit. Gibraltar was a small, very British enclave, but he'd never forgotten that Viktor Grekov had unfinished business with him. Or that a nameless Soviet agent may simply want revenge for the loss of a female colleague. He didn't lose sleep over it, but it kept him wide awake.

Chapter 37
Gibraltar, 1936

The nurse evidently held a post of responsibility, there was a navy blue stripe around each of her cuffs. Her uniform appeared to be made of cardboard, and she wore a cap starched in concrete, with an expression to match. "Her pulse is too fast and she has a fever," she said accusingly at Davina. "We shall have to admit her."

A porter and wheelchair were summoned. The porter helped the emaciated Cristina into the seat and tucked a rug over her knees. Davina bent down to place the baby in her arms.

"And what do you think you are doing?" The nurse's accent was broad Scots, the tone outraged authority.

"Giving her her baby," replied Davina, not daring to make eye contact.

"Are you mad? She is undoubtedly contagious. I repeat, undoubtedly contagious."

"But . . ."

"No buts here, missy . . ."

Missy! Missy! Davina heard her mother's voice say, *And who, precisely, are you calling missy?* She stood up straight and thrust the baby into the nurse's arms. "Then you hold him."

The nurse accepted the little bundle as a reflex action then hissed, "We cannot have this child in the ward!"

"You'd better put him in the nursery, then, or find him a wet nurse, because he needs to be fed." Davina marched swiftly to the door of the infirmary.

The nurse, breaking a cardinal rule, ran after her, saying, "We cannot take this baby."

The new Davina, whose voice and manner were brisk and crisp, turned and looked the nightingale in the eye. "I am sorry, but *we* have done all *we* can do. This baby needs to be with his mother. A child should never be separated from its mother – no matter how good or bad one might judge them. I am not her family, and I cannot look after this baby until his mother is recovered, because I have got nowhere to live and nothing to feed him."

"But there are rules!"

"Yes, I'm sure there are. There is also your Christian duty. I have done mine, now you do yours. Get that poor girl better, and don't take her child away from her. She's already lost her mother, her husband and goodness knows who else in this madness."

"Ah, so she's a Spaniard from Spain. She's not even Gibraltarian."

"Neither am I, and neither are you, Nurse. Thank you. Goodbye."

Davina's hands were shaking and her heart was pounding as she stepped out of the smell of disinfectant and back into the noisy street. Sito was lounging against the cart smoking a cigarette, but he threw it down and stubbed it with his foot the moment he caught sight of her face. He stepped forward to greet her then turned, shouting, "Hey you! Clear off!" and ran round the side of the cart where a group of boys were helping themselves to his cargo.

By the time Sito had chased the boys away and returned, Davina had pulled her precious Gladstone bag from under the seat and was folding the waterproof cape over her arm. "I had better take this. You never know, I might need it again one day."

"Are you going now?"

"Yes, my dear. You have to sell your goods," she gestured to the cart, "before they all get stolen, and I have to find a room for the night, and passage to England tomorrow, if possible."

"But . . ."

"My goodness, what a lot of 'buts' today!" She was barely holding back the tears. The tension of the scene in the infirmary, the tiredness and the horrors of the past week had caught up with her. Above all else, she didn't want to lose this boy who had done so much for her.

Sito pulled a little notebook and a stub of pencil from a trouser pocket. "Tell me where you are going, señora."

Davina took the notebook and opened the pages. It was full of scrawling, forward-leaning handwriting. She looked at Sito questioningly. He shrugged, "I write things down."

"So I see. I hope you haven't written anything about me."

"No."

"And I hope you're not lying." Davina put the little book on the seat of the cart and wrote: *Crimphele House, Tamstock, Cornwall, England.* Then, underneath, she wrote: *Plymouth, then take train to Callingford Junction.* "There is a telephone, but I've forgotten the number. About Marina . . ."

"I shall find her for you. You will see her again soon. And I will kill that stupid Pedro!"

"If Franco doesn't shoot him first."

"Hmm, that's true."

"If you do meet him again, don't harm him. I have no quarrel with Pedro."

Sito shrugged, "As you wish. When I find Marina, what do you want me to say?"

Davina sighed. "Oh, I don't know. Whatever you think is right. We have a lot of truths to tell sooner or later. Tell her what you want her to know. But only if you think she is strong enough to take it. If you want to, and your grandmother agrees, come to England with her." She did not say she didn't believe a word they were saying: that she couldn't believe she was going to see her daughter again or that he would ever leave Spain. Putting her arms around the boy's shoulders, she hugged him. She was crying. "Go now, and make sure you sell all those dreadful melons before you start back."

"Every single one. And I'll tell my Gran why they give her indigestion."

"No, don't! Not a word to anyone – ever. Promise?"

Sito looked at her with a sheepish grin, "We Heredias are good at keeping secrets."

Davina arranged the cape over her arm and picked up her bag. "You haven't written anything about what happened, have you Sito?"

"What happened?"

"Oh," Davina waved a hand in the air, "just about everything." She tried to smile and said in English, "Bye-bye."

Chapter 38
Gibraltar, 1936

Leo noticed the woman struggling up the street with the Gladstone bag for three reasons: she had an unfashionable mass of long golden hair blowing romantically in the autumn breeze, she was carrying what appeared to be a waterproof cape on a bright, sunny day, and she was wearing the Madonna-blue dress. It was the woman he had seen on the cart earlier that morning. As he neared her, he noted that she was older than he had first assumed and, as their paths crossed, realised the long romantic tresses were unusual for a woman of her age. Under other circumstances he would have found an excuse to speak, to help her with her bag, but he had important matters to attend to, plus he wanted to exploit any possibility of the Maharani viewing his private, ex-biscuit tin collection in the shop. Apart from all that, indeed, on top of all that, the Barodas were linked by marriage to the lavishly spending, bright young things of Cooch Behar, who were among the P&O Liners' best passengers. Business was business, especially as profits from *all* sales were being directed into his new Gibraltar bank account.

*****

Davina lugged the bag up the hill, stopping now and again to look in a shop window or examine the outside of more modest hotels. She was also keeping an eye open for somewhere to sell what she thought of as her loot, and some sort of shipping office. A bookseller's sign caught her attention. Books in English. How wonderful, she would come back and buy at least one for her voyage home. There was a copy of *Jane Eyre,* but the prices were in sterling and she only had pesetas. She would have to change Doña Mercedes' housekeeping money at a bank. First, though, selling the old woman's jewellery was a priority. Unless she found a room first . . . Her head was spinning. "Oh, God, what a mess," she sighed.

Taking refuge on the edge of a water trough, Davina tried to gather her thoughts and put them in order. She sat there for a while, gazing down the street at nothing in particular. Her stomach rumbled; she hadn't eaten since very early that morning, and even then it had been only a crust of stale bread and a drop of water. No wonder she was dizzy. In the distance a man stopped to look directly at her. Embarrassed, she tried to wind her loose hair back into a bun, but she had lost all her hairpins.

Davina flushed hot and cold; she hadn't put up her hair after that first night in the clearing. The pins would be on the ground where she had slept under the cart. A little nest of straw-coloured English hairpins. Evidence. A sneaking, unwanted doubt crawled into her head. What had Sito written in his little book? He owed her no favours. She was after all – from his point of view – responsible for his family's poverty and his mother's unhappiness. Was Sito going to report her to the British police? Or tell the Spanish Guardia Civil she was a thief, an arsonist and a murderess?

"Will this ever end?" she said aloud and got to her feet again.

Leaving the commercial area, Davina wandered down Rosia Road looking at houses bearing B&B signs and selected one because she liked the name: Roseland. The landlady showed her a room. It was stuffy and flowery but not unpleasant. Bright pink curtains festooned with posies, a pale green flounced counterpane of oversized roses and everywhere a lingering odour of lavender-scented furniture polish.

"Yes, thank you, this will be fine," Davina said. The landlady handed her a key and stood waiting. "Oh, um, yes, sorry. I've only got Spanish money at the moment."

"No, no. Good heavens, lovey, this is a boarding house not the Ritz. I'm not after a tip. I was wondering if you would like a cup of tea, you look a bit a peaky."

Davina slumped on the soft bed, "That would be wonderful."

The landlady hobbled off down the landing and Davina sat staring at the curtains, trying to summon enough energy to open a window. She was nearly asleep when the landlady returned.

The woman bustled in with a loaded tray; tea and biscuits, and a little bottle of Scotch. "I should've said – thought about it while the kettle was on – my name's Emma Sangster." She looked at Davina, who was trying to sit up and be polite. "No, my duck, you drink this and have a good sleep. I know a troubled heart when I see it. Should do, I've had three husbands and never been married to one of them. I know what it is to be in what my old mum called 'troubled times'. She settled the tray on the small bedside table then folded the far side of the counterpane over Davina's legs. "I said you looked done in," she muttered. "Have a good sleep and we'll see what later on brings in the wind."

As the plump landlady closed the door softly behind her Davina sank back into a feather pillow. She slept until late in the afternoon and woke with a start. The room was stifling. She got up and staggered to the window. It opened onto a spectacular sea view. Gulls swooped down over rooftops, further below there was the banging and clattering of the naval base. It was all so alien and yet strangely familiar. "I shall stay for as long as I can," she said to the Atlantic Ocean. "I shall stay here and get myself sorted out before I go home and start again."

Davina suddenly felt lighter, fresher, eager to be doing something. She stripped off her dirty dress, washed her hair with the meagre froth from a lump of yellow Sunlight soap then gave herself a thorough stand-up bath at the washstand. After putting on a clean but very crumpled frock from her dusty bag, she spoke aloud to the newly single woman in her wardrobe mirror, "I'll buy some cologne or maybe some real perfume. From now on, I'm going to do what I want, when I want. No grieving or regrets. It's time to look forward, not back. Time to find the real me and take her back to England."

Her new resolution and positive attitude lasted less than two hours.

*****

Leo recognised her as the icon lady from the cart the moment she walked through the door. She had tied her hair back with a scarf, but it was definitely the same person. He also recognised her situation: she had come to sell and she was embarrassed because she needed money. He stepped forward, "Good morning, may I help you?"

Arnold, who was polishing candlesticks at the back of the shop, looked up to see what was going on. Leo saw his head peering round a glass case of ceramic thimbles and little bells, and winked. Arnold's eyes narrowed and he returned to his polishing.

J. G. Harlond

The woman was holding a Gladstone bag in two hands before her. She stared around the shop, taking in the glass cabinets, the open trays of silver spoons and fancy cake knives, the shelf of Babushka dolls in red dresses, a filigree fire-screen and its accompanying poker. Her eyes came to rest for a moment on the brass cobra, still rearing, forever unsold, at a very mottled mongoose. "What an Aladdin's cave!" she said.

Leo grinned with pleasure. "It is, isn't it?"

She moved towards the Georgian table in the centre of the shop to get a closer look at the mother-of-pearl pill boxes and jade-handled paper-knives displayed on its polished surface. "I saw the rings and things in your window. You say 'gold bought', so I've . . ." Her bag bumped against the edge of the table and she jumped back. "Oh! Sorry! Gosh, I had better be careful here."

Leo knew the voice: the 'gosh'. Where? When? He couldn't remember, so he said, "Would you like to show me what you have brought us? Over here." He led the lady, for she was a lady, to his leather-topped desk, and held out a chair. She sat down, pulling the large bag close to her chair, patting it with her right hand as if it were a pet dog.

Once she was settled, Leo lowered his large frame into a bentwood chair facing her and said, "I'm sure you have something special for us." His tone was reassuring. Out of the corner of his eye he watched Arnold moving closer, selecting another item to clean within earshot.

The lady – Leo calculated she was in her mid to late thirties – opened her bag and hurriedly removed some items from a side pocket. "I have these." She laid out some earrings.

"I hope you have their partners."

"What? Oh, yes. That was silly." She rummaged again, "Here they are."

Leo picked up an eye-glass and examined two sets of drop earrings.

"Those ones are from Columbia, I think, well the stones are," she gushed.

"Yes, yes. And this pair is set in white gold. Quite unusual. What else?"

Looking a little more confident, the lady opened the bag wider and delved in. She laid out various pearl necklaces, a diamond brooch, a sapphire pendant and then an array of mismatched earrings and bead necklaces. Leo touched the pearls to his teeth – imitation. The ones on the shorter strand with a broken clasp were real. The diamond brooch was paste. Everything else was jumble sale gewgaws.

Nevertheless, Leo examined each item professionally without speaking. The Colombian emeralds were of value; the rest was very ordinary. He removed his eye-glass and portioned the items into three groups. The woman watched his hands and flushed scarlet. She looked up and met his gaze.

Leo started to say something but she interrupted him. "It's all macaroon, isn't it? Scaramouch!" she blurted in a panic.

"Scaramouch?"

"What's the word for worthless diamonds?"

"Mackbar?"

"That's it. Mackbar. Base diamonds."

"Yes. Do you know about diamonds?"

"No! No, nothing. I – someone told me once." She began to scoop the jewelry on the table together. "I'm sorry. I didn't mean to waste your time."

"Stop, please." Leo tried to stay her hand with his but she snatched it away as if he were a leper. Confused, he said, "We shall be pleased to buy everything."

"Ai, ai, ai," murmured Arnold from beside the centre table.

Leo went to the till and removed the entire day's takings. He counted it then added a ten-pound note from his own wallet. Arnold, who was watching him, cleared his throat meaningfully. He ignored him, put the money in a buff envelope and returned to his desk.

"Now if you can just tell me your name and address, for our records, we shall be all fair and square." He took a sheet of paper from the desk drawer and sat down again to write, saying, "One hundred and twenty pounds, seven shillings and sixpence to Miss? Mrs . . .?" The lady just stared at him. "No receipt needed?" Leo cocked his head on one sided, questioningly.

"No, thank you." The woman grabbed the envelope and crumpled it into her fist without looking at it. She stood up ready to go, knocking the chair backwards with her legs.

"Is there anything here in the shop you would like, perhaps?"

"I don't want to buy anything, thank you."

"As a small gift, I meant."

Arnold, who was now examining the empty till, slammed it shut with a clang. The shop bell pinged and the lady was gone.

Leo looked about him, surprised and thoroughly unsettled by the stampede exit. Then he lunged from his chair, grabbed the Gladstone bag and rushed for the door.

"Quick, you've nearly lost her!" shouted Arnold with all his old sarcasm.

*****

"D'you want to talk about it, lovey?" said Emma Sangster. "I'm the only discreet landlady in the whole world. You can trust me not to tell a livin' soul. What you say stops in this kitchen, right here in this teapot. Anyway, no one's listened to a word I say since my boy Jacko went to France and never came home again." She poured tea into a wide eau-de-nil cup and rattled on, "I bought a budgie after that, back in 'fifteen. He never talked to me, neither. He was a good listener, though, 'til he died. Got a bit o'seed stuck. I never got another one. Just lookin' at 'em now makes me think of that war."

"That's how it started," mumbled Davina, "with the war."

She began at the Armistice party and went on through two more cups of thick tea uninterrupted, until she killed a man in a clearing by a reservoir and then travelled four more heart-stopping days in a mule cart with a girl probably suffering from typhus and her baby, and arrived on the Rock of Gibraltar, only to come face to face with the father of her lost daughter.

There was a silence. Eventually Emma Sangster said, "And I thought I'd lived." She got up, "You need a brandy, my girl. This tea'll rot our guts, the way we're goin'." She bent down and pulled a bottle from a peppery smelling sideboard, then put two tumblers on the table. "So now what you goin' to do?"

"You tell me, Mrs Sangster."

"All right then. Tea might rot your gut but the leaves come in handy." She pointed at the dregs in Davina's cup, "Swill that lot round and tip it in the sink. . . That's it. Now hand it over 'ere and let's see what's what."

There was a rat-tat-tat on the back door.

"Sit down. Don't answer it – we're busy. Now, give me that cup."

As Davina handed her the cup, the door opened.

It was Leo. Behind him stood a policeman.

"I said give me the cup, not rub the sodding pot!" laughed Emma Sangster, too loudly. "Here sit down, girl, before you fall down – I'll deal with this."

Chapter 39
Gibraltar, 1936

Emma Sangster, landlady of *Roseland Guest House*, Rosia Road, bustled to the door, "I've got a front door, you know, what you two doing coming round the back like the baker's boy?"

The policeman saluted. The gentleman in the navy serge suit raised his hat. Davina tried to pretend she didn't know him and did as her landlady insisted – let her deal with it.

"Come in, if you must," Emma Sangster huffed. "Just watch yerselves, this lady has gone and picked up a touch of something very nasty. I shouldn't be surprised if it isn't highly contagious, so don't come too near."

Neither of the men moved to enter. The policeman eyed Davina with alarm, "You first, sir," he said, addressing the gentleman at his side.

"No, no officer. You are in uniform and on duty, you first." The man's eyes registered the kitchen and the contents of the table. Davina felt herself being assessed, scrutinised from the back door. She stared, unspeaking, first at him then, white-faced with terror, at the policeman.

"Yes, right, I won't take up anybody's time, just need to ask Mrs Sangster a couple of questions on behalf of the sergeant," the British bobby said.

Emma Sangster flapped her fat arms, "Oh, come in, come on in. Do I put the kettle on or are you really not stopping?"

She spoke to the policeman, but Davina could see she was keeping a beady eye on the big man in the dark suit carrying her travelling bag.

"He's classy and no mistake," she whispered into Davina's ear as she returned to the kitchen table to stand protectively at Davina's side.

The bobby removed his helmet and smoothed back his gingery hair. 'D'you remember me, Mrs Sangster? I stayed here a couple of years ago with my missus, when our flat got flooded. Gordon Scott from Cardiff."

"Oh, yes, the Welsh Scotts. Pretty as a picture, your wife."

"That's what I tell her, Mrs Sangster. Mind you, she's put on a bit since she was here. Got a sweet tooth, and after the last nipper, well . . ."

"Another one, oh dear. Are you wanting to stay again? I'm awful sorry, I'm fully booked."

Davina looked at Emma Sangster, it wasn't true. Why should her landlady do herself out of business to protect a woman she didn't know?

"No, no, this is official, not . . ." The Welsh policeman swivelled his eyes in Davina's direction meaningfully.

"Shall we go into the sitting room then, where it's private?" Emma Sangster said.

"Good idea."

The landlady and the policemen left the kitchen, but Leo – Davina was certain it was Leo – was still at the door. She couldn't breathe: had he had gone straight to the police with her stolen goods? What sort of man would do that after . . .? Or had it been Sito? Had he gone to the Gibraltar police to tell them everything after all? She wondered if the man could hear the beating of her heart against her ribs – then she wondered if Emma Sangster might not be right, she had picked up something nasty. "Please, God, let it not be typhus," she whispered, closing her eyes.

When she opened them again Leo had stepped over the threshold and removed his hat. Davina tried to think of him as just a man – any man – as simply the jeweller who'd examined her loot. But she couldn't, because this particular man was her daughter's father.

And right at this moment he was standing within a yard of her, examining a variety of knick-knacks and souvenirs on her landlady's crowded sideboard. One by one, he picked up a wooden lighthouse with razor shell inlays set on a cockle shell rock that said 'A present from Scarborough' and various vaguely identifiable animals with shell ears and tails from Southsea. He put each one back in its place, then stooped to examine more closely 'Our Lady of Lourdes' done out in a crinoline of varnished winkles. Smiling, he turned to look at her, "Fascinating – such a lot of work, such patience. I have brought you your bag, by the way." He indicated her travelling bag by the door.

"Thank you."

"We do know each other, don't we?"

"Yes."

"You are the diamond Dymond girl with a 'y' – but I have to make a confession, I have forgotten your first name. It begins with a D, only it's not Daphne or Dorothy." He gave her a heart-stopping lopsided, one-dimpled grin, "Something beginning with D, though, isn't it?"

"Davina."

"Of course, 'Davina'! London, and the uncut stones. I have never forgotten, and I have never done that since, you know – shown a girl how to judge diamonds. I should have guessed at the 'mackbar'. I am getting forgetful in my old age."

"Middle age. We are middle-aged now."

"Actually, not quite, I am as old as the century and this is 1936, so not the middle – well, yes, of the human span, I suppose. You don't look middle-aged at all."

"I certainly feel it and a lot more. Mrs Sangster is right – you had better not come too close."

"Look, I'd be blind not to see the effect that uniform had on you. Can I suggest that your fever demands immediate quarantine? Up you go to your room, and no one to be admitted except the good landlady and myself. You have, after all, spent the last few days in my constant company, so I must be immune."

He was bossy and bustling, but Davina had no energy to stop him organising her.

"I don't think that bobby is here for anything related to what one might call a 'personal nature', though," he continued. "There are at least two thousand refugees on the Rock now, not enough drinking water, and typhus has come in from across the border."

"That's where I have come from – across the border."

"Yes, I think I saw you. But that's good, much better. There's serious fighting in Ronda and Seville and I don't know where else. You are much safer here. Only you arrived at least a week ago, don't forget that. I can vouch for it, if necessary."

Davina looked at Leo – she had never forgotten *his* name. Why was he trying to help her? Why offer her an alibi, what could he possibly know? She put a hand to her brow and pressed down on her eyes. "I'm sorry, I do feel very unwell."

"Up you go then." Leo was taking charge again. He helped her to her feet and guided her by the elbow into the hall. "Can you manage the stairs all right? My God, what a carpet! Enough to make anyone dizzy. There you go."

As Davina let him assist her up the stairs, she came to her muzzy senses and was just fast enough to close her bedroom door sharply in his face.

For a moment she leaned her head against the glossy painted wood then turned and slumped to the floor on her bottom like a rag doll. How dare he barge in after nigh on twenty years and start telling her what to do. Her left temple throbbed, her left eye-lid flickered. She scrambled to her feet and got to the basin just in time before she was sick. Migraine: hardly surprising. Davina washed out her mouth, reached up to close the curtains then vomited again and staggered to fall face down on the bed.

When she awoke, there was a fresh sea-breeze in the room and a vase of roses with a card tucked into them on her dressing table. As if by telepathy, Emma Sangster appeared with a tray of lemonade and ginger biscuits. "You're awake, then?"

"Yes, I think so. What day is it?"

"Monday."

"Monday!" It was still only a week since Alfonso had died. "What happened on Sunday?"

"I made roast beef and Yorkshire pud and Mrs Crabbe, who's got Bella Vista two doors down, came in for a chat. Oh, and your Mr Kazan came round in the afternoon with these nice roses. Now, can you get up? There's a bath running with some of my lavender bath-salts and then he wants to see you."

"And you think I ought to see him."

"I do. He's got lovely manners, nice eyes, and a few bob in the bank by the look of him. And it's about time you had a bit of fun." Emma Sangster stood back, arms folded over her ample bosom. "Mind you," she chortled, "I always was a terrible judge of men."

Davina didn't hear her, she had remembered the policeman. "What did the bobby want?"

"Nothing to do with you, dearie," Mrs Sangster replied, moving to the window to open the curtains. "The sergeant wants to stay here while they're doing up his new flat."

"Oh, for heaven's sake! Sorry, what did you say about men again?"

"Men? Can't remember. Come on then, up you get and into that nice bath. You'll feel brand new after."

Leo and Davina dined in a small sea-front restaurant on the Atlantic side of the Rock. They chatted about how Gibraltar felt like an island, about Arnold Mackay and laughed about his obsession for dusting and polishing, about rare items in the New Oriental Curiosity Shop; about Spanish wine and the serious problem of drinking water; about absolutely everything except themselves. Coffee was served, Spanish brandy poured and darkness fell. Gradually the golden drink worked its magic, Davina began to feel the tension in her neck and shoulders relax, she leaned back in her chair and smiled.

Leo returned her smile then, after a brief pause, said, "I have three secrets I want you to know."

"That sounds like three too many, and far too serious."

"That is why I have kept them secret." He swilled the brandy around its globe and avoided looking at her. "I have a daughter, a father I do not know how to talk to, and a fortune's worth of uncut stones in a bank vault."

Davina laughed. "Well, if you want to play 'truth, forfeit or dare', I have a daughter, who does not know her father; I've stolen jewels that unfortunately weren't worth a fortune – and I think I killed a man. So there. Oh, and I lost my virginity to a passing stranger when I was eighteen."

Leo looked at her and burst out laughing. "My lady, you leave me speechless."

"Good, because I really, really do not want to continue this conversation."

The waiter came to the table with a box of Havana cigars and halted the macabre game.

Davina gazed out to sea while Leo selected a medium-sized cigar, cut and lit it. For a few moments he puffed at the Cuban tobacco then he said, "I'm sorry, but I wanted you to know."

"My husband died just over a week ago, and my daughter has run off with her young man to join this damned civil war, and it is all so dangerous . . . I'm sorry, as well, but this is all too soon for me. I should like to go back to Mrs Sangster's now. Tomorrow I have to arrange my passage back to England."

"Tomorrow! Can't you stay a little longer?"

Davina shook her head without looking at him.

"I shall accompany you on the voyage, then."

"No! I want to go home by myself."

Leo leaned across the table and patted her hand, "Sshh. I'll pay the bill and we'll go."

They walked in silence up the steep streets of the Rock. Gharries were available but Davina wanted to walk. As they traversed the unusually silent town, she said, "I was being selfish in the restaurant. You wanted to tell me about your daughter."

"It's not important."

"Yes it is. You wanted me to know."

They stopped in the Alameda gardens and sat on a bench. The scent of jasmine hung like a zenana screen in the still night air, separating them from the real world. Slowly, Leo told Davina about his old-fashioned courtship of Kitty, how he had asked her father for permission to marry her and how he had left her for months and months on end to go travelling in foreign countries. He told her about his lovely little girl called Ellie and stopped after Millicent Cleaver's account of the fire, unable to continue.

"Does this daughter know she still has a father?" asked Davina quietly.

"Yes."

Davina sighed, "Good."

"But it is all so difficult." Leo squeezed Davina's hand. "She is with my father. She's quite safe because I know Millicent will look after her but . . ." He sighed, "It's too much to tell in one night."

"Why, Leo, why is it too much?"

"Because . . . Do you believe in the Wheel?"

Davina shook her head. "You mean, 'what goes around comes around'?"

"No, not that exactly – although, yes, I suppose you could see it like that. I mean, I knew my father existed when I got to London and met you. I actually half knew about him when I was a boy in Bombay. Various people insinuated, but they never actually told me outright and I was too young to do anything about it – so – well, I pretended I didn't know anything about him. I pretended I hadn't got a father – because I had chosen someone else for that role. I didn't want to be a Russian, I wanted to be English. I didn't want to be one of Britain's old enemies. So I ignored him and spent as much time as I could with an Englishman." Leo paused and folded Davina's fair, freckled hand gently into his.

"So who looked after you when you were little?" she asked.

"I grew up in a British orphanage, and sort of spent a lot of time with a high ranking IPS family. That's why I speak the way I do. English people think I'm frightfully old-fashioned la-di-da, but it's the way I learned to speak you see. I copied them."

"So who is Millicent?"

"How do you know about Millicent?"

"You just told me. You said Ellie is all right because she's with Millicent."

"Did I?"

A blackbird hopped among branches above them, pinking a warning, telling them to go home. Davina said, "Blackbirds always make me think of England. Whenever I hear them, I can see them hopping around the sundial in Tamstock."

"Mmm," Leo was suddenly back in a leafy London street, he lifted Davina's hand and kissed it then noted her furrowed brow in the moonlight and leaned over to kiss her nose. "Sitting down there at that table, I was thinking what life might be like if I hadn't . . ." He faltered, his charm, his skill with words, his talent for getting what he wanted, all forsook him in a moment of truth. "I came back to see you in London," he said. "The maid told me you'd married and moved to Spain."

Davina said nothing.

There was a sudden guffaw of laughter, followed by obscenities. A group of drunken sailors swayed into the gardens. One stopped to throw lewd comments at them but on catching sight of Leo's scowl in the lamplight, turned away.

"Actually, I thoroughly dislike Gibraltar," Leo said, watching them stagger off.

"Then go back to India, spend time with your daughter and make peace with your father, if he will let you. Honestly, Leo, I think we both need to sort ourselves out before . . ."

He sought her lips, kissed her, then her words sank in. "Before what? If you are talking about priorities, this is what

I suggest: I have a beautiful suite of rooms with spectacular views of the harbour, some new gramophone records –"

"Oh, no," Davina laughed, separating herself and straightening her dress. "Not so fast. Not this time."

"Ah, well, we have time. Now I have found you I am *not* going to let you run away again," he replied, grinning his dimpled grin. "Forget booking a passage anywhere. I simply shan't let you go."

Davina turned and looked him in the face. "What gives you the right to give me orders? I said I wanted to go home, back to England, and you're treating the matter as a whim."

Amused by her annoyance, Leo kissed her on the forehead and said, "But you do want me to escort you back to Mrs Sangster's now, like a proper gentleman."

"Absolutely. Like a proper gentleman."

At the gate to *Roseland*, Davina put her arms up around his neck and Leo was tempted, very tempted, to pick her up and carry her back to his hotel. Then she froze. "A policeman," she whispered, seeing a bobby walking his evening beat. The uniform made her shudder. "One day the Spanish police will trace me to Gibraltar. I'm sorry, I have to go, and as soon as possible."

*****

The next day, Davina reserved a berth on the *Ranpurna* for the following Friday. The ship was returning to Tilbury, calling at Plymouth. Very soon she would be safely back in old Tamstock.

For each of the remaining days, Davina met Leo in the afternoon. They dined together at the new Rock Hotel, where Leo did indeed have a beautiful a suite of rooms on the top floor. Their lovemaking was tranquil and joyous. It was as if they had been lovers for years. Two happy people who never tired of each other's face, of kissing eyelids and gently biting lower lips, of running hands over bodies that were now fuller and softer, and so very easy to understand.

Leo told her he loved the opulence of her breasts, their roundness, the hard, darkness of the nipples. He said he liked the texture and smell of her hair when it fanned out across the pillows. Then he said he loved her.

"Utterly, completely and all the superlatives you can think of."

"Oh, Leo," Davina laughed, "only you could mix love and grammar."

"Is that a criticism?" Leo rolled away from her, hurt at what he considered a criticism.

"No, silly, I think it's lovely," Davina reached out for him, but he sat with his back to her on the side of the bed and ignored her touch.

"A pity I don't smoke," he said, "this would be a good moment." There was a silence between them. Leo pulled on his dressing gown and went to the window.

Davina bit back tears and started to get dressed. She had insisted on returning to Roseland before each night was over, knowing that if she stayed one whole night she might never leave Gibraltar, and she had good reasons to go. This time round, she told herself, she must let her head rule her heart.

Standing at the door to the room she said quietly, "I'm sorry, Leo. I do love you very much, but I *have* to go. I can't walk out of one life straight into another, not when my heart is dragging me home as well. I yearn for my home. Can't you understand that?"

Leo spoke without moving. "Not really. I would like to say I do, but I don't, not really. I suppose – I've never really thought about it – but I suppose I've always put people before – what – land? A place? Bit ironic considering what I was doing for so many years, but I was doing it for people . . . not a country."

Confused, Davina came to his side. "What do you mean?"

Leo shrugged, "Water under the bridge."

"But is there nowhere that calls you back? Have you never had a proper home?"

"No." Then Leo spun round, "But I'd like to make one with you."

"In England? Oh, Leo that would be wonderful! Come to England – but not yet."

"Not right away, not on the steamer with you?"

"Give me a few weeks to get settled, a month, say. Give me some time to myself, please."

"Why, so you'll have time to write to me and tell me not to come, a 'Dear John' they call it, don't they?"

"No! I shan't do that. I love you."

"Then what is your doubt?"

Davina shook her head slowly, "I don't have a doubt – not like that, not about us. It's – I just need to be on my own for a while – at peace. I want to find myself, if that doesn't sound too silly."

Leo put his arms around her and Davina let herself fall against his wide chest. He made her feel safe, protected, he loved her and she loved him: why then did she want to get away from him and be on her own? It was absurd.

"You'd better give me your address," Leo said, as he walked her back along Rosia Road.

On the Friday morning they stood side by side on the North Harbour quayside waiting for the *Ranpurna* lighter.

Davina watched a swoop of raucous gulls heckling a fishing boat and her heart beat faster. Facing the sea, she pulled the ozone into her lungs and wanted to laugh and cry all once.

"We don't have to stay here in Gibraltar," Leo said. "I mean I don't *have* to stay here because of the shop. I'll be going back to India before the end of the year, anyway. We could go there together."

"What?" Davina hadn't been listening.

"Look," he continued, squeezing her shoulders, "I know you said it was too soon for you, but I think even if I have only been in your life these few short days . . ."

Davina didn't hear the rest. She was lying in a young man's arms in a stuffy room behind velvet curtains; she was arching her back in the sweat and agony of childbirth; she was watching two sturdy legs and a bob of black hair whoosh down a slide: *'Look, Mamá, look!'*

"Leo," she said, "you have been in my life for *all* my life. What are you saying?" She flung her arms up around his neck and hugged him until her feet came off the ground. "Are you asking me to –?"

"Come with me to Bombay."

Davina's heart sank. "No."

"But why?"

"I told you. We have to sort out our lives first. Go back to your daughter. Make sure she is all right. She must miss you terribly. Then come to England. I want to see you by the river. I know it's silly, but I want to see you in a place where I know I belong."

"In that case," said Leo, hurt beyond words, "you had better have this now." He reached into an inner pocket and extracted a flat, square package wrapped in white linen. "Please don't open it until you have passed Trafalgar."

Davina accepted the gift and began to stow it in her travelling bag. Leo winced and said, "Better keep it on you, just while you get aboard – bags get lost sometimes." She started to put it in her handbag. "No, really, much safer if it's actually on your person. Can you get it down the front of your dress?"

Davina laughed, "No much room there for this."

"Try, it'll be safer."

Davina opened her front buttons and pushed the package down as far as her waistband. She laughed, "I look like Mrs Sangster now!"

Before she climbed into the ship's lighter, Davina said, "Come to England Leo, please. Come to Cornwall and see me where I have been happy." There were tears in her eyes and her voice caught on a sob.

Leo nodded but kept his own misted eyes lowered, "Soon, I'll come soon."

*****

As Leo waited until the lighter reached the *Ranpurna* a sense of loss settled under his left rib cage. Losing so much in one single morning nearly unmanned him. He turned and strode away from the quay without looking back, torn between three loyalties: his daughter, his country, and the woman he loved.

*****

Davina defied Leo's instructions and opened the package as soon as the ship was under way. It was a white buckskin box lined with gold satin. Nestling among the gold fabric was a necklace studded with tiny emeralds, diamonds and pearls. There was a big pearl in the centre and below that, a huge pear-shaped emerald pendant. It was beautiful and obviously worth a fortune. Davina had never heard of the Empress Emerald.

Chapter 40
Gibraltar, 1936

Arnold heard the door-bell and looked over the counter. Leo, not a customer. He registered the harrowed expression and said nothing.

Leo went to his evaluation desk and sat down, his hands palms-down on the leather pad. Arnold carried on polishing the till in silence. Eventually, he said, "She's gone then?"

"Mmm."

"For long?"

"Forever, I'm afraid."

"Is she that special?"

"More than special."

"Why did you let her get away, then?"

"She wanted to get back to her home in England."

"Well, you're a fool, and a damned great fool at that," retorted Arnold.

Leo shrugged, "What could I do?"

"Do! What you do with every other bint and bibi worth the rogering; charm her prostrate and keep her there. Leo, you get all the girls you set your hat at. I've watched begums and mems make eyes at you with their husbands in the same room. Now, suddenly, you're mooning around like a love-sick calf over losing a middle-aged Englishwoman who doesn't know one end of a lipstick from another. Where's the sense? She's neither rich nor sophisticated, nor particularly gorgeous."

"That's the point."

"And what about Kitty?" Arnold said in a low voice, quietly making his way round the counter to stand beside a brass dancing Shiva. Duster raised in his right hand, as frozen in action as the immobile dancing deity, Arnold awaited his moment. He had spent twenty years feeling jealous of Leo Kazan and he was about to see him crumble. He wanted to see the expression on his face, savour his misery: would he, *could* he cry? *Vengeance is sweet and it is mine,* he thought. "Poor Kitty," he whispered a little louder. "What about your dear little wife, darling Kitty?"

"Kitty died two years ago."

"Diwali, I remember it well." Arnold shivered, despite his cold-blooded intention. "Poor, poor Kitty, you should have looked after her properly. *I* wouldn't have gone away and left a treasure like that behind."

"You were there?" Leo's tone was accusatory.

"There? Oh, no, but one of Lionel's runners came in. As soon as I heard what was going on I did try to get there. Lionel came with me. We couldn't move, streets were jam-packed in all directions. I did try. I've told you all this before. I tried to get there, so did Lionel."

"Tell me your version again."

"What d'you mean, 'my version'? It's what happened. Didn't that Cleaver woman tell you how brave she was saving the child from an inferno of flames?" Arnold forgot his intention to stay calm, paced to the back of the shop indignantly and put the yellow duster back in the broom cupboard.

Leo said, "Just, tell me again."

Arnold came back to stand by him. "That day, when the rioting started, Millie Cleaver was on her way to your father-

in-law's shop for some ribbon, wool, or God-knows-what . . .
She was always hanging around. Always watching out for
you. Mystery you never noticed, frankly. Pretty rubbish spy
that doesn't know he's being stalked, if you ask me. Kitty was
coming back from somewhere with the baby. You know all
this. They threw a fire bomb in . . ."

Arnold was still angry about it. The police had done
nothing to break up the demonstration in its early stages and
three good people had died because of an English name
painted on a shop window. And, to top the lot, this oh-so-
suave, oh-so-international, clever-arse Kazan hadn't been
there. Away as usual on some glamorous mission, swanning
around Europe, wining and dining traitors. Mr Soviet-
connection Espionage Kazan, whose reports sent shivers
down IPS backs and London ministers into huddles. But he
hadn't been there to prevent a bunch of chanting coolies
throwing home-made fire bottles into the home of a
completely innocent, half-Indian family. It made his blood
boil, thinking about it. And now, the one man who should
have been there – and probably could have prevented it, with
all his street Marathi and chameleon personality – was
whimpering over the past because he'd fallen flat with a
wench who hadn't been to a hairdresser in twenty years! He
removed a bank statement from his jacket pocket and turned
to face his adversary in triumph, ready to make the final
thrust – but Leo was slumped over his desk.

Some of Arnold's accumulated anger and resentment
evaporated. He reached out and timidly patted Leo's
shoulder. "Maybe Millie Cleaver knew about the
demonstration, or she was worried when she saw what was
happening, or maybe it was just divine coincidence."

"There's no such thing as 'divine coincidence'." Leo's
voice was muffled and as petulant as an adolescent's.

"And you just happening to be within five yards when a leopard damn near jumps on Hermione Pinecoffin, what was that, then? I doubt even you could fiddle that one." Arnold stared at Leo's head, but got no response. "The fact is, Millie Cleaver's got your little girl, and that's good – but only for a short time. She's no chicken, Leo, she's at least in her sixties and she can't look after Ellie forever."

Leo responded to this with a self-indulgent sigh, which relit Arnold's original flame. He marched to the shop door and turned the sign to 'closed' then slowly walked back to big man and said, "It's time, isn't it? Sit up and listen to me, damn you. It's time to get things clear. Time for you to explain –"

"None of you tell me anything about my mother." Leo mumbled into his arms.

Arnold put the bank statement on the desk, where Leo would see it, and inched onto the chair opposite. "Didn't he tell you, your father? Didn't he tell you all this himself?" Arnold stretched up, short spine ramrod straight, and stared at the bent head before him. *'Information is power, Arnold.' Too true, Lionel, too true.* "Your real mother is in *her* mother's house in Goa. Her father died some time ago, but *her* mother, your grandmother, is still alive. Ancient, but alive. Your mother's called Catalina – you know that, it's on your birth certificate – she lives in her old bedroom surrounded by her Portuguese dollies. After they found her wandering in the streets, searching for you, she was very ill, but they looked after her and she got better, only not completely. Physically she is fine, but she'll never be right in the head. Under the circumstances, it's probably a blessing."

Leo sat up. "Thank you." There was a pause then he asked quietly, "Do you think I should see her?"

"See her, don't see her, it makes no difference to me. You should, however, see this." Arnold pushed the bank statement under Leo's nose and waited for the reaction.

"Ah," Leo said.

"You stupid, arrogant bastard, did you honestly think I wouldn't find out?"

"Maybe I wanted you to."

"No wonder you're so comfortable in that hotel, no wonder you . . . What? What d'you mean, wanted me to find out? What's all this about?"

"Maybe I wanted you to know what it felt like to be cheated."

"Oh! As if I don't know, eh? As if I never minded you getting invited to Hermione's tea parties, taking rides with Sir Lionel in gharries, going to fancy parties on Malabar Hill all dolled up like a blasted peacock."

"I never went to a fancy party with Lionel. What are you wittering about?"

"Ah, we're starting to take notice, are we?" Arnold slithered from the chair and grabbed the flimsy bank statement. "I want it back, every penny – and more."

"More, why should I give you more?" Leo was alert now.

Arnold felt a smile crawl around his lips, he couldn't help it. He was enjoying every moment, and why not? It had taken years but he was finally getting his own back. "Because I know what happened to the Empress Emerald."

Leo looked him in the eye. "What emerald?"

"The one you pinched from Mrs Whatsit's dressing table. There's still a reward for it all these years on, and d'you know why? Because it's worth a *fortune*. It belonged to Catherine the Great – "

Leo burst out laughing before the words had left his lips. Arnold was furious, incandescent with anger.

"I bet old man Craven hiked the price up nicely with that one. Catherine the Great!" Leo scoffed.

"It belonged to your mother!"

Leo went silent. "You mean old man Craven and his son, and you, you all knew you were selling something that belonged to . . . I can't believe it. You were all that dishonest."

"Dishonest! Us? That's rich coming from someone who pinched anything shiny like a bloody magpie and hid it in a biscuit tin under floorboards." Arnold's scorn seared into the final phrase. If he didn't get a penny back from Leo Kazan it wouldn't matter now because he'd reduced him, broken him down to size, belittled him. Then a thought struck him, "Let me have it now and I'll see you right."

"The emerald? I don't have it. It was under floorboards, as you so rightly stated, in my father-in-law's shop."

"I don't believe you. You've still got it."

"No, sorry, I really don't have it. And if I did, I'd return it to a very sad woman in Goa. Just a thought, but Leonid – my father – was at that fancy party you mentioned, how come he didn't see it and claim it there and then?"

Arnold shrugged, "Leonid Kazan, that old buffoon. We did laugh, though. One of life's little ironies, Clive said."

"As you say, ironic," Leo pushed the chair back and stood up, his bulk a looming shadow cast by the late afternoon sun beyond the window.

Arnold suddenly felt vulnerable, but he wasn't going to give in. Holding the edge of the table for strength he said, "She's got it, hasn't she? You've given it to the Englishwoman." It was a stab in the gathering dark, but it went right home.

"Mm, and you won't find it now."

Arnold put a hand to his mouth and bit his forefinger. He wouldn't find it now *without difficulty*. The woman, whoever she was – and he *could* find out because she'd been staying somewhere local – the woman had slipped past his observers, perhaps on numerous occasions. He knew nothing about her. But that would be remedied. "I wonder what she'll say when the policeman turns up at her English door accusing her of theft," he hissed, as if to himself.

His feet left the ground. He was lifted across the shop in one movement and dumped in the damp confines of the broom cupboard. The door slammed shut and the bolt knocked home before he could even scream for help.

"Open the door!" Arnold yelled, bashing with both fists on the rough wood. "Open the bloody door, Leo! Let me out! Let me out!"

There was no reply. He leaned back against a low shelf and waited, panting with exertion and panic. Silence. Then a sort of dragging noise. Then he distinctly heard the door-bell jingle – open and closed.

It took him over an hour to get out of the cupboard using the broom handle and the metal dustpan as a battering ram. He cut his hands to shreds on splinters trying to widen the hole.

It was pitch black by the time he was out. Lighting the lamps, he made a rough inventory of his stock. Nothing had been taken. Except, yes, the contents of Leo's desk drawer, whatever they had been.

Chapter 41
Gibraltar, 1936

Emma Sangster looked down at the funny little man on her front doorstep and wondered if there was a circus down on the race-course. She liked a good circus. The funny little man tried to raise his hat with a bandaged hand.

"Been in a fight?" she asked.

"No. Yes, in a manner of speaking."

"What can I do for you, love? I'm full to bursting, and if you've come selling forget it. If you've come about evacuating me, you can forget that, as well, I haven't got nowhere to go and no one who'll take me in, so that's that."

"Actually, no. One of your neighbours directed me here. I'm looking for a woman."

"Sorry, duck, I'm not that sort of establishment."

"No, no, I mean, I mean I'm looking for . . . my cousin. She's taller than me – obviously – and um, fair hair, long fair hair."

Emma Sangster sniffed. "Perhaps I should have explained, I'm a police billet, have been for years. Your cousin isn't here, sorry. Has she got lost with all the evacuees?"

"Er – maybe."

"Well there you are, then, you go down to the police station and ask there. PC Scott said he was trying to make a list of who was being taken off the Rock, but it's a right old job, what with so many coming in all the time."

The midget went white in the face and said, "Evacuees – that's why she was selling. I didn't think about that. Are there lists I could –"

He was interrupted by an almighty boom and Emma Sangster grabbed her door jamb. When the reverberations petered out, she said, "Testing those guns again. Least ways I hope it's only testing. Some says as how that man Franco's going to fire on us for rescuing people. Not that I can believe it, but there's that many strange things happening these days, you don't know what to believe." She stepped out of the doorway and looked out over the coast. "Can you see any ships what aren't ours?"

There was no reply. She turned back to speak to the little man again and found him flat out on her front path. Bending down, she gently shook his shoulder to see if he was unconscious. "You all right, sir?" she asked when he opened his eyes.

"No, actually."

Emma got down to her knees and lifted him using her elbows like the nurse had showed her with her second, George, when he was in the final stages and couldn't feed himself. "That's it. Let's get you inside and get a hot cuppa in you. I can't help you with that lady you're looking for, but I can help *you*, if you'll let me? In a spot of bother are you?"

Chapter 42
Plymouth, England, 1936

Davina sat on a wooden bench watching the early autumn rain flatten the plants in the station-master's window box across a railway track. She felt chilly and conspicuous in her foreign summer frock and old-fashioned cape. A gaggle of farmers' wives waddled down the platform carrying oversize wicker baskets covered in red gingham cloths. They each wore a bright headscarf and looked as if they had just stepped out of a Beatrix Potter colour-plate. As the country train chuntered into the station and came to a noisy halt, Jemima Puddleduck ushered her companions into a carriage, then held the door open until Davina had lugged in her much-travelled carpet bag.

"You on then, m'dear? You look chilled to the bone. Had a nice holiday have you?"

"No. Yes. I suppose so."

The farmer's wife smiled at her. It was such a genuine, uncomplicated smile that Davina wanted to hug her.

Five of the country wives settled themselves across the front bench seats of the carriage with their backs to the engine; the remaining four sat in the double seats facing them. As one, they arranged their baskets on their laps and picked up their conversations where they had left off. Davina chose a middle seat a few rows down the carriage and stared out of the window in a daze, not registering anything until they slowed down for the next station. Then she noticed the glorious profusion of fluffy hollyhocks and tall weeds lining the sidings. The station itself was immaculate: yellow marigolds in cut-down barrels, lobelia still swinging bright and blue from hanging baskets despite the autumnal weather. She was home and it was all so familiar – and all so strange.

A young ticket inspector hopped into the carriage. One of the headscarves nudged another in the ribs, "Here he is, Rose, your beau."

"Doris!"

"Morning officer," said one of the older ladies. "You polished your buttons this morning? We've got Rose with us, you know."

"Mabel," simpered Rose, "leave him alone."

"Morning ladies," said the young ticket inspector, trying to ignore their teasing, "tickets, please."

"Tickets?" said Jemima Puddleduck, "Oh my, who bought the tickets? Any you girls got a ticket?"

The head scarves nodded left then right and then left again, in perfect unison. Davina had to put a hand over her mouth to stop herself laughing out loud. The ticket inspector turned round to see who was watching his weekly humiliation, his face as red as pickled beetroot.

"We bought tickets last week. I got them 'ere somewhere. Will they do?" Doris pushed her hand down into her basket and came up with the hairy root-end of a leek. The ladies cackled with pleasure, "That's a leekit, mother!" said one. "He wants a teekit."

"Oh, I got one of those," shouted a headscarf tucked into a corner seat. She pushed her hand under the cover of her basket and pulled out a round yellow disc. "Ah, no, silly, this is a *tea biscuit*. What was it you wanted again, boy?"

"Come on now, ladies, you're not the only travellers today. I got to punch other people's tickets before we get to Callingford."

"Rose says you can punch her ticket as often as you like, boy," said Doris.

Rose dropped her head over her basket, consumed with naughty giggles.

"Right, then . . ." The pink ticket inspector turned on his heel, walked a few paces down the carriage and leaned over to receive Davina's peace offering. He nodded his gratitude and went to stand by the door. There was a kerfuffle in the rear seats and a headscarf called, "Here they are, boy, I've found them."

The tickets were punched and the poor young inspector was rewarded with a bulbous currant bun and a pot of jam. The fun was over and everyone settled down to look at the scenery – big red-brown cows knee-deep in mud, and hedgerows glistening with raindrops in the morning sun. The clouds parted as they only ever do over England: it was the start of a beautiful day.

Davina sighed with satisfaction and relief and wondered if she had had a nice holiday.

Chapter 43
The Star of India, 1936

The voyage became tedious two days out from Gibraltar. Leo was in no mood to socialise or occupy himself with any of his usual on-board distractions. He had met no one interesting or anyone that merited fleecing at cards. His dining companions were dull and worthy: a school principal, a senior cleric and an upper-ranking ICS officer. Their wives were dowdy and much taken with the related topics of hygiene and housing. They lamented the number of Indian street children, 'poor little urchins' they called them, but could identify no solution to the distressing sight of emaciated toddlers begging on the public highway. There was some mention of the European situation, but, as one of the wives pointed out, they were going a long way away from any possible fighting. The Germans had surely learned their lesson after the last do.

Each evening, as soon as dessert was over, Leo was on his feet and making his excuses before he could be included in the gentlemen's smoking coterie; he really couldn't be bothered to be sociable and he became more and more edgy as his destination slowly approached.

George Randall, the very pukka ICS-wallah at Leo's table, waited until they had passed Port Said before he made his move. He and Leo coincided while taking a morning turn on deck. They stood together as the Gulf of Suez merged into the Red Sea.

"You've seen this a few times, I dare say," said Randall.

"Lost count," said Leo.

"Me too, but it's always a pleasure to get back into eastern waters. Home for you, eh?"

Leo cocked his head on one side, picking up a warning signal. "Yes and no."

"But you're more at home in India than on our good King's chilly isle."

"I live in Gibraltar, actually."

"Yes, I know. Mediterranean climate, very pleasant they tell me. Not so safe a fortress as it used to be, though. That chap Franco's got more about him than our government wants to admit. I'm told he could send in his Arab horsemen at midnight and have the whole bally garrison beheaded by sunrise."

"I think that's a bit of a picturesque overstatement. The British garrison is on alert and well prepared to protect itself, and us, or so I'm told."

"Us?" responded George Randall, sounding surprised. "Well, now that is excellent. *Carpe diem*, as they say. Testing times, though, eh?" He looked about him like a naughty schoolboy about to scrump apples. "One has to be very careful who one's talking to nowadays. Friendly natives, well-educated aristocrats in their own right, you know – sort of people with whom one dines and then has to put under house-arrest. Can be damned embarrassing, I can tell you. We really have to watch our words. Of course you're used to that, eh?"

Leo looked out to sea, refusing to give Randall any encouragement.

But the ICS officer ploughed on regardless, "Nehru's taking much too strong a lead of the Congress Party, you know. It'll sink 'em sooner or later. Demanding total independence from Britain is a huge mistake. What with Jinnah giving the Moslems even more reasons to get fractious, one is literally walking on shards of glass. Not to mention the commies stirring up trouble for the sake of it. No doubt about it, Kazan, we need you back in harness. None of my crew can say more than 'cheers' in Russian. Congress and the commies are most definitely in cahoots – as the chaps you ferreted out years ago proved, of course. Frankly, I never understood Sir Gerald's attitude. You were worth your weight. They needed anything, you could find it. Sir Lionel said it, and he was damned right. Prevention's better than cure, as our good ladies at dinner are so keen to point out." He opened a silver cigarette case and offered it to Leo, who declined. "Curious coincidence meeting like this on board - *carpe diem,* as I said, eh. I've got a letter for you from the India Office in my cabin."

"Me, Mr Randall? I think not. I'm afraid you have mistaken me for someone else, I have an antique shop in Gibraltar."

"Yes, yes, excellent cover, I know about that. Domiciled at the Rock Hotel, I know that, too. Must cost a pretty penny."

Leo was about to ask why the letter hadn't been left there if they knew his whereabouts but didn't. They had their watchers: someone – Arnold Mackay most likely – would have tipped off Randall about him leaving. There was no such thing as a coincidence, but being on the same vessel as Randall was a nasty one. He stayed silent, watching a dhow plough its honest way through the coastal waters.

The Indian Civil Service man, discomfited by Leo's attitude, delved in again, "As I say jolly fortunate us being on the same ship. Call me George, by the way. I'll get enough of 'Mister this and mister that' the moment we disembark."

Leo inclined his head in acknowledgement but still refused to enter into conversation. So George Randall proceeded without him. "I knew it had to be you from the dining roster. Of course you have an unusual name, but then my wife confirmed it. She used to take tea with Lady Hermione, when she first came out and I was very junior, before we went into the Punjab. In fact Joan was with Lady Hermione only a couple of weeks ago. We were staying with family in the West Country."

"Hermione Pinecoffin? I thought she was dead."

"Good heavens, no. Bright as a button, and still chattering on about you and that blessed leopard. Hermione has rather concertina-ed time, if you know what I mean? She tends to forget she was a grown woman, wife and mother and all that, when you were billeted on them."

"That is incorrect. I was never billeted on them."

"No, but you *were* Lionel's golden boy, and unfortunately Hermione still prattles on about you all the time. That's one of the reasons you had to be rested, you know. No one was sure who she was talking to, or who was listening, more to the point. Went a bit loopy after poor Lionel passed away. Got stuck in a time groove and just kept on repeating the same stories, some of which were not for the public ear. I mean, I know no one listens to loopy old dames, but there again in Bombay she used to mix with all sorts, and there was a constant stream of visitors after the funeral – all colours and creeds, as they say. Not like Joan, she sticks with her own. Anyway, Hermione's safely back in the family country home now, out of the way. Pinecoffin must have told her everything that was going on. Can't for the life of me think why."

The triangular sails of the dhow shifted and the boat headed back to shore. For a moment Leo was tempted to jump overboard and swim to it: start a new life in a new land.

Then he heard Davina's soft voice say, *'What about your little girl?'* And a round-faced, adorable child called out *'Daddy!'* Davina was right, denying the child was wrong.

Leo eased his shoulders and said, "What you say may be true, Mr Randall, I cannot verify or deny it. However, I was 'rested' as you put it, and as a consequence my life has taken a different turn, for which I am very grateful. I would like to leave the past in the past."

"Gone native, have you? Gerald said you would."

"I *am* native. And proud of it. I belong to a nation blessed with a vast mineral wealth and a tremendous cultural heritage, as visiting royals are so fond of repeating. But we have been used, sometimes not unkindly, that I will grant, sometimes with misguided best intentions on your part, but in the main we have been abused, Mr Randall, exploited and mistreated. That has got to end. India must make her own decisions for her own well-being, build her own future. That is an imperative."

George Randall leaned over the rail and flipped his cigarette into the waves below. Avoiding eye contact he said, "Quite a speech. You should go into politics."

"I plan to."

The Englishman frowned, unsure whether it was a joke or sarcasm then looked away again out to sea. With his face averted, he said, "It's not on, you know. Not possible old chap. Not in anyone's best interests. India needs Britain; the country will collapse in chaos if you let the coolies take over."

"I find ignoring insults like that to be best. I'll say good day to you, Mr Randall. I regret I am not wearing a hat; if I were I would doff it deferentially." Leo turned on his heel to go.

Randall blinked, saying hastily, "Before you go – as I mentioned before, it was my wife who confirmed your identity." He slowed his words. "She also remembers a young

Sikh at about the same time – we were at a dreadful fundraiser – '17 or was it early '18? Whatever, whenever it was – this young chap caused a quite a sensation among the ladies, positively gasping for him, they were. Wearing a great egg-sized ruby in his turban and eyes as green as emeralds, she said, which is another coincidence because that very night a priceless necklace known as the *Empress Emerald*, disappeared. Do you remember? Hermione Pinecoffin reminded Joan of it not one month past."

Leo smiled a wry, one-dimpled smile. "I don't know how well you were acquainted with Sir Lionel, Mr Randall, but it is quite clear to me that you are a civil servant and he was Political Service." He turned his back on the crass civil servant once more and started towards his cabin.

As he walked away, Randall said, "We'll get you, you know. You'll be top of our list for solitary confinement."

Chapter 44
Bombay, 1937

Leo was returning from a meeting in the city with other Home Rule activists. They had been discussing how to spread greater awareness of the need for independence in outlying villages. Lost in thought as he walked up the hill towards his father's bungalow, Leo didn't notice the policemen until he was right at the gate. There were two constables. They were waiting for him.

"Evening, gentlemen," Leo said. "Are you visiting, or is this an official visit?"

"Official, sir," said one. "Would you come with us, please?"

"To? Why?"

The policemen looked at each other, "A few questions only, sir," said the second policeman. "Down at the station."

"But this is not an arrest?" Leo said. "No, of course not, what could you possibly arrest me for?" He cast a furtive glance at his escape routes. The quickest and safest was through his father's rose garden, over the wall and then down through other gardens until he got to the bottom of Malabar Hill and across town into the labyrinth of streets he had known so well as a child. There was at least one brothel where he could claim sanctuary. The girls had taken him in before – and when he'd acquired the Empress Emerald all those years ago.

Leo looked at the two men in uniform. "Could I just go in and say goodnight to my daughter, and maybe get a jacket, it'll be chilly later on?"

Not giving them time to think, Leo put his hands between the bars and iron birds of the gate and opened it from inside then hastily walked round to the back of the bungalow, ignoring the houseboy who was standing on the front step with his hands over his mouth – whether in shock or horror – Leo couldn't decide.

His father was sitting on the terrace with a guest. The guest was George Randall.

Leonid made rapid hand movements and blinked dramatically as if trying to warn Leo, but whatever the reason and whatever he was trying to convey, it was too late.

Leo shot a glance at the path to the rose garden then turned back to George Randall. "Father, Mr Randall, good evening. To what do we owe this surprise, Mr Randall?"

George Randall smirked and nodded at the two policemen. They stationed themselves where they could block Leo's exit via the front garden gates.

"Mr Randall has been asking me to translate some Russian, Leo," Leonid said hastily. "He has a letter – or I think it's a letter – I don't see it all just some lines."

"A letter? In Russian? Curious." Leo looked at George Randall, who was now positively beaming. "You have acquaintances in Russia now?"

"Contacts more than acquaintances, I'd say. But yes, it is a letter. From your friend in Moscow, Mr Kazan. Viktor – with a *k* not a *c*." Randall handed Leo a piece of paper.

Leo took it, willing his hands not to tremble, keeping his expression firmly under check. "I think you are mistaken, Randall, I have received no letter from any *Viktor* with a *k*."

"Ah, no. I should have been more specific. The letter is not *to* you, Mr Kazan, it is *about* you."

Leo turned to his father. His father looked away. Leo wanted to say, '*I'm not a communist, father. I am not one of your enemies*' but in doing so he would be playing straight into George Randall's hands. He began to rattle off a few words in Russian, "This man is after something. Don't take too much notice, he's a nobody . . ." but even as he spoke he realised he had misjudged Randall, and the visit was a lot more serious than he wanted to admit. He looked back at the path leading to the rose garden – and abandoned any idea of escape. His father would assume the worst if he ran. He tried to meet his father's eye, but the old man looked away.

"They said you were fluent," Randall said.

"I was just saying the roses will be looking nice this evening, I can smell them from here, lovely."

Randall's mouth twitched but he said nothing.

Leo tried to catch his father's gaze again, and failed. He turned back to Randall saying, "So, can I ask what this Viktor is writing about me?"

"I think we had better discuss that down at the police station, Kazan," Randall said.

"Why? What could this piece of paper say that might require me to visit a police station? May I see it, by the way?" Leo held out a hand.

Randall picked up the sheet of paper, folded it neatly then put it in his jacket pocket. "Later, perhaps," he said.

Trying to keep his patience, Leo said, "You do know *who* I was working for in Britain, don't you? You know I was visiting Soviet Russia – and why – I hope."

"Oh, yes indeed. Splendid work, yes," Randall gushed. Then his tone changed and in an icy voice he said, "What we didn't know was that you were also doing splendid work *for* the Soviets."

"Sir Gerald knows all about it. How and why. Look in my reports. It's all there in Sir Gerald's office – in his blasted filing cabinet."

Randall made an exaggerated grimace, "Yes, it was. Unfortunately, someone got into his office and raided your file. Only thing left is the folder – can you credit it? Right under the secretary's and his assistant's noses."

Leo clenched his fists. He hadn't taken anything about his Soviet work, but they'd got him all the same. "I thought you said you were a civil servant, Mr Randall. This is Political Service work."

"Ah, well, we civil servants come in many shades. And it doesn't do to snub us, you know." Randall gave Leo a knowing look. "Shall we go? There is a police inspector assigned to this bit of business. He's waiting for you as we speak."

Randall got to his feet and put on his hat. The two constables arranged themselves either side Leo. Leo judged distances: he wouldn't make it to the rose garden let alone over the fences and rooftops.

"The police inspector was delighted to see your name, as it happens," Randall said conversationally as he strolled down the path to the gate with Leo behind him. "Something to do with a robbery here on Malabar Hill twenty years ago, I think." Then Randall suddenly sidestepped and doffed his hat, "Forgive me, Mr Kazan senior," he said, addressing Leo's father, "I omitted to bid you farewell. Don't worry about your wayward son here. He'll be in safe hands. At worst he'll be sent to the Red Fort in Delhi – rather apt, under the circumstances. The Red Fort for a Red sympathiser, what?" He smiled at Leo, "Our girl tells us you've known Viktor Grekov since you were a student in St Petersburg, or whatever it's called nowadays."

"That would be Mary-Marietta, the Bulgarian girl, I suppose," Leo said, half to himself, wondering what she or they had concocted against him. Not that it mattered. The fact was that without his father's support he had no one to turn to, nowhere to run to, and no way to convince anyone he had only ever done what he thought Lionel Pinecoffin wanted of him. Then he stopped in his tracks, causing the policemen to grab each of his arms. "My daughter!" he exclaimed. "I haven't kissed her goodnight."

Chapter 45
Cornwall, England, 1937

A roll of white mist curled around the many-cornered house, sidled up the chimneys and settled down to await the sun. Below, the old river barely moved.

Davina awoke from a dream about swans. She buried into the feather down of her white pillow and pulled a blanket up around her ears. She had been poor Elise, alone in her prison garret. High above circled her white-clad brothers. She called and called, but they didn't hear her. They were looking, but they could not find her. She sighed heavily, pushed the sheet down over her stomach and slowly got out of bed.

By the time she got downstairs the post-boy had already been. There was a letter on the mat. Davina looked at the stamp and at the handwriting then took the letter into the family sitting room to read it in a chair. She didn't trust her knees not to buckle.

Dearest Mamá,

By the time you get this I shall be in France, I hope. We have been in Barcelona for a few weeks but Pedro has decided I cannot stay. I have been translating for some Welsh miners and some Americans but now we are being bombarded all the time and Pedro is sending me across the border to

Port Bou. He says his wife and baby need to be safe. Yes, Mamá, you have got a married daughter and now you are going to be a granny!!

Give my love to everyone and tell them I am quite safe, and as happy as it is possible to be under the circumstances.

All my love, and do not worry. I feel very well, not sick at all . . .

Davina rolled her hand over her own swollen abdomen. *'Not sick at all', you lucky girl. Perhaps, my darling, you are going to be a mother and sister in the very same month.* She started to laugh and cry with relief.

The outer envelope that had enclosed Marina's unopened letter dropped to the floor. It was embossed with the García del Moral monogram and had been addressed in what looked exactly like Alfonso's forward-slanting scrawl. So Sito was getting into the house and the bureau was intact – that meant the house had not burned to the ground at all. What was going on there? Why hadn't he popped in a few lines about himself and what was happening in Jerez? Marina said *'do not worry'* – dear Lord, there were so many things to worry about. Still, it was the best Christmas present she had ever had.

Mary Peach put her head round the door, "I've left some apple tarts and mince pies in the kitchen. What's the matter?"

"Oh, Mary!"

The kind woman crossed the room and gathered Davina into her arms. "That's it, my dear, have a good cry. It's what you need."

"Mary," sobbed Davina, "why are people so good to me these days? Nobody said anything nice to me for years and years and now, when I don't deserve it, you are all being so good to me."

"Well, I don't know anything about those Spaniards, good Christian folk they're s'posed to be, but you're back home now and you're lovely and we're going to look after you, don't you fret. Your baby is going to be as strong and healthy as a Cornishman should be."

Davina put her head back and laughed. She couldn't be sure what nationality his father was, Spanish or – whatever Leo was – but he would be born a Cornishman. She hugged Mary. "Thank you, you are an angel. Let's have a mince pie and a schooner of sherry – it is Christmas Eve."

They moved into the kitchen. Davina removed the cloth from the plate of sugary little pies and said, "How do you know it's a boy?"

"I don't know. Just seems like it'll be a boy."

It was a boy. He was born on a blustery night in early May, when the wind rattled the Crimphele chimney pots like the devil himself was trying to get in. A perfectly formed healthy baby with every baby's deep blue eyes and his very own halo of spun-gold hair.

The midwife said, "There you are m'dear, give him a cuddle and your milk'll flow easy."

"What you going to call him?" asked Mary Peach.

"I'd like to call him Tristan, but it seems – I don't know – can't decide."

"Nice name that. A good Cornishman even if he was from Brittany, ruined by a married woman, if I remember right."

"Mary! I sometimes forget Parry Jones was your father. Tristan was a good Celt, wasn't he?"

"He was. Han'some and brave. Roll on your side a minute. There you go. That better?"

"Much better. Poor Tristan and Iseult. Trapped by love."

"Love potion, weren't it? Not natural love. Mind you, that's a worse trap, if you asks me." Mary Peach held out her arms, "Now, give your little Tristan to me and he can sleep here in his crib while you rest. Mrs Jenkins and I'll go down for a cup of tea, if that's all right? Been a long night. You close your eyes – you got a busy time coming now."

The two women tiptoed out of her room and Davina rolled over to gaze at her new son. He was so beautiful. God bless him. And, please, God, take care of Marina and her baby, and keep these children safe from the outside world.

"Mary!"

Mary Peach stepped back into the bedroom.

"Mary, are we born the way we are, or does life make us?"

"Bit of both, most like. I'd say we are born who we are, but life makes us what we become in the end, if you see what I mean?"

"Like poor old Morrigan."

"She weren't so poor: your family looked after her pretty well. Your pa even rented a cottage for her down here when she retired."

"Did he? He didn't tell me that."

"No, well he had a soft heart for all that your mother wanted her gone in case she blabbed about you. She did go dotty . . . Anyway I think we make our own destiny, one way or another. And if it's not what we want, we've only got ourselves to blame."

"Yes, I think you're right. It just took me thirty-five years to find out."

"Well, that's normal. Most women seems to spend their young days trying to be someone they think they ought to be, or that they'd like to be, so they go along with what other people want and expect from them. Then, when they're married and they got the kids to look after, all that goes out the window and they're just themselves. And one day they see the fancy ideas they used to have don't fit in real life: bit like finding you can't squeeze into your best frock any more. But that don't matter, cuz with the little ones around there's no need for fancy dresses anyway. You are what you are. Happens about mid-thirties, I'd say. Leastways, it does round these parts."

"Mary Peach, how did you become so wise?"

Mary sighed a long heartfelt sigh, "I ain't wise, I just seen a bit too much of life. It's rubbed off the illusions. Being married to a boozer does that to you. And I've got my Gwenny to think of. I sometimes wonder if she isn't a bit simple."

"But Gwendolyn is gorgeous. She's as pretty as –"

"As is a constant worry to her ma that she don't fall in the same man trap as I did."

"*We* did."

"Yes, well, enough of this philosophising. You got your little one to think of now. And he's safe here with a proper mother to love him and a fine roof over his head. Get some sleep, while he'll let you."

Chapter 46
Cornwall, 1940

The peace of the summer morning was cut to shreds as yet another bomber squadron took to the air. Davina kept her eyes focused on dead-heading the roses in the lower garden. She had on two occasions watched what were now called 'dog fights'. The first time, the English plane came tumbling down to earth; on the second occasion she saw the skirmish up over the estuary, then within seconds both planes appeared to plunge head first into the sea. Once, a plane had flown so low over the house she had seen the pilot's helmet and goggles. Her greatest fear was that the war would come crashing down on her own hard-won peace: that her beautiful old house sitting comfortably by the river dressed in summer wisteria mauve would be violated by the world of men.

It had taken Davina a long time to settle and then a long time to learn how to enjoy independence. She had spent most of her life on her own in one way or another, so being in the old house with just Tristan for company did not worry her, and Mary Peach and her daughter Gwenny gave her a hand with the housekeeping so she did have some company. She had plodded along, coping with her situation – until one morning, for no apparent reason, she awoke, stretched her arms up to the ceiling and sighed, "Heaven." No one to answer to, no one to criticise or nag her, and a whole day to

"

do whatever she wanted. From that moment on, the little rituals of daily life became a pleasure. Save for persistent worries about Marina and her little girl's well-being, and less persistent but more intrusive, invasive replays of words spoken by Leo, she was content.

Now, a plane from the RAF squadron had turned and was charging back inland, trailing smoke like a black parachute. Davina instinctively ducked. "No, please, no," she gasped. Then she called out, "Tristan! Tristan, where are you?"

Tristan had lost interest in the real-life battles raging above him, far more interested in his own games. He raised a caterpillar arm and called, "Here," from somewhere among the jungle of roses and rhododendrons that surrounded the old house.

"Come over here, sweetheart."

"In a minute."

Davina smiled and returned to her pruning. There was no point going indoors; if the plane did crash and they were inside, it would be infinitely worse. Another plane was suddenly overhead; she kept her eyes resolutely focused on her hands, dropping each dead bloom into her garden trug, making room for regeneration.

She did look up, however, when the post-boy wheeled his bicycle round the wooden door.

"Alright, then?" It was a question requiring no answer, his normal salutation. "Got a bundle for you this mornin', Mrs Moral," he continued, waving a handful of buff and white envelopes in his hand, "and a telegram from your daughter."

Davina tucked her shallow flower basket up onto her left arm, pulled off her gardening gloves and stepped out from among the thorny bushes. There was a big cream envelope from Alfonso's lawyers – the document inside would require careful reading; and a letter from the Dymond accountants.

Matthew was a self-obsessed, surly devil but he kept her informed about the family firm and she received a monthly income for her share in the Bristol sherry business. The third envelope was small and bore an Indian stamp. She tried to give it no importance and placed it with the other unopened letters among the cracked rosehips in her flower trug. Indian stamps always made her tummy turn, but when Billy the post boy handed her the flimsy brown telegram her hands began to shake. She tore it open: *PEDRO SENT TO LABOUR CAMP COMING TO YOU NOW.*

"Good news, then, is it?"

"Yes, Billy. Not excellent news, not for my daughter, but good news for me."

"Alright then, I'll be off. Bye."

Davina read the telegram again and popped it into the pocket of her flowery summer frock. She would read the business letters from Jerez and the Bristol accountants later. But she wouldn't open the envelope with the Indian stamp until she was safely alone in her own room. Pulling her gloves back on she returned to her roses.

"Mummy!"

"Yes, dear."

Round little Tristan, his golden curls tucked away under a yellow sou'wester, staggered down the path from the house wearing gumboots and carrying his favourite book of bird stories. "Mummy, look, I'm the duckly ugling."

"No you're not, silly," laughed Davina. Stepping back onto the path and bending down, she gathered him to her. "You are a very beautiful and very hot little boy. You are not ugly in the very least. Take that hat off sweetheart; you'll boil in this sun."

"*Alright* then," Tristan mimicked Billy the post-boy exactly. He struggled out of her arms and scuttled back in the direction of the kitchen and Mary Peach's preparations for lunch.

Davina moved on up the row of dry brown petals and seed heads. Pushing her hair away from her face with the back of her hand, she continued with her gardening, speculating on the contents of her letters.

She felt, did not see, the garden door open once more. And she knew who was standing there. He had arrived before she had even opened his latest letter. He was absurdly well dressed for a Cornish summer morning.

Then Tristan was beside her again, tugging at her skirt. He was now wearing a black woollen hat and had a white tea towel tied around his neck. Ignoring the man at the garden door, he pulled at her skirt with one hand and indicated behind him with the other. "Look, Mummy, look," he insisted, until she followed him to a vast lavender bush, in the midst of which lay a nest of sticks and unravelled wool.

Having achieved his objective, Tristan turned and acknowledged the presence of the stranger. "Who's that?" he said.

"You had better ask him."

Tristan looked up at her for reassurance, and when she nodded he ran off down the path and gazed up at the tall stranger.

The stranger felt his stomach lurch. It was exactly, exactly as he remembered. A woman and child in a terraced garden full of roses. It was exactly, exactly what he wanted.

"Come and look," said the boy. "I've made a nest."

Leo came to stand beside Davina. She smiled at him. She had eyes as blue as the summer sky, and freckles. Leo reached for her hand. Davina bit her lip; she was laughing and crying at the same time.

"Look!" demanded Tristan again.

They stared down at the mess of twigs and wool. It was very like a real nest. A nest containing three silver apostle spoons, some gold toffee papers, two fancy hairpins and a beautiful necklace – its huge pear-shaped emerald glinting in the sunlight.

"Are you my daddy?" asked the boy.

Leo hunkered down beside the child and poked a finger into the nest. "Well, it certainly looks like it."

"*Alright* then!" Tristan gave him a big kiss on the cheek as if he had known him all his short life then skipped off up the path singing, "I'm a little magpie, black and white, here's my nest, shiny bright."

Davina and Leo looked at each other and burst out laughing.

"Introductions over," said Davina.

Leo picked the necklace out of the nest and stood up.

"It's stolen property," said Davina.

"A magpie?"

"One or two, along the way. It's famous – infamous."

"Oh."

"I read about it in an article on famous jewel thefts the day I went to see the doctor because I was expecting Tristan. There was even a picture."

"And?"

"Oh, someone stole it from a maharani in Simla or somewhere and then, when it reappeared, it was stolen again."

"You haven't done anything about it?"

"No. At the time my life was quite complicated enough without getting involved with the police. I assume the person who 'acquired' it sold it to you for the same reasons I came to your shop. That rather gave me pause and made me think. Anyway, I'm never going to have a reason to wear the dratted thing, so unless a little magpie, black and white, chooses to put it in his shiny nest and shows it to anybody else, I think it's quite safe here."

"Good."

"Let me show you the garden."

They wandered around the rhododendrons, along the paths between the fruit bushes and the area set aside for vegetables. Davina named plants and chattered about how long it had taken her to get the garden back into shape after years of neglect. Then she said, "Now, what about you? I want to know all the things you have left out of your letters. What haven't you been telling me?"

"Oh, about complications, mostly no longer complicated, thank goodness. Ellie is staying with my father and Millie, but they have a young *ayah* looking after her now. They have moved up to the hills permanently. My father has taken out Indian citizenship and adopted the religion of our forbears. It suits him. He dispenses wisdom over a hookah and goes to the mosque every day so he has plenty of new acquaintances and he's as happy as a dispossessed person can be. Millie has a child to care for and she's doing it remarkably well for her age, as I told you. And Ellie has completely taken to her new *ayah*, which helps. They have plenty of other domestic help of course. Ellie is safe, going to an English school and content for now."

"And you?"

"Yes, well, I ran into *even more* difficulties with your countrymen, which they engineered very tidily after they released me in Delhi. They confiscated my passport and actually tried to bully me into working for them again, would you believe? After locking me up for two years it's suddenly 'Oh, Mr Kazan this' and 'Oh, Mr Kazan that'. At one point I wondered if I was going to be arrested again. That's why my letters became so few and far between. I very much fear they intercepted yours. They'll know where I am now, anyway. I had to be very careful who I was talking to and what I was saying."

"So how did you get here – now?"

"It's all rather strange. They had me watched day and night. 'Minuted' as Sir Lionel used to say – but I was used to that. I was afraid, to be honest, they'd find another excuse to put me back in prison, and I couldn't have borne that, but they didn't. Then, out of the blue, after making at least a hundred attempts to get my passport back and a passage to England to see you, I am informed that Mr Churchill wants to consult me – of all people – and I've got to get to England as fast as possible. So I was put on a plane three days ago and, via various military bases on the way, here I am."

"Mr Churchill! Gosh."

"Gosh indeed, except he's going to say something rather stronger than that when he hears the answer to what I think he's going to ask me – about what we expect for increasing our war effort. Mr Churchill doesn't have a very high opinion of us Indians."

"So you are going to London?"

"No, he's somewhere down here in a secret government residence on the Helford River. A perfect coincidence; and I always said coincidences didn't exist."

"Mummy!" piped Tristan, trotting towards them. "Aunt Mary says is the man staying for lunch?"

"Are you?" asked Davina.

"If I may?"

"Good. I have a lot I want to tell you, but it will have to wait until our little magpie is out of earshot."

"And I have a lot to say as well. As you can see, I have got my life in order 'before', as you demanded – and I've spent a lot of time thinking about what will come next."

"More or less." Davina spoke the words looking at Leo's face then turned away. "You've got your life in order – more or less. Perhaps less, I'm afraid." Then she gushed, "You have another daughter, Marina, and she's a mother now and so you have a granddaughter as well."

Leo opened his mouth to speak, but he was speechless. Tristan arrived back at the site of the nest before he could find anything to say.

"Don't take anything, please," Tristan said, looking up at Leo. "It's *my* nest."

"You need a biscuit tin."

The little boy cocked his head on one side, considering the suggestion, "To put things in?"

Leo nodded and the child grinned.

"Are you going to stay with us now?" he asked.

"I think I'd better, if Mummy will let me." Leo looked at Davina. Her face lit up.

"Can you stay?" she whispered.

"Do you want me to?"

But Leo didn't hear Davina's answer because Tristan pushed between them. He put one hand in his mother's hand and the other in his father's hand, and tugged them toward the house. "Lunch is ready," he piped. "Come on, I'm hungry."

The End

Author's Note

A great deal of research went into writing this novel, but four books I went back to time and time again were: *Raj – The Making and Unmaking of British India,* by Lawrence James (Little, Brown and Company, 1997); *The World of Diamonds,* by Timothy Green (Spanish translation *El Mundo de los Diamantes* Editorial Planeta, 1981); *Pasión India,* by Javier Moro (Editorial Seix Barral S.A., 2005) and *Gibraltar – Rock of Ages,* by Hubert Caetana (Gibraltar Books Ltd., 2003).

If you would like to read about Leo's wicked Italian ancestor, Ludo da Portovenere, look for *The Chosen Man* (Penmore, 2015).

If you have any questions about *The Empress Emerald* or would like to know more about the real house in Cornwall that I have called Crimphele, go to my web page: www.jgharlond.com

About The Author

J G Harlond

Jane G. Harlond grew up in Devon and studied in Bristol, Portsmouth and the USA before finishing her academic studies with an M.A. in Social and Political Thought at the University of Sussex. She has lived and worked in a variety of different countries and is married to a retired Spanish naval officer. Harlond has two sons and five step-children, all of whom now have their own careers in diverse parts of Europe.

IF YOU ENJOYED THIS BOOK
Please write a review.
This is important for the author and helps
to get the word out to others
Visit

PENMORE PRESS
www.penmorepress.com

All Penmore Press books are available directly through our website, amazon.com, Barnes and Noble and Nook, Sony Reader, Apple iTunes, Kobo books and via leading bookshops across the United States, Canada, the UK, Australia and Europe.

PENMORE PRESS
www.penmorepress.com

The Chosen Man

by

J. G Harlond

From the bulb of a rare flower bloom ambition and scandal

Rome, 1635: As Flanders braces for another long year of war, a Spanish count presents the Vatican with a means of disrupting the Dutch rebels' booming economy. His plan is brilliant. They just need the right man to implement it.

They choose Ludovico da Portovenere, a charismatic spice and silk merchant. Intrigued by the Vatican's proposal—and hungry for profit—Ludo sets off for Amsterdam to sow greed and venture capitalism for a disastrous harvest, hampered by a timid English priest sent from Rome, accompanied by a quick-witted young admirer he will use as a spy, and bothered by the memory of the beautiful young lady he refused to take with him.

Set in a world of international politics and domestic intrigue, *The Chosen Man* spins an engrossing tale about the Dutch financial scandal known as tulip mania—and how decisions made in high places can have terrible repercussions on innocent lives.

PENMORE PRESS
www.penmorepress.com

HEAVEN CRIES

BY

STEPHAN

SILVA

When Artemio Battaglia joins the *Regia Aeronautica* to become a fighter pilot at the beginning of World War II, he's inspired by the romanticized patriotism of the Fascists. His idealism is challenged when he witnesses atrocities committed against indigenous populations in North Africa, shattered after the officials he informs do nothing to stop the murderers. Their response is to transfer him to the most dangerous front in the war.

A disillusioned Artemio returns to Piacenza only to find his city occupied by ruthless German soldiers. He enlists in the war again, this time as a member of the Red Brigades. With a renewed sense of purpose, Artemio repeatedly places himself in peril, sabotaging German supply lines and giving aid to the Allies. But when his comrades capture a downed Italian pilot and schedule a hasty execution, Artemio recoils at the senseless violence. Once again he is called to act in accordance with his conscience and embarks on a bold plan to set things right.

Based on the experiences of the author's great uncle, *Heaven Cries* is a story of a young man who confronts the brutalities of war armed only with a courageous heart and an unshakable faith in moral decency.

PENMORE PRESS
www.penmorepress.com

Fortune's Whelp
by
Benerson Little

Privateer, Swordsman, and Rake:

Set in the 17th century during the heyday of privateering and the decline of buccaneering, *Fortune's Whelp* is a brash, swords-out sea-going adventure. Scotsman Edward MacNaughton, a former privateer captain, twice accused and acquitted of piracy and currently seeking a commission, is ensnared in the intrigue associated with the attempt to assassinate King William III in 1696. Who plots to kill the king, who will rise in rebellion—and which of three women in his life, the dangerous smuggler, the wealthy widow with a dark past, or the former lover seeking independence—might kill to further political ends? Variously wooing and defying Fortune, Captain MacNaughton approaches life in the same way he wields a sword or commands a fighting ship: with the heart of a lion and the craft of a fox.

PENMORE PRESS
www.penmorepress.com